Praise for

Heidi Swain

'Lose yourself in this heart-warming story of romance, community and secrets. The perfect story to read by the fire!' **Phillipa Ashley**

'Sweet and lovely. I guarantee you will fall in love with Heidi's wonderful world' **Milly Johnson**

'A little slice of joy' ***Heat***

'Sparkling and romantic' ***My Weekly***

'A true comfort read and the perfect treat to alleviate all the stress!' **Veronica Henry**

'The queen of feel-good' ***Woman & Home***

'The perfect read to relax and curl up at home with' **Caroline Roberts**

'A story that captures your heart' **Christie Barlow**

'Fans of Carole Matthews will enjoy this heartfelt novel' **Katie Oliver**

'A wonderfully uplifting story with a picturesque setting you'll wish you could visit' ***Culturefly***

Also by Heidi Swain

The Cherry Tree Café
Summer at Skylark Farm
Mince Pies and Mistletoe at the Christmas Market
Coming Home to Cuckoo Cottage
Sleigh Rides and Silver Bells at the Christmas Fair
Sunshine and Sweet Peas in Nightingale Square
Snowflakes and Cinnamon Swirls at the Winter Wonderland
Poppy's Recipe for Life
The Christmas Wish List
The Secret Seaside Escape
The Winter Garden
A Taste of Home
Underneath the Christmas Tree
The Summer Fair
A Christmas Celebration
The Book-Lovers' Retreat
That Festive Feeling
The Holiday Escape
Home for Christmas
Best Summer Ever
All Wrapped Up
Walking on Sunshine

Heidi Swain

Falling for You

SIMON & SCHUSTER

London · New York · Amsterdam/Antwerp · Sydney/Melbourne · Toronto · New Delhi

First published in Great Britain by Simon & Schuster UK Ltd, 2026

1 3 5 7 9 10 8 6 4 2

Simon & Schuster UK Ltd, 7th Floor, 199 Bishopsgate, London, EC2M 3TY

Simon & Schuster Australia, Sydney
Simon & Schuster India, New Delhi

www.simonandschuster.co.uk
www.simonandschuster.com.au
www.simonandschuster.co.in

The authorised representative in the EEA is Simon & Schuster Netherlands BV, Herculesplein 96, 3584 AA Utrecht, Netherlands. info@simonandschuster.nl

A CIP catalogue record for this book is available from the British Library

Paperback ISBN: 978-1-3985-3876-4
eBook ISBN: 978-1-3985-3877-1
Audio ISBN: 978-1-3985-3878-8

Typeset in Bembo Std by Palimpsest Book Production Limited, Falkirk, Stirlingshire

Printed and Bound in the UK using 100% Renewable Electricity
at CPI Group (UK) Ltd

FSC www.fsc.org
MIX
Paper | Supporting responsible forestry
FSC® C013604

To Dad,
You were the inspiration behind this one.
Thank you x

Chapter 1

As I set off on the long journey south on the first of September, I willed myself not to look back. Highfell Hall, set in the stunning Yorkshire countryside, was now consigned to my past and, for the first time in over a decade, the course of my life was set to dramatically change.

For reasons beyond my control, my entire world had altered during the last eighteen months and consequently decisions had to be made, and now was the moment to fully embrace them. The future resembled nothing like the one I had for so long assumed was ahead of me but, even though the prospect was daunting, I had no choice but to face it. As I had recently turned thirty I supposed the beginning of a new decade was an appropriate time for a fresh start . . . at least I hoped it was.

I cleared my throat, swallowed over the lump lodged there and resolutely looked ahead. In less than a minute I would leave the sweeping drive and reach the road, and the hall, where I had so happily worked as an events organiser, would be far behind me. In terms of distance at least. I would always carry a piece of it in my heart along with my treasured memories of the parties, weddings, balls and many other celebrations I had been a part of.

Despite my determination, my gaze flicked to the rear-view mirror, and I caught a brief glimpse of my former home, sitting statuesque and securely planted in the sunshine-filled early September landscape. Tears began to sting my eyes, and just at that moment, my mobile rang out and made me jump.

'Rafe,' I said, as his name lit up the screen and I connected the call via Bluetooth. 'Rafe,' I said again. 'Hi.'

'Skylar, darling,' he responded, his deep and reassuring voice filling the car. 'I know I said I wouldn't call, but I was worried about you and just wanted to check you're up to the journey. My offer to send someone along to drive you to Norfolk still stands.'

'No need,' I told the kind and thoughtful man who was my father but whom I had never called Dad. 'I'm on my way. But thank you.'

'You've set off already?'

'Just a couple of minutes ago.'

My eyes returned to the view behind me, but the hall had passed out of sight and perhaps it was no bad thing I hadn't watched it disappear.

'Any idea what time we can expect you?'

By 'we' he meant himself and his two much-loved cats, Socrates and Plato.

'According to the satnav,' I surmised as I checked the screen, 'sometime around midday, but I'm planning to stop for something to eat along the way. I couldn't face breakfast, so it will probably be nearer half one or even just after when I do finally land. Will that be all right?'

'Yes, absolutely,' he confirmed. 'Perfect in fact because by then everything will be unloaded and the movers will have long gone. You'll be able to walk in and relax.'

'I'm not sure I can remember how,' I tried to joke, but he knew there was truth in what I said and his next words proved it.

'Which confirms exactly why we're embarking on this exciting adventure, doesn't it?'

It was a comfort to hear him say that he still thought it was going to be an adventure. There had been times since I'd taken up his offer to move in with him while I decided what I was going to do next with my life that I had succumbed to some serious doubts that I was doing the right thing, so at least one of us was certain it was going to turn out well.

Rafe had always been in my life, but we'd never had what most people would consider a conventional father–daughter relationship. He and my mum, Faye, hadn't been a couple since their late teens and it was a chance meeting, years later at a party, that had resulted in the creation of me.

My father, who until just a few months ago had lived in the US, generally preferred the company of men and Mum favoured flying solo so she had raised me alone but kept in touch. Consequently, as I grew up, I had got to know Rafe through letters, emails and video calls and occasional visits when he was in the UK. Then, when I was old enough, I began to fly out during the summer to stay with him in the States. Even so, we hadn't spent more than a couple of weeks together. Until now . . .

'It does confirm that,' I rather belatedly agreed as my thoughts returned to what he had said. 'I could do with a break.'

'I'm delighted to know that you've finally accepted that,' he said, because I had taken some convincing. 'And even happier that I'm able to offer you the opportunity to move in with me and take one! Are you looking forward to seeing the house?'

'Given the minute detail of the video tour you gave me during your last viewing, I feel like I already have,' I smiled. 'The former owners must have had the patience of a saint to let you do that while they were trying to pack.'

'Such a lovely couple,' he said wistfully. 'Had it not been for their still growing family, I'm certain they wouldn't have even considered selling up.'

'Which would have been unfortunate for us.'

'It certainly would,' he agreed. 'Houses in Nightingale Square rarely come up for sale so we were lucky to secure it, and being so close to Dad is going to be wonderful.'

'It certainly is,' I agreed, feeling warmed that he had included me when he was the one who had done all the securing.

Rafe's father, Grandad George, was a resident in a care home situated not all that far from the square in the centre of Norwich and I knew that had been the determining factor in the decision to make an extremely generous offer on the four bedroomed, detached house. Well, that and the fact that the area was so idyllic and had a thriving community garden.

Now he had permanently returned to the UK, Rafe was determined to throw himself into local life. I, on the other hand, having lived literally miles from neighbours and shops for a decade, had an inkling that I was going to find the transition trickier to negotiate than my gregarious father, and that was why I'd hedged whenever my long-term future came up in conversation.

'And I'm certain that as soon as we're unpacked, the words will start to flow again,' he continued, sounding hopeful. 'With an increasingly looming first draft deadline, they certainly need to.'

He was an award-winning, bestselling and critically acclaimed crime writer who had never experienced writer's block before. His books were all set in the US but since he'd moved, he hadn't been able to locate his muse and feared it had opted to stay on the other side of the Atlantic without him.

'You haven't made any headway at all then?' I ventured to ask.

'Frustratingly not. But don't tell my agent that. He's already having a minor meltdown. The problem is, I've got this idea for a new book—'

'Would this be the allure of the shiny new idea when your current plot isn't behaving?' I interrupted him.

'Huh,' he harrumphed. 'I should never have given you that insight into the writing life, should I?'

'You should not,' I laughed. 'Especially now we're going to be living together. I'll be on your case morning, noon and night until I've found another job to keep me occupied.'

'There's no rush to do that,' he reminded me.

'I know.'

'But none the more for that,' he continued with a laugh, 'don't start nagging and make me regret stepping in and offering you a home when your mother unexpectedly sold up! Have you heard from Faye, by the way?'

Mum, or Flighty Faye as Rafe called her, had very recently returned to Goa. She'd had a lifelong love affair with the area and had decided that it was time she moved there for good. I hadn't taken her chatter about it all seriously – she always seemed to have some far-fetched idea brewing – but when she called to say that she'd sold the house and was off, I had no choice but to take note. She was now running a beachside bar with a friend and working part-time in a yoga retreat with no plans to ever return.

Selfishly, at the time, I felt her decision couldn't have come at a worse moment for me because I had planned to move in with her once my time at Highfell came to end. But it had turned out all right because Rafe had kindly come to my rescue. He was by far the steadier and safer parental option, so it was bound to be for the best.

'Not since she emailed to update me about landing the yoga job,' I told him.

'Um,' he said. 'Me neither. I'm not sure if that's a good or bad thing.'

'With everything else I've got going on,' I said wryly, 'I'm considering her silence as golden.'

Rafe chuckled at that. 'Yes,' he said. 'You're right. I'll do the same. Now, I'd better let you get back to your journey.'

'Okay. I'm just about to join the road through the valley.' The hall nestled among the hills was a fair way behind me now. 'Send positive thoughts for a straightforward trip with no hold ups, will you?'

'That sounds more like Faye's territory, but I'll see what I can manifest for you, my darling,' he said. 'See you later.'

'Yes,' I swallowed. 'I'll see you this afternoon.'

Clearly, our manifesting skills needed some refining because I had to endure the journey from hell. Not only were there long tailbacks as a result of a three-car crash and a broken-down lorry, but I was also acutely aware that it had been quite some time since I'd driven in such heavy and fast-moving traffic and that did nothing to settle my already present nerves.

When I did eventually stop at a service station for something to eat, I could barely swallow the sandwich I had picked out, and the coffee I'd opted for made me feel jittery rather than soothed. Having messaged Rafe with an amended arrival time, I set off again, secretly wishing that I'd taken up his luxurious offer of sending someone to collect me and my car and drive us south.

The unexpected hold-ups meant it was almost three o'clock when I finally reached the road I needed and then pulled into Nightingale Square. The house was the first on the left as you turned onto the one-way street that looped around the central green. There were seven houses set around it in total. All detached, some were larger than others, and even though they had what looked like generous plots, I couldn't help thinking how close together they all seemed.

The sweeping valley views and wide-open landscape I was used to were a long way behind me and I had to blink hard to suppress the rush of tears which filled my eyes as I carefully pulled onto the drive and in front of the garage at the side of the house.

'You've just endured a dreadful journey,' I told myself. 'So, you're bound to feel out of sorts. You'll feel completely different after a decent night's sleep.'

The pep talk wasn't helping, so I scooped my bag off the passenger seat and quickly climbed out of the car. My legs felt a little wobbly and I'd barely set foot on the path to the front door when it was opened from inside and a woman, looking back over her shoulder and laughing, stepped out.

'Skylar!' came Rafe's unmistakable voice from behind her. 'Here you are at last, my darling. I was beginning to get worried.'

The woman, who was wearing jeans and an oversized shirt, turned to beam at me and when she looked at Rafe again, I noticed she had a pencil tucked behind one ear.

'He really was,' she smiled, when she turned back to me. 'But you're here now. Safe and sound. I'm Lisa,' she added and held out her hand which I went to shake but she pulled me in for an awkward hug. 'You must be all in after that drive.'

'Yes,' I said, when she finally released me and looked at me intently. 'It wasn't the best.'

I was taken aback by her demonstrative welcome and wasn't really in the right frame of mind to exchange pleasantries or take in any of the information she then started to bombard me with, despite acknowledging the difficult drive I'd just had. She told me the names of everyone who lived around the square along with the details of what they did in the community garden across the road.

'I'm a writer, too,' she excitedly finished up. 'Just like your dad, but a rather different genre. And you know what, with your gorgeous green eyes and long chestnut hair, you could have the look of my next lead character, Skylar!'

'No one too racy, please Lisa,' Rafe laughed. 'Skylar is my daughter, after all.'

'Don't worry,' she quipped, making me feel even more self-conscious. 'The names are always changed to protect the innocent!'

I wasn't sure if that made me feel better or worse.

'We've been comparing notes about writer's block,' Rafe explained when I didn't say anything.

'It's going to be fantastic having someone literally across the road who I can talk to about the highs and lows of writing for a living,' Lisa said as she pointed to the house where she and her family lived. 'Your arrival, Rafe, is going to stop me bending my husband's ear and that will make him very happy indeed!'

'I'm delighted to hear it,' he beamed.

'Well, that's fantastic,' I said to them both when I realised it had been some time since I'd said anything. 'Really great, but if you don't mind—'

'Oh love!' Lisa gasped. 'I'm so sorry. I literally popped over to say welcome to the square and as usual I've got carried away and chatted on for far too long. You must be dying for a cuppa. And a tour. Your dad said you've not even seen the place in person yet! I still can't believe I missed spotting you when you came to view it Rafe, and Heather and Glen never said a thing . . .' her many words trailed off. 'I'm doing it again,' she tutted. 'I'll leave you to it, but if you need anything, anything at all, just knock.'

'Do you think they're all like that?' I asked, as we watched her walk away and then wave from her doorway before she disappeared inside.

'I hope so,' Rafe grinned. 'The level of community spirit the vendors and agent kept talking about really sold this place to me. That is, after being so near to Dad, of course. Now come inside and I'll show you around.'

Chapter 2

With the front door finally closed, I took a deep breath and felt my shoulders relax as some of the tension I'd carried with me on the journey, and during my rather intense welcome to the square, started to ebb away.

'What do you think of the door?' Rafe asked, as I put down my bag and slipped off my shoes. 'The panels are original to the house, but the previous owners had them set into a new frame and door.'

The geometric shapes the stained-glass panels were made up of were both striking and colourful and added an authentic touch to the entrance of the house.

'I think it's beautiful,' I told him. 'And I love that the last residents did this, it shows how much they cared for the house. I hope the sun catches it at some point during the day. It will look even lovelier then.'

Rafe looked delighted with my response. 'I couldn't agree more,' he smiled. 'So, full tour first or a comfort break and a cuppa?'

As I looked around the hallway I was already somewhat familiar with because of the detailed virtual tour he had given me, I could feel a welcome surge of excitement starting to bubble up and wanted to forge ahead.

'I tell you what,' I suggested. 'Why don't you make us a brew while I freshen up, and I'll drink it as you show me around?'

'Sure?'

'Completely,' I nodded. 'I don't want to wait another minute.'

I didn't venture further than the downstairs cloakroom and waited in the hall, again admiring the detailing on the door and the ornately tiled floor, until Rafe returned with tea for both of us.

'Is that all right?' he asked as he handed me a mug. 'I'm never sure if I make it strong enough for you, what with you being used to a Yorkshire blend.'

'It's perfect,' I told him as I gratefully took the first comforting sip. 'Thank you. Now,' I smiled, inclining my head to the right, 'I'm guessing this door is closed because the boys are in there?'

'They are,' Rafe confirmed. 'I was going to hold off letting them out of their crate until you arrived so you could look at both sitting rooms and decide which you'd prefer, but with the time drawing on they were getting a bit antsy, so I thought it best to give them some space. I hope you don't mind?'

'Of course not,' I told him. 'We'll look in there last, shall we?'

As my father and I had never spent much time together we'd agreed to have our own sitting rooms. They would afford us some privacy as we got used to living under the same roof. It might prove to be unnecessary, but I was grateful for the option of a domestic breakout space.

'Yes, that's a good idea. I'm hoping to introduce them to

the house slowly. They'd only just got used to the rental after the trauma of their trip here from the States . . .'

'I'm sure they'll adjust just fine,' I said, because he looked worried. 'They'll probably settle in sooner than me.'

'Do you think you might have trouble settling in?' He frowned and I instantly regretted what I'd said. I did think it was going to take me a while, but I really didn't want to add to his concerns.

'Of course not,' I backtracked. 'I was just saying that to try and make you feel better about the cats.'

'That's all right then,' he said, clinking his mug against mine. 'Drink a bit more and then we'll make a start.'

The room to the right of the front door, where Rafe was acclimatising the cats, had previously been used as a family sitting room and had originally functioned as a dining room when the house was built. I knew this from the detailed video tour he'd treated me to. The room to the left was smaller, but with the same style of bay window to the front and the original fireplace with a not unattractive faux fire insert. There were deep wooden fitted shelves either side of the chimney breast with practical cupboards underneath.

Rafe had asked the movers to deposit my much-loved William Morris fabric covered sofa and armchair in there and I couldn't help thinking they looked like they had been made for the space. I thought my books, which had been briefly kept in storage with most of my other things as well as everything Rafe had shipped from the US, would look right on the shelves, too.

'This room was the kid's playroom,' Rafe explained. 'The chap who surveyed the property said the chimney could quite easily be reinstated.'

'But why would you want to?' I shrugged, as he flicked a switch next to the fireplace and the flames leapt into life. 'I think it looks lovely as it is. Real fires are beautiful of course, but do you really want the trouble of cleaning, laying and tending it? And in a room of this size, it's most likely unnecessary, so would rarely be lit.'

'Um,' he said. 'I hadn't really thought about that aspect of it. I suppose it would be a lot of work for an occasional real fire.'

'And with this, you can have the look of the fire without the hassle.'

'You're right,' he agreed. 'We'll leave it as it is.'

'And I'd like to take this room,' I said, looking around. 'If that's all right with you?'

'You aren't just saying that because your furniture is already in here, are you?' he asked. 'It's smaller than the old dining room.'

'I don't mind the size. In fact, I like it. It feels cosy, and don't you think the furniture looks like it's meant to be here?'

He cocked his head and took the space in further.

'Actually, it does look right. As if it's been in here for ever,' he nodded. 'But don't completely make up your mind until you've seen the other room later.'

'All right,' I said, but in truth I was already sold on the snug little space.

'Kitchen next,' Rafe said and led the way back through the hall which had storage built in under the stairs and the cloakroom I'd already visited. 'The kitchen and dining area is part original and part extension.'

'Oh wow,' I gasped as I stepped into the room. 'This looked

impressive when you showed me on your phone, but it's even lovelier in real life and it fits the house perfectly. What a sympathetic addition.'

'I'm so pleased you think so,' Rafe said as he also looked around. The extension was light and airy thanks to the pitched skylights and bifold doors that led out to the garden. 'And it will be even lovelier once we've unpacked and got rid of all these boxes.'

As well as my few pieces of furniture, some kitchen paraphernalia had also been transported from Yorkshire ahead of me and now I could see our combined accumulation of boxes all together, I was looking forward to unpacking the contents and seeing them in situ.

'I agree,' I said on an out breath. 'With Highfell being sold and packed up, I've felt like I've lived in a holding area for months. It will be good to be able to walk about without boxes and crates hindering every step.'

'Yes, I feel the same way myself. Though I do appreciate your situation is different to mine, because I wanted to move.'

'Yes,' I said, then changed the subject because I didn't want to spoil my first look at my new home with the memory of having just left my former one. 'Let's have another tea and carry on.'

'And how about a slice of this Victoria sponge Lisa carried over with her? The jam is homemade and the eggs came from the hens in the community garden which, incidentally, is called the Grow-Well. How lovely is that?'

'Very lovely,' I said as I thought I might owe Lisa an apology for my unenthusiastic arrival. 'I'd love a slice. Thank you.'

Upstairs, there were four bedrooms. The two large doubles

both had en suites and the two smaller rooms shared a family bathroom. Given that a growing family had lived here before us, the place was remarkably pristine and wouldn't need decorating in a rush.

I picked the double room at the back of the house because it offered a view of the garden and a huge oak tree in another property in a street behind the square, and Rafe was keen to take the one at the front because it had a double aspect.

'I'm pleased that's settled,' he said as he checked his watch. 'Because the new beds will be arriving within the hour. It would have been a nuisance to have to wait to set them up or move them if we hadn't properly made up our minds and needed to switch them.'

'Yes,' I agreed. 'I don't think we could manage to do that on our own.'

'I'm sure Lisa could have found us some help.' I didn't doubt that for a second. 'I'm going to set up to write in the other bedroom at the back, so I hope my typing won't disturb you.'

'I'm rather hoping that it will,' I contradicted. 'Because it will mean you've found your muse again.'

'That's a good point,' he smiled. 'Here's to many interruptions to your day!'

We went back downstairs and quietly went into the room where the cats were acclimatising to their most recent changes. Socrates, black with white paws, was hunkered down behind some boxes, but the tabby, Plato, had stationed himself on the broad window ledge to check out the neighbours and have a good wash.

'I hope Socrates is okay,' Rafe frowned.

'Given how nosy I know Socks usually is,' I said, using the

black cat's nickname, 'he won't be able to resist joining Plato soon.'

'I daresay you're right,' Rafe agreed.

'Give it a few days and it will feel like we've been here for years,' I said, optimistically. I knew it was likely to take me longer, but there was no harm in hoping. 'And I know you've already told me off for saying it, but I really am grateful to you, Rafe. I don't know where I would have ended up if you hadn't offered to put a roof over my head.'

'And some respite to go along with it,' he reminded me again. 'I know you've previously told me off for mentioning it, but I mean it Skylar. Ten years you've been working without any proper time off. You need to make the most of this opportunity to rest and recalibrate.'

'I know,' I nodded. 'And I promise I'm going to try.'

'Good,' he said and closed the gap between us to give me a hug. He kissed the top of my head and I felt myself relax. He felt strong and solid and knowing I could depend on him was a huge comfort. 'Good,' he said again.

He looked bright-eyed when I stepped away, so I went to make a fuss of Plato and, with perfect timing, Lisa walked by and waved when she spotted us through the window. Life in Nightingale Square was going to be extremely different to what I was familiar with, but I'd soon get used to it, wouldn't I?

The beds arrived a little later than expected and just as the van pulled up to deliver them, my mobile began to ring.

'Oh,' I said, no doubt sounding surprised. 'It's Mum. I'll ring her back once the beds are up.'

'No, don't do that,' Rafe insisted. 'Talk to her now. I can

manage this. It's only a case of telling the driver and his mate where we want them set up. Say hi to Faye for me.' And with that, he went to let them in.

'Mum,' I said, as I closed my sitting room door and answered her call. 'Hi, how are you?'

'Skylar!' she answered. 'I'm fine! How are you? It's today, isn't it? Moving day, I mean. How are you feeling? Was it a wrench to leave Highfell?'

I closed my eyes and took a deep breath. Tact had never been Mum's strong point.

'It could have been worse,' I lied. 'And it's not as if I haven't had time to prepare for it, is it?'

'I suppose not,' she sighed. 'But even so . . .'

My departure had been in the offing for months, so it wasn't as though the change had been sprung upon me. My former employers and the owners of the hall, Madeline and Tobias, had decided they were ready to slow down and retire abroad – both well into their seventies that was hardly surprising – but, with no children to pass it on to, that meant Highfell had to be sold and the new owners weren't interested in holding events there.

It struck me then that as well as losing my former home and place of work, I'd also lost the found family that Madeline and Tobias had become. The hall was quite isolated and consequently we had been close. My time living there had given me an idea of what it felt like to be part of a normal family, and I'd often wished my mum hadn't been quite so flighty and that I could have experienced a similar kind of stability when I was growing up.

'How's the house then?' Mum asked, when I didn't elaborate on my feelings.

I looked around the room as the sound of boxes being lugged upstairs reached me through the door.

'It's absolutely beautiful,' I told her. 'The former owners clearly loved the place and even though they've done some quite extensive remodelling, they've kept loads of original features.'

'I still can't understand why Rafe wanted somewhere so old and so central to the city,' Mum commented. 'His place in LA was modern and practically rural. I hope he's going to like it, for both your sakes.'

'He already loves it,' I insisted. 'And you do know why he picked here, Mum. It's so he can be near to Grandad George.'

He was also keen to embrace some genuine community spirit but not knowing if he'd shared that desire with Mum, I decided not to mention it. I had the feeling she'd find that rather amusing.

'You're right,' she said. 'Of course. And I know I sound a bit negative for someone who usually looks on the bright side.' That was putting it mildly because on any given day she could usually give Pollyanna a run for her money! 'But I'm worried about you, Skylar. I know you're not going to find the transition easy, especially when you've got nothing to keep you occupied while you negotiate it.'

I couldn't help rather uncharitably thinking it was a little late in the day for her to find some deep maternal feelings. I had always known Mum loved me, but as she had always been caught up in her own dreamy world, I had become independent at quite a young age. That made the fragility I was currently experiencing feel even more unsettling, and I felt blessed that Rafe was willing to nurture me through it.

'I'll be fine,' I said. 'As Rafe keeps reminding me, it's been far too long since I took some time off, so the luxury of not having to worry about looking for and starting a new job straightaway will give me the chance to properly bed in here and explore the area.'

By the time I'd taken an extended holiday I was certain I'd be raring to go again and ready to take on a new job, but I was going to keep that thought to myself.

'You sound more like me than I do,' Mum teased. 'Who'd have thought it?'

'Not me, that's for sure.'

'Well,' she said, sounding more like herself, 'as long as you really are okay, I'd better let you go. I bet you've got loads to do and I should get back to work before I'm missed. It's heaving in the bar tonight.'

Ducking out at an inopportune moment sounded more like her.

'All right,' I said. 'Thanks for checking in.'

'Don't worry if you don't hear from me again for a while, will you?'

'I won't,' I told her.

I was so used to her flitting in and out of my life, it would have been more of a worry if she'd said she'd call again next week or even next month!

'Take care.'

'You too.'

And with that, she was gone.

Chapter 3

I wasn't someone who generally went to bed particularly early, and Rafe certainly wasn't, but by the time we'd made up the beds, given the cats a good fuss and shared a takeaway – which was delivered to the house, what a novelty – we were both flagging. I didn't expect to nod off so quickly in a different bed in a new home situated in a city at the opposite end of the country to where I was used to, but I went out like a light and didn't wake until I heard Rafe cursing on the landing the following morning.

'What's going on?' I asked, as I joined him.

We were both still in our summer pyjamas, but Rafe's thick, dark hair looked nothing like the tangled nest I suspected that I was sporting.

'Plato made a dash out of the sitting room door when I went to check on him and Socrates, and now I can't find him,' he said worriedly.

'Are there any doors to outside or windows currently open that he could have escaped out of?'

'Thankfully not,' he said, sounding relieved as he looked down from the landing. 'But the little sod could be anywhere. Oh damn! And there goes Socrates, too!'

In his haste to locate Plato, Rafe had neglected to close the sitting room door before coming upstairs and now Socks had made a bid for freedom, too.

'So much for keeping them in one room for a few days,' Rafe groaned.

'Come on,' I said. 'Let's follow Socks. He'll probably lead us straight to Plato.'

We quietly went downstairs and headed for the kitchen, which was the direction Socks had gone in.

'There,' I laughed. 'What did I tell you?'

The pair were wantonly basking in the sunshine that was streaming through the bifold doors and neither looked the worse for wear following their adventure beyond the confines of Rafe's sitting room.

'What do I do with them now?' Rafe frowned. 'Take them back to the other room or leave them to get on with it?'

'Given that they're not looking at all bothered, I think I'd leave them if I was you,' I said. 'They can go back to your sitting room if they're feeling unsure and, in the meantime, we'll just have to be super careful about external doors and windows.' Given that it was such a sunny morning, it would have been lovely to open the doors to the garden, but it couldn't be helped. 'How long do they have to stay inside for?'

'Two weeks,' Rafe sighed. 'At least.'

'That time will pass in a flash,' I said stoically, as I reached for the kettle. 'Now, I don't know about you, but I could do with a coffee and some breakfast.'

Once we'd toasted most of the loaf Rafe had thought to bring with him and had a fix of caffeine, he showed me an online shopping order on his phone and asked what I'd like to add.

'Of course, I'm planning to shop locally as much as I can,' he told me. 'There's a street not too far away with shops selling pretty much everything we'll want to eat and drink, but while we get set up and as we need to stock up on some of the basics, I thought a bulk delivery wouldn't hurt.'

'It's a good idea,' I agreed, as I scrolled. 'Though having things delivered isn't what I'm used to. And being able to walk to the shops is going to be as much of a novelty as having our dinner arrive on the doorstep.'

'Yes,' he said thoughtfully. 'I'd forgotten how remote you'd been at Highfell.'

'You've missed off cleaning supplies,' I pointed out. 'And that reminds me, I haven't got a vacuum cleaner. Have you?'

'No,' he said. 'I've nothing like that and I'm not sure we'll need a proper one as I was thinking of asking Lisa if she knows of a cleaning firm or even a local person who could take care of the domestic side of things for us.'

'There's no need for that,' I told him. 'I'm more than happy to clean. I enjoy it and it will give me something to do. I'm going to need something to fill all the time I've got.'

Rafe didn't look convinced.

'I'm sure we can find you something more exciting to do than cleaning,' he tutted.

'Perhaps, but in the meantime, leave the housework to me.'

He eventually acquiesced but insisted that we should have two cordless vacuums. One for upstairs and another for down, so I wouldn't have to carry one up to the bedrooms. Clearly, my father was used to a different standard of living than me. Back at Highfell I'd had to drag an ancient and very heavy cylinder vacuum about when the housekeeper needed a hand.

It had been a nightmare to balance on the stairs until you got the knack.

The rest of the day was spent unpacking boxes and starting to settle in. There wasn't a huge amount to do, but Plato seemed to think everything we were doing was for his amusement and had a great time following us about and diving in and out of the empty boxes, and a couple of the half unpacked ones too. Socrates stayed mostly in the kitchen, observing from afar and soaking up the sun.

Along with the sofa and chair, my books, framed photographs, few ornaments, mirror and paintings all looked perfect in the little sitting room and the addition of a lamp from Rafe completed the cosy aesthetic. The sight of it all made me feel far happier than I had expected to when I had set off from Yorkshire the morning before.

'Skylar!' came Rafe's voice from his room. 'Could you please give me a hand?'

He had sourced second-hand, or more likely fifth or sixth hand, the loveliest worn leather Chesterfield sofa and now wanted it moved to a slightly different position.

'If we can't shift it on our own, I'll ask Lisa if we can borrow her other half.'

'I'm sure we can manage it between us,' I said and quickly put the words into action. I might have been feeling better than the day before, but I wasn't ready for another neighbourly encounter just yet. 'How's that?' I puffed.

'Perfect,' Rafe nodded and stretched out his back. 'I think we're almost done.'

I still had my bedroom to sort, but that wouldn't take long.

'Let's have a break then,' I suggested.

The kitchen was where our individual things had been most combined and I loved the clashing mismatch of items on the open shelves. My pieces were more practical while Rafe's were decorative by comparison. Our two styles complemented each other well and I imagined many a meal cooked together in the months to come. With autumn just around the corner there'd soon be warming stews and deep filled pies bubbling away in the range oven.

'Do you have a favourite mug in this collection?' I asked as I flicked the kettle on. 'I didn't think to ask at breakfast, but we hadn't unpacked this lot then, had we?'

We'd used the plain white mugs Heather and Glen, the former house owners, had kindly left us along with a packet of biscuits, a pint of milk in the fridge and a 'welcome to your new home' card.

'I do,' Rafe smiled. 'It's the Emma Bridgewater with the cats on.'

'Of course it's that one,' I laughed. 'I should have known, shouldn't I?'

'What about you? Pick any you like.'

He already had quite a few, and I knew he was intending to add more.

'This one,' I said, unhooking one that had words written around it in black.

'That's from the Black Toast range,' he told me. 'It's a little plain for my taste—'

'You don't say?' I interrupted and he laughed.

'But it's a Bridgewater classic, so I had to have it.'

'Of course you did,' I smiled. 'Now, would you like tea or coffee?'

We spent the remainder of the day further sorting and arranging and then set to flattening the boxes. Rafe thought it would be a good idea to pass them on to someone else who was moving, but I wanted to keep them.

He hadn't seemed impressed with the idea, doubtless because it inferred that I wasn't planning to make Nightingale Square my forever home, but if I found a job some distance away after my time out, then I wouldn't be able to carry on living here, would I? In the end we opted for a compromise. With the cats securely shut in Rafe's sitting room and until he could ask locally where he could advertise them, I carried them out to the shed.

The next morning, I spotted Lisa looking animated on her doorstep and shouting back into the house. A minute or so later, three children of varying ages appeared and, after some squabbling, reluctantly piled into the car on their drive. They were wearing school uniforms, and I realised it must be the first day of the new autumn term.

September was a month I usually looked forward to because, rather than the back-to-school feeling, it heralded a slight lull for me. Most of the weddings and events had taken place during late spring and throughout the summer and it was finally time to take my foot off the gas, as Rafe was prone to say. This year however, my foot had already been off the throttle for a while. Madeline and Tobias had kept bookings to a minimum this season as they prepared to leave Highfell and now I felt rather adrift and unsure as to what to do with the onset of autumn. As well as the rest of my life . . .

'Are the cats in the kitchen with you, Skylar?' Rafe called to me a short while later. 'There's someone at the door.'

'Yes, they're both here!' I called back and jumped up. 'Give me a second and I'll close the door.'

I waited with bated breath as I tried to work out if I knew who it was – that would only be Lisa – or if it was one of the ever-increasing number of deliveries for Rafe.

'Come on through to the kitchen,' I heard him say and I sprang away from the door. 'Come and meet my daughter, Skylar. She's in here with the cats. One of whom is already intent on escaping.'

I gave Plato an accusatory look. He was annoyingly keen to expand his horizons and proving quite the magician with his disappearing act when either Rafe or I wanted to go into the garden. That said, I was pleased he wasn't feeling unsettled.

'Here we are,' Rafe said as he opened the door and I braced myself for another potential neighbourly bombardment.

I didn't know why I was still feeling so reluctant to meet people. It had been a big part of my former job, and I'd never struggled with it before. Perhaps it was the proximity of everything that was throwing me off. Whatever it was, I hoped it would soon pass, and I'd feel more like my sociable self again.

'Skylar this is Kate. Kate, meet Skylar,' Rafe told the woman who came into the kitchen with him. 'Kate is one of the owners of Prosperous Place,' he added for my benefit. 'She lives there with her partner, Luke.'

I knew that Prosperous Place – which was located just opposite the square – was a large Victorian property with extensive grounds and that the popular community garden was located there.

'And our two girls,' Kate added. 'I've just taken them to school and thought I'd drop in on my way home and introduce myself.'

'Would you like a coffee?' Rafe offered.

'No, no,' she said. 'But thank you. I'm not going to linger, because you've probably still got tonnes to do.' I was warming to her already. 'Moving house is such a trial, isn't it?'

'It's lovely to meet you,' I smiled. 'And yes, it does have its moments. Though Rafe has been the one bearing the brunt of most of them.'

'Oh?' she said, looking between us.

She was probably wondering why I hadn't called him Dad. People generally tended to be curious about that.

'I've bought the house,' Rafe explained, though he didn't need to. 'But Skylar and I are going to share it.'

'I see,' Kate nodded. 'I own one of the houses a few doors along. It's where I lived when I first moved here following my divorce.' Clearly, she had no qualms about sharing either. 'And Luke and I co-own another place almost opposite here, too. That's where our head gardener, Freya lives. It was the garden that I wanted to talk to you about actually.'

'I know we haven't made it over to the Grow-Well yet—' Rafe started to say but she put up a hand to stop him.

'Of course you haven't made it over there yet,' she laughed. 'You've only just arrived! No, I wanted to let you know that you're more than welcome to explore the whole of the garden if you'd like to. It's looking rather beautiful, even though the summer is coming to an end, and the walks around it are lovely. Very peaceful.'

Given that I'd moved from such a remote spot, it would be a genuine blessing to have somewhere peaceful to visit practically on my new and, to me at least, crowded doorstep.

'Well, that's very generous of you,' Rafe smiled. 'Isn't it Skylar?'

'It is,' I agreed. 'And much appreciated.'

'Here's the code to the gate,' she said and handed Rafe a slip of paper. 'Lisa said she'd forgotten to give it to you and was going to come over, but I said I'd call in. I know I shouldn't have written it down. We have a friend staying with us and he's always saying we should change it regularly, but I struggle to remember anything more than my bank card PIN and there'd be so many people to tell!'

I felt a pang of sympathy for their friend. It was an issue I had always tried to address at Highfell, but Madeline and Tobias had insisted the security codes shouldn't be changed either.

'We'll commit it to memory and shred the note,' I promised Kate.

'A new shredder!' Rafe said loudly and Kate and I jumped. 'Something else for the list.'

'And just when you thought you'd remembered everything,' I smiled.

'And on that note,' Kate said, with a nod to the paper, 'I'll leave you both to it. Come and look around anytime, won't you? You'll find the community garden if you follow the path to the right once you're through the gate and the rest of the garden to the left and around the house.'

'Thank you,' I said as she made for the door.

Rafe followed her and I checked I had eyes on both cats.

'If you want to meet everyone en masse, then I suggest you come to the Grow-Well at the weekend,' Kate said and I made a mental note to avoid weekends for now. 'That's when you're likely to find most people popping in and out.'

'Lisa said there's a rota?' Rafe questioned.

'There is. But we'll get you added when you're settled. No rush.'

I closed the kitchen door and let out a breath, grateful that we had a bit of respite before we had to do that.

'There,' Rafe said, when he came back to the kitchen. 'How fantastic was that?'

'This is exactly what you were hoping life in Nightingale Square was going to be like, isn't it?' I smiled.

'To a T,' he grinned. 'And I hope you're going to love it, too.'

'I'm very much looking forward to visiting the garden,' I told him. 'In fact, I think I'll go tomorrow as the forecast is still set to be sunny and you've made plans for us to see Grandad George on Saturday. Will you join me?'

'I think I'll head over on Sunday when everyone's most likely to be there.' That didn't surprise me. 'And in the meantime, I have an idea I really need to go and get down . . .'

He hurried off and I hoped his muse had come calling. I was tempted to ask if the idea related to the book he was supposed to be writing or the tempting new idea he'd mentioned but as I didn't want to distract him, I let him go, hoping it was the former.

Chapter 4

My first Friday living in Nightingale Square dawned sunny and warm and I was looking forward to exploring the garden at Prosperous Place. The evening before, Rafe had given me more of a run down on the history of the connection between the square and the Victorian mansion house across the road.

It had been built and originally owned by an ancestor of Kate's partner, Luke, called Charles Wentworth. He was a philanthropic shoe factory owner who took as much care over the life of his staff as he did his own. The properties in Nightingale Square had been built to house the factory managers and supervisors, and there had also been streets of small, terraced homes for the general workers.

Given that Luke had opened the grounds of Prosperous Place to the people now living in the square to create the community garden Kate had played her part in setting up and running, he sounded every bit as generous as Mr Wentworth himself, and I felt privileged that Rafe and I would become a continuing part of the square's history.

The insight also gave me further understanding as to why Rafe had picked the place to buy as opposed to somewhere more modern as Mum had assumed he would. My father and I were both keen on history and I was looking forward to discovering more about the area.

'Are the cats with you, Rafe?' I called as I pulled on my plimsolls in readiness for my first foray beyond the front door. I had picked my time to leave with care and was hoping to be safely through the garden gate before Lisa returned home from the school run. It wasn't that I disliked her. She'd been nothing but friendly the day I arrived, but I was planning to slip into the garden and explore alone, for this first time at least, and I had the feeling that if she spotted me, she'd insist on acting as a well-meaning guide.

'No,' Rafe said, as he opened the door to his writing room upstairs and popped his head out.

'Sorry, I didn't realise you were working.'

'It's okay,' he yawned. 'It's probably time I took a break.'

His usually tidy hair was ruffled, and he was wearing the same shirt as the day before.

'Have you been writing all night?' I frowned.

'If it's Friday morning,' he laughed, 'then yes. Hooray for the return of the muse!'

'Hooray indeed,' I agreed.

'I take it you didn't hear me bashing away at the keys.'

'I did not,' I confirmed. 'I'm guessing the cats are in the sitting room then?' I added with a nod to the closed door.

'They are,' he said as he walked down the stairs. 'And they can stay there a bit longer as I'm expecting some deliveries. I don't want to risk them, or should I say Plato, making a run for it.'

'Do you want me to wait and help you unload everything?' I offered. 'I don't mind.'

'No, no,' he said, as he turned me towards the front door. 'You go and enjoy the garden. You've been cooped up here with me since you arrived. You need to stretch your legs.'

'All right,' I willingly relented. 'I'll see you later.'

Even though it was early, it felt comfortably warm as I took a deep breath and stepped outside. I had wondered if my light cotton dress and cardigan combo would be a bit chilly, but I needn't have worried. Autumn still felt a long way off, but then August had been such a scorcher, it was no surprise that the warmth was lingering during the first week of September.

I stopped on the path before the gate and cocked my head. I could hear the distant drone of traffic, but given the hour, it wasn't as loud as I had thought it might be and I was grateful for that. Feeling hemmed in was one thing, but having to get used to traffic roaring by at proximity every time I ventured out of doors would have been another level of claustrophobic all together.

'One, nine, eight, seven,' I quietly said, once I'd crossed the road, located the garden gate and keyed in the code.

The wooden gate was set in a brick wall which looked as old as I knew the mansion house to be and it was high, too, and in places covered in ivy. I turned the gate handle and felt excitement bubbling up as it opened. I had the impression that I was about to discover somewhere truly magical. A place of peace and tranquillity that had the potential to help me adjust to the many changes I was negotiating when I needed a moment of calm.

'Oh, my goodness,' I gasped as I stepped inside and carefully closed the gate behind me. 'Wow!'

It was even more beautiful than I had imagined and as I

slowly walked through and around the garden, I became utterly entranced and lost all track of time. As well as borders still in bloom, there were many mature trees, stretches of manicured lawn and a winter garden that, according to some signage, came into its own between November and February, depending on the weather. There were also stunning metal sculptures, and this was all before I'd even caught a glimpse of the Grow-Well.

Along with figures of hares in different poses, I'd also spotted metal dragons tucked behind plants, scaling walls and peeping out of pots. I'd read something about Norwich having a dragon connection and was now eager to know more.

Without my phone to tell me, I truly had no idea what the time was, but my tummy was starting to rumble, and I found I needed a drink, too. I was just thinking it was probably time to leave when I spotted a hidden fern garden and decided that a few more minutes exploring wouldn't hurt. It wasn't as if home was any great distance away.

'Another dragon,' I smiled, as I spotted a small one scaling what I thought was a tree fern.

'They're lovely, aren't they?' said a voice behind me and I spun around to find a woman with the longest hair I'd ever seen, holding a pair of secateurs in one hand and a bucket in the other. 'Sorry,' she apologised. 'I didn't mean to make you jump.'

My hands had flown to my chest, and I could feel my face was flushed.

'Don't apologise,' I told her. 'I was in a world of my own. You could have crunched your way along the gravel path, and I wouldn't have heard a thing. In fact,' I laughed, 'I suppose you did.'

'I did,' she smiled. 'But that's the magic of this garden. It transports you to a different place entirely. I've always found it beguiling.'

'I can understand why,' I agreed, as I looked back at the dragon. 'It's my first visit and it certainly won't be my last.'

'I'm Freya, by the way,' she told me. 'I'm the head gardener here and this is Nell.'

I hadn't noticed before but there was a little fawn-coloured dog standing behind her. 'She's a bit shy.'

'Hello Nell,' I said quietly. 'I'm Skylar. I've just moved to Nightingale Square with my father and I'm feeling a bit shy, too.'

'Kate mentioned that I was probably going to see you,' Freya smiled again. 'How are you settling in?'

I took a moment before answering.

'So far, so good,' I said.

'Lisa told us you've come from Yorkshire.'

Why did that not surprise me?

'She's right,' I confirmed and decided to elaborate before Lisa had the chance. 'I was an events planner at a place called Highfell Hall, and compared to the square, it was literally in the middle of nowhere.' For some reason, Freya looked rather taken aback. 'The owners decided to sell, and my father convinced me to take some time out before I look for another job, so here I am.'

'You must be finding it quite an adjustment,' Freya said astutely.

'Yes,' I nodded. 'It's certainly different.'

'I remember . . .'

'Sorry?' I frowned.

'You probably won't believe this,' she said as she put down the bucket and secateurs, 'but your journey to Norwich sounds very similar to my own.'

'How so?'

'Before I started working here,' she explained, 'I was a gardener at a country estate in Suffolk called Broad-Meadows. When the owner, my dear friend Eloise, died, her nephew inherited and there was no longer a place for me in his plans, so I had to leave.'

'I don't believe it,' I gasped in surprise.

'It's true,' she smiled. 'Kate and Luke came to the rescue with both a job and a house when I least expected it and I've worked and lived here ever since.'

'What are the odds?' I laughed.

'Millions to none.' Freya laughed too, but then her expression grew serious. 'So, I do know.'

'Know what?'

'How hard it can be to go from living out in the sticks to being suddenly surrounded by people, property and traffic. It's a tricky transition.'

I felt a lump starting to form in my throat and swallowed hard.

'You don't think I'm making too much of it by feeling a bit overwhelmed then?' I croaked.

'Absolutely not,' she said. 'It's a total life change and when it's been thrust upon you as opposed to choosing it for yourself, it's that much tougher to get your head around.'

She stepped forward and reached for my hand then gave it a squeeze before releasing it and I felt that all the feelings I'd been experiencing but had tried to suppress were justified after all.

'I can't tell you what a relief it is to hear you say that,' I told her in a rush. 'I thought I was being a bit of a drama queen.'

'You're not,' she said. 'You're really not. And if you want my advice . . .'

'Yes, please.'

'Make the most of this time you've got to settle in and enjoy the autumn. Don't rush into making any big decisions and certainly don't pretend that you're feeling fine when you might not be.'

'Much of that sounds like what my father would say,' I smiled. 'Though I haven't told him the whole of how I'm feeling.'

'Well, perhaps you should,' Freya said. 'And you can always talk to me. I mean it, Skylar. This is such a great place to live, and I really hope you'll take your time and give it a chance to grow on you.'

'The garden has already made a good start. I really love it here.'

Freya looked at me for a moment.

'And talking of love,' she grinned. 'Is there anyone special in your life?'

'If you mean a partner,' I quickly and rather dampeningly said, 'then no, there's not.'

'In that case, you'd better watch out. Whenever someone moves into Nightingale Square, love soon follows!'

'Not for me,' I insisted. 'I've got more than enough on my plate without adding romance to the mix.'

'Perhaps you're right,' she said. 'But then, since when have our hearts ever waited for the right moment for us to fall in love?'

'That's a conversation for another day,' I told her as my tummy rumbled. 'Right now, I need to go and have some lunch.'

'All right,' she said. 'But remember what I said. Anytime you want to chat, come and find me.'

'I will,' I told her. 'Thank you, Freya.'

I set off back towards the gate thinking what a coincidence it was to find someone so lovely who had experienced practically the same situation as I now found myself in. Freya might have moved to the square with a job, but she knew the complications of moving from rural living to city dwelling and it felt good to know there was a kindred spirit I could call on should I need to.

However, where her pronouncement about love was concerned, she was entirely on the wrong track because it wasn't going to find me here. Having spent my life watching my mum, Flighty Faye, flit from one casual relationship to another and personally negotiating the resultant messy aftermath, love was something I took very seriously indeed.

It was all or nothing for me and it hadn't been anything for quite some time. Not since a three-year relationship with farmer, Reuben, had come to an end. We'd cited our lack of leisure time as the final deciding factor in calling it, (we both worked long hours and lived some distance apart) but it had been an amicable ending and we'd wished each other well.

Whatever Freya thought, I certainly wasn't in the right headspace to go looking for love now. A few months down the line perhaps, once I'd settled on my next steps and made some decisions about what I was going to do with my life. But for now, I was ringfencing my heart and no matter who I met in the square, they wouldn't be falling for me or I for them. I wasn't even certain that I'd be staying in the area long-term so that didn't bode well for my Big Love rule, did it?

With my head down and my heart dismissing all thoughts of romance, I walked quickly back to the garden gate. I hoped there was something to eat at the house. I hadn't thought to check before I left.

I was so preoccupied with my empty belly that I didn't notice the rapid approach of footsteps on the gravel until the last second and when I looked up, I found my path blocked by a tall, wide, furious-looking man with bright blue eyes, scruffy dark blond hair and even scruffier stubble. Had I not zoned back in, I would have walked right into him.

'Can I help you?' he demanded and I took a step back.

'No, I don't think so,' I swallowed. 'Though you could give me a bit of space.'

He realised then just how close he was and how intimidating his sudden appearance must have been and he also took a step away.

'What are you doing here?' he asked crossly. 'This is private property. How did you get in?'

Clearly not everyone in the vicinity was friendly. I shifted my gaze to fully meet his and felt his blue eyes fix fast on my green ones. His Adam's apple bobbed as he swallowed and his expression softened, but only a little and just for a moment.

'I am aware this is private property,' I told him, while thinking he was the first person I'd ever met who had truly cerulean-coloured eyes. I'd read about them in romance novels but never come face to face with a pair. 'And I got in using the key code Kate gave me.'

'Oh,' he said, his eyes still on mine. 'Right.'

'You wouldn't happen to be her partner Luke, would you?'

'No,' he said and shook his head. 'No, I'm not Luke.'

I hadn't really thought he could be because he wasn't anything like the match I had imagined for lovely Kate at all. When he didn't then offer me a name, I decided I wasn't going to tell him who I was either. I'd intimated that I had permission to be in the garden, and he'd have to be satisfied with that.

'Well, thank goodness for that,' I huffed. 'Now if you wouldn't mind getting out of my way, I'm expected at home.'

He had no choice but to move aside when I took a quick step towards him again and I stomped back over to the square feeling furious that my visit had been tainted by the rudeness of a stranger.

I knocked on the front door – just in case the cats were on the loose – and when Rafe answered, the expression on my face quickly banished the smile on his.

'What's happened?' he asked as I shrugged off my cardigan and eased off my plimsolls without bothering to undo the laces. 'You've been gone ages, so I thought you were having a good time.'

I took a moment to compose myself.

'I was,' I told him and conjured up a smile. 'The garden is stunning. And I met Freya, the head gardener, too. She was lovely and we soon realised we have quite a lot in common.'

I didn't mention Mr Blue Eyes coming along at the last minute and throwing a spanner in the otherwise happy works. I couldn't seem to stop thinking about him though, even though I was trying to recall the details of the dragon sculptures and the scent of the many roses.

'Well, that's great,' Rafe said as we headed to the kitchen

and the source of the delicious smell of bread. 'Though it doesn't explain the frown you walked in wearing.'

'Sorry, I guess I've just got a lot on my mind.'

Rafe looked concerned. 'That's no good,' he tutted, as he opened the oven door to retrieve the delicious looking sourdough baguette he'd warmed through. 'The whole point of you being here is to ensure that you haven't got *anything* on your mind.'

'I was only worried that we hadn't got anything in to eat,' I blagged. 'And that I'd faint from hunger before I'd worked out where the shops were.'

'Oh well,' he grinned, as he added the warm bread to a platter already loaded with fresh olives, cheese, tomatoes and charcuterie and carried it to the table with a flourish. 'I found the shops earlier, so that's that problem solved.'

'Indeed, it is,' I agreed and joined him at the table.

Chapter 5

I woke early the next morning, and felt grateful that I had an excuse not to begin the day with another walk around the gardens at Prosperous Place.

Knowing that I needed to remain at home while Rafe was out (more deliveries were due) and until we were going to visit Grandad George together later, meant that my being bound to the house was justified and had nothing to do with my deep-seated desire to not run into the angry man on the other side of the garden gate again.

Given the effort I'd been going to, to put all thoughts of him out of my mind, he was still resolutely present, but that was probably because of the manner of our meeting. I wasn't someone who thrived on conflict and the hostile encounter had unsettled me far more than his mesmerising blue eyes . . .

'Skylar!' Rafe called from the hall a while after he'd returned from another foray into the area and after I'd taken in a couple of parcels. 'Are you coming?'

Curled up in my sitting room with Socks on my lap, I hadn't realised just how late it was but a quick look at the clock told me that I'd wasted far too long staring into space thinking about . . . the garden.

'On my way,' I called back.

'Oh, you're in there,' Rafe said, when I emerged with the cat in my arms. 'I thought you were upstairs. Stick him in here with Plato and we'll get going.'

'You might want to run a brush through your hair and remove the pencil from behind your ear before we head out,' I grinned. 'Have you already been out looking like that?'

Rafe groaned as he stared at his reflection in the hall mirror, then removed the pencil and ran his hands through his dark hair, which fell obediently into place. I wished mine did that, but I'd got Mum's hair, which needed coercing into behaving, which was why she always wore hers up. My eyes were green like hers, too.

'Would you look at the state of me,' Rafe tutted. 'And yes, I did go out like this. Anyone would think I didn't care what I looked like.'

He wasn't a vain man, but he did like to look his best and had a penchant for scarves, whatever the season, and a kind of effortless, slightly bohemian elegance that couldn't be contrived. You either had it or you didn't and my father had it in spades. He also had a way of making men and women fall in love with him with just a look, but unlike Mum, he didn't leave a trail of broken hearts behind him. He had the knack of making people feel cherished, me included, and I appreciated that for both myself, and everyone else who crossed his path.

'Throw a scarf on and you'll be fine,' I teased, then ducked as he went to ruffle my hair.

'Do you know where we're headed?' he asked, as we locked

the house and walked to my car, which was still parked on the drive rather than in the garage.

'Not a clue,' I told him. 'But my satnav should provide the answer. I hope it isn't too far. I'm not used to driving on busy city roads yet.'

'I suppose the traffic here is different to what you've been used to, isn't it?' he mused.

'Everything is different here,' I said with emphasis as I remembered what Freya had said about letting my feelings be known rather than bottling them up.

'Yes,' Rafe nodded. 'I'm sure it is.'

'Come on then,' I said, because thoughts of Freya automatically led to memories of Mr Gruff. 'We'd better getting going, otherwise we'll be late.'

Our arrival at the Cavell Care Home was a little later than planned, and a quick look at a map on my phone before we went in suggested that it would have been easier to walk the distance than try to negotiate a section of the ring road that took us close to the city football ground where something was happening that afternoon. My eyes had been firmly on the road, so I had no idea if it was a match, but I hoped I could find a different way back to the square.

'Are you all right?' Rafe asked. 'I thought you handled that rather well.'

'I could do with a stiff drink,' I confessed, 'but as I've got to get us home again, I'll have to wait until tonight to recover my wits. Why didn't you ever learn to drive, Rafe?'

'I never felt the need, I suppose,' he shrugged and readjusted his scarf. 'I'll treat you to a dram of my Laphroaig once we're back. That'll set you straight.'

'I'll hold you to that.'

I hadn't seen Grandad George for a long time and, knowing that his health hadn't been what it was when he moved into the care home, I was bracing myself for some dramatic changes in his physical appearance, but I needn't have worried. Once we'd signed in at reception, with Rafe being welcomed like the celebrity he was to some, and I had been introduced and also made to feel welcome, the sound of shouting met our ears from the direction of what my father told me was the main day room.

'That's Grandad George, isn't it?' I gasped.

'Sounds like it.' Rafe chuckled. 'Come on. Don't worry, Helen,' he said to the woman behind the reception desk. 'I know the way.'

I followed Rafe to the room where the din was coming from and we found Grandad George seated opposite another elderly gent who looked, in style of dress at least, much like my father. The pair seemed to be engaged in a loud debate as to the legitimacy of a word one of them had just added to the Scrabble board that was set up between them.

'Fetch the dictionary, Beth!' Grandad George demanded. 'Freddie's cheating *again*!'

'Fetch it yourself,' the woman he'd addressed responded and I had to put my hand over my mouth to stop a rush of laughter escaping. 'I've got better things to do than referee for you two, *again*. Besides, we've got visitors.'

The two men turned to the door and Grandad George's expression was transformed.

'My darling girl!' he called out, looking bright-eyed. 'You're here!'

I rushed to give him a hug and breathed in the scent of mints and cedarwood aftershave that I associated him with.

'Hello Grandad,' I beamed as I squatted at the side of the table to see him properly. 'I'm sorry it's been so long.'

He held on tightly to my hand, and it was a struggle not to cry. I might have left found family behind, but in Norwich I had not one, but two blood relatives to further bond with.

'Never mind that,' he said and leant forward to kiss my cheek. 'You're here now.'

'Are you going to introduce us?' the man I knew was called Freddie, requested.

'This,' Grandad George said proudly as I stood up, 'is my delightful granddaughter, Skylar. She's just moved to Norwich and is sharing a house in Nightingale Square with my son, Rafe, who you've already met.'

'It's a delight to meet you, my dear,' Freddie twinkled. 'And I know the square, of course. I've spent many happy times there enjoying the garden and parties in the Grow-Well.'

'And,' Beth, the reluctant referee, said, 'I know it too because I live there.'

'Do you?' I gasped.

'Yes,' she said, 'with my partner, Eli. We're just a couple of houses away from where you and Rafe are in Heather and Glen's place. Or should I say, old place, given that it's yours now?'

'What a coincidence!' I laughed and looked at Rafe who smiled.

'Beth is the activities manager here,' Freddie put in. 'She keeps us all entertained, but not necessarily out of mischief.'

I got the impression that Beth most likely had her hands full with some of the sprightlier residents.

'In that case, Beth,' Rafe said, 'may I ask if you walk here from the square?'

'I do,' she nodded.

'That's good to know,' I puffed. 'I'll be picking your brains later about the route you take, if that's all right. We drove here today and it was not pleasant.'

'I can imagine,' Beth shuddered. 'If you come on foot and take a couple of shortcuts I've discovered, you can be here in no time. I'll draw you a map.'

With that decided, she went to set up the net for table tennis at the far end of the room where the windows overlooked a large garden.

'Come on,' Grandad George said as he, a little stiffly, eased himself upright. 'Let's find somewhere a bit quieter to properly catch up.'

'We'll continue this later then, shall we George?' said Freddie with a nod to the board.

Grandad George pretended not to hear him and as he moved away from the table, he somehow flipped the board completely over.

Freddie let out a roar of frustration. 'You old sod!' he objected. 'You only did that because I was winning.'

'You were not,' Grandad George shot back. 'Now, if you don't mind,' he added with dignity, 'I want to spend some quality time with my granddaughter.'

For the second time since I'd arrived, I had to suppress a laugh and Rafe looked amused too.

'He's a blatant cheat,' Grandad George told us as we followed him out. 'Blatant.'

Rafe shook his head and I felt very happy to find my

grandfather in such high spirits. Though that said, I wouldn't have wanted to swap places with Beth when it was time for the rematch!

Having been given a snail's pace tour of the ground floor of the home and admired Grandad George's large and comfortable room, Rafe and I then explained how we'd divvied up the rooms in the house along with what the cats had been up to.

'Well, that sounds very sensible,' Grandad George said in response to us telling him that we each had our own sitting room. 'I had been wondering how the pair of you were going to rub along, having never spent longer than a summer holiday together.'

'Do you know,' Rafe said, 'that thought has never crossed my mind. Though,' he added, with a look to me and a shudder, 'I bet it would have crossed yours, Skylar, if you'd had to move back in with your mum.'

'Given your shared history, there must be something about her that you like?' I chuckled.

'I don't think we need to know the details of Flighty Faye's appeal where your father is concerned,' Grandad George tutted. 'It'll be dinner time soon and I don't want my appetite curbed. It's fish and chips on a Saturday.'

Rafe shook his head and rolled his eyes.

'Fish and chips,' I said wistfully. 'I can't remember the last time I had fish and chips.'

'We can have them tonight, if you like,' Rafe offered. 'Rumour has it, there's a great place in the city that delivers.'

'I'm tempted,' I swallowed, my mouth watering at the thought, 'but will they complement the whisky you promised me?'

'Only one way to find out!' Grandad George grinned.

'Oh well,' I said. 'Knowing what a connoisseur you are, if it's Grandad George approved, fish, chips and Laphroaig it is.'

With that settled, it was time for us to go, but not before Beth came to find us and gave me a simple looking map of the walk she took to and from the square to the care home.

'This looks easy enough,' Rafe said, when I gave him the paper. 'How about I head back on foot,' he suggested, 'and we'll see if I'm back before you get there in the car?'

'No chance!' I objected. 'I'm not making that journey on my own.'

'Fair enough,' Rafe accepted. 'It wasn't really fair of me to suggest it, I suppose. We'll go back together and I'll see if I can use my phone to offer some different directions to your satnav to avoid the ring road.'

'Whatever you do, don't listen to him, Skylar!' Grandad George shouted. 'He couldn't find his way out of a paper bag. Heaven knows where you'd end up.'

'Hey!' Rafe grumbled. 'I'm not that bad.' I gave him a look. 'Well, perhaps I am . . .'

'We'll stick to whatever the satnav says just this once,' I said. 'But thank you for the map, Beth. We'll use that the next time we come.'

'You won't leave it too long, will you?' Grandad George asked.

'I won't leave it many days at all,' I promised him.

'And neither will I, Dad,' Rafe smiled. 'And we'll have to see about getting you to the house soon, too.'

'Oh, yes,' I said. 'It will be lovely to show you around.'

'And introduce you to the Grow-Well,' Beth suggested. 'Then

you'll be able to compare notes about what it's like with Freddie, won't you George?'

'We're yet to introduce ourselves to the Grow-Well,' Rafe told her. 'But I'm planning a visit tomorrow.'

'I'll probably see you there then,' Beth smiled, then had to rush back to the day room where someone had started playing 'Great Balls of Fire' very loudly on the piano.

'That's Freddie,' Grandad George tutted. 'He's such a show off, but he does have a knack of keeping everyone's spirits up and joints in working order!'

I tried not to imagine the scene that would meet Beth's return, but I was grateful for Freddie's timely musical performance because it meant there had been no opportunity for her to ask me if I would be joining Rafe in the Grow-Well the next day. I had been feeling shy about meeting everyone before but wondering if the guy who had challenged my presence in the garden might be there too was now my main reason for not wanting to go over. That said, I'd have to face it soon, because the lure of the garden was beckoning . . .

Citing my desire to try out the new vacuum cleaners and give the house a good dust and airing – the fish and chips the evening before had been delicious, but the smell lingered – as a reason for not wanting to accompany Rafe to the Grow-Well, I shut the cats in his sitting room once he'd gone and set to.

With my summery Spotify playlist filling my ears and plenty of rooms to clean, I soon wasn't thinking about what my father was doing, or who he was getting to know. The only rooms I left were Rafe's bedroom and en suite. He'd insisted that he'd sort those himself, and when I reached it, I decided I wouldn't touch his writing room, either. Now the muse had retuned, I didn't want to do anything that might send it packing.

'Come on then, you two,' I said to Socks and Plato who shot out of the room the moment I opened the sitting room door.

I'd double-checked all the windows were closed again and the bifold doors locked before releasing them and then shut the pair in the kitchen in case Rafe returned while I was vacuuming and I didn't hear him knock. I didn't think he'd be too much longer because the smell of the beef joint he'd put in the slow cooker at the crack of dawn was now temptingly permeating every nook and cranny and it would soon be time for him to start making the crunchy on the outside, fluffy on the inside roast potatoes he was an expert at. My mouth watered at the thought, and I resisted the urge to lift the lid on the beef.

I'd just put the vacuum on to charge when he returned looking wind-blown but very happy and carrying a jute bag.

'How did you find the garden?' I asked him.

He held up the bag. 'It's amazing! Fruit, veg, hens, honey, cats and the loveliest mix of people.'

'You met some more of the neighbours then?'

'I did,' he nodded. 'And you must soon, too. Not everyone was there, but our nearest neighbours Carole and Graham were, along with Beth and the head gardener, Freya, and her partner, Finn. He was a sight to behold, but nothing like as fearsome as he looked.'

'What do you mean?' I asked as I wondered if he might have been the guy I'd run into.

'He's pure Viking,' Rafe grinned. 'Really long braided hair, arm ring, the lot.' That didn't sound quite like who I was thinking of. 'But surprisingly quiet. I had to coax the little conversation we had out of him. Everyone asked after you, Freya especially.'

'She did?'

'Yes, she asked me to ask you if you'd like to go over tomorrow afternoon and she'll show you the Grow-Well. She also said to tell you that there likely wouldn't be anyone else there, unlike today, if that makes a difference. Does it?' Rafe frowned.

'No, but I might take her up on her offer anyway.' If I was with her, I'd be less likely to be confronted again. 'Did she say what time?'

'She gave me her mobile number,' Rafe said, handing me his phone so I could find it, 'and said she'd call round after she's had her lunch tomorrow and the two of you could go over then, if that suits you. How does that sound?'

'Ideal,' I said rather distractedly, because I'd spotted a notification and email on my phone that I hadn't been expecting as I keyed in Freya's number. 'I'll message her later and say yes.'

'Great,' Rafe said and drew in a breath. 'Now, that beef smells good. I better get the potatoes on and maybe you could wash these?' He held up the bag.

'What's in there?'

'Freshly dug carrots and just picked French beans,' he told me with a grin. 'Prepare yourself for a flavour sensation and our first taste of the good life in Nightingale Square!'

Chapter 6

Our Sunday dinner was delicious, but having read what the email was about, along with checking the Instagram notification which had also landed, I was unable to reach the same levels of ecstasy over what the veg tasted like as Rafe did. Fortunately, he didn't notice my dip in mood and waxed lyrical about the potential having the community garden to tend and harvest was going to offer us. Apparently, our vitamin D levels were going to be fully topped up and our diet much enhanced.

Knowing he was keen to get writing again once we'd finished eating, I insisted I would clear away and load the dishwasher, and I didn't hear another peep out of him. I sat in my sitting room and fell to brooding, then didn't sleep well, so wasn't feeling at my best when Freya came to meet me after her lunch break the next day.

'Ready?' she smiled, when I opened the door.

There had been a definite downturn in the weather, and it was cool and rather breezy, so I pulled a jumper on over my long-sleeved T-shirt before locking the door and slipping the key into my jeans pocket.

'I am,' I nodded. 'It was really kind of you to offer to do this.'

'It's no trouble.'

'No Nell today?'

'She was with me this morning, but there was no budging her just now. She's not a fan of windy weather, so I've left her curled up in her basket.'

'Sensible Nell,' I sighed.

'Are you all right?' Freya frowned.

'Yes,' I said. 'Sorry. I had some news yesterday, and I suppose it wasn't entirely unexpected, but it's still made me feel a bit . . . sad.'

'Do you want to talk about it?' she asked, as she keyed in the code to the garden gate once we'd crossed the road.

'I daresay I'm being over the top,' I shrugged. 'It's a silly thing really—'

'Nothing's silly if it upsets you,' Freya cut in. 'What might be completely insignificant to one person can mean the end of the world to another.'

'Well,' I said. 'It's not the end of the world, but it isn't insignificant, either. Not to me, anyway. I had an email from the people I used to work for letting me know that they'd decided to delete the Insta account attached to the hall. They were still getting email booking enquiries, although there was a pinned post explaining that Highfell now has different owners.'

Madeline and Tobias had also been keen to know how I was settling in and if Rafe and I were getting along but Freya didn't need to know that.

'Did you think they might keep the account going, even though they no longer live there?' Freya asked.

'I hadn't really thought about it,' I told her. 'I suppose it wasn't very likely but by the time I'd read the email and then gone to look for one last time, the account was already gone. I would have liked to have taken some screenshots of the grid . . .'

'Maybe you could ask them if there's any way you can access the photos you wanted to save?' Freya suggested.

'It's not so much about that,' I sighed again, struggling to explain. 'I was the one who took most of the photos, so they're all on my phone anyway.'

'Well, that's something.'

'I suppose . . .' I continued, still struggling to find the words, 'I guess this has made me properly realise that part of my life is now completely over. I probably should have grasped that when I packed my car and drove away last week, but this was the last connection to the place I had and having it severed before I had a chance to prepare for it, feels . . . well, I don't know exactly, but rather like another blow.'

Freya put an arm around me. It was a kind, but unexpected gesture from someone I'd only just met, but I gratefully rested my head on her shoulder, nonetheless.

'I completely understand,' she said. 'I think it all stems from it not being your decision to leave. I know that impacted on me when I left Broad-Meadows.' She'd said something about that before. 'Go with the flow and allow yourself to feel these emotions, Skylar. Don't try to dismiss them because ultimately that won't help you come to terms with the changes.'

'You're right,' I swallowed, aware that she was talking total sense. 'I know you are.'

'Endings are tough,' she said and squeezed me closer.

'But they're also the gateway to new beginnings.'

She smiled at that and let me go. 'Who said that?'

'I read it on a tea towel somewhere,' I smiled.

'Great,' she grinned. 'Not really what you want to hear when you're in the midst of something traumatic though, is it?'

'No,' I agreed. 'Now come on, show me where all this fruit and veg that my father has fallen into raptures over is growing and what he's supposed to do to help it make the journey from seed packet to saucepan.'

'This way,' Freya pointed, thankfully not saying that I was supposed to play a part, too.

However, I was barely through the Grow-Well gate before I realised why Rafe had been so smitten. Created within the original and sheltered Prosperous Place walled garden, the scene before me wouldn't have looked out of place in a self-sufficiency magazine six-page spread. That number of pages would have been needed to do it all justice.

There were raised beds full of healthy looking veg, some ready for harvesting, various varieties of fruit bushes and trees growing both near and along the brick walls, a hen house and spacious run, complete with half a dozen clucking hens and the cutest bothy with two cats stretched out along the window-sill where it was doubtless warmer than reclining outside in the wind.

'That's Violet and Dash,' Freya told me. 'Brother and sister, born and bred here and always up to some mischief.'

'That sounds like my father's cats, Socrates and Plato,' I smiled, my former upset about the Highfell Insta account for the moment forgotten. 'One is quieter than the other but still far too easily led astray.'

'Cool names,' Freya approved. 'This pair are neck and neck on the mayhem front. What one doesn't think of the other one does.'

I laughed at that.

'Is that an oven?' I asked, pointing towards what I thought looked like a traditional pizza oven.

'It is,' Freya confirmed and headed over to where it had been built. 'Lisa's husband John is head chef and this is where we hold various parties and celebrations throughout the year. Even right through the winter if it's dry.'

There were tables set out and chairs of all kinds, along with bunting flapping in the lowest branches of a vast oak tree.

'How lovely,' I smiled.

Even though I had been reluctant to join Rafe and meet everyone the day before, I could see the appeal of a party in the Grow-Well and perhaps I might at some point develop an urge to pitch in with the growing and so on, though I would need guidance because I was no gardener.

'The whole place is an oasis in the city,' Freya said wistfully. 'Though,' she added, as she looked around, 'it's currently getting a bit out of hand.' It looked fine to me, but then I wouldn't know a weed from a wallflower. 'Graham and Carole mostly take the lead because they're retired, but Graham hasn't been well this year, though he's on the mend now.'

I remembered Rafe had mentioned them as our nearest neighbours. He hadn't said that Graham had been poorly but given that it was the first time he had met them, it wasn't likely to have come up in conversation, and he wouldn't have noticed if Graham looked different because he hadn't known him before.

'I'm sorry to hear that,' I said. 'Though obviously pleased that he's recovering.'

Freya went to say something else, but a sudden spattering

of cold raindrops landed with the next gust of wind and she shrieked instead.

'Shall we wait it out in the bothy?' I suggested as it started to rain harder.

'No,' she said. 'Come on. I've got a better idea!'

I followed her back out of the Grow-Well and along a path I hadn't been down before.

'I'll introduce you to my partner, Finn,' she said, as we briskly walked side by side. 'He's got a studio where he creates his art just along here.'

'His art?'

I tried to match the description of the Viking that Rafe had given me with my idea of an artist.

'Yes,' Freya said, filling in the blanks for me. 'He's a sculptor. He made the hares and dragons in the garden, among other things. Did I not say?'

'Wow!' I gasped. 'No, you didn't. What an amazing talent to have.'

Further conversation was halted as the rain came down even harder and we both squealed and made a dash to get under cover. Had I known what was waiting for me on the other side of the large door, I might not have been so keen to rush through it. However, by the time I'd realised who one of the deep voices inside belonged to, it was too late.

I came to an abrupt halt and Freya had to nudge me further in to close the door behind us.

'Well,' she laughed, 'this wasn't in the forecast. There goes my plan to cut the main lawn this afternoon.'

'That's my fault,' I apologised. 'Giving me a guided tour has held you up.'

She shook her head at that. 'I would have hardly got started,' she said kindly, making me feel better.

I was looking everywhere but at the two men standing opposite us but I knew Freya wouldn't put the moment of introduction off for ever.

'I didn't expect to find you here, Erik,' she continued, 'but I'm pleased I have because that kills two birds with one stone. Erik, Finn may I introduce you to Skylar. Skylar, this is our friend, Erik, and my partner, Finn.'

I took a deep breath and looked up. I looked at Finn first and found him to be everything Rafe had described.

'Hello Skylar,' he smiled. 'I met your dad yesterday.'

'Yes,' I nodded. 'He did say.'

'He mentioned me?' Finn blushed.

'He did,' I confirmed.

'Crikey,' he said and fiddled with one of the leather bracelets he was wearing. 'I hope I didn't make a fool of myself. I'm a total Rafe Harding fan and to be honest, I didn't really know what to say to him.'

I smiled at that. 'He didn't say you were anything other than lovely,' I reassured him and Finn blushed deeper. 'And I'm a huge fan of yours, Finn. I had the best time on Friday spotting all the dragons as I got to know the garden. Not to mention the hares. They're outstanding.'

'Don't say another word, Skylar,' Freya laughed. 'He's already wishing the floor would open up and swallow him.'

Clearly, Finn was as shy as Rafe had guessed, but what about Erik? I didn't much want to talk to him, but I could hardly ignore him, could I? I shifted my gaze to look at him. He was wearing jeans and boots with the laces undone and a ruby coloured linen henley shirt which I realised, when my eyes travelled up to his face, annoyingly enhanced the blueness of his eyes. It was an accomplishment I wouldn't have thought possible because they were already bright enough.

'Hello,' I nodded.

On meeting him again, I couldn't help thinking he looked familiar, but whether that was because he had been annoyingly in my thoughts during the last few days or another reason, I couldn't decide. Either way, here he was, the set of his jaw almost as rigid as it had been during our first encounter.

'Hi,' he responded and that was it.

Freya, obviously realising that neither of us were going to say anything further, carried on.

'Until you and Rafe arrived,' she said to me, 'Erik was the newest member of the clan.'

'Is that right?' I said and turned to look at her.

I wondered if he'd taken a dislike to me for taking his place as the newbie, but that would have been ridiculous, wouldn't it?

'He was Luke's friend first and now he's . . . well, I suppose you're the unofficial property manager and maintenance guy here, aren't you, Erik?' Freya said.

I wondered if he was the person responsible for trying to get Kate to change the security codes and how he was feeling about Freya telling me things that he clearly had no desire to volunteer himself. I turned back to look at him to find he was already staring at me. It was most unsettling.

'Something like that,' he said, his eyes still on mine.

'I suppose that explains why you were so rude to me when you spotted me in the garden last week, doesn't it?' I blurted out. 'I daresay you thought I was trespassing. You would have made me feel better if you'd explained that.'

I sensed Freya and Finn exchanging a look.

'You've already met?' Freya asked.

'Sort of,' I shrugged.

'You didn't mention it, Erik,' Finn said.

'I didn't think,' he also shrugged as he finally looked away and as the rain began to drum more loudly on the studio roof. 'I need to go.'

'Not in this!' Freya protested. 'You'll get soaked without a coat.'

'I told Luke we'd look at some quotes for clearing the gutters ahead of winter,' he mumbled. 'I'd hoped to do it myself, but . . . anyway, I don't want to keep him waiting.'

Clearly, I wasn't going to get either an apology or even an acknowledgement that he could have made me feel better before.

'Take this then,' Finn said, as he moved to grab a waxed coat from a hook.

'Thanks,' Erik said and shrugged it on.

He looked even more rugged in the oversized coat, and I stepped aside as he made for the door in a reversal of the dance we'd had at the gate on Friday.

'See you tonight!' Finn called after him, but he was gone.

'He's not usually like that,' Freya frowned looking from Finn to me.

'I can't say that makes me feel any better,' I smiled brightly, even though I felt a fool. And not for the first time where he was concerned. 'Though thank you for telling me.'

'No, I'm sorry,' Freya tutted. 'I don't suppose it would.'

'Coffee?' Finn offered, holding up a jar.

'I should get back really,' I said and looked towards the door Erik had just fled through.

The rain was still hammering down.

'But you haven't got a coat either,' Freya pointed out.

'And I haven't got another spare,' Finn added. 'So, you might as well wait until it slackens off a bit.'

'And I'm not going anywhere,' Freya said. 'I can't do much in this and certainly nothing I'd got planned.'

'All right,' I agreed. 'I'll stay and coffee would be great, thank you.'

Finn gave me a tour of his studio. His work was mostly made from scrap metal which made it sustainable as well as stunning and Freya made me laugh when she explained that Nell was only allowed inside if she was wearing little bootees to protect her pads from any sharp bits of metal that hadn't been swept up.

'What a sensible precaution,' I smiled as I imagined what Nell must look like. 'Does she mind wearing them?'

'Not at all now,' Freya told me. 'She waits at the studio door for me to put them on. She's a clever old thing.'

The image of Nell lifting one leg and then the other while Freya or Finn slipped the bootees on was an amusing one, but as soon as it popped out of my head, my second encounter with Erik burst back in.

'You're not thinking about Erik, are you?' Freya asked perceptively, when Finn went to rinse out the mugs.

'No,' I fibbed. 'I just remembered about the Insta account being deleted, but I'm grateful to you for the distraction this afternoon. You've stopped me dwelling for too long.'

'Well,' she said, 'dwelling is fine for a while.'

'But not a life plan,' I nodded as Finn came back into the room.

'Another tea towel saying?' Freya nudged.

'It could be, couldn't it?' I laughed.

'What's this?' Finn asked.

'While Skylar's between jobs, she's been thinking about printing a range of inspirational quotes on tea towels,' Freya told him, deadpan.

'Oh right,' he said, looking from her to me. 'Well, that sounds—'

'She's joking,' I interrupted before he had to struggle to find the words to say something positive about the made-up venture. 'I might not know what my next job is going to be, but it won't be that!'

Chapter 7

The next day, I had no desire to disturb Rafe, who was immersed in his first draft, so I waited until the rain had cleared and then took myself off to see Grandad George. Armed with the map Beth had given us and an umbrella just in case, I thoroughly enjoyed the walk from the square, even though the weather had completely changed from the week before.

I had arrived in Norwich on a wave of warm late summer sunshine, but now, exactly one week on, autumn seemed to have landed and there was a coolness in the air that I couldn't imagine the temperature would recover from until next spring.

'Hi Skylar,' Beth greeted me once I'd signed in at the care home and gone to see if Grandad George was in the day room. 'I take it you walked here,' she added, with a nod to the umbrella. 'How did you find the journey?'

'So lovely. It was easy to find my way, thanks to your instructions, and completely stress free, so I'm really grateful.'

'Excellent,' she smiled. 'I'm pleased to have been able to help.'

'You don't happen to know where George is, do you?'

'He's off doing something at the moment, but you're welcome

to wait for him in here, if you like. I'm just about to serve tea and biscuits ahead of the quiz. Would you like a cup?'

There wasn't a spare seat in the packed room and the trolley in the doorway was loaded with cups, saucers and everything else required for an afternoon cuppa.

'No thank you,' I said. 'But I'm happy to help you, if that's allowed. You look like you've got plenty of takers.'

'Oh yes, please. That would be great,' she said. 'If you could hand out the biscuits, that would save me no end of time. Everyone's allowed two to start with and there are no dietary restrictions with anyone in here, so they can have what they like.'

With both of us on duty it didn't take long to serve everyone and that freed Beth up to get the things together for the quiz. Grandad George still hadn't appeared and, having noticed there was a resident set a little apart from everyone else, I went to say hello.

'Would you mind if I sit here?' I asked, indicating the fabric footstool next to her chair. 'Only there's nowhere else to sit and I'm waiting for my grandad.'

'I don't mind,' she said quietly, and I gingerly sat down hoping the stool would take my weight, which it did.

'How's your tea?' I asked.

'It's all right,' she said, peering into the cup. 'Not quite as strong as I really like, but it's drinkable.'

'Would you like me to make you another?'

'No, you're all right. I'll stick with this.'

'I like my tea strong, too,' I told her. 'I put it down to years of living in Yorkshire.'

Her gaze shifted from looking at the tea in her cup to my

face. Her eyes looked a little dull and tinged with sadness and her complexion was pale.

'You're not a Yorkshire lass though, are you?' she frowned. 'You don't have the accent. My husband was from Scarborough, and you don't sound anything like him.'

'Was he?' I smiled. 'I've visited the North Bay Beach area and really liked it, but no, I wasn't born and bred there. I moved to Yorkshire for my work, but that's come to an end and I'm living with my father in Norwich now.'

'I thought I recognised you,' she said, sounding a little more animated. 'You were here last week with Rafe Harding, weren't you?'

'That's right. He's my father. I'm his daughter, Skylar.'

'Well, I never,' she said. 'I love his books.'

'I'll tell him that,' I nodded. 'He'll be thrilled!'

'Oh no, don't,' she said and her cheeks flushed. 'I'd be embarrassed and I've got enough on my plate without worrying about him knowing that . . .'

'What have you got on your plate?' I asked forthrightly. 'Is something the matter?'

'Oh, it's nothing really.'

'If it's troubling you . . . sorry, I don't know your name.'

'Mabel. My name is Mabel.'

'Well, if it's troubling you Mabel,' I said kindly, remembering the conversation I'd so recently had with Freya, 'then it's something rather than nothing.'

She looked at me and sighed. 'I suppose I'm having a bit of a time of it, adjusting to life in here,' she blurted out. 'I'd lived on my own since my Arthur died and I was managing fine, but then I had a fall and our daughter, who works abroad a lot of the time, panicked that I wasn't safe on my own and suggested I should come here.'

'But you didn't want to?'

'It's not that there's anything wrong with the place,' she said. 'And the staff are lovely, but no, I didn't want to. Not really. But I didn't want to be a burden either, so I agreed to move.'

'I'm sorry to hear that you're unhappy, Mabel,' I swallowed, feeling choked.

'I've got used to my own company since my Arthur died. He was the love of my life you know,' I smiled at that. 'And I'm finding it a bit . . . full on in here. There are all these activities every day, but I'd like to be left to my own devices and have a quiet chat with someone every now and again but there's been no chance of that.'

I could see how someone who was used to living on their own might find the busyness overwhelming. On the one hand, I could appreciate how important it was to keep the residents active and engaged, but clearly it didn't suit what everyone needed.

'Have you told anyone how you're feeling?' I asked.

'No,' she said and shook her head. 'I don't want to be a bother. Look,' she added, 'here's your grandad. You go and see him, my love. After all, that's what you've come for. And I'm all right really.'

'It's okay, I'm happy to chat.'

'No,' she insisted. 'You get along and remember, not a word to your dad that I'm a fan.'

I didn't want to leave her, but she was adamant and so I left her to it, wondering whether I should say something to Beth about how she was feeling. Would that be overstepping? I'd only handed out a few biscuits and that hardly made me staff.

'Skylar!' Grandad George welcomed me before I had decided. 'How long have you been here?'

'Just a few minutes.'

'Thankfully long enough to help me stop the scavengers nabbing more biscuits than they should,' Beth put in.

'Oh blast,' Grandad George grumbled. 'I didn't realise how late it was. Have I missed my afternoon cuppa?'

'There's plenty of tea left,' Beth said, 'but biscuit-wise, it's Rich Tea or nothing.'

'No chocolate digestives?' he tutted.

'Nope,' she said and showed him the inside of the tin to prove the point.

'Well, I call that feeble,' he sulked but took two Rich Teas anyway.

'Well, you should have been here at the right time then, shouldn't you?' Freddie teased as he ostentatiously popped half a chocolate digestive into his mouth and crunched with relish.

'I hope it gets stuck in your dentures,' Grandad George scowled.

'I'll have you know,' Freddie began to bluster, but I cut him off.

'Yes,' I asked. 'Where were you, Grandad?'

'He was setting—' Freddie interjected before Grandad George had a chance to tell me.

'Thank you!' he snapped. 'If I want my granddaughter, or anyone else in the day room to know where I was then I'll be the one to tell them, not you, Freddie show-off Fanshawe.'

Beth and I exchanged a look.

'Well, I didn't know it was a secret, did I?' Freddie huffed back.

I looked over to see what Mabel was making of the noisy

exchange which seemed to be amusing everyone else. Her expression was vacant and she was staring out of the window at the rain that had started up again.

'Come on, Skylar,' Grandad George said as he linked his arm through mine. 'Let's go and talk in my room where we won't be overheard!'

We made our way along the corridors. The place felt like a maze to me. Perhaps I should ask Beth for another map until I could find my way to Grandad's room unassisted.

'Do you really not like Freddie?' I asked, when we were out of earshot of the day room.

'On the contrary,' Grandad grinned. 'He's my favourite person in here.'

'Really?'

'Absolutely. There's nothing like a little lively debate and some cross words to keep the brain active and the wits sharp.'

'I'm not sure Mabel would agree with you,' I sighed.

'Mabel?'

'Never mind,' I said. 'This is your room, isn't it? I remember the number.'

As instructed, I closed the door while Grandad George rooted around in the nightstand for what turned out to be a secret cache of chocolate digestives.

'All that fuss,' I pretended to scold, 'and you've got a stash in here anyway!'

'I didn't want anyone else to figure that out, so I had to make a show of missing out. It costs a fortune for me to be here, so I might as well have what I'm due.'

'Right down to a chocolate digestive biscuit apparently,' I smiled.

'Quite,' he grinned. 'Help yourself.'

I took one then sat in the armchair he'd allocated for visitors while he made himself comfortable in the one that had a mechanism for helping him sit down and stand up again.

'Now, he said, once he'd finished dunking and drinking, 'tell me how you're settling in. It's a week today since the big move, isn't it?'

'It is,' I nodded. 'And for the most part, very well. The house is absolutely lovely, the cats are settled and Rafe's writing again.'

'So, that's the bricks and mortar, the feline occupants and my son accounted for,' he reeled off, 'but I was asking about you, Skylar. How are *you* adjusting to city life?'

I got the impression that blagging about how I was really feeling wasn't going to work with my grandfather. And having taken on board what Freya had said, I thought I shouldn't attempt it.

'Well, given how quiet the square is and with the addition of the beautiful garden and community space across the road at Prosperous Place, it doesn't really feel like city life,' I began. 'Though it isn't anywhere near as remote as Highfell, obviously.'

'Obviously,' Grandad George echoed. 'And how are you enjoying not working? Are you making the most of the time and having a proper rest which, in my opinion as well as Rafe's, was very much overdue.'

'Aside from taking on the cleaning in the house, I'm doing absolutely nothing,' I told him. 'Nothing at all.'

He was quiet for a moment. 'And that's a problem, because?' he asked.

'I didn't say it was a problem,' I frowned.

'Not directly, but your tone did.'

'Oh,' I swallowed.

'Go on.'

'It's not *really* a problem. I'm just not used to having nothing to do, and with so many hours to fill I'm starting to find myself either stuck in the past or beginning to fret about the future.'

There, that was a truly honest statement.

'Oh dear,' Grandad George sighed. 'I know it's early days, but that's not what Rafe had in mind for you at all, my dear. He was hoping this time would help you rest. He didn't want you to be brooding and looking backwards or worrying about what would come next.'

'I know,' I sighed, 'and that's why I haven't told him. As far as he's concerned, I am resting. You won't say anything, will you?'

'I'd hate to think that we're keeping him in the dark—'

'But like you've just said,' I interrupted, 'it's early days. By this time next week, I might feel completely differently.'

Grandad George handed me the biscuits, and I helped myself to another one.

'But then again,' he said, 'you might not and I think I know what you need.'

'What's that?'

'Something to anchor you in the present,' he said eagerly. 'Something that will take up some of the many empty hours you're struggling to currently fill with . . . well, nothing.'

'I'm not sure how Rafe would react if I told him I was looking for work just a week after I've moved in with him.'

'Who said anything about work?' Grandad George shrugged. 'Why not take up a hobby or try your hand at something different for a while. Try your hand at a few different things until you hit on something you feel passionate about. Anything to stop you brooding.'

'I suppose I could . . .'

'And you might find that the distraction, or distractions, unscramble your thoughts about the future. You could even discover an entirely different career to pursue as a result.'

'I wouldn't go that far,' I said, before he got further carried away. 'I loved my job at Highfell. Yes, it had its stressful moments, but at the end of the day, when the niggles were all resolved, turning client's celebration dreams into reality was amazing. I really loved it and I'll definitely want to do it again even though that will most likely mean I'll have to . . .'

'Even though that will most likely mean you'll have to what?' Grandad George frowned when my words trailed off.

In the unguarded moment, I had been about to say that, depending on what jobs became available in the future, it would most likely mean moving again, but thankfully I'd stopped the words spilling out. I might have been honest with Grandad George about a lot, but I wasn't going to share that. I wasn't going to tell anyone that my time in the square might potentially have an expiration date.

'Find an inventive way of explaining the gap in my employment history on my CV when it comes to finding a new job,' I said, thinking on my feet.

'I'm sure you'll come up with something,' Grandad George smiled. 'Given that your heart is set on this career that you love.'

'I'm sure I will, too.'

I'd got away with it, but only just.

'And talking of love,' Grandad George went on, completely

changing tack. 'Have you or Rafe spotted any eligible men in Nightingale Square?'

'Grandad!' I gasped. 'We've only been here a week.'

'Your father can be a fast worker when someone takes his fancy.'

'Honestly,' I tutted, though I knew he was right. 'Well, I can't speak for Rafe, but no, I haven't seen any eligible men in Nightingale Square.'

He didn't need to know about attractive 'Ol Blue Eyes' across the road. Even if Erik was available he either made me angry or feel a fool and neither emotion was a base to build any kind of relationship on.

'Well, keep your eyes peeled.' Grandad George winked. 'A bit of a fling could be the ultimate distraction.'

I rolled my eyes at that and went to stand up.

'You know very well that I don't go in for flings,' I told him as I brushed biscuit crumbs into my hand and dropped them in the wastepaper bin. 'Mum's track record has put me off casual relationships for life. I'd rather go without.'

'Fair enough,' he said, because he knew what the situation with Mum was like and the impact her love life had had on me. 'Are you going?'

'Yes,' I said, with a nod to the window. 'It seems to have stopped raining again, so I'll dash back now. It was a much quicker journey on foot, but I've got my brolly, just in case.'

'Good idea. Though you're very welcome to stay, of course.'

'I know I am,' I said, and leant down to kiss his cheek, 'and thank you, but I'd better get back. Rafe forgets to eat and drink when he's writing unless he's summoned, and it's time he had a break.'

'All right,' Grandad George said, and squeezed my hand. 'And if you don't come back soon, that will be no bad thing because it will mean you've found something to fill your time, but don't leave it too long, will you?'

'I won't,' I promised. 'And I know Rafe will be here tomorrow.'

I left him with his newspaper and made my way back through the warren of corridors to the reception area. All sounded calm and quiet in the day room, so the quiz must have gone smoothly. Either that or Beth had given everyone a silent time out!

'Skylar!' said the woman herself, just as I reached for the security pad to open the door. 'Have you got a sec?'

'Of course. Is everything all right?'

'Absolutely fine. I just wanted to say thank you for talking to Mabel earlier.'

'I enjoyed it. She's lovely.'

'She is, but she's been like a fish out of water since she arrived,' Beth said worriedly. 'Did she happen to mention anything about what's bothering her? She insists she's fine whenever I ask her, but she's clearly not.'

Given that she had asked me so directly, I decided to share what Mabel had told me in the hope that Beth could make some adjustments to accommodate her going forward.

'We hate to think of residents staying in their rooms, but it sounds like Mabel would appreciate the peace,' Beth sighed, once I'd filled her in. 'Most residents who have lived alone before they arrive tend to embrace the company and what we offer, but it's not a fit for everyone . . .'

'Mabel isn't there just yet,' I confirmed. 'But what you offer here is amazing.' Rafe had given me a rundown of the weekly schedule, and it was packed and full of variety. 'And I'm sure she'll want to take part eventually, but for now she just wants peace and the odd quiet chat.'

'Okay,' Beth said. 'There is one thing we haven't got set up here that might be useful.'

'What's that?'

I couldn't imagine there was anything missing at Cavell Care.

'I'll come back to you when I've given it further thought,' Beth said and then added with a nod towards the sky. 'You better head off. It looks like it's going to chuck it down again any minute and I don't like to leave the reprobates to their own devices for too long!'

Just as she said that Freddie struck up on the piano.

'And I can hear why,' I laughed. 'I'll see you again soon.'

Chapter 8

My conversation with Grandad George gave me plenty to think about. I swiftly concluded that he was onto something when he had suggested that finding a new hobby or different pursuit to occupy my mind might be just the thing to stop me ricocheting between reminiscing about the past and fretting about the future. But what could I do? It had been a long time since I'd had free time, and working out how to fill the plentiful empty hours I now had at my disposal was suddenly proving to be a fulltime occupation.

'So, what are you up to today, Skylar?' Rafe asked while we sat in the kitchen and ate breakfast on the Friday morning. 'Now the weather's cleared up a bit, you could further explore the Prosperous Place garden or maybe put in an appearance at the Grow-Well.'

I had mulled over the possibility of offering to help in the community garden but had held back for two reasons. Firstly, I was no gardener and wouldn't want to get anything wrong. Freya had already said that there were certain areas getting out of hand and I wouldn't want to make them worse by pulling up the wrong thing. And secondly, there was the matter of a certain blue eyed Prosperous Place resident who I was still keen to avoid. The less said about him and how often he slipped uninvited into my thoughts the better!

'I'm not sure,' I told my father as I took another bite out of a warm, buttery and jam smeared croissant, 'but one thing I do know is that I won't be heading back to Blossom's again today. Having that bakery practically on the doorstep is far too tempting.'

With Rafe so engrossed in his writing, he had armed me with a shopping list at the beginning of the week and sent me out into the nearby street to pick up some food and drink. Consequently, I had spent some time every day since getting to know the area and the shops located there. There were lots of small businesses, including Greengages Grocers where Nightingale Square resident Poppy worked and Blossom's the bakery which had yet another neighbour, Mark, behind the counter and filling the ovens.

Rafe had told me about Poppy and Mark before I made my first recce and suggested I should introduce myself if I saw them, but I hadn't, even though they both wore name badges to identify them. I had started to regret keeping quiet now because when I did finally meet them it might be awkward if they remembered serving me and it became obvious that Rafe had mentioned them, and I hadn't then said hello.

There was also a busy coffeehouse on the same street, a packed vintage emporium and a second-hand bookshop. From what I'd seen, the street was as idyllic as Nightingale Square. The only place I hadn't been in was a pub called The Dragon. It was one of those old, dark buildings you could easily over-look, and I thought I might soon spend some time there but didn't mention it to Rafe because I didn't expect to end up there that day.

'I agree about Blossom's,' Rafe said as he swallowed the last of his croissant. 'My waistline doesn't need any extra padding this early in the autumn. I don't mind a couple of pounds going on over Christmas, but we're still months away from that.'

Rafe had always been health conscious and made a point of staying fit and trim. I had wondered if that was the LA lifestyle rubbing off on him. If it had been, he'd obviously carried it back with him to the UK when he moved.

'Well,' I said. 'I think you look fabulous.' He appeared mollified by that. 'And you'll soon find somewhere to exercise again if you really want to.'

'Um,' he said thoughtfully. 'Lisa sent me a text a couple of days ago suggesting an afternoon walk around a lake with her during the week. She thought it might be just the thing to give us the chance to get away from the screen and discuss plot problems and timelines and so on. She said she often goes for a stomp around Whitlingham to think things through ahead of the school run.'

'Right,' I said, drawing the word out. 'But I thought you preferred to keep your writing process and all the rest of it, to yourself?'

'I always have in the past,' he confirmed. 'But perhaps it's time for a change now I'm trying something new.'

I looked at him and frowned. He'd turned quite pink.

'You are currently working on the crime novel you're contracted to write, aren't you?' I quizzed.

'I've actually got a couple of projects on the go,' he said

cagily. 'You could come with me and Lisa if you like? Some brisk walking might be good for you, too.'

'I appreciate the offer, but I'm fine on my own for now and besides, I wouldn't want to hamper your creative conversation.'

He accepted that and rushed off to message Lisa and tell her he'd take her up on her offer beginning the following week and I swiftly got ready to head out before he tried to rope me into going with them again!

I wiled away the morning further exploring the shops and was just trying to make up my mind whether to walk back to the coffee shop or visit The Dragon, which I'd then arrived at, when the decision was made for me. Heading briskly in my direction, as I dithered on the pavement outside the pub, was Erik. I didn't think he'd spotted me, so I quickly turned around, pushed the door open and ducked inside.

Had my heart not been trying to beat its way out of my chest, I would have been instantly charmed, but it was a minute or so, when I was certain that Erik must have passed by, before I could take in the interior of the place and appreciate its Lilliputian proportions.

As well as being small, it was rather dark, even though it was relatively bright outside and the place smelt comfortingly of woodsmoke though there was currently no fire burning in the grate. The low ceiling was beamed, and I spotted a subtly backlit dragon sculpture scaling the wall that just had to be of Finn's making.

'It's quite something, isn't it?' commented the man behind the bar as I walked closer and took the details of the dragon in.

'The whole place is quite something,' I said, turning to smile at him. 'It feels like somewhere out of a fairytale.'

Finally mesmerised by the cosy atmosphere, I'd almost forgotten about Erik being somewhere in the vicinity.

'We get told that a lot,' the barman nodded. 'Either that or it reminds customers of The Prancing Pony in Hobbiton.'

'Actually,' I said, thinking of the film adaptations of The Lord of the Rings trilogy, 'that is a better description.'

'I take this is your first visit?'

'It is,' I confirmed. 'Am I too early for a bite to eat?'

With the pub looking so lovely and remembering about there being the possible danger I could run into Erik along the pavement if I left, I decided to play it safe and stay put.

'No, you're fine. Here's a menu, and while you're having a look, can I get you a drink?'

I opted for a half pint of locally brewed bitter as it felt most befitting and settled at a table for two next to the fireplace in anticipation of the chips which came highly recommend, and a fresh Cromer crab sandwich.

'So,' the barman asked when he came back a couple of minutes after delivering the food to check everything was okay, 'how are you finding it?'

'Absolutely delicious,' I told him. 'It's all divine, but the crab is sensational.'

'Excellent,' he smiled. 'I'll leave you to it then.'

The pub had filled up a little since I'd started eating and I felt thoroughly relaxed as I ate and watched the customers come and go. Or I was feeling relaxed until the door swung open and Erik stepped inside, effectively filling up every inch of space that was left. I hunkered down in my seat and attempted to become invisible. Though it only then dawned on me that I really needn't have worried about being spotted then or out on the street because given our track record he was hardly likely to seek me out for a cosy chat, was he?

Unfortunately, it turned out that I was wrong about that . . .

'Skylar?' I heard him say. 'I thought I saw you a few minutes ago but then you just seemed to disappear.'

I looked up and found his blue eyes trained on mine and a frowned etched across his forehead, but I didn't comment. To be fair I was still chewing the last bite of sandwich so could be excused for not responding. He was wearing another henley shirt, an unbuttoned navy one this time, and I wondered if he purposefully picked out his clothes to enhance the colour of his eyes.

'So,' he carried on in the face of my silence, 'you've found The Dragon then . . .'

'Apparently so,' I said quietly, once I'd swallowed. 'Is it a haunt of yours?'

Depending on his answer it might well end up being somewhere else I wanted to avoid. That got me virtually crossing my fingers in the hope that he would say no it wasn't his usual hostelry because I already loved the pub and would like to make it my local. I'd never had one before but could imagine myself spending quiet afternoons here with a book and a beer as the autumn days grew chillier.

'Erik!' called the barman, which gave me an answer, but not the one I had been hoping for. 'Pint of the usual?'

'Just a sec,' he called over and looked down at me again. 'Freya told me earlier that you haven't been back to the garden. She said she'd been expecting to see you because she thought you liked what you'd seen, but you hadn't shown up. Though I suppose, she might have missed you . . .'

'No, she's right,' I told him. 'I haven't been back.'

He raked a hand through his already unkempt blond hair and sighed.

'And I'm guessing that's probably my fault, isn't it?'

I was almost tempted to say he thought a lot of himself, but given that he was right, I swallowed the words away.

'Well—' I began.

'You don't have to deny it,' he said, cutting me off. 'I honestly can't account for my behaviour the previous times we've met Skylar, but I can apologise for it. I'm truly sorry for my less than warm welcome and I really hope it hasn't put you off visiting Prosperous Place.'

I hadn't been expecting him to say anything to me, but if I had attempted to guess the words that were going to come out of his mouth if he did, I wouldn't have reckoned on any of the ones he'd just said. He was quite transformed, in both conversation and looks. His features had softened and the expression in his eyes told me he was in earnest. In fact, he looked almost desperate that I should accept his apology.

'In that case,' I relented, 'how about we completely forget about what's gone before and I buy you a drink to prove it's behind us?'

'No,' he grinned, his eyes attractively crinkling at the corners. 'I'll buy you a drink. It's the least I can do.'

'All right,' I smiled back.

'What will you have?'

'I've just finished a half of the local bitter, so the same again would be great.'

'I think I'll go for that, too and some chips. I'm famished,' he said and headed to the bar.

It took a few minutes before he came back, because everyone seemed to know him and wanted to have a word with him and I got the feeling that it was down to more than just recognising someone you sometimes saw in a pub. I hadn't forgotten that I had previously thought I knew him from somewhere, too, and given that we were now on a friendlier footing, I decided to outright ask.

'Thank you,' I said, when he put my drink in front of me and sat in the chair opposite. He was so broad, his bulk effectively blocked my view of the entire place. 'I hope you don't mind me asking, Erik, but I can't shake off the feeling that I recognise you, but I'm pretty certain that we hadn't met before last week.'

He took a mouthful of his pint and ducked his head.

'I used to play rugby,' he said self-effacingly. 'Some people know me from that.'

'Of course!' I said and clicked my fingers as the penny dropped and his image fell into place. 'You're an international player, aren't you? I've seen you on TV *and* in the papers. My former boss was a huge rugby fan. How did I not twig before?'

Given his fame and talent, I thought the way he'd expressed his hugely impressive career was very modest, but I'd rather he was that way inclined as opposed to someone who bragged and became big headed.

'I *used* to be an international player,' he said with emphasis. 'I had to retire from the sport entirely at the end of last season because of a recurring knee injury.'

'Oh crikey,' I swallowed, wishing I'd known that before I'd gushed. 'I'm so sorry. That must be really tough to get your head around, especially at your age,' he looked taken aback. 'Sorry,' I winced. 'I shouldn't have said that I—'

'Yes, you should,' he interrupted. 'In fact, I'm thrilled that you did.'

'You are?'

'Yes,' he said again. 'It's what people I meet in public are always thinking but they hardly ever come out and say it, and to be honest, I wish they would because it is tough. So tough, and it would be great to be able to talk about it without making anyone feel awkward.'

I was relieved that I hadn't put my foot in it but also sad that he felt that way and that he was having such a difficult time.

'I guess you thought playing rugby was going to be your entire career, didn't you?' I sighed.

'I did,' he nodded. 'And even though it wouldn't have lasted much longer at international level, I thought I'd got a fair few years left playing at club standard.'

The barman came over with Erik's chips, and we didn't pick up the conversation until he'd gone.

'So,' I said, having given some thought to what Erik was currently doing in terms of work at Prosperous Place, 'if you don't mind me asking?'

'Ask away,' he said and dipped the end of a chip into the bowl of ketchup before popping it into his mouth.

I had to look away as he licked the salt off his lips.

'How is it that you find yourself working as the unofficial property manager and maintenance guy at Prosperous Place? That's as far removed from playing rugby as you can get, isn't it?'

'That's kind of the point.' Erik nodded as he reached for another chip. 'Dive into these if you want some, won't you?' he offered.

'I've already had a small bowl,' I confessed, 'but that one

does look rather tempting,' I added and reached for one of the biggest, which made him gasp in protest, but good humouredly. 'So, Prosperous Place?'

'Well,' he started to explain, 'I had a very rough of time of it, mentally I mean, when it came to adjusting to the changes when I stepped away from rugby. Or rather, limped away, given the nature of my injury.'

'I can appreciate that there would have been a lot to get your head around.'

'It wasn't just the eighty minutes on the pitch that disappeared, but literally the entire structure of every single day,' he recollected and shook his head. 'In the early days, I felt completely adrift.'

I wondered if he had family who had supported him but didn't want to ask in case that wasn't the case.

'It was when I was at my lowest that someone recommended this mental health charity and it was through them that I met Luke,' he carried on. 'Have you been introduced to him yet?'

'No,' I said. 'Not yet.'

'He's an amazing guy. He's always been really open about his mental health challenges and he and the therapist I worked with helped me so much while I clawed my way out of the deep pit I'd fallen into.'

'Jeez, Erik,' I swallowed, as a lump formed in my throat. I thought he was extremely brave to talk so honestly about what he'd been through, especially given that I barely knew him, but I supposed that was the point. It was high time these sorts of conversations were normalised. 'That sounds really bad.'

'It was for a while,' he nodded. 'But once I was able to start thinking about what had happened as an opportunity to try something new, I gradually began to feel hopeful again. I'd been channelled in one direction for so long, that it was quite a revelation when I started to look around for something different to do.'

'I see,' I said, as I started to join up some of the dots. 'And because Luke and Kate needed someone to look after . . .'

I stopped talking as Erik shook his head again.

'No,' he said, 'they didn't need anyone. Not in the beginning anyway. We became good friends and they offered me a place to stay, no strings attached. However, as I got better, I began to feel uncomfortable about not contributing, so I started doing things around the house and grounds, just odd jobs really and that led to taking some other things on and the role just kind of grew from there.'

'And you're enjoying it?'

'I'm absolutely loving it!' he declared. 'It couldn't be any further removed from what I did before, but it's just what I need. I'd love to stay for good, but I don't think that will pan out. But,' he briskly added, 'it's what I need for now and if I've learned anything in the last few years, it's to live in the present and not get bogged down looking too far into the future.'

'That's hard though, isn't it?' I frowned, thinking of my own situation.

Obviously, it was nothing like what Erik had found himself facing, but it was impacting on me, nonetheless.

'Are you worried about the future, Skylar?' Erik asked. 'Do you not see yourself living long-term in Nightingale Square?'

I mulled that over and let out a breath.

'Obviously you don't have to tell me anything,' Erik said hastily. 'But a problem shared and all that and, despite my disastrous first impression, I'm a good guy really and the soul of discretion.'

I looked over at him, wondering how we'd got so badly off on the wrong foot when actually he was so lovely. I guess I'd just caught him on a bad day and given that Kate had previously said that someone was nagging her and Luke to change the security codes, it was obviously down to Erik to make sure no one uninvited was on the premises . . .

'I'm not sure,' I began thoughtfully. 'But the future is on my mind. As you probably know, I've moved here with my father.'

'The famous crime author.'

'He's not that famous,' I smiled.

'Don't let Lisa hear you say that.'

'But what you won't know is that we've never lived together before. We haven't previously spent any longer than a couple of weeks together over the summer every year.'

'And how's it working out?'

'Really well, so far. Thank goodness, but the circumstances which led to the move weren't great.'

'Go on.'

'Well, Rafe invited me to move in with him when my former work as an events manager came to an end. I'd previously lived on-site in a historic hall in the Yorkshire Dales, but the hall was sold and I lost my home and my job.'

'I see,' Erik sighed and puffed out his cheeks. 'So, just like me, you had choice taken away from you.'

'Yes,' I agreed. 'Just like you. I never would have chosen to leave.'

'How long had you been doing the job and living there?'

'A decade,' I sighed. 'And it was amazing. Though I've realised now that I was a bit of a workaholic. Rafe had already sussed that and insisted that rather than look for another job straightaway, I should move in with him and take a break.'

'What a great dad,' Erik smiled. 'He knew exactly what you needed.'

'He did,' I nodded. 'He does.'

'So, is there an end date to this break?'

'No, I think Rafe's hoping that I'll find something local and settle here permanently.'

'But you don't want to?' Erik frowned.

'To be honest, I don't know what I want.'

'Well, given that you've only been here a week and a half that's hardly surprising.'

'I suppose not,' I said and bit my lip. When it came down to how many days had passed, I don't suppose I had been particularly patient with myself. 'Though even if I did want to stay, I'm not sure I could find a role similar to what I had before around here . . .'

'Maybe it's time for you to do something different, too?' Erik suggested. 'It's certainly working for me.'

'But I love my job,' I sighed. 'And I also loved being a part of the family and living on-site.'

I didn't add that I'd had an unsettled upbringing and that the years with Madeline and Tobias were the closest I'd ever experienced to regular family life.

'Intense though,' Erik cleverly pointed out. 'You've already conceded that you were a bit of a workaholic, and I can't imagine you had much opportunity to switch off when you were literally living on the job.'

'That's true,' I agreed with a frown.

'Look,' Erik said and I stared deeply into his eyes. 'You haven't got to figure it all out today, have you?'

'No,' I said and relaxed my shoulders which had stealthily inched up to almost around my ears. 'There's no pressure on me to do anything right now.'

'In that case,' he announced, 'I think you need a distraction to stop you fretting. Something to take your mind off all the things you don't need to be thinking about while giving you a sense of purpose. I'm guessing you're feeling as untethered as I was when I retired from rugby.'

I wouldn't have gone that far, but he was on the right track and I smiled.

'You sound like my grandad,' I told him. 'He said *exactly* the same thing earlier in the week about me needing something to do.'

'Great minds. And I know just the thing. You can start helping in the Grow-Well. Graham could really do with a hand now autumn's landed.'

'I'd already thought about that, but I'm no gardener and I—'

'That's no problem,' Erik shrugged. 'The Grow-Well isn't really a garden, is it?'

Chapter 9

Erik and I walked back towards Nightingale Square together and carried the conversation on as we went. I couldn't help noticing that a couple of people who walked around us nudged one another as we passed them, but Erik didn't react to his star attraction and that made me like him even more.

'So,' I surmised as we walked along, 'you're as smitten with living where we do as everyone else, are you?'

'For the most part,' he said, 'I do love it.'

I was intrigued by his answer.

'What's the part you're not so taken with?' I asked curiously.

'Oh, it's nothing major,' he shrugged.

'Please tell me,' I insisted. 'So I know what to look out for.'

'It's nothing terrible,' he said, rather reluctantly. 'Just something that I've become increasingly aware of.'

'I see,' I nodded, though of course I didn't. 'Well, you don't have to tell me if you don't want to.'

'No, it's okay,' he said. 'I think I will.' I waited. 'The thing is,' he explained, 'that everyone who lives in the square and obviously at Prosperous Place, is one half of a couple.'

'And you're not?' My heart suddenly did that annoying racing thing again, but as I was having to walk quickly to keep up with Erik's lengthy strides there was no need to attribute the sensation to anything else. 'You're single?'

'Yes,' he said. 'I'm single.'

'But you don't want to be?' I swallowed.

'Oh, I want to be single,' he insisted and my heart thumped again but to a different beat. 'Happy to be single, because I'm in no position to look for a relationship. I've still got so much to come to terms with. Throwing love into the mix would be a disaster. I'm more than content on my own, but . . .'

'But?'

'But sometimes, when I'm at a Grow-Well party or helping out with a garden open afternoon or something, I do feel it a bit, well . . . you know?'

'Yes,' I nodded, because when I had taken some rare time off and gone out after Reuben and I had ended our relationship, I'd also experienced the occasional awkwardness of flying solo. 'I do know.'

'You're single too?'

'I am and I'm in the same boat as you, Erik. I'm not currently looking for love, either,' I said honestly. 'Not with everything else in my life having only just changed. A romance would be disastrous for me, too.'

'In that case,' he nudged, 'you can share my oars if you like and we'll paddle the same boat together.'

'Thank you.' I smiled and nudged him back. 'In fact,' I suggested, 'why don't we take it a step further and buddy up at any future events? That way, neither of us will feel rudderless or out on a limb.'

'That's a brilliant idea,' Erik laughed. 'We can be each other's platonic plus one.'

'I love that!' I laughed. 'Platonic plus one. Brilliant! I've never been a PPO before.'

With that agreed and feeling astounded that a conversation and a shared bowl of chips could have transformed our relationship to such an extent, I left Erik at the turn into Nightingale Square. I crossed the road feeling far more optimistic than I had in a long time.

It had felt cathartic to talk to someone who was facing such big changes to their own life and Erik's were even more dramatic than my own. That had helped to give me some perspective, because I knew that once I'd had a break, I could return to the role I loved whereas Erik was unable to play professional rugby ever again. Not that he seemed too downcast about that now, but I could tell he'd been to hell and back to reach his current optimistic and hopeful viewpoint. We might have got off to a rocky start, but Erik now felt like just the single friend I was going to need, and I hoped he felt the same way about me, too.

With a spring in my step and feeling full of bonhomie, I didn't duck out of sight when I spotted Lisa corralling her clan up their garden path. In a complete attitude turnaround, I decided to no longer put off saying sorry for my lacklustre conversation the day I arrived in the square and she had been so affable.

'Lisa!' I called before she disappeared into the house. She turned to look at me as I hurried along the pavement. 'Have you got a minute?'

She came back down the path and opened the gate.

'Skylar,' she smiled warmly, as welcoming as the day I'd met her. 'How are you, my love? Are you all settled?'

'Pretty much. The house was left in such great shape; we only had to unpack.'

I knew the previous owners, Heather and Glen, were good friends of hers and had played an active part in the Nightingale Square community.

'I'll tell Heather that,' Lisa grinned. 'She was vacuuming as she reversed down the hall for the last time, so she'll be delighted her efforts haven't gone unnoticed. If we ever left here,' she laughed, with a look back at her own house, 'well, let's just say, it wouldn't be quite as pristine as your place was.'

'I'm sure it would be just fine,' I smiled back.

'Mum!' someone bawled from the hallway. 'Archie's got the biscuit tin!'

'You can have two each,' she hollered back. 'Just two and remember, I've counted how many are in there!'

'Have you really?' I laughed.

'No,' she said resignedly. 'No point, they always pinch more than two so the inevitable scolding after the daily raid is justified.'

'I love that you have a system in place.' I grinned but didn't want to hold her up. 'I better let you get on,' I said, backing off.

'No,' she said, 'you're all right. Is there something I can do for you?'

'Actually,' I said, 'I wanted to do something for you.'

'Oh?' she frowned. 'What's that?'

'I wanted to apologise.'

'Apologise?' she blinked. 'Whatever for?'

'The day I arrived,' I said, feeling shy. 'I know I came across as—'

She put up a hand to stop me and shook her head.

'You were fine,' she said seriously. 'More than fine given that you'd just endured the journey from hell. I was the one at fault—'

'No, you weren't,' I cut in. 'You were being neighbourly and kind and—'

'Far too Lisa!' she interrupted again, this time with a chuckle. 'I don't *think* I usually go full-on Lisa so soon, but I was so excited to discover that I'd got Rafe Harding and daughter for neighbours that I let myself get completely carried away and let the full-on version of myself out before either of you had got used to the tame one!'

'Oh, Lisa!' I laughed out loud.

'I'm being serious. I try so hard now to ease my larger-than-life personality in when I meet new people but where you two were concerned, I completely failed. If there's anything I can do to make it up to either of you, just say the word.'

'Rafe's fine,' I told her. 'He thinks you're just the author chum he needs.'

She flushed scarlet when I said that.

'So, his message to say he'll walk at Whitlingham with me wasn't a sop then?' she asked. 'He really does want to come?'

'Believe me,' I told her, 'Rafe doesn't do anything he doesn't want to and has no qualms about saying so. If he's said he's up for lakeside walks to talk about all things writing related, then he means it.'

'Excellent!' she nodded. 'But what about you, Skylar? Is there anything I can help you with?'

'There is,' I said, grasping the nettle Erik had handed me.

'Name it.'

'I was wondering if you'd introduce me properly to the Grow-Well team so I can make a start helping with whatever needs doing. With some strict guidance of course, so I don't get anything wrong.'

'Well, that's just made my day!' Lisa clapped. 'I'll let Graham know and we'll go over in the morning. He's the best person to get you up and running. We all have various roles we take on but he's the one who's ultimately in charge, so he'll be best placed to tell you what's what.'

'Excellent,' I said. 'Thanks Lisa.'

'I'll come and meet you at yours at ten,' she said as a louder argument in the house broke out. 'That'll give me just about enough time to get this lot back under control and hand over the reins to John.'

With the arrangement made, I headed home and waited until Rafe had shouted me the 'cats all-clear' signal before slipping inside. It was just a few more days until they could start to explore the garden and I felt as though my future, the immediate one anyway, was happily aligned with my feline friends. We were all destined to explore more of the great outdoors this autumn.

I was feeling a bit jittery the following morning as I waited for Lisa. I hadn't told Rafe what I was planning to do because I didn't want a fuss and the second I spotted Lisa crossing the square, I shouted a quick goodbye to him and went out to meet her.

'Ready?' she asked.

'Ready,' I said. 'Though I haven't got any gloves or tools or anything. Will that be a problem?'

'If Graham sets you straight on with a job, you can borrow a pair of my gloves,' she generously offered. 'I'll show you where they are in the bothy and there are tools there too, that we all share, so no need for you to have your own.'

'Okay,' I said and let out a breath. 'Great.'

'Are you all right? You seem a bit nervous?'

'I am nervous,' I told her. 'I've never done anything like this.'

I'd laid awake half the night swinging between cursing and thanking Grandad George and Erik for their encouragement to try something new. Fingers crossed by the end of the day I'd only want to thank them, but time would tell.

'You've never gardened?' Lisa asked. 'Or grown anything before?'

'I haven't so much as pulled up a weed,' I told her. 'I couldn't even identify one. Which is why I'll need very detailed instructions about everything.'

'Don't worry,' she said, as she keyed in the gate code and opened it. 'Graham will gladly take you under his wing.'

She was right, too. He was kindness itself and delighted to have an apprentice. His rather bossy wife was also lovely and supplied endless mugs of tea between telling her husband to pace himself and not get carried away.

'So,' Graham said, once he'd given me a more official tour than the one with Freya, and told me what was what, 'we'll get you started on something right away, shall we?'

'Okay,' I said, 'but only if you tell me *exactly* what to do Graham because my biggest fear is pulling up your prize parsnips or something.'

'The parsnips stay in the ground until at least the first frost,' he said seriously, 'so they're not ready to come up yet.'

'Noted,' I nodded, though I had no idea what a parsnip top looked like.

Accepting that I was a total novice, he set me up with something failsafe – clearing a bed of bolted salad leaves and then emptying out a couple of pots. I took my time pulling the plants up, putting them in the wheelbarrow and then depositing them on the compost heap with any weeds that had made their home there, too. Graham had explained that not every weed could be composted but those in the bed I was working on would be fine.

I then added some well-rotted manure and forked the bed over so it looked as good as new and was ready for whatever would be going in next. The plants in the pots came out leaves, compost and all because they'd dried out.

'Our watering rota went a bit awry at the end of the summer holidays,' Graham sighed, when he came to inspect my work. 'So, these have gone over a bit earlier than they usually would.'

'Have you considered installing an automatic watering system?' I suggested, as I ran a hand over my brow. It was a chilly day, but I'd worked up quite a sweat, and I realised then that I hadn't thought about anything other than what I'd been doing since I'd started. So far, my efforts were proving to be the ideal distraction. Grandad George and Erik would be as thrilled about that as I was. 'I did a bit of googling about growing veg last night and some of the irrigation systems looked very impressive.'

'It has crossed my mind, but I haven't looked properly into it. I might run the idea by everyone at the party.'

'What party?' I echoed.

'Oh,' Graham said, with a nod to the garden entrance. 'Stand by your beds. Here comes the boss.'

I turned around to find Kate coming towards me with a man I'd never seen before. He was very good looking.

'Lisa said you were making a start today, Skylar,' Kate smiled at me.

'And I thought it was about time I introduced myself,' the man said. 'I'm Luke. It's a pleasure to meet you.'

'Likewise,' I said, 'I would shake your hand, but I've got a bit mucky, even with Lisa's gloves on.' They were too big for me, so I'd buy some of my own ahead of my next visit.

'We don't stand on ceremony here, so no worries,' Luke smiled. 'How are you finding life in the square?'

We chatted for a few minutes and then Beth arrived with her partner, Eli. It was certainly a day for meeting people, but I found I didn't mind that. Eli didn't linger because he needed to get to his work, but Beth stayed.

'So, Graham,' she said. 'Do you think the weather's going to hold for the party? It's not anywhere near as warm as it was last week, is it?'

Graham refused to be drawn on the weather saying it was as changeable as a woman's moods. This earned him a look from his wife and stifled laughter among the rest of us.

'We always have an evening gathering here to celebrate the autumn equinox,' Kate explained for my benefit.

'How lovely,' I smiled.

'It is,' Luke agreed. 'We have a meal together and talk about the year so far.'

'It's nothing as grand as the autumn festival we attended last year,' Kate said, linking her arm through Luke's. 'But it's fun in its own way.'

'An autumn festival,' I said wistfully. 'That sounds wonderful.'

'It was,' Kate nodded. 'My brother, Tom, and his wife, Jemma, live in this lovely Fenland town called Wynbridge with their kids, and it has an autumn festival now that runs for weeks.'

'They had some really fun activities,' Luke added. 'Great stuff for the kids to do.'

'Where are your girls today?' Beth asked him.

'Erik's taken them to a crafting workshop at the castle,' he explained. 'Jasmine was really keen to take part, and he volunteered to take both her and Abigail along.'

I had wondered if he might come and find me as Lisa had mentioned I was here, but clearly not if he was off-site. I found the thought of him in the 'fun uncle' role most endearing.

'If only we weren't all so rushed off our feet with other commitments,' I heard Kate say as I tuned back into the conversation, 'we might have been able to organise a couple of extra things to do at the party here this year.'

'Everyone's lives seem far busier than when we set this garden up originally,' Carole said. 'The square has seen so many changes over the last few years, but we keep going and I'm proud of how we all still manage to come together.'

'Me too,' agreed Luke. 'The Grow-Well is such an integral part of Prosperous Place, I can't remember life without it now.'

'That's because you hadn't been moved in five minutes before we were setting it up!' Kate reminded him and kissed his cheek.

'And I know Rafe wants to get over here to help,' I told them all. 'And of course, if Graham's happy to keep telling me what to do, I'm happy to pitch in as much as I can. In fact,' I added as inspiration struck, 'I'd be happy to take on organising some things for the party if you like. Assuming,' I quickly added, 'I wouldn't be standing on anyone's toes.'

'You wouldn't be,' Kate rushed to say. 'But are you sure you can spare the time?'

'Time is the one thing I currently have an abundance of!' I laughed. 'And I'd be delighted to fill some more of it.'

'You used to be an events organiser, didn't you?' Beth asked.

'I still am,' I told her. 'I'm just between jobs at the moment but keen to keep my hand in if it would be any help?'

'Come over to the house,' Kate beamed. 'And we'll give you more of an idea of what usually happens, and I'll look up the Wynbridge Autumn Festival details online, too, in case you want to take a look.'

'All right,' I accepted. 'I will.'

'But not until you've brushed out and given those pots you've just emptied a good scrub,' Graham said with a smile. 'The job needs finishing. Come on and I'll show you where the brushes and detergent are kept.'

'We'll see you in a bit then,' Luke grinned.

'I'll join you as soon as I'm done,' I promised and followed Graham over to the bothy.

Chapter 10

Just after lunchtime and armed with a couple of fresh eggs and a rumbling tummy, I said my goodbyes at the Grow-Well and walked over to the house. I arrived just as Erik turned up with two very excited girls who raced off ahead of him.

'What have you been up to?' he asked me. 'You look really grubby.'

'Well, hello to you, too,' I laughed. 'If I look that bad, perhaps I'd better head straight home.'

He stared at me for a moment and then gave me the brightest smile.

'You've been in the Grow-Well, haven't you?' he said, sounding genuinely delighted.

'I have.'

'It was an easy guess because you've got some leaves caught in your hair.'

He took a step towards me, and I realised he was going to pull them out.

'There,' he said, as he gently lifted them away and let them fall.

'All gone?' I asked, my voice catching.

'I think so,' he reassured me.

'The garden was brilliant,' I smiled.

'Don't say another word,' he said. 'Let's use the tradesmen's entrance,' by which he meant the side door. 'You can clean up some more in the cloakroom and then tell me all about it. And I can introduce you to Luke.'

'I've already met him,' I said as Erik led the way. 'He and Kate were in the garden earlier and invited me over to tell me more about the upcoming equinox party.'

'Great,' Erik said over his shoulder. 'I'd forgotten about that.'

Having handed Erik the eggs for safekeeping, I shrugged off my jacket and short wellies in the boot room and tidied myself up, as much as I could, in the warm cloakroom. Erik hadn't mentioned that I'd somehow managed to smear compost right across my forehead, or that my ponytail was bumpy. I pulled the band out and shook my hair loose. I noticed my complexion looked rather rosy thanks to my exertions and I didn't hate the look.

'Do you need anything, Skylar?' Kate called from the other side of the door which I then opened because, I realised, I had taken a few minutes to get myself together.

'No, I'm all good,' I told her. 'That is as long as you don't mind the scruffy look. I don't think I'm going to deposit any mud about the place.'

'You're fine,' she said. 'And you look as a fresh as a daisy. The autumn air obviously agrees with you.'

I felt my cheeks turn even warmer because of the compliment.

'I was nervous when I started, but I had the best time, and everyone was so friendly and helpful. Graham especially. I think I'm going to learn a lot from him.'

'You're not alone,' she said, as we walked along a short corridor towards the kitchen, 'I don't think there's anything he doesn't know about sowing and growing. Now, come and have some lunch and I'll put the kettle on. Though I would imagine, Carole has kept you full of tea.'

'She has,' I confirmed. 'And I wasn't expecting lunch but thank you that would be lovely.'

'It's only soup and sourdough,' Luke said as we walked into a kitchen which rivalled the size of the one at Highfell.

He was standing in front of an Aga and stirring a huge pot, while Erik sliced the loaf on a vast scrubbed pine table. It was an idyllic scene of domestic bliss.

'Well,' I said, as I looked around, 'it smells delicious. My tummy is rumbling in anticipation.'

Once the thickly buttered bread, squash and sweet potato soup and drinks were served, the four of us sat at the table to enjoy the unexpected but most welcome repast.

'So,' Luke said to Erik, who was sitting next to me, 'did the girls behave? The crafts they came back with looked impressive and I can see you've got glitter in your hair.'

'They were as good as gold,' he grinned and Kate tutted.

He made no attempt to get rid of the glitter which I could then see sparkling in the light, and without thinking, I leant over and brushed it away. His eyes met mine and I felt even rosier than before.

'Just returning the favour,' I said quietly and he grinned.

'They're always better behaved for you than me,' Kate sighed, thankfully not seeming to notice my face was even pinker than when I'd walked in.

'Only on this occasion because I said I'd take them for a

Happy Meal if they didn't bicker,' Erik confessed. 'That's why they haven't hung around for soup.'

'Well, I wouldn't want to switch this soup for chicken nuggets,' Luke said.

'Me neither,' I agreed. 'Is it homemade? It's delicious.' For some reason it felt imperative for me to focus on something other than my now glittery hand. 'I've practically lapped this up.'

'It is,' Kate said. 'I made a huge batch fresh this morning, so there's some for the freezer. You can take Rafe a serving if you like?'

'Yes, please,' I said. 'He'll love that and probably quiz you for the recipe.'

'I can give you that, too,' she generously offered.

'And the bread came from Blossom's and was made by a neighbour of yours, Mark,' Luke told me. 'Have you met him yet?'

'Not yet,' I said. 'But I am familiar with the joy of Blossom's. I joked to Rafe only yesterday that we'll soon be putting on our Christmas weight before Halloween!'

'Along with the equinox, that's something else we celebrate here,' Luke said.

'Christmas or Halloween?' I asked.

'Both!' he and Kate said together and laughed.

'I'm excited to hear about the imminent celebration,' I added, turning the conversations further towards why I had been invited. 'You must fill me in on the details.'

'Not before you've told us about your morning in the Grow-Well,' Erik nudged. 'I want to hear all about that.'

It didn't take me long to fill them in about what I'd been

up to because I hadn't done all that much, but I did make a point of saying, just like I already had to Kate, how much I'd enjoyed it, along with what a total distraction it had been.

'I didn't think about anything else the whole time I was tidying and forking,' I said in wonder. 'And the time just flew by.'

'How lucky you bumped into someone yesterday who suggested you give it a go,' Erik said rather smugly.

'Yes,' I said, letting him enjoy the moment. 'Wasn't it?'

'You aren't worried about anything though are you, Skylar?' Kate asked.

'No,' I said, my eyes still on Erik. 'Not really. I've just been finding it a bit of a challenge to keep occupied. I'm not used to having no work to do. Before, even on my days off, I was thinking about events and quite often ended up doing something work related because I lived on-site.'

When I had been going out with Reuben I'd been as preoccupied with my work as he was with his family's farm, so it was little wonder the romance had fizzled out. Not that there'd ever been much fizz, I now realised. Previously I'd assumed the relationship we had was what a Big Love settled down into, but now I wasn't so sure it had ever been a Big Love in the first place . . .

'Hence your offer to help with the equinox party,' Luke guessed, as he pushed back his chair and stood up and I refocused on the conversation. 'Would anyone like another ladle of soup?'

Erik had another bowlful, but Kate and I both declined. I could easily have eaten more, but Kate had mentioned cake to go with the tea, so I needed some room left for that.

'Yes,' I answered Luke. 'I've never been a part of an equinox event before, so this will be fun, and Rafe, who wants me to take a proper break because I haven't had time off for so long, won't object because this is something for the community. And hopefully it will be far less stressful than overseeing a wedding with two hundred guests!'

'Two hundred guests,' Erik whistled.

'That was the average,' I told him. 'Sometimes it could be far larger.'

'No wonder you need a break!' Kate gasped. 'You'll be able to do this standing on your head, as long as you really want to.'

'Oh, I do,' I nodded. 'I really do.'

She and Luke went on to tell me that it was a simple gathering where everyone came together to enjoy the Grow-Well harvest, share a meal made of ingredients grown in the garden and generally make the most of the last of the light evenings before the days started to grow shorter, colder and darker.

'Carole, Poppy and I will be doing most of the food prep,' Kate finished up.

'I'm sure Rafe would love to contribute something, too,' I said. 'He's a fabulous cook.'

'The more the merrier!' Kate accepted gratefully.

'And John makes the most amazing pizzas, using the dough bases Mark supplies,' Luke added.

'I'm looking forward to seeing the oven fired up,' I said keenly. 'So, what exactly do you need me to do? The food is clearly all in hand.'

'If you could take care of setting up, decorating and ambience,' Kate asked. 'That would be fantastic. Everyone seemed to have more time to go all in before, but we're all so busy with other things now that it's mostly just simple meals we come together for.'

'Which are still lovely,' Luke said.

'But it's not quite the same,' Kate finished up.

'Well,' I smiled, 'atmosphere and special touches happen to be my forte, so you can leave all of that to me. And what about this Fenland autumn festival you mentioned? What's that like?'

It was mid-afternoon by the time we finished chatting and looking at the pretty festival online and we only came to a halt then because Kate and Luke's girls came bursting into the kitchen claiming they were famished.

'Anything but soup!' clamoured the eldest, Jasmine.

'I want cake!' demanded Abigail. 'Or dippy egg,' she said, eyeing my eggs on the worktop.

'Those belong to Skylar,' Erik said as he scooped them up. 'Come on, Skylar. I'll walk you to the gate. Anything to get away from this racket. No more Happy Meals for this pair if they're not going to keep their end of the deal for more than a couple of hours.'

The sisters were instantly silenced and sat at the table as though butter wouldn't melt.

'Thank you for lunch,' I said to Kate and Luke, while Kate ladled some soup into a container for me to give to Rafe. 'It was all delicious.'

'The joy of homegrown,' Kate sighed happily as she handed me the lidded pot. 'And I'll text you the recipe.'

We'd thought it would be a good idea to all exchange numbers, and Rafe and I were now added to the Grow-Well WhatsApp group, too.

'And thank you for taking on some of the party planning,' Luke said. 'It's a weight off our minds but do feel free to ask about anything you're not sure of. We're not going to just dump it all on you and run.'

That was good to know, but exactly what I expected. I was beginning to understand the true meaning of community and I rather liked it. I hadn't expected to, or not so quickly at least, but it felt wonderfully inclusive.

'I know where the tables and chairs are stored,' Erik said to Luke, 'so I can show Skylar all that along with the other bits and pieces I know you've used for parties in the past.'

'Thanks, Erik,' I said. 'Nice to meet you girls.'

'What do you say?' Kate encouraged the still quiet pair.

'It was nice to meet you, too,' they echoed sweetly and Luke rolled his eyes.

It took me a minute to pull my wellies on again and do up my jacket and Erik waited with the eggs in one hand and the soup in the other.

'You don't need to walk me to the gate,' I told him, when I took both from him.

'Yes, I do,' he grinned. 'Unless you can juggle, and besides, I've got a favour to ask you.'

'Oh?' I said and followed him out.

The wind was keen and there was the odd raindrop blowing about in the breeze, too. Autumn seemed to have properly arrived, even before the equinox.

'Will you come to the pub with me tonight?' Erik asked, once the house door was closed behind us.

I whipped round to look at him. Was he asking me out? Surely, not given that we'd only just agreed to be friends.

'Freya and Finn will be there and Mark and Neil,' he said and the penny dropped. I felt myself blush again, this time for jumping to the wrong conclusion. 'I want to go, but not on my own.'

'I see.'

'I thought it could be our first official PPO outing,' he grinned and I found myself smiling back.

'As long as Rafe isn't expecting an evening of conversation,' I told him. 'I'll be there.'

Rafe heated up the soup the moment I handed it over. Dug deep into his writing cave he hadn't eaten all day and the cats were looking martyred because he hadn't given them their lunch, either.

'I thought you might have fed them,' he said as he blew on the soup, 'but now I think about it, you went out this morning, didn't you?'

'I did,' I confirmed, as I weighed out the cat food and the pair twined themselves around my legs and mewed pitifully. 'Stop that,' I said in protest of their weaving, 'otherwise you'll have me over.'

I pushed between them, put the bowls down and left them to it.

'And you haven't been back all day?' Rafe asked.

'I haven't.'

'Where have you been?'

'Working in the Grow-Well,' I smiled. 'Then having lunch with Kate, Luke and Erik in Prosperous Place.'

'Well, I never,' Rafe said. He sounded surprised. 'That's a turn up and no mistake. What made you decide to do that?'

'It was something Grandad George said,' I explained. I didn't mention Erik because he'd already come up in the conversation once and I didn't want my father making more of our friendship than he should. He'd recently bemoaned my single status, overlooking the fact that I was content with it. 'He suggested that it might be a good idea to use the time I'm not working to try something new.'

'Good old Dad,' Rafe cheered in approval. 'You won't find me arguing with that. Something new is just what you need.'

I decided not to mention helping with the equinox party just yet. I didn't think he would object, but kept it to myself, nonetheless.

'I didn't think you would argue,' I smiled. 'I'm going to see Grandad again on Monday and I'm sure he'll be thrilled.'

'I'm seeing him tomorrow, but I won't mention it. I'll let you fill him in.'

'And what are you up to tonight? More writing?'

'No,' he said. 'Not tonight. I've got a date.'

'A date?'

'Yes,' he laughed. 'A date. You don't need to sound so Lady Bracknell about it.'

'I'm just surprised is all,' I shrugged. 'Given how long you've spent writing every day, I didn't think you would have had time to set up a date. It isn't someone you've met online, is it?'

'No,' he said firmly. 'It isn't. I'm beyond all that. What about you?'

I felt my cheeks flush.

'What about me?' I squeaked.

'What are you doing tonight?'

I wilted a bit.

'Oh,' I said, 'I've been invited to The Dragon with a few of the neighbours. Do you think I should go?'

I already knew what he'd say to that but hadn't predicted the addendum.

'You should,' he said mischievously. 'You might find a date yourself.'

'No, thanks,' I responded primly and stood up again. 'As I've told you before, that's the last thing I need.'

Chapter 11

I don't know why, but I faffed for ages trying to decide what to wear for the trip to the pub. The weather had turned a little milder as the afternoon turned to early evening and that gave me more outfit scope, which didn't help with the unusual bout of indecisiveness. It was just an evening in the pub so it really didn't warrant such careful thinking about, but I had got out of the habit of socialising in a group, and this felt a bit more formal than working with neighbours in the Grow-Well where a holey jumper and well-worn jeans would suffice.

I had just settled on smarter jeans and a shirt with a long-sleeved T-shirt underneath, on the assumption that the tiny pub might be packed and I could lose a layer if I got hot, when a text from Erik landed saying that everyone was going to convene at the entrance to the square at seven so we could walk to The Dragon together. That gave me time to have something to eat, but having had such a filling lunch, I thought I'd wait until later. Another bowl of those delicious chips would be the perfect addition to the evening.

'You look fabulous, Skylar,' Rafe smiled when I walked down the stairs just before seven. 'I can't remember the last time I saw you wearing make-up. That copper eyeshadow really suits the colour of your eyes.'

'Thank you,' I said. 'You don't think it's a bit too much for a trip to a pub, do you?' I used to wear make-up for work but generally didn't bother otherwise. 'Does it look like I've made too much of an effort?'

'Not at all,' Rafe reassured me, as he helped me into my jacket. 'But what would be wrong with making an effort, anyway? I don't think enough folk do these days and you've hit just the right note with the look you've gone for.'

I hoped he was right because a quick glance at the clock told me it was too late to change my mind.

'That's all right then,' I said and stood on tiptoe to kiss his cheek. 'Thank you for the confidence boost. And you smell divine. I hope he's worth it.'

'So do I,' he grinned. 'Have fun tonight and don't forget your key. I'll leave the cats in my sitting room, so don't worry about them escaping when you come back in.'

'All right.'

I picked up my small bunch of keys from the hall side table.

'That's assuming you do come back,' he added. 'You might get lucky.'

'I'll definitely come back,' I told him. 'And I'm not sure that's average talk for a father and daughter.'

'Since when have we been average?' he laughed, putting air quotes around the word. 'If I thought we were that I'd be sorely disappointed in both of us.'

'I'll see you later,' I laughed with him and headed out.

I could see everyone waiting for me and, even though it was quite dark already, I felt rather self-conscious as I walked around the square to join them. They probably weren't even looking at me, but it felt like they were.

Erik and Finn were a clear head taller than the other two men and I was relieved to see Freya was wearing smarter clothes. Her long hair was loose but there were braids either side with gold thread woven through them which shone in the streetlights. She looked like the perfect shield-maiden for Viking Finn.

'Skylar,' Erik said as he stepped forward to greet me.

'Hello,' I swallowed as I looked at everyone. 'I'm sorry if I've kept you waiting.'

'You haven't,' said the man I guessed must be Neil because I knew he wasn't Mark. 'Mark got the time wrong, so we were here a bit early.'

'I'm keen for a pint tonight,' Mark said with a grin that almost looked impish. 'So, I *might* have got it wrong on purpose.'

Neil rolled his eyes.

'And us three have only just arrived,' Freya said, accounting for the others.

'I'm Neil,' the guy said cheerfully, 'and this is my husband, Mark.'

'Hello,' I smiled at them both.

'I think I recognise you, Skylar,' Mark said. 'You've been to Blossom's Bakery a couple of times, haven't you?'

'Far more than a couple,' I joked. 'Rafe, that's my father, did say that a neighbour worked in there, but I wasn't sure if that was you or not.'

'Yep,' he said. 'That's me! Helping to expand waistlines right across the city.'

'Um,' I said, feeling relieved that the moment of introduction had passed with a simple explanation as to why I hadn't said hello before, 'so I gather.'

'I hear you're working in the Grow-Well now,' he said and linked his arm familiarly through mine. News really did travel fast. I had thought country gossip moved at the speed of light, but apparently close-knit city communities had an efficient network, too.

'I am and I'm really enjoying it,' I said as we all set off.

'Erik has just told us that you've already visited The Dragon, Skylar,' Finn said, over his shoulder. For a man with such a commanding presence he was so quiet, you could almost forget he was there. 'What did you make of it?'

'I loved it,' I said enthusiastically. 'And I instantly spotted one of your dragons scaling the wall, Finn. It's exquisite and a real treat to be able to admire it closer than the ones in the garden.'

'Thank you,' he said and ducked his head.

'Now you've made him blush,' Mark teased.

He was proving himself to be the joker of the pack that I had immediately imagined him as.

'Leave him alone,' tutted Neil, and Mark laughed then slipped his arm from mine to scoot off and walk the rest of the way with his husband.

Erik fell into step with me and we let the other four stride further ahead.

'Thank you for agreeing to come tonight,' he said quietly.

'Don't thank me yet,' I told him. 'The evening hasn't started, and you might end up regretting asking me if I prove to be a bore.'

'That's the last thing you'll be,' he said, and our eyes met. 'I just know it's going to be a fun night.'

He was right, too.

The pub was still relatively quiet when we arrived, so we bagged a table big enough to accommodate us all and put in our orders for drinks and food. I had wondered whether to go for something other than chips, but then a heaped bowl was carried out for another customer and I caved. I went for a cheeseburger, too.

'Oh crikey,' I said, when it was put in front of me. 'I'm not sure I'll eat all of this. I'm hungry, but not *that* hungry.'

'Have no fear,' Neil said. 'We won't let anything go to waste.'

'Hey,' I objected when Erik then immediately pinched the biggest chip from my bowl.

'Just returning the favour.'

'Fair enough,' I laughed, because I had taken his prize chip the day before.

As I tried to work out how best to tackle the huge burger, I felt amazed that it wasn't all that much longer than twenty-four hours ago that Erik and I had had our heart to heart at the next table. So much seemed to have happened since then and all of it had gone a long way to making me feel further settled in Nightingale Square. It had been a truly great day, and it wasn't over yet.

I finally decided that some burger tower deconstruction was needed, much to the dismay of Mark who somehow managed to get his mouth around the whole stack of his. It didn't matter how I devoured it, every mouthful was delicious, but I couldn't finish the chips so left those in the middle of the table for everyone to dip into.

Freya was sitting on my left and I couldn't help noticing that her hair looked even more impressive close up.

'Your hair looks gorgeous, Freya,' I commented. 'It must take ages to braid it like that.'

'Thank you,' she smiled and ran her fingers down the length of one of the intricate plaits. 'You'd be surprised how quickly Finn can do this, even when he's incorporating threads or beads.'

'Finn did it?'

Having admired his own hair, I should have realised he was an expert.

'Years of practice,' he said to me, having heard what we were talking about.

'He keeps offering to do mine now it's longer,' put in Erik and I looked at his messy shoulder length blond hair. 'But I've haven't been tempted yet.'

It was doubtless long enough, so I thought that was a shame.

'You should let him,' I said, 'I think it would suit you.'

'My dad would have forty fits!' he laughed.

'Why does it matter what your father thinks?' I shrugged.

'Your dad is clearly very different to mine,' he commented intriguingly.

'My father is different to everyone's!' I laughed, thinking of the conversation we'd had before I left the house. 'We're far from what most people expect.'

I didn't say more than that and neither did Erik and the conversation turned to an announcement Mark and Neil had previously made about putting their plan to become parents on hold after their second adoption attempt had failed. It was the only time throughout the evening that Mark looked downcast.

'I'll be back in a sec,' he said and headed off to the gents.

'Is Mark, okay?' Freya asked Neil.

Having only just met the pair, it felt to me, even though neither of them had thrown awkward glances in my direction, that this was a conversation for close friends rather than brand-new ones and therefore I also excused myself.

'I'll just go and get another round in,' I said and slipped away.

The bar was packed, so it was going to take a while, but that would give the others plenty of time to chat. I hadn't been waiting long before Erik joined me.

'I thought I'd give you a hand,' he smiled down at me.

'Thank you,' I smiled back. 'You'll probably get served faster than me.'

'What, because I'm a local?' he asked. 'You're a local now, too, Skylar.'

'No,' I nudged, 'because of your star status!'

He shook his head. 'I definitely haven't got star anything,' he blushed.

His words were instantly contradicted because the next second someone clapped him on the shoulder and offered to buy him a pint and I noticed a woman on his other side staringly adoringly up at him, completely starstruck.

'Of course, you haven't,' I grinned and inched forward in the queue.

With two trays full of drinks and a variety of snacks to save us having to make another trip to the bar for a while, we slowly made our way back to the table.

'I hope you're enjoying your first evening as my PPO,' Erik said unguardedly.

'What's a PPO?' demanded Mark before I'd had a chance to answer.

I hadn't realised he was right behind us and jumped. Given that the level of chatter in the pub had increased as more people poured in, I was surprised he'd heard.

'Never mind,' I said. 'Look, I got you another pint.'

'Thanks,' he said and took it. 'Now come on, spill the beans. I could do with cheering up. It'll help me get my mind off Neil and I putting our plans on hold.'

'I'm so sorry you're having to do that,' I said sympathetically.

He ducked his head. 'I'm feeling better about it than I was but I'm still struggling to talk about it, even when it is in the company of friends.'

'In that case,' I said, 'I'll say no more. But I'm still not telling you what a PPO is.'

'Spoilsport,' he tutted, then as soon as we'd sat down again, shouted out, 'Do any of you lot know what a PPO is?'

I looked at Erik and could tell from his expression that he didn't want to elaborate any more than I did.

'Something to do with the post office?' Finn suggested.

'No, it's something to do with health insurance, isn't it?' frowned Neil.

'I don't think so,' Mark said, looking first at Erik and then me. 'What do you think, Skylar?'

'I think you should drink your pint,' I said deadpan, 'and stop trying to give Puck a run for his money.'

Freya laughed, Neil almost spat his drink out and Finn nodded.

'Skylar's got you sussed already,' Finn delighted in pointing out to Mark.

'Um,' Mark pretended to huff. 'I think she has.'

Fortunately, Erik and I were saved from further questioning

because music started to play loudly and it was impossible to carry a conversation on other than between tracks and that only lasted a few seconds. Having consumed more alcohol than I had in a long time I found myself singing along with everyone else and we stayed in The Dragon, drinking and laughing until last orders and then set off to Nightingale Square in a rather wobblier formation than we'd arrived in.

It was a crisp night, and the chill air sobered me up enough to remember that we hadn't talked about the equinox party. I had wanted to pick everyone's brains for ideas and memories of celebrations in the past.

'Will any of you be heading over to the Grow-Well tomorrow?' I asked.

'That depends how my head feels in the morning,' Mark said, giving his temple a rub.

'If we do, it'll most likely be in the afternoon,' Neil said. 'We're due to put some hours in and I've been a bit too tied to my desk of late, so working outdoors for a while will do me good.'

During the evening, I had discovered that Neil was an architect.

'I'm a bit gardened out this week,' Freya yawned.

'But I might pop in,' Finn said.

'What about you Erik?'

'Same answer as Mark,' he grinned.

'I'll probably see some of you there then.'

'Assuming you're not hungover,' Erik pointed out.

'Even if I am, I'm sure I will have rallied by the afternoon.'

We were back at the entrance to the square by then and as we said our goodbyes, I noticed Mark was watching Erik and me.

'No kiss goodnight?' he said, his head cocked as I went to walk away.

His remark was confirmation that he had assigned himself the role of mischievous matchmaker, and given the way Erik stared at his feet, I knew he had sussed that, too. I decided to call Mark's bluff.

'Oh, go on then,' I said and quickly went to grab the front of his jacket. 'Just the one.'

'No!' he squealed, loud enough to wake the dead as he leapt out of reach. 'Not me!'

'Well, make up your mind,' I tutted and everyone laughed. That said, Neil didn't look overly impressed with his husband's antics.

'Mark,' he scolded. 'Behave yourself before you wake up the neighbourhood. You'll have Lisa and John out here demanding to know what's going on!'

That was enough to rein Mark in, and we all headed off to our respective homes with smiles on our faces.

Chapter 12

I'd remembered to drink a glass of water before I'd got into bed after my evening in the pub with my new friends, but my head still felt a little fragile the following morning, and so I decided to treat myself to a Sunday lie in once I'd retrieved some things from downstairs.

Rafe's bedroom door was closed, and with no sign of him having surfaced in the kitchen, I released Plato and Socrates from his sitting room, quickly fed them and left Rafe a note warning him not to be fooled by their demands for further food. Armed with tea, toast and my laptop, I returned to my room ready to snuggle back down in bed for a restorative hour or possibly even two.

Besides sleeping in it, it wasn't a room I had spent much time in, but as I took a moment to properly admire the original and ornate tiny cast iron fireplace and the view of the magnificent oak in the neighbouring garden, I realised I'd been missing out. It was a pretty room, further enhanced by my floral sprig bed linen and curtains, and while I drank my tea, I sat on the padded window seat which had a capacious storage space underneath and, from the perfect vantage point, admired the tree in its entirety.

I'd only been in the square a week and a half but already I could see the leaves had changed and I thought it might be nice to take a photograph of the view, with the tree front and centre on a set day every month to record its transformation throughout the seasons.

'No time like the present,' I said and took a snap on my phone. I then ate my toast, climbed back into bed, pulled up the duvet and reached for my laptop. 'Wow,' I gasped as I looked at the Wynbridge Autumn Festival website Kate had directed me to along with an Instagram account called Autumn Everything, that the festival's chief organiser curated.

There were plenty of ideas for me to jot down to potentially include in our equinox party to make more of an event of it, and I found myself wishing there were more canines than just Nell in the square because the dog's fancy dress photos looked hilarious.

I knew we had at least four cats in proximity, but I couldn't imagine them tolerating being turned into pumpkins and ghouls! Rafe's pair certainly wouldn't so that put two out of the running straightaway.

As I continued to scroll, there was a light knock on my door.

'Come in,' I said, but not so loudly that it made my head thump.

The door opened and my father stood there, filling the space and looking rather rumpled.

'I just wanted to let you know I'm back,' he said croakily.

'Back?' I frowned, then realised he was wearing what he'd had on when I left the house the evening before. 'Have you been out all night?'

I hadn't heard him open the front door or come up the stairs.

'Um,' he said, looking sheepish, but he needn't have worried because I wasn't going to give him a telling off, though I was surprised he hadn't let me know he wasn't coming home. 'Sorry I didn't message,' he apologised. 'The time just seemed to run away with us.'

I noted the 'us' and thought his date must have gone well. Very well.

'I see,' I said. 'Well, you're a grown man and you don't need to explain anything to me, so—'

'We spent the entire night—' he interrupted.

'No!' I said loudly. 'I just said you don't need to explain anything!'

'Talking,' he grinned. 'We spent the whole night talking.'

I had to smile myself then.

'What about?' I asked, feeling interested rather than panicked.

'Everything,' he said soppily. 'Nothing.'

'And all the things in between?'

'Something like that.'

He didn't sound like himself at all.

'And will you be seeing him again?' I ventured.

Where Rafe was concerned sometimes, no matter how well a date had gone, that wasn't always a given.

'Oh, yes,' he said. 'I'll be seeing him again.'

I resisted the desire to ask more about this man who had got my father looking so smitten. No point getting invested just yet. That was something I had learnt at a young age, but it came from my flighty mum's behaviour rather than Rafe's.

There had been a couple of guys who had lasted longer

with Mum than a month and I had enjoyed their company around the house. But, just as I began to get used to having them around regularly and imagined us all playing happy families, Mum would get tired of them, call time, and it would just be the two of us again.

'Would you like me to get up and make you some breakfast?' I offered Rafe.

'No, you stay there,' he told me. 'I'll bring you another tea up if you like.'

'Yes, please.'

'What are you up to?' he asked with a nod at the laptop. 'Not doom-scrolling, I hope?'

'No,' I said, 'nothing like that. Just catching up with a few things.'

I had decided I wouldn't mention my part in planning the equinox party until I'd gathered what I wanted together and could prove to him that it wasn't anything like work and wouldn't have an impact on my rest and recuperation time.

'I'll be back in a minute with your tea,' he said and took my mug and plate with him.

'I've fed the cats!' I shouted after him, in case he didn't spot my note or the cunning felines had hidden it.

He was much longer than a minute and while he was downstairs, I could hear him talking in a low voice on the telephone. Surely that couldn't be his current beau calling already. He was certainly eager if it was, but then Rafe had appeared keen, too.

While I was waiting for my tea, I thought I should check my inbox. I'd completely fallen out of the habit of keeping up with anything online now I didn't have notification alerts constantly landing on my mobile and interrupting my train of thought.

The first thing I noticed was an email from my friend, Alisha. She was someone I'd met in year seven at high school, and like me, she had a parent who moved around a lot. Unlike me however she was often taken abroad and was fluent in Spanish and Italian as a result. We were both seen as something akin to nomads by the rest of our classmates and formed a friendship which shifted to email when I was moved on before she was.

We hadn't seen each other in a long time, but we still exchanged news about our lives. She had recently settled in Ottawa, and having admired the photos she sent, I shared the details of my move to Norwich, attaching the photo of the oak tree.

'What are you so engrossed in?' Rafe asked when he eventually came back.

I was working my way through the rest of my unread mail by then.

'An email from Mum,' I told him and turned the laptop around so he could see the photos I'd downloaded that she'd also sent.

'Does she usually email?'

'No, not as a rule. Generally, when she's away I don't hear from her from one month to the next.' I never worried about her being incommunicado because where Flighty Faye was concerned, that was the norm.

'What has she got to say for herself then? Anything life changing?'

'Not as far as I can tell. And I've read between the lines in as much detail as I can. I think she just wanted to prove to me that she was properly settled.'

'Well, that's life changing in itself, isn't it?' Rafe pointed out.

'Yes,' I agreed. 'I suppose it is. Either that or she thinks she'll make us jealous that we're heading into autumn and winter while she's basking in an azure-coloured ocean.'

The intense colour reminded me of Erik's eyes . . .

'Well either way, I'm pleased you've heard from her,' Rafe yawned. 'I'll leave you to it. Say hello from me if you reply.'

'Are you going to bed?'

'Shower first, then just a nap. I want to get some more words down this afternoon before I go and see Dad.'

'I'll try not to make too much noise when I get up, and I'll be heading to the Grow-Well again later.'

'Have fun,' he said and took himself off.

I replied to Mum, then checked I hadn't missed anything else. Just as I was about to log off, an email from Tobias and Madeline's Highfell address landed. I initially assumed it must have been sent in error, but when I opened it, I realised I was wrong.

'A Mr Thomas Fuller, who owns a country manor house and estate in Devon, has asked us to forward to you the attached document,' I read aloud, having first been warmed by their excitement about finally having moved into their house in Portugal. Building work had held them up but they were properly settled now. 'We know you're taking a break from work but wondered if it might be of interest? He asked us for your email, but we told him you would contact him directly if you wanted any further details.'

I downloaded the document wondering what it was that

Mr Thomas Fuller wanted with me. It didn't take many seconds of further reading for me to find out.

'It's a job,' I gasped as I scanned the page again. 'A fantastic job!'

Apparently, Mr Fuller had attended a wedding at Highfell Hall and been extremely impressed with the organisation. He mentioned that he had spoken to me but given the number of people I talked to at every event, I couldn't place him. Our brief conversation however had left a lasting impression on him. He had also talked about event management with Madeline and Tobias, and they had stressed the importance of having a committed, organised and unflappable manager which they considered me to be. How delightfully flattering.

Now Mr Fuller planned to start offering his home as a venue for weddings etc., and having discovered that Highfell had changed hands and that I was no longer working there, he had contacted Madeline and Tobias directly to ask if they knew if I was looking for another position.

My eyes flicked over the renumeration package. It was extremely generous and the situation and role sounded very similar to the one I had come from in that it would mean living on-site and taking on the management of all events. The salary was higher than I'd had before and with living costs kept to a minimum there would be scope to save for the future.

'Wow,' I whispered, as I googled the manor house and looked at the images of a stunning home set in a beautiful landscape.

Mr Fuller was potentially offering me the opportunity to pick up my career exactly where it had just been cut off. I felt confident that I was more than capable of sliding seamlessly into the role. I sat back and gave the proposition further thought.

I soon realised that I would also be back to working all hours, ironing out niggles long into the night because I lived on-site and probably yet again never be taking days off or the full holiday entitlement that was due to me. Is that what I really wanted?

Surely, I owed it to Rafe to properly immerse myself in this time that he had gifted me and think about it as the chance to explore making changes as Grandad George had suggested even if it was only to the structure of my working week in a similar position. This offer from Mr Fuller might have been familiar and therefore comforting, but was it *too* familiar?

It was all food for thought but I couldn't help wishing that I hadn't checked my inbox. Given how well the last couple of days living in Nightingale Square had gone, I was just starting to feel fulfilled and at home and useful, too. Now I feared my head was going to be preoccupied with an offer that I might come to the conclusion was too good to turn down . . .

Knowing that Rafe was having a nap, I sent the document to his printer, then snuck into his writing room to retrieve it and put it in the drawer on my nightstand. Having not made up my mind what to do, I knew I wouldn't gain anything from trying to talk to my father because his opinion would be completely one-sided, but with what he considered to be my best interests at heart, and that would doubtless make me feel further conflicted.

No longer in the mood to languish in bed, I washed and dressed then packed up an apple and sausage roll which Rafe had sourced in the local butchers and walked over to Prosperous Place. I took a quick wander around the garden, lingering to look at Finn's dragons in the secret fern garden, which was fast becoming my favourite spot in the whole place, then made my way to the Grow-Well.

'Good morning, Carole,' I said when I found her in the bothy where I was going to leave my lunch.

'Morning, Skylar,' she said back. 'I've just boiled the kettle if you'd like a drink.'

'I could do with a coffee.' My head was feeling better, but I didn't have much oomph.

I wasn't sure whether that was the impact of the night in The Dragon or the shock of Mr Fuller's job offer and the tumult it had kicked off.

'Decaf or fully loaded?' Carole offered.

'Better be fully loaded,' I smiled. 'And I'll make it. You kept everyone topped up yesterday.' I glanced into the garden as I prepared my drink. 'I thought I might see a few people here today, but perhaps I'm a bit early.'

'Finn and Neil have been and gone. And I've told Graham he's to stay indoors today.'

'Oh, that's a shame, about Finn and Neil, I mean. I thought they were coming over later than me.'

'Neil told me he wanted to get out of the house while Mark was swearing he'd never drink again,' she laughed. 'And Finn was eager to get to the studio because he'd had an idea for a new sculpture.'

'Both valid reasons for putting in an early appearance,' I said as I stirred my coffee and inhaled the restorative aroma. 'A shame though because I was hoping to talk to them, and anyone else who might be here, about the equinox party.'

'We're all very excited to have an expert in charge of it,'

Carole said, making my temperature rise a little because I hadn't specifically agreed to that.

'Oh crikey,' I puffed. 'You've made me feel nervous now. And I'm not completely in charge; I know the food and drink is already taken care of. I was going to ask if there were any specific likes or dislikes, or dos and don'ts that I should be aware of.'

'I can help you there,' Carole offered. 'We're an easy lot to please and if you can add anything to the usual meal it's bound to be well received. Just don't stress over it. Do what you feel would be appropriate for this time of year.'

'So, I've got free rein to add things to the celebration as long as they're seasonal?'

'I'd say so.'

That made me feel happier to forge ahead. Carole and Graham were the Grow-Well guiding hands and if Carole herself was giving me carte blanche to include some extras, then I couldn't possibly go wrong, could I?

'Has anyone mentioned budget?' she asked.

'No,' I said. 'I meant to ask Luke and Kate if there was a Grow-Well pot, but it slipped my mind.'

It turned out there was some money available, not much, but I was an expert at making funds go far and promised I would make every penny count.

'I'm sure you will,' Carole nodded in approval.

'So,' I said and looked out of the bothy window again, 'now that's sorted, what's on the to-do list for today?'

The most pressing thing was cleaning out the hens, and it wasn't going to be a quick job either. The monthly clean and sanitise was a few days overdue, and with the weather on the turn and the hens likely to spend more time indoors, Carole was keen to get it done.

'Do you ever let them out into the garden?' I asked as they were currently contained in a large run.

'They're excellent at cleaning bugs out of the empty raised beds,' she told me, 'but obviously we must follow the rules about how to house them during outbreaks of bird flu and we're mindful of foxes, too. For now, they're being kept in their run.'

Given the size of the run and the various structure and enrichment additions, I didn't think the girls would ever be bored and they looked very healthy and engaged.

'Erik!' Carole called and I turned around to find him walking through the gate. 'You don't fancy giving us a hand, do you?'

'That's actually why I'm here,' he said as he walked over. 'I'd just got back from the gym when Luke remembered it was his turn to do the hens but as he's catching up with some admin, I offered to take his place.'

'That's very gallant of you,' Carole said. 'Thank you.'

'And I've done it plenty of times before, so it won't take long,' he reassured us.

'It's a complete clean out today,' Carole reminded him.

'I know the drill for that,' he nodded. 'Why don't you leave me and Skylar to it? I'm sure there are plenty of other things you could be getting on with.'

'Well, if you're sure?' she said hesitantly.

'Why don't you go and check up on Graham?' I suggested.

'Um,' she said and looked at her watch. 'That might not be a bad idea. I have been here a while.'

She reminded Erik about how much disinfectant to use and

then went back to the square leaving the pair of us to get on with the rather mucky job of cleaning out the henhouse. I'd never been in such close proximity to live poultry before, but Erik was clearly used to scooping them up and tucking them under his arm. I thought I'd have to work my way up to feeling that confident and familiar, but I did enjoy the cleaning process. The house and run looked quite transformed by the time we'd finished.

'Are you all right?' Erik asked, as the job neared completion. 'You're very quiet this morning. You haven't got a sore head after last night, have you?'

'No,' I said, 'nothing like that. Or not now, anyway.' The truth was that while I had scrubbed and swept, my mind had returned to thinking about the job offer, but I didn't want to get into that. 'I'm a bit preoccupied with thinking about the equinox party. It's going to be the smallest celebration I've ever had a hand in helping with, but it feels like the most important!'

That wasn't a lie, even though it hadn't been the reason why I had been quiet while we worked.

'Have you seen anyone else to ask about it, like you mentioned you were going to last night?'

'Only Carole,' I told him. 'And she said not to stress and just go for it. I had planned to catch Neil and Finn too, but they'd been and gone before I got here even though I arrived earlier than they said they might come over.'

'I wonder what prompted that?' Erik frowned.

'Mark's hangover,' I smiled. 'And Finn's creative brain.'

'Ah,' Erik nodded. 'I daresay both made for very early starts and you haven't forgotten that I said I'd help with the party if you'd like me to, have you?'

'I haven't. Thank you. And you must have been up with the lark, if you've already been to the gym,' I pointed out. 'Do you go as often as when you were playing rugby?'

'No,' he said. 'Nothing like as much, but if I don't keep on top of my fitness and physio then my knee soon lets me know about it.'

'That must be a nuisance.'

'Not really,' he said. 'Because it's as good for my mental health as anything else and gives my mind space to think about other things.'

'Such as?'

He looked thoughtful. 'There is something specific I'm mulling over but I'll fill you in when I've got a bit further with it.'

'Fair enough,' I accepted.

'And there's another advantage to going to the gym.'

'Oh?'

'I get to walk by Blossom's on the way back and the bakery is open by then.'

'Isn't that counterproductive?' I pretended to frown.

'It's all about balance,' he said, sounding zen. 'I know exactly how long I need to be in the gym to earn myself a brownie or an éclair or—'

'I get the idea,' I cut in. 'I've got a sausage roll in the bothy for my lunch. Do you think cleaning the hens out warrants eating it now?'

'Probably, because you have worked hard,' he said with a smile. 'But it would taste even better if you shared it.'

'Point taken,' I grinned. 'Let's finish tidying up and give it the attention it deserves.'

Chapter 13

That evening in my cosy sitting room, with Plato curled up in the armchair next to me, I sent an email thanking Madeline and Tobias for forwarding Mr Fuller's offer and fell to thinking about it again. No matter how hard I tried to focus on pulling together ideas for the equinox party instead, my brain kept tracking back to the sheet of paper now on the arm of the chair, and in the end, I had to banish it from sight before I found any peace.

It all made for a rather restless night, but I was looking forward to seeing Grandad George the following morning and telling him I'd taken his idea about finding a distraction to heart and how it was working out. Rather less well than it might have done given I now had something else to think about that complicated the point of my moving to the square, but I genuinely had enjoyed my two stints in the Grow-Well, and wouldn't mention the job offer.

'No secret meeting or appointment today,' I commented when I found him and Freddie sitting with their heads together in a quiet corner of the care home day room.

'Skylar!' Grandad George beamed. 'How lovely to see you.

No, nothing clandestine today. In fact,' he said mysteriously, 'I think my work there is done.'

'Given what you've just told me,' Freddie joined in, 'I think you're right, old man. Mission accomplished. Very well done.'

'If anyone ever dared to assume that folk are over the hill and out of the loop when they move into residential care,' Grandad laughed, 'then they'd be seriously underestimating us, wouldn't they?'

'That they would,' Freddie wholeheartedly agreed.

I shook my head as the pair high fived and felt grateful that I didn't know what had been afoot, and given that it was 'mission accomplished' I preferred to forget rather than fuss over it.

'I think I'll leave you to it,' Freddie said and kindly offered me his seat. 'I'm going to telephone my friend, May. I'll thrash you at dominoes later George. Lovely to see you again, Skylar.'

'Likewise,' I smiled and sat down in his place.

I scanned the room and noticed Mabel was absent. I hoped she was all right.

'So,' Grandad George said, 'how are you, my dear? You look a little tired, if you don't mind me saying so?'

'That's because I'm a bit worn out,' I told him, then added, 'but that's your fault.'

'Oh?'

'Don't look so worried, because it's with good cause. I took on board what you said last week and I'm now helping in the Grow-Well. I've been over twice since I saw you and you were right, it's a great distraction and I'm learning lots of new things, too.'

'Oh Skylar,' Grandad George clapped, 'that's the best news.

I'm so pleased. What have you been doing over there? You know, your father never said a word when I saw him yesterday. I take it he knows?'

'He does,' I confirmed. 'But I asked him not to say anything because I wanted to tell you myself.'

'Go on then. Fill me in.'

I told him how I'd cleared beds and pots and then given the henhouse a deep clean and been rewarded with more of the freshest brown eggs I'd ever had. There had even been a feather attached to one.

'Well, how about that?' he said, sounding astounded. 'I've never had you down as an outdoorsy type, but this 'something new' seems to have perked you up no end, even if it has tired you out.'

'It certainly has and that's not all. I've had an evening in a local pub with some of the neighbours, too, and I'm feeling much more settled as a result.'

Had it not been for the details of the potentially too good to turn down job offer, I might have felt *completely* settled, but the email wasn't up for discussion.

'I was already in a good mood, but you've made me even happier!' Grandad George glowed. 'What are the locals like? As friendly as Rafe reckons or has he got his rose-tinted specs on? I know how keen he is for this move to be a success for both of you, so he might be a bit blinkered . . .'

'No, he's right,' I was happy to say. 'Everyone is friendly and so kind and helpful.'

Even Erik had come good and if you'd told me that just a week ago, I never would have believed it. He hadn't been able to explain why he'd been off with me, but I had assumed his initial bad mood had been prompted by fears of a Prosperous Place security breach. Whatever the reason, he had apologised and that was good enough for me. I was already enjoying being his Platonic Plus One and had just about managed to rein in my tendency to moon over his beguiling blue eyes.

'Well, that's marvellous.'

'And there's something else marvellous, too,' I continued. 'But I haven't mentioned this to Rafe in case he thinks it sounds too much like my line of work.'

Grandad George looked concerned.

'It isn't work,' I said quickly. 'Not in the employed and paid for sense anyway.'

'Go on.'

'I've offered to help organise the Grow-Well autumn equinox party and include some extras,' I told him. 'The neighbours come together throughout the year to celebrate the seasons, along with feasting on what they've grown, but recently everyone has been so busy there hasn't been an opportunity to do more than share the meal. Now however—'

'You've come along,' Grandad George cut in with his smile back in place, 'with time on your hands and being an outstanding organiser, you've offered to step in and embellish things.'

'I don't know about being an outstanding organiser,' I laughed at his high praise, 'but yes, that's the gist of it. What do you think?'

He took a moment to consider.

'Three things,' he said and held up the corresponding number of fingers.

'Go on.'

'One, I think it sounds like a brilliant idea and the perfect way to further keep you occupied while you're taking time out from the real world of work.'

'Agreed.'

'Two, I very much hope I can blag an invitation to attend, even though I'm not a resident of the square.'

'I'm sure I'll be able to smuggle you in,' I giggled. 'What's the third thing?'

'You must tell Rafe before someone else does. It's bound to come up in conversation with one of the neighbours, and he'll be hurt if he hasn't heard it from you.'

'I just don't want him jumping to the wrong conclusion,' I sighed.

'Well, that's exactly what he'll do if he thinks you're trying to hide what you're up to. And to be honest Skylar, this is nothing as dramatic as something like letting him assume you're resting while secretly applying for jobs. You're making too much of it, my love.'

I bit my lip and nodded. 'Perhaps you're right,' I swallowed and again pushed away thoughts of the unexpected offer.

It wasn't as if I'd applied for that job, it had landed in my lap.

'This is a small gathering for people you and Rafe are starting to think of as friends. It's going to be fun. No pressure, no bridezilla expectations, just neighbourly fun.'

'To be fair,' I said, though it was hardly the point, 'the grooms could be equally as bad.' Grandad George gave me a look. 'But I get what you're saying. I'll tell him today.'

I hoped Lisa hadn't got to Rafe first, because having heard what Grandad George had to say about it, I could see that I had made rather a mountain out of a molehill.

'Good. And you know how much your father loves a good party,' he reminded me. 'He might have an idea or two to contribute.'

'Assuming he isn't too preoccupied,' I mused.

'With his writing you mean?' Grandad George asked. 'Or the man he spent the whole of Saturday night talking to?'

'He's told you then,' I realised. 'It must be serious. I hope he's a nice guy.'

'Don't look so worried. I have it on very good authority that he's a very nice guy indeed. Now, here comes Beth with something fun for me to do. Will you stay?'

Having decided that I should tell Rafe about my involvement with planning the equinox gathering with all possible haste, I decided not to join in with what Beth had got lined up, but I did make a point of nabbing her. In fact, that was a mutual thing because she wanted to talk to me, too.

'I don't want to hold you up,' I told her. 'But I was just wondering where Mabel is today. I haven't seen her at all.'

'She's in her room.'

'Oh right,' I grimaced, hoping that was okay.

I knew Mabel craved peace, but I hoped she wasn't hiding away.

'Don't worry, it's all good,' Beth elaborated. 'She's just having some time out after the early birds' senior tai chi session. It was her first go at it today.'

'I see,' I said, drawing the words out because the activity and Mabel's participation in it had taken me by surprise. 'Well, that's definitely progress, isn't it?'

'It is,' Beth agreed. 'She might have picked the quietest activity to try, but she did it and I've been making sure she hasn't been pestered into coming out of her room when she doesn't want to. She's now got some balance to her days.'

'She did mention the opportunity to have some quiet chats, too,' I remembered. 'Though I imagine the staff don't have much time for that, and I know you're always on the go.'

'That's actually what I wanted to talk to you about,' Beth smiled.

'Oh?'

'Our conversation about Mabel got me thinking over something I've been considering for a while now.'

'Which is?'

'Setting up a befriender service,' she explained. 'Made up of a small group of volunteers who'll come in once a week initially, to chat with people like Mabel, who would benefit from something more peaceful to what's generally on offer in the day room.'

'I think that sounds like an excellent idea!' I smiled. 'Mabel will be thrilled.'

'I've settled on trying it on a Thursday,' Beth continued. 'Perhaps even starting it in a small way this week if I can sign anyone up.'

'Even better.'

'So, what do you think?' she asked and I realised the direction the conversation was taking. 'How do you fancy being our first volunteer and taking Mabel under your wing while she settles here?'

It took me less than a second to decide.

'I'd love to!'

'I was hoping you'd say that,' Beth beamed. 'There'll be various safeguarding and reference checks to undertake, but as long as you're in the day room with other staff around until that's done, we can make a start straightaway.'

'In that case, I'll come in on Thursday then.'

Beth was delighted.

'If you could be here around ten, we could get the ball rolling with the forms and so on and then there'll be time to talk to Mabel for a while before lunch.'

'Yes,' I confirmed. 'I can easily manage that.'

With just the party details to prepare, sparing a few hours on a Thursday wasn't going to pose a problem. It didn't strike me then but given that I hadn't hesitated to accept Beth's offer, it said a lot about what I was really thinking about the one Mr Fuller had made me.

'See you Thursday then,' Beth said as a bit of a hubbub broke out in the day room. 'Unless I bump into you in the Grow-Well before then.'

'Either way, I'll see you soon,' I said, as she rushed off. 'Thanks, Beth.'

Rafe was ensconced in his writing room when I arrived back and by the time I'd zoned back in after a stint of party planning, I realised that the noise that had made me jump was the front door closing and him heading out.

'It doesn't look like I'll get to talk to him today then, does it?' I said to the cats as I read the note Rafe had left me telling me not to expect him back until the next day. 'Let's just hope he doesn't bump into anyone from the garden before he comes home.'

Before I had arrived in the square, I had wondered how the pair of us were going to rub along living under the same roof. Were we going to get on, or find the proximity too intense?

That was obviously wasted worrying time because often we were proving to be ships that passed in the night, rather than in each other's pockets. I supposed that was no bad thing as it gave us each some space, but it was frustrating now I wanted to talk!

The next morning, I checked the calendar and realised there were just eight days left until the equinox. I had already come up with some affordable but meaningful ideas for the party and needed to get on with some of them if I was going to get the things I needed in time.

I had wondered about running what I had in mind by Kate and Luke but then remembered that Erik had offered to help and sent him a text asking if he was free to meet me in The Dragon for lunch the next day.

He had messaged back within minutes, and with that arranged, I read the job offer from Mr Fuller again. I wasn't sure when the shift had occurred, but I couldn't in all honestly say that it felt as appealing as it had initially. He hadn't written that there was an expiration date to the offer, but it didn't feel fair to keep him hanging on now I'd decided.

With the paper resting on the arm of the chair in my sitting room, I opened my laptop ready to formulate a reply and just at that moment my father rushed into the room.

'Crikey Rafe!' I gasped.

With one hand I'd slammed the laptop shut, while the other slid the sheet of paper between the arm of the chair and the cushion so it was out of sight.

'What are you up to?' Rafe laughed as he came far enough into the room to face me. 'You look positively furtive.'

'Nothing,' I said guiltily. I could feel my cheeks were blazing but I could put that down to him making me jump. 'When did you get back? I didn't hear you arrive.'

'Just now,' he said. 'I suddenly remembered it was D-Day and wanted to make the most of it as the weather's decent.'

'D-Day?'

'The boys can go outside today,' he said brightly. 'It's a fortnight since we arrived and as they're so settled, I thought we'd give them access to the garden. Supervised though, of course. Do you want to watch how they react when I open the doors?'

'I'd love to,' I said as my heart rate settled and I stood up. 'I don't know about you, but I actually feel like we've been here far longer than a fortnight.'

'I feel the same. And I'm delighted to hear you say that because it hopefully means that you're feeling as content as I am.'

'The transition has definitely gone smoother than I expected it to,' I told him, while I remembered how I had been worried about being hemmed in by so many houses and nervous about driving on busy roads. Though that said, I hadn't driven since our trip to see Grandad George. 'The garden at Prosperous Place and the Grow-Well have really helped and I'm sorry I snapped just now,' I said sheepishly. 'While we're keeping an eye on the cats, I'll tell you what I was doing when you made me jump.'

Or my tweaked version of it. This was the ideal opportunity to explain about the party and hopefully allay any lingering suspicions he might have had about my shifty reaction to him unexpectedly arriving. I could tell him about the befriending service I was going to be a part of at Cavell Care, too. I now had more reason than ever to start putting down roots in Nightingale Square and the sooner I sent that 'thanks, but no thanks' email the better, but it would have to wait for now. Cat freedom beckoned.

'Come on then,' Rafe said cheerfully. 'Who do you think will be first out the door?'

'You're not really expecting me to answer that, are you?' I said and rolled my eyes.

'Come on boys!' he called as he walked out. 'It's time to expand your horizons and we're sure it will be Socks who's first to explore!'

Having assumed it would be Socrates who made a bolt for freedom the second he had the chance, we were both wrong because it was Plato the tabby who tentatively stuck his nose out and joined us on the patio while his unusually cautious companion watched on. I remembered that Plato had also been the bolder of the two the day we moved in.

'He's all talk,' Rafe said to Plato but with a nod to Socks, which made me laugh. 'You better not let him forget your bravery, Plato, my pal.'

It didn't take long for Socrates to creep out, and Rafe and I watched as they prowled around the walls of the garden which currently had a thin border running down each side, a large patio the width of the house outside the doors and a square block of lawn. I imagined it had been functional for a growing family with toys, bikes and play equipment but knew Rafe would be eager to make changes the second spring arrived. If not before.

'What are your plans for out here?' I asked.

'I haven't made any yet,' I was surprised to hear him say,

'because I'm still trying to decide whether to have a garden office installed somewhere towards the end of the lawn.'

If he did go ahead, that wouldn't leave much space for plants but then with the acreage across the road, I supposed that didn't matter. It would certainly mean less to maintain here.

'What do you think?' he asked.

'I think that whatever you decide will be wonderful and with that huge oak in the garden behind us, I think you've hit the jackpot.'

'Yes,' he agreed and looked admiringly up at it. 'I certainly intend to make the most of what the professionals call "borrowing the landscape".'

I told him about my plan to take a photo of the tree every month and showed him the first one.

'We could have them printed on a calendar to use the following year,' he suggested.

'I like the sound of that. As long as I don't forget to take a photo one month!'

'Put a reminder on your phone,' he said sensibly. 'And when you've done that, you can tell me what you were beavering away at earlier.'

Once I'd done as he suggested, I put my phone down and looked at him.

'Well,' I said, still choosing my words with care despite Grandad George's prediction that Rafe would be thrilled, 'I've taken on a bit of a . . . project.'

'That's not your way of saying you've found a job, is it?'

'No,' I said. 'Absolutely not. At least not in the sense that you're thinking.'

'Go on.'

'It is event planning,' I conceded and he opened his mouth to object, but I pushed on without pause, 'but for the Grow-Well,' he closed his mouth again. 'They have various celebrations throughout the year and it's the autumn equinox one next. Everyone usually chips in and some neighbours still are, but generally no one has the time to do much now, so I said I'd take it on. The finer details, anyway.'

'I see.'

'So, it is work, but nothing like—' I began to justify my decision.

'I think it's a brilliant idea,' Rafe cut in. 'I do appreciate that it must feel strange trying to fill so many hours when you're used to not having any to spare and this is something you can really get stuck into. Like working in the Grow-Well.'

He sounded over the moon and that made me feel even happier and even more certain that turning down Mr Fuller was the right thing to do. Perhaps Grandad George was right and that doing something in a similar vein, but not exactly the same as I'd done before, might open up other avenues for me to consider.

'And as of this morning,' I carried on, 'I've got something else to do, too.'

Rafe loved the sound of the befriender service and that my kindness to Mabel had been noticed.

'Not everyone's like me and your grandfather,' he said thoughtfully. 'I suppose we take change a bit more in our stride than some other people, don't we?'

'Me included.'

'Oh, I don't know,' he said, then jumped up because Socrates had leapt to the top of the back wall and was looking interested in the garden on the other side. 'I think you've taken to living here like a duck to water.'

I was surprised but very happy to acknowledge that I actually had no reason to disagree with that!

Chapter 14

Rafe and I spent the rest of the day and evening together and Grandad George had been right about me making too much of telling my father about the 'work' I had volunteered to do. I supposed the longer we lived together, the better we would get to know one another and how each of us were likely to react to things. That was a prospect I was looking forward to.

'Are you heading out?' Rafe asked late the next morning when he noticed my bag and shoes by the front door.

I was in my sitting room putting my laptop into a tote bag and getting ready to walk down and meet Erik later in The Dragon. I thought it would be easier to show him what I had in mind for the party on a bigger screen than my phone and I still hadn't had an opportunity to reply to Mr Fuller, so I planned to get that sorted, too.

I hadn't sent a response the previous evening because Rafe and I had enjoyed a few glasses of wine with our supper and I had a rule where I never messaged or emailed anyone with alcohol in my system. And Rafe had been flitting in and out and chatting all morning, so I still hadn't had a moment to compose what I wanted to say.

'Yes,' I said. 'Erik, from across the road, and I are meeting in The Dragon for lunch.' Rafe raised an eyebrow. 'He's helping with the party,' I said lightly and quickly added, 'so he needs to know what I have in mind.'

That should have nipped any potential Mark-like comment about my lunch date in the bud, and it did.

'In that case,' was all Rafe said, 'I'll walk with you as far as the pub.'

'You're not writing today?'

'Later, but first there's a reference book I need to pick up from the bookshop. The owner, Colin, is proving to be a genius in tracking things down that I haven't been able to find.'

'Given how far you must be into writing the book, isn't it a bit late for research?' I asked. 'Or are you one of those authors who does it as you're going along?'

I wasn't sure how his writing mind operated but had an idea that every creative had their own way of tackling things.

'A bit of both,' he shrugged. 'Now come on. I'm ready if you are.'

With him standing in the doorway, I decided not to retrieve the paper with the job details on it from down the side of the chair because that would have drawn attention to it. I would dispose of it later.

'I'll just grab a jacket,' I responded. 'And then I'll be all set.'

I arrived at the pub early and had plenty of time to compose my email to Mr Fuller. I hadn't wanted to send a blunt response and spent some time writing a paragraph explaining that I wasn't currently working but would be in the future. I had learnt from Madeline and Tobias that venue owners talked, and you never knew who might become a useful contact in the future. I didn't want to burn any bridges by coming across as brusque.

I had pressed send and was looking at a crafting website when the pub door opened and Erik walked in. He was wearing a cord jacket with the collar turned up and his trademark boots with the jeans caught in the tops and a new addition, a beanie. I let out a long breath as I took him in. He wasn't my usual type – darkish-blond hair, blue eyes and much taller than me – so why did my heart kick every time I saw him? I couldn't remember a time when it had *ever* done that when Rueben walked into a room.

Erik hadn't spotted me and was waylaid as soon as he crossed the threshold. I watched him pull the hat off. His hair was as messy as usual and I reckoned Finn was right, it was long enough to braid. I realised I was staring as he tucked a stray strand behind one ear while giving the person he was talking to his full attention. I grabbed my phone to distract me and was looking at nothing of importance when he walked over.

'Skylar, hey.'

I gave it a second before I looked up even though I'd known he was there.

'Hey, Erik,' I swallowed.

Even though I wasn't looking for any sort of romance and was more than happy to be his friend and PPO, I was still struck by how good looking he was close up. I wondered if I always would be . . .

'Am I late?' he asked as he shrugged off his jacket. 'You look as though you've been here a while.'

'No,' I said, 'you're not late. I came along early because I had some admin to do.'

'Have you still not been connected to Wi-Fi at the house?' he frowned. 'Because if that's the case, I'm sure Kate and Luke wouldn't mind you jumping on theirs. Especially if it's party stuff you're dealing with.'

'It's nothing like that,' I explained. 'The Wi-Fi is fine at home; I just fancied a change of scene. But thanks for suggesting that.'

'Okay,' he said. 'Let me get us a drink and we'll get straight down to it, shall we?'

'Yep,' I swallowed again. 'Let's get straight down to it.'

While he was at the bar, I opened a couple of tabs on my laptop so I could show him my party ideas and when he came back with lemonade for me and a Coke for him, he took the seat next to mine so we could both see the screen.

'Just a sec,' he said and leant back to secure his hair with a band from around his wrist, and in the process, treated me to a waft of whatever deeply masculine, but not overpowering aftershave he was wearing. 'That's better.'

'I think Finn was right,' I commented. 'Your hair is definitely long enough to braid.'

'Um,' he said. 'I've been thinking about having it cut. I've never grown it this long before and it's at what Finn has told me is an awkward stage. Apparently, I've got to stick it out because when it's longer it will be easier to tie up.'

'I'd agree with that,' I told him. 'There's always an in-between few months that drives you nuts. And I've always thought you can do more with long hair.'

'My father would not appreciate you encouraging me, Skylar,' Erik nudged and drank some of his Coke.

I remembered that he'd mentioned his father in the same

sentence as his hair the night we came to the pub with the others. His tone had suggested disapproval then, too.

'I take it he's not a fan?' I ventured.

'Of me or my hair?' Erik asked.

His tone implied that he wasn't joking.

'I meant your hair but—'

'He's not keen on either at the moment, but I won't bore you with the details.'

I was curious, nonetheless.

'Does he live nearby?'

'No, not very close,' Erik smiled. 'He's in Sweden.'

'Sweden?'

'Yes, my mum was Swedish and Dad took her name,' he said, and I noted the past tense. 'She died when I was in my teens, and Dad moved to Sweden permanently when I was in my twenties.'

'I'm sorry about your mum,' I said softly. 'Do you have any brothers or sisters?'

'Nope,' he said. 'It's just me. Do you mind if we change the subject?'

He sounded almost gruff and I was taken aback.

'Of course,' I said, feeling hot. 'Sorry, I didn't mean to pry.'

'You haven't,' he said more gently, then nudged my arm with his again and nodded at the laptop. 'I'm just keen to know what you've come up with for the party.'

I didn't believe that was the reason he wanted to draw a line but pulled my laptop closer and refreshed the page. I didn't get the chance to explain anything however, because Mark then bounded in and made a beeline straight for us.

'What's this then?' he asked as he looked down at us. 'A cosy lunch for two?'

I shook my head.

'Do you see any food here?' Erik asked and looked at the table.

'And the pub's getting busy,' I pointed out. 'So, it's hardly cosy, is it?'

'In that case,' Mark said as he moved to sit opposite us, 'I'll join you.'

'No, you won't,' Erik said and stuck his foot out to stop Mark moving the chair. 'We're busy.'

'Doing what?' Mark frowned.

'Equinox party planning,' I told him. 'And I don't want anyone other than me and Erik to know what I'm considering otherwise it won't be a surprise.'

'And don't think about sitting back there so you can look over our shoulder either,' Erik said and looked behind us. 'In fact, come on Skylar, let's move to that corner table we had last week before someone else nabs it.' I noticed Mark's eyebrows shoot up at the mention of us having been in the pub together before, but he didn't comment. 'That way we can keep an eye on him.'

'No need for that,' Mark objected. 'I'm not staying. I've just come to collect something from the kitchen that Blossom's lent and needs back.'

'In that case,' I said as Erik and I moved to the slightly quieter corner anyway, 'you'd better get on with it, hadn't you?'

Having watched him leave and as the smell of delicious food cooking began to reach us, we decided to put in our lunch order first and then look through my ideas.

'A ritual?' Erik commented when I opened the first tab and before he'd read anything about it. 'I don't think they've tried anything like that before.'

He sounded a bit doubtful about it.

'It's straightforward,' I told him, 'but meaningful and if there's some way we can have a fire for the burning part, I thought it would be perfect. Have a proper look.'

I waited while Erik read the details and then turned and gave me a gorgeous smile.

'You like it?'

'I love it,' he nodded. 'It's a brilliant idea and you don't need to worry about the fire aspect because Finn has made these great braziers that are used for winter celebrations. We'll be able to borrow a couple of those and not have to tend to them as much as we would a bonfire.'

'They sound perfect,' I said, feeling relieved. 'So that's one thing sorted. Now, what do you think of this?'

I waited again while he looked at the next idea I'd found.

'Perfect,' he beamed. 'Again.'

'Really?'

'Really and I'm sure Freya can sort out enough terracotta pots for every household and more to spare,' he enthused. 'We won't have to tell her what you're planning to do with them, and they'll be so much nicer than plastic alternatives.'

'I still have to source the bulbs,' I said, thinking aloud.

'I know where there's a garden centre,' Erik responded and reached for his phone. 'We could have a road trip.'

We looked again at the details of what I had in mind. It was only simple when compared to the kind of thing I had previously been responsible for but knowing how much it was hopefully going to mean to my new neighbours and friends I was taking just as much care over it.

'The party is only a week away now,' I said, 'but I'm confident there's time to arrange all of this.'

'Absolutely,' Erik agreed. 'And if the weather lets us down, then everything can easily be transferred into the house.'

'Apart from the braziers.'

'There's a huge fire in the sitting room and I'm sure Kate and Luke would be willing to light that for us,' he said, solving the problem. 'And Greengages will have everything you need for the table decorations.'

'Thank goodness for you, Erik,' I said gratefully. 'You know all the best places.'

'And so will you soon, now you're a local,' he smiled. 'Look, here comes our lunch.'

He moved his chair a little away from mine and we talked further about the party while we ate. Erik had a steak sandwich and a bowl of chips, while I enjoyed a crab salad. He kept offering to share the chips, but I resisted. Just.

'I'd better get back,' he said eventually, having checked the time on his phone. 'I've been gone ages. Are you staying?'

'No,' I told him, 'I'm going to head back too, so we can walk together, if you like.'

We'd just finished deciding when to go to the garden centre when we caught sight of my father and a man I didn't recognise walking towards us on the other side of the road.

'Hey, look,' Erik said. 'There's your dad.'

He went to call out but I put a hand on his arm to stop him.

'No,' I said. 'Don't say anything.'

'Why not?' Erik frowned, as I ducked behind him in case Rafe happened to look across and spot me. 'Don't you want him to see us? I can't imagine he'll make comments like Mark and try to shove us together.'

'So, you've picked up on Mark doing that, too?'

'How could I not?' Erik laughed. 'But don't worry, he'll soon get bored and move on to teasing someone else.' The sooner the better as far as I was concerned. 'But what's the deal with your dad?'

I watched as Rafe and the mystery man, who was something of a silver fox, passed by. They were completely engrossed in their conversation and looked to be of a similar age, height and build. Rafe was carrying a tote bag from the bookshop, but I was certain the man with him wasn't Colin, the shop owner.

'I have a feeling,' I told Erik, 'that the guy Rafe is with is someone he's just met and is rather taken with.'

'They look equally taken with each other.'

'You're right, but Rafe hasn't introduced him to me yet and I'd hate to force his hand.'

'Ah right,' Erik said and we moved off again.

'I can't believe he's met someone he really likes already,' I said in wonder. 'We've only been living here a fortnight.'

'But you've already met lots of people that you like in that time.'

'You know what I mean.'

'But that's how it works sometimes, isn't it?' Erik said. His eyes were focused on his feet now rather than where he was going. 'I mean, I've only just met you, Skylar, but I know I really like you.'

'You do?' I squeaked, feeling myself go warmer than the weather warranted.

'Of course,' he said and gave me a fleeting glance. 'I mean, you're the perfect PPO for a start, aren't you?'

I'd foolishly jumped to the wrong conclusion, but to be fair his words were ripe for misinterpretation.

'Well yes,' I said, feeling flustered. 'I really like you in that way, too Erik. And this is the perfect street for people spotting, isn't it?' I forged quickly on.

'Why? Who else have you seen?' He looked up from the pavement and behind him to see who might also be around.

'I meant in general.'

There was no point trying to backtrack because the smile Erik was now wearing told me he'd realised I'd put my foot in it, and my flushed complexion was probably a bit of a give-away too. In trying to steer the conversation in another direction I'd dropped myself right in it.

'So, I did see you here in the street last Friday!' He teased. 'And you saw me and took off to avoid me, didn't you?'

'Maybe,' I blushed.

'But why?'

'Why do you think?' I tutted. 'It may have slipped your mind but on the two previous occasions we'd met, you'd been rather mean to me.'

He was quiet for a few steps.

'Well, yes,' he said, and puffed out his cheeks, 'I suppose I was a bit of a bear, but I promise I'll never be horrible to you again.'

'I should think not,' I recovered. 'Us Nightingale Square singletons have to stick together.'

Chapter 15

With lots of other things to think about and my time now fully accounted for, I set aside the embarrassment I'd felt over how I'd let slip to Erik that I'd gone out of my way to avoid him, and with the email to Mr Fuller sent and no reply having been received, I forgot all about his unexpected job offer, too.

I was up early the next morning and looking forward to my first Thursday session as a befriender at Cavell Care Home. It was unlike anything I'd undertaken before, and Grandad George had been right in his prediction because there was something exciting about that. The opportunity also made me feel good about myself. I wasn't only taking the role on to fill some time; I was also doing it for the benefit of other people. Lovely Mabel initially and more residents in the future.

The future . . .

It struck me as I made my first coffee of the day that the assumption I could now acknowledge I'd arrived with – that I had chiefly moved to Nightingale Square to please my kind father and take the time he insisted I needed to rest while between jobs – was fading further into the background. At just over a couple of weeks in I was feeling safe, settled, occupied and happy to simply go with the flow, for a while longer at least, and there was something very comforting about that.

Beth was waiting for me in the care home reception, and having signed in, in a different capacity to usual, she gave me a lanyard with my name and volunteer status and walked me to the office to meet Sandra, the home's manager. She didn't strike me as someone who would be very hands on with the residents, but then I supposed her role was nothing like those of the carers who worked intimately with everyone on a twenty-four-hour basis.

'Don't mind her,' Beth whispered, as we walked back down the corridor away from Sandra's office, 'she's not best known for her people skills.'

'I could tell,' I grimaced. 'Though I can't imagine she has the easiest of jobs, balancing budgets, allocating funds and so on.'

'You're right,' Beth agreed as we squeezed into her office, which was the size of a broom cupboard. 'Funds are always tight, but on that note, you can claim expenses as a volunteer for your travel to and from here. I meant to tell you on Monday but forgot.'

'Don't worry about that. I won't be expecting you to work out how much shoe leather I get through on the walk to and from the square.'

'Well, if the weather turns bad and you need to drive, do make a note of your mileage and I can compensate you for that.'

If the weather turned bad, I'd still be walking because I didn't fancy having to face the convoluted trip around the ring road. Once had been enough.

'Thanks, Beth,' I said, nonetheless.

'Now, let's go through the safeguarding and I'll show you what's currently on the activities schedule, then you can go and see how Mabel's feeling today.'

We found Mabel in the currently quiet day room, and she was delighted to see me. When I explained that I would be coming in on a weekly basis from then on for a cuppa and a chat she was even more thrilled.

'Beth has just shown me the activities schedule,' I told her. 'And I noticed there's tai chi happening first thing in the morning a few times a week. I've never tried it myself, but I do wonder what it's like.'

'I've been doing that,' Mabel confided. I had hoped she would. 'I've only just started and I'm not very good at it but it's relaxing and very peaceful.'

'That sounds right up my street. I've never been one for exercise classes or going to the gym.'

Mabel put a hand over her mouth to stifle a laugh. I didn't think the image of me exercising was that hilarious, but I was pleased to see her looking happy.

'I'm not laughing at you, Skylar,' she explained. 'Your mention of exercise classes just reminded me of something.'

'Well, you have to tell me what it is,' I said. 'Come on, share the joke.'

She looked at me and smiled.

'You probably won't have heard of this,' she began, 'but back in the eighties, keeping fit with Jane Fonda in her leotards and legwarmers was all the rage. There was a local weekly class offering something like she did and a couple of friends and I used to go along.'

She shook her head at the memory which had obviously amused her.

'Did you get fit?'

'Hardly,' she grinned. 'We used to pick up fish and chips on the way home every week as a reward for our huffing and puffing.'

'Oh Mabel!' I laughed.

Her admission made me think about Erik stopping at Blossom's on the way back from the gym. He still hadn't elaborated on what he'd been thinking about while he was working out, but I bet it wasn't leotards and leg warmers!

'And we certainly never looked like Jane Fonda. Not before or after the months of going along!' Mabel giggled. 'I was already in my forties and never going to be the size ten I'd aspired to be in my twenties, but it was good fun.'

'I've heard of Jane Fonda,' I said, and unlocked my phone, 'but not her exercise classes.'

A quick search online had us both in fits as we giggled over the brightly coloured exercise outfits that left little to the imagination and then watched a couple of clips of the classes themselves.

'No wonder you needed a chippy tea after that!' I exclaimed.

'Exactly,' Mabel said and wiped the happy tears from her eyes. 'We never would have made it home without something to sustain us after all that jigging about.'

The morning whizzed by in a similar vein and I set off back to the square having also spent a few minutes talking to Grandad George and telling him that he'd been right about Rafe's reaction to what I was doing.

'And how are the plans for the party coming along?' he asked.

'Very well. I'm going to pick some bits and pieces up at the weekend and then it will just be the setting up and celebrating.'

'A doddle compared to what you've been used to, then?'

'It is,' I agreed, 'but I can appreciate how hard it would be for anyone else to do extras like this when they're so busy with other things.'

'Lucky for the neighbours in Nightingale Square that you aren't busy then, hey?'

I agreed with that, too.

I had a real spring in my step as I signed out and walked the increasingly familiar route home. I felt so happy to see Mabel's mood so vastly improved because of something as simple as a conversation and a couple of hours reminiscing. She'd said she was going to stick to the tai chi and would enjoy fish and chips on a Saturday at the care home even more now she'd remembered the workouts with her old friends.

'How did you get on?' Rafe asked me after I found him in the kitchen with Plato curled up on his lap.

He'd found a fabulous sofa on a local selling site and had it delivered and deposited in front of the previously empty wall on the far side of the kitchen. I'd always had a hankering for a sofa in a kitchen and loved it.

'Absolutely brilliant,' I told him, as I spotted Socrates prowling about the garden. 'The resident I was with today had the funniest tale to tell. Do you know who Jane Fonda is?'

'Of course,' he nodded. 'She's an American actress and activist, but to be honest, I'm more familiar with her through her fitness regimes and videos. Well, DVDs now, I suppose. Everyone was doing her classes back in the eighties!'

'Even you?'

'I decline to comment,' he laughed, which obviously meant yes. 'I've probably still got the leg warmers somewhere . . .' he then added, which confirmed my assumption and gave me an image amusing enough to rival Mabel's!

'Well, don't rush to dig them out,' I smiled. 'What shall we have for lunch?'

I was inclined to suggest fish and chips but as there was loads of Grow-Well salad in the fridge I went for that instead.

Having messaged Erik the next day to check the location of the garden centre he'd recommended for us to visit on Saturday, I looked the details of it up online and found it was family run, which I loved, and a few miles out of the city, which I wasn't so keen on. He'd offered to take us, but I had a feeling that my desire to drive was going to further diminish if I didn't get behind the wheel soon and that wouldn't be a good thing, even though it would be easier than battling my demons. Consequently, I said we'd take my car as it needed a run but that he'd have to bear with me feeling jittery as I wasn't used to city roads.

I was ready early Saturday morning and tried not to keep tuning in to the distant drone of traffic which I'd never focused on before.

'All set?' Erik smiled, but then his face dropped. 'What's up? You look pale. I know you said you were feeling a bit nervous, but if you're not well—'

I put up a hand to stop him.

'Other than feeling like my stomach's going to drop through the floor, I'm perfectly healthy,' I attempted to joke, but it was completely true.

'Listen,' he said. 'You're going to be fine. I've got every faith in you. You've negotiated narrow, winding, hilly Yorkshire roads for years, so you can handle the flat of Norfolk.'

'It's more about the volume of traffic than the terrain.'

'Slow moving traffic for the most part,' Erik said bracingly. 'And I'm a brilliant passenger. I'll support you every mile. And my insurance covers me to drive any car, so I promise we'll just stop, and I'll get behind the wheel if you really have problems.'

With his kind words and assurance, I began to feel better.

'And I have got my satnav,' I told him as I unlocked the car.

'Honestly, Skylar,' he said as he climbed in and adjusted the seat to accommodate his long legs, 'you've got this.'

With his kindness and encouragement ringing in my ears, we set off. I didn't much enjoy the first part of the short journey, but once we were out of the city, the rest was easy driving. My hands were nonetheless a little shaky as I pulled into a parking space, but as I turned the engine off, I began to feel euphoric.

'You did it!' Erik grinned, once we'd climbed out.

'You were brilliant!' I said and rushed round the car to where he was standing.

He put up his hand to high five me, but I was too full of adrenaline to take any notice and practically flung myself at him. I gave him the tightest hug. He felt solid, but safe rather than like a brick wall.

'Feel good?' he asked, as he wrapped his arms further around my back so there wasn't a millimetre of space between us. 'About the drive, I mean,' he added, sounding a little flustered. 'Do you feel good about accomplishing that?'

'I feel amazing!' I laughed and pulled away a little. 'You

were such a help, Erik, especially around the ring road.' I looked up at his face and the intense closeness of him, which I'd instigated, suddenly hit me. As did the nearness of his beautiful blue eyes. 'Sorry,' I blustered and took a step back. 'I didn't mean to gush . . .'

'Don't apologise,' he swallowed and ran a hand through his already mussed up hair. 'I'm really pleased you did it, Skylar, and if you'd like a passenger any other time while you're driving around the city, you only have to ask.'

My PPO was proving to be perfect in every way. Kind, supportive and now I knew he was a wonderful hug provider, too.

'I might take you up on that.'

'I hope you do.'

I then realised I'd locked my bag in the car and went to retrieve it.

'Now, come on,' I said. 'This place looks huge, so they're bound to have what we need.'

'That's why I suggested it,' he laughed and we went to find the entrance.

We only really needed to pick up a couple of things, but I was so overwhelmed by the variety of autumn decorations I knew I could adorn the house with we'd soon had to switch out the baskets we were carrying for a small trolley.

'Remind me again, what were the variety of daffs you wanted?' Erik requested once he'd dragged me away from the aisles of autumn leaf garlands and fly agaric ornaments.

'Narcissus Paper White. And the hyacinths are Pink Pearl and Anna Marie.'

'You're in luck,' he said and held up a bag of the narcissus. 'It looks like they've got the lot!'

'Excellent,' I clapped. 'Let's have a count up of how many we're going to need.'

It took a while to do that, and I also hunted down some autumn themed pot labels that I thought would be handy. It all took longer than I had expected, but I knew that was my fault because I'd got carried away with the sundries.

'Are you needed back at the house soon?' I asked Erik as we loaded the bags into the boot of my car.

'No, there's nothing urgent. Why?'

'Well,' I said with a nod back to the garden centre, 'I want to thank you for guiding me here and for your infinite patience while I cooed over the autumn aisles.'

'What did you have in mind?' he asked, sounding a little mischievous.

'Tea and a scone,' I said, which wasn't what I had really wanted to say.

'You're my kinda gal, Skylar Harding,' he grinned.

'I'm Skylar Shawe,' I corrected him. 'I have my mum's surname, but I'm delighted you approve of the payment.'

The scones were huge, the cream was thick and the jam was ruby red. I hadn't thought I'd be able to devour all of mine, but with the help of a seemingly endless supply of tea, I rose to the challenge and managed it. Erik and I barely spoke, other than to make suggestive noises of appreciation while we tucked in. We didn't even have the traditional 'jam or cream first' conversation slash argument!

'Crikey, that was good,' Erik sighed, as he wiped the cream out of his stubble, which was almost long enough to be classed as a beginner beard.

'I couldn't agree more,' I told him as I let out a breath. 'We did get everything I wanted, didn't we? I'm worried I got too sidetracked to notice.'

'We got everything,' Erik laughed. 'I checked the list while you were unloading the trolley at the till.'

'That's all right then.'

'I tell you what might not be all right though,' he frowned. 'Have you checked the forecast for next week?'

'Nope,' I answered. 'I've given it up. Not checking the weather is now one of my rules to live by.'

Erik looked confused. 'Can I request an explanation?'

I suppose it did need clarifying.

'When I was working at Highfell,' I explained, 'the weather played a huge part in planning an event. If it let us down, I needed a watertight quick change contingency plan to ensure it didn't impact, and now I don't have to worry about it, I've given up looking.'

'Ah, right,' Erik said. 'I see. That must have been stressful.'

'It could be. So, what does the forecast say for here? What's happening overhead next week?'

'What are your other rules?' Erik asked, rather than share the outlook. 'You said that not checking the weather is one of your rules. Tell me another.'

I thought of the one I'd most recently applied.

'Never send messages or emails when I've had alcohol.'

'That makes sense,' Erik laughed. 'Did you learn the hard way?'

'I did,' I confirmed. 'Egged on by a friend who I keep in touch with online, I sent a message to a guy I thought I liked. It was in a moment of gin-soaked madness and I'm not going to elaborate on the consequences . . .'

When he'd flirted with me and asked for my number, I had no idea he was engaged. Thankfully, the wedding didn't take place at Highfell. Assuming it still went ahead. For the sake of the bride, I hoped it hadn't.

'Did you not have another friend on hand to talk you out of it?' Erik asked.

'I didn't really have friends my age at Highfell,' I shrugged.

Erik's face dropped. 'That's a bit sad.'

'I've never really been a close friend kind of person,' I continued. 'Mum moved me around so much when I was growing up, it was hard to form friendships that lasted. Don't look like that,' I said when Erik's expression fell further. 'I was fine and I do have one pal who had a similar upbringing to mine. She lives in Canada now and we still email.'

'Did you make friends at university?'

'I didn't go. I went into work at eighteen. That's how I've got all the years of experience that make me so brilliant at my job.' I was trying to make him smile, but he didn't. 'I'm making friends now I have more of a chance. You, Freya and Finn being the first.'

'Well, that's good,' Erik nodded. 'Here's to a happy future in Nightingale Square that's packed full of friendship.'

How long was that future going to be, I wondered. Perhaps, I was beginning to believe, longer than I'd originally thought . . .

'And packed full of fun, too, if this party turns out how I hope it will,' I said, moving us on. 'But is the weather really looking grim?'

'It's not looking great,' Erik winced and I guessed it was predicted to be the opposite. 'But on the bright side, we can move everything other than the pizza oven into Prosperous

Place if needs be. You'll just have to decide before we start setting up on the day.'

'That is a sensible alternative,' I said. 'But we'd better check with Kate and Luke that they really won't mind everyone descending on them if the heavens open.'

'Believe me,' Erik smiled, 'they're used to it.'

'And I suppose if we do end up celebrating inside, I could decorate the room we'll be in with some of the decorations we've just loaded into the boot of my car before I put them up at home. That would justify me buying so many, wouldn't it?'

'Autumn decoration overload completely rationalised!' Erik laughed and toasted my idea by clinking his cup of tea against mine.

Chapter 16

Despite my conviction not to check the forecast, I did succumb and Erik had been right. There was going to be a swathe of rain sweeping right across the country from west to east with the longest spell for Norfolk set to arrive early on the 23rd – the day of the equinox.

Consequently, it was decided in advance that the celebration should take place indoors and everyone was notified via the WhatsApp group. Consensus was that this was the best plan, though John was still hoping he'd be able to fire up the outdoor oven as long as someone was willing to hold an umbrella and help with ferrying the pizzas to the house.

The day dawned disappointingly dull, but I refused to let it dampen my spirits and, straight after breakfast, I began to get everything together ready to take over to Prosperous Place for setting up.

'What's all this?' Rafe asked, when he wandered into my sitting room and stretched out his back after a long stint at the keyboard.

'Don't look too closely!' I commanded. 'It's stuff for the party tonight.'

'What *all* of it?'

'Well, no,' I said, looking at the bags of decorations as well as the boxes of flower bulbs, 'some of it is mine. I got a bit carried away buying autumn decorations at the garden centre, but they'll look lovely in the house after I've used them tonight.' Rafe laughed at that. 'What's so funny?'

'Decorating for fall was very big in my neighbourhood in LA,' he explained. 'And I shipped quite a lot of my own stuff back with me. It's currently in boxes in my writing room because I didn't see the point of putting it in the loft when we arrived because autumn was so close. I was going to suggest we decorate the house this weekend.'

I hadn't considered that my father might have decorations of his own. I'd never visited him in the fall, as he endearingly called it, but knowing the US was so big on Halloween, I probably should have realised.

'The best dressed house in the square is bound to be awarded to us then!' I laughed.

'I think you're right,' he said with a nod to all the bags. 'We'll be able to festoon every room with this lot and don't worry about the cats.' I hadn't considered them either when I'd been piling garlands into the trolley. 'Just like the Christmas tree, they've never been interested in any of it before.'

That was a relief to hear. I'd seen enough cats going crazy with Christmas decs on social media to belatedly realise that could have been an issue!

'Are you missing LA?' I asked, because Rafe had barely mentioned the US since we'd moved in together.

He came properly in and sat on the sofa, and I flopped down on the armchair. As I did so, I heard the sheet of paper with the Devon job details on crinkle, and I realised I'd never thrown it away. The recycling bin was due for collection that day, so I made a mental note to stuff it in there when I left.

'I'm not missing it at all.' My father smiled. 'I have my memories, mostly good ones, and it was time to come home. And of course, all my best people are here.'

I glowed at that.

'Don't let Mum hear you say that,' I warned him. 'I'm sure she thinks she should be included as one of your best people.'

'You're right,' he laughed. 'And actually, she is a favourite of mine because she gifted me you.'

'Oh, Rafe,' I sighed happily.

'I mean it. You're the best thing I've ever done, Skylar.'

'Even better than winning your Dagger Award?'

'Hey now, that's not fair,' he pretended to sulk. 'How can you make me choose between you and that?'

'I'm only joking. I wouldn't do that to you.'

'You know,' he said, 'you do remind me of your mum.'

My glow was replaced with a glare.

'I hope you don't mean that,' I huffed. 'I've spent my entire life attempting to be the complete opposite to her in every conceivable way. You know the carnage she leaves in her wake and if you think—'

'If you let me finish,' my father mildly butted in, 'I meant in looks not personality.'

'Oh.'

'You have her gorgeous green eyes. You're nothing like her otherwise and I'm most grateful for that.'

'Sorry,' I said, feeling chastened.

'And I'll tell you who else has got gorgeous eyes,' Rafe went on, my defensive reaction apparently forgotten.

'Who?'

'Erik who lives across the road.'

I had been expecting him to say his beau, but so far all I knew about him was what he looked like at a distance from the day Erik and I had spotted him (assuming that was him) and Rafe during our walk back from the pub. And apparently, it was going to stay that way.

'Has he?' I shrugged, making out I hadn't noticed. 'I didn't know your paths had crossed.'

'I've met everyone at Prosperous Place and from the square now.'

'You've done better than me then,' I said and stood up. 'I've still got a couple of neighbours to go, but I'm not sure who they are. Anyway, I'd better get on. I want to make an impact and a good impression tonight, so the sooner I start setting up, the better.'

'And don't forget to tell Kate and Luke that I'll be arriving a bit early to welcome Dad and former Nightingale Square resident, Harold, who are sharing a taxi from the care home.'

'Already done.'

'Efficient as ever,' he said, and kissed my head on the way out. 'I'm making a coffee; would you like one to take with you?'

When I was ready to leave, I stuffed the job sheet into the recycling bin and loaded everything else into my car. The short journey wasn't really justified, but it would take more trips to and fro on foot to carry everything than I had time to make. Erik had opened the gates to the drive so I could pull straight in, and as soon as I had we began unloading.

'There's even more than I remember,' he laughed as we ferried everything to the house.

'I think it's breeding when I turn my back,' I quipped. 'I'm sure the garlands are twice as long as before!'

The Prosperous Place kitchen smelt divine as everyone contributing food had decided to get together and make and bake en masse. The scene was both charming and convivial, and it was an ideal demonstration of the strength of community spirit the square enjoyed.

'Skylar,' Kate smiled, 'tell me what you want me to do? Is there anything you need?'

'Just Erik,' I said and immediately blushed. I thanked my lucky stars that Mark hadn't been around to hear that. 'What I mean is, Erik knows what I've got planned, so he's going to help me set it up. That way it'll be a surprise for you and everyone else.'

'That's a brilliant idea,' Carole, who was stirring a huge pot on the Aga, commented. 'We're all very excited to find out what you've got lined up for us, Skylar.'

'It's only a couple of things,' I said, hoping they wouldn't be disappointed.

'But a brilliant couple of things,' Erik chimed in as he arrived with the last of the bags. 'Now come on, we'd better get on. Where do you want this lot?'

As the table in the kitchen was large enough to accommodate everyone, with the youngsters sharing a smaller table, I decided that would be the best place to set up the first activity. It didn't require much preparation so didn't need doing until after we'd eaten. Once I'd put the box of supplies next to the dresser, and asked everyone not to look inside it, that was it for in there.

'So,' I said to Erik, as he showed me the drawing room where the open fire was already laid and would just need lighting later in the day. 'Once the first part has been completed in the kitchen, we can come in here in lieu of Finn's braziers and then move on to the dining room for the messy bit.'

'Perfect,' Erik nodded. 'And as that's the room that's going to need the biggest transformation, let's head there now.'

The first thing we did was cover the table with a felt backed table protector that Luke came in and showed us, and then, with him banished, we covered the whole of the surface with a thick layer of brown paper which could be recycled. I then set to decorating the centre of the table with my silk leaf garlands and battery-operated fairy lights while Erik went to collect the terracotta pots Freya had found and cleaned up for us.

He stopped in his tracks when he staggered back in with the crate of heavy pots, and I rushed to close the door behind him in case anyone else was about.

'What do you think?' I asked. I noticed his hair and shoulders were wet and guessed the promised rain had arrived. 'Will it do?'

While he'd been gone, I'd piled up some small pumpkins and gourds in strategic places around the room and lit them with more lights and battery-operated flickering candles. There was also a wreath on the back of the door and autumn incense burning to add a layer of seasonal scent. I didn't intend to leave it burning longer than a minute or two in case any of the neighbours had asthma, but it would be enough to enhance the seasonal ambience.

'Will it do?' Erik laughed as he put the crate down. 'Skylar, it's perfect.' I felt my shoulders relax. 'I had been going to say it was a shame we couldn't celebrate in the Grow-Well, but then I stepped outside, and with the rain pouring and the wind getting up,' and right on cue a fierce gust rattled the window casing, 'I realised how lucky we are to have an indoor alternative and your efforts have made me even happier.'

'You like it then?' I said, grinning like the Cheshire Cat.

He looked down at me and shook his head. Rafe was so right about Erik's eyes but then I already knew that.

'I love it,' he beamed and I had to force myself to look away.

Having then helped a little in the kitchen, I only had time to drive back to the square to get changed ahead of everyone starting to arrive. Rafe was just leaving as I rushed in. He was carrying the cake he'd baked the day before and looking rather grim.

'If you hang on,' I said, 'I'll only be a minute and I'll drive us both back over. There's a lull in the rain, but I don't think it will last, and it'll be a travesty if your cake gets soaked.'

'No,' he said, his eyes not quite meeting mine, 'you're all right. It'll be fine in the tin. I'll go over now so I'm in good time to meet Dad and Harold.'

'Is everything all right?' I frowned.

'Fine. Why wouldn't it be?'

With the time ticking, I didn't have time to enquire further, and when I arrived at Prosperous Place, having dashed across the road on foot, because it was only then starting to rain again, I found Erik's mood had changed somewhat, too.

Both the men in my life seemed suddenly out of sorts, though no one else seemed to notice because they were all so busy and my father and Erik were putting a brave face on things. However, I could see their smiles were fixed and when they thought no one was looking, their façades dropped faster than the temperature outdoors and they looked strained.

I didn't have time to talk to them because I was trying to remember names and faces and make sure Grandad George and Harold were comfortable in their seats at either end of the table. Not that they were short of Nightingale Square neighbours willing to tend to their every whim. Grandad George was ecstatic to be included and was entertaining the children with his party trick of producing coins from behind their ears. I'd forgotten he could do that.

'How fabulous is this?' Lisa said ecstatically as she looked around the kitchen. The room was huge, but it felt full with everyone in it. 'John's gone to do a recce, but I've told him he can't cook pizzas in this.'

It was still possible to make out the sound of the whistling wind even above the noisy level of chatter, so I knew she was right.

'Tell him it will give us an excuse for another gathering,' I suggested.

'That's a brilliant idea,' she agreed. 'Now, can you remember who everyone is?'

I went around the room and named everyone.

'Almost perfect,' she praised. 'You just muddled up Eli and Jacob. Eli is Beth's partner and Jacob is Poppy's.'

I'd only very briefly met Eli before, so that was allowed and saying hi to Jacob was a first hello, just like with John.

'And Poppy mentioned her brother . . .' I faltered.

'Ryan. Sadly, he's had to carry on working so he won't make it now.'

'One less name for me to muddle up,' I joked and Lisa laughed.

'Oh, here we go,' she said. 'Kate's windmilling for everyone's attention, so you'd better join her.'

I was a little nervous when I went to sit next to her, but I needn't have been. Kate commented on the beautiful table decorations which I'd had to scale down when I realised how much food there was going to be and she also thanked me for stepping in to plan the evening's entertainment. Everyone applauded, which made my face flush and then Luke stood up and said a few words about the significance of the equinox and how it was a time to celebrate the Grow-Well harvest – which John, who was back, toasted loudly – and also reflect on our personal experience of the year so far.

Given what I'd got planned for our first activity, this was the perfect moment to explain what was going to happen after we'd eaten, so before Luke finished talking, I stood up, and having spotted my move, he handed over to me.

'I know you're all dying to tuck in,' I began and John cheered again, 'so I'm not planning to hold us up. I just wanted to say a couple of things. Firstly, thank you so much for making my father and I so welcome in Nightingale Square and for extending an invitation to my grandfather this evening. It's so great that all three of us are here together and given what Luke has just said, I don't think we could have moved at a more significant time. I know I'm certainly contemplating the changes in my life, and I would imagine Rafe is, too.'

Everyone called out something kind and welcoming and

Rafe raised his glass to me and smiled. I still didn't think he looked quite like himself, but I'd get to the bottom of what was bothering him after the party.

'And secondly,' I quickly continued, 'I thought it would be the ideal time for us to perform a simple equinox ritual, and further prompted by Luke's words just now, it feels like the perfect fit. I haven't done anything like it before, but while you eat, it would be helpful if you could consider something meaningful to you that you're grateful for this year and something you feel ready to let go of, something you've outgrown or a habit you want to leave behind, for example. I'll explain more later.'

I sat promptly back down and Luke stood up again.

'I'm intrigued, Skylar.'

'But hungry, too, I'm sure,' I said and everyone laughed.

'You're right!' he applauded. 'So, let's eat!'

There were sausage, squash and apple traybakes adapted to accommodate meat eaters and vegetarians alike, corn on the cob, swimming in salty butter, a hearty vegetable casserole with dumplings which had gone crispy on the top but were light as air underneath, dishes piled with green beans and spinach and tiny honey glazed carrots with some of their tops still attached. And that was just what was within my reach. Poppy had supplied the chutneys and pickles which were her speciality and Mark had added rustic, seed topped loaves and the promise of a choice of desserts.

As plates were filled, Kate and Luke made sure everyone had a drink and Beth and Rafe helped Grandad George and Harold to whatever they fancied. The level of chatter slowly quietened, even where the youngsters were sitting. I looked around the table and again thought how lucky my father and I were to be so included. That said, Rafe *still* looked preoccupied and Erik's expression put me more in mind of his former rather than latter self.

I hoped he might be focused on his gratitude and releasing his thoughts, but when he stood up and walked out, I could tell that wasn't the case. I went to push back my chair, but Luke, who happened to be doing the rounds and filling glasses, put a hand on my shoulder.

'Is it his knee?' I asked. 'He looked uncomfortable when he walked out.'

'I think it is playing up,' Luke shared. 'He's probably overdone it a bit this week.' I hoped that wasn't my fault. 'And I know how frustrating he finds it not being able to just get on with things without a second thought.'

'It must be so hard,' I sighed, thinking how the physical aspect of his situation must also impact on everything he had to think about and adjust to.

'And he might not say much,' Luke carried on, confirming my thoughts, 'but he's still coming to terms with everything. His life has changed so much . . .'

His words trailed off as Erik came back in and, after a word with Finn who twisted around and patted him on the arm, he then took his place again and Luke moved away.

'So,' said Graham, who was sitting next to me, 'how are you finding your first Grow-Well celebration, Skylar?'

'I'm loving it,' I told him. 'It's the epitome of what my father was hoping to find when he moved here.'

'And you?'

'To be honest,' I said, 'I didn't really know what to hope for and if you'd told me I'd adapt so quickly to going from living in relative isolation to being surrounded by people all the time, I probably wouldn't have believed you.'

I might once have been surprised to hear myself speak so frankly, but there was something about these people that inspired openness.

'But Carole told me you were an event planner,' Graham frowned. 'Surely you were surrounded by folk all the time doing that.'

'Only for the events themselves,' I pointed out. 'The hall was pretty remote and there were only a couple of other full-time staff on-site.'

'That is a big difference to living here then,' he acknowledged. 'And you know, you aren't the only person sitting at this table who's arrived in the square during so much change in their lives. You're in the right place, my love.'

Given what I knew of Freya's past and Erik's too, I believed that.

Once everyone's plates had been emptied and, in some cases, emptied again, Kate suggested that half of us should switch places to ensure we got a chance to talk to everyone, which was a brilliant idea. Another good idea was saving the desserts for later as we were all so stuffed! The youngsters however were served theirs and allowed to eat in the playroom if they wanted to while everyone else turned to me in anticipation of the ritual.

'So,' I said, feeling pleased to have heard a couple of people talking together about their year, 'I'm going to give you each two slips of paper. On one you write something you're grateful for that has real meaning, and on the other, you add the thing, or things, that you're ready to shed and release. That should be something that you want to make a commitment to freeing yourself from.'

'Are we going to share what we've written?' Beth asked.

'Absolutely not,' I said seriously. 'This is something that's just for you, so don't hold back. I'll hand out the paper and pencils now and then we'll have a few minutes of proper quiet to think and make our notes. Each thing can be as simple as one word or a couple of sentences. It's entirely up to you.'

I had wondered if everyone would take it seriously, but a quick look around the table proved they were. Erik looked to be covering every bit of his paper, and I pondered if that was his gratitude or release note . . .

'Do you think everyone's finished?' I quietly asked Freya who was sitting next to me.

'I think so,' she said. 'What happens next?'

'We need the fire for that,' I told her and her eyes widened. 'Okay, everyone,' I said more loudly. 'If you're all ready.' They were. 'Then bring your notes and follow me.'

We walked in reverent silence to the sitting room where Luke had got the fire brightly blazing. The room smelt of woodsmoke, the ultimate autumnal scent, and was even warmer than the kitchen.

'Right,' I said. 'The plan is for us to keep the note about what you're grateful for somewhere safe as a reminder of this year's blessings, and we're going to burn the note with what we want to release written on, and while we do it, we're going to visualise whatever we're casting out, literally falling away.'

'Brilliant,' Finn said, as he stepped forward. 'I love this, Skylar.'

'We were planning to use your braziers,' I told him, 'but the weather had other ideas.'

'It's the start of the wild hunt,' he said, but I hadn't heard of that. 'Odin is getting in early and preparing us for winter.'

'Well, let's hope we can enjoy autumn before then,' Freya laughed. 'I take it you're going first then, Finn?'

It took a while for everyone to cast their notes into the fire and Harold requested some help with his and then he and Grandad George made themselves comfortable while the rest of us went back to help tidy the kitchen. With everyone doing something, the room was soon cleared, and I went to check everything was as it should be in the dining room.

'I'll bring everyone along in a minute,' Erik offered kindly. 'Save you having to come back.'

'Can you give me five instead?' I requested. 'I want to make sure the room's perfect.'

'It already is,' he smiled, 'but all right.'

'Are *you* all right?' I asked, because his smile still wasn't quite reaching his eyes.

'Of course,' he said unconvincingly. 'This is a brilliant celebration.'

'I didn't ask about the gathering. Is it your knee?'

'It is giving me a bit of trouble, but . . .'

'Go on.'

'It's a family situation that's come up at the same time as something else,' he said and I could tell he was trying to make whatever it was sound trivial, even though to him it clearly wasn't. 'Go on,' he said, with a nod to the door. 'Go and check the room.'

I collected Grandad George and Harold on the way and the number of gasps and smiles as everyone else, the youngsters included, filed into the room a few minutes later was gratifying.

The decorations were much admired and then when I explained that every household was going to be planting up hyacinth and narcissus bulbs in time for Christmas flowering, the excitement rippled around the room again.

'That's the loveliest idea,' Kate said.

'I can't take the credit for it,' I said honestly. 'I found it online and worked out that the timing would be perfect.'

'I wondered what you wanted the pots for,' Freya said as she and Finn moved further around the table to an empty spot.

'I know you could have helped me,' I told her, 'but I wanted it to be a surprise.'

'And it is. A truly lovely one.'

Erik and I had made sure there were plenty of bulbs to go around, including ones to take back to Cavell Care once they'd been started off in a cooler environment. I thought the bothy might be useful for that and Freya agreed.

'We'll need labels, so the pots don't get muddled up though,' she said sensibly and Erik appeared at my elbow with the pack I'd picked up at the garden centre. 'I see you've thought of everything,' Freya smiled in approval.

It didn't take long to plant the bulbs and add the labels, but there was going to be some tidying up required because the compost had got everywhere. I made Kate and Luke promise to leave it for me to sort as soon as I was back from my befriending session at Cavell Care the next day. They didn't really want to leave it for me, but I insisted.

'My idea, my mess,' I said. 'And this is the sort of clean up that's easier to do on your own.'

With the pots grouped on the table, ready for carrying to the bothy, we all went back to the kitchen and sat down to bowls of apple crumble, pear tart, blackberry and cinnamon galette and a damson cobbler. There was cream, custard and ice cream and how any of us managed to get home afterwards was a mystery to me.

But home we all eventually headed, with full bellies and even fuller hearts.

Chapter 17

After the evening's excitement, I had expected to sleep like the proverbial log, but I lay awake for a long time thinking about my father and Erik and wondering what was at the very heart of the dip in mood they'd both seemed to succumb to.

I also mulled over what it was that I had decided to write down, keep and release during the equinox ritual. Just a couple of months ago it would have been impossible to even contemplate that I would be grateful that my job at Highfell had come to an end, but that was the thing I had felt moved to be thankful for because it had already transformed my life in so many positive ways.

The habit I had chosen to release was fretting about the future. I knew I had already gone a long way to achieving it, but I didn't think a little bit of a boost courtesy of the magic of the season would go amiss.

'Skylar! Are you up yet?'

I sighed in my restless sleep and felt myself resurface.

'Isn't it your volunteering day?'

My eyes flew open and registering the time I leapt into action.

'Are you going to eat before you go?' Rafe asked when I bowled into the kitchen and flicked the kettle on.

The cats, looking startled, scarpered from the room and I took a deep breath.

'No time,' I said and reached for an insulated cup and the instant coffee. 'I'm sure Beth will be able to dig me out a biscuit.'

'Here,' Rafe said and handed me an Eat Natural bar, 'take this, just in case.'

'Thank you.' I stuffed it into my pocket. 'Did you have a good time last night?'

'I had a super time and so did Dad. I thought what you came up with was perfect.'

'I'm so pleased you liked it. Everyone else seemed happy too, didn't they?'

Why was the kettle taking so long. I drummed my fingers on the countertop, willing the water to boil faster.

'More than happy,' Rafe said. 'In fact, I can't help thinking it's a shame that . . .'

His words trailed off as I flicked the kettle off and poured the almost boiled water into the cup. A little splashed down the side and I only narrowly missed scalding my hand.

'What's a shame?' I frowned as I mopped the spilled water up.

'Nothing,' he said.

'It's clearly something,' I said back, stopping for the first time since I'd rushed in to look at him.

His expression suggested he was as tired as me. Either that or he was still worrying about something.

'You're going to be late,' he said with a nod to the clock. 'We'll talk about it later.'

'I'll hold you to that,' I said as I headed to the hall, because

I really did need to go. 'Don't forget I'm clearing up at Prosperous Place before I come home, but we will talk.'

'Watch the roads!' he called after me as though I were a careless teen rather than a fully grown woman.

Though given how flustered I was, it was good advice.

'Sorry I'm late!' I panted breathlessly the moment I arrived at Cavell Care. 'I overslept.'

I headed back outside again to shake out my umbrella, which would have been a health and safety nightmare had it dripped all over the floor.

'Don't panic,' said the carer behind the reception desk. 'You're not late, my love. And you can stick your brolly in the bucket in the lobby.'

I did as instructed and mopped up the drips, then signed in and went to find Mabel. I spent the time chatting to my new friend who had more tales from her past to share, including some of her time courting Arthur who she said again had been the love of her life, even though she had been seeing someone else when he arrived on the scene.

'How did you know that Arthur was the one?' I asked and she smiled.

'Because I couldn't stop thinking about him from the moment I clapped eyes on him,' she confided, 'even though I was almost engaged to someone else. Every time Arthur walked into the shop where I worked my heart went berserk. It didn't take long to figure out.'

'That sounds like love at first sight.'

'I'm not so past it that I can't remember there was some lust at first sight, too,' she giggled and my mouth fell open in surprise.

'Mabel,' I grinned and she changed the subject.

Before heading off, I had a few minutes with Grandad George who was in his room resting, but buoyant, following his fun night out. It was so good to be able to pop in and see him whenever I wanted to and I felt determined to make up for all the lost years when Mum had been moving me about.

By the time I knocked on the door at Prosperous Place, I was feeling the lack of breakfast despite having devoured the snack bar from Rafe on the way back.

'You look like a drowned rat!' Erik said as he opened the door.

'That's why I came round the back. I didn't want to drip all over the hallway, and thanks for that description.'

'I only meant—'

'I know what you meant and I'm only getting wetter standing here! Are you going to ask me in or what?'

'Yes,' he said and stepped back. 'Sorry.'

'And I'm sorry for snapping,' I apologised as I peeled off my soaked coat and Erik took charge of the umbrella that hadn't been much use on the windy walk back. 'I hoped I'd be feeling serene this morning after the ritual last night, but now I'm soaked and starving.'

As I stood up from undoing my boots, my stomach gave the loudest rumble to prove the point.

'You're hangry,' Erik said with a smile and I tried not to feel mortified that he'd heard. 'Tired and hungry are never a good combo. Come on, I'll fix us some lunch.'

With a plateful of a combination of leftovers to tuck into I began to feel better. Not quite serene, but certainly better.

'Where are Kate and Luke?' I asked, once the painful pangs had started to subside.

'Out somewhere,' he told me. 'But they haven't stopped talking about last night and the girls were full of it before school. Everyone had such a great time. It was a perfect celebration thanks to you, Skylar.'

'I really appreciate you saying that.' I blushed. 'Though I'm not sure Rafe would agree with you.'

'Oh?'

'He's got something on his mind, but I haven't had a chance to get to the bottom of it yet. And I haven't forgotten you weren't at your happiest last night either.'

'How can you be so sure?' he quizzed. 'You haven't known me long enough to see me at my happiest.'

'Don't digress,' I tutted. 'You said it was a family situation, so what's going on? A problem shared, remember? Your PPO has the right to know.'

'That would be a fun slogan,' he said and I couldn't suppress a smile. 'It rhymes and everything. Though it would only work if the world knew what PPO stood for and as we're keeping it to ourselves . . .'

'Enough of that,' I commanded. 'Now, come on. Out with it, Mr Svensson.'

He emitted a little shiver.

'Don't call me that,' he said and dithered again. 'It reminds me too much of my father.'

'And is your dad the reason why you're out of sorts?'

Erik leaned back in his chair and folded his arms across his broad chest, then, perhaps realising how defensive the gesture looked, unfolded them again and rested his elbows on the table. I tried not to think about how big his biceps had looked in the close-fitting sweater he was wearing.

'Partly,' he said. 'But there's other stuff, too.'

'So, tell me then. I promise it will help to share. And I can say that with absolute authority because I've felt heaps better about everything since our heart to heart in The Dragon a fortnight ago.'

Given how much had happened since, it felt much longer ago than that.

'September is a tough month,' Erik began with no preamble. 'It's the start of the rugby season and a stark reminder of everything I've lost. I've been trying not to think about it, but then I happened to see some training photos online after we'd set up for the party yesterday and my head started to go over it all again.'

'Did you stumble across the photos? Or did you go looking for them?'

The look he gave me was all the answer I needed.

'I know,' he said, sounding frustrated as he rested his head in his hands so I could only see the top of his head. 'It was a classic self-sabotage manoeuvre, and combined with further interference from my father, I've been mentally paying for it all last night and today.'

'You know, you've never sounded happy when you've mentioned your dad. What's the deal with him?'

Erik looked up again and sat back in his chair.

'I do try and be patient with him,' he sighed and screwed up the paper towel he was using as a napkin. 'But sometimes I boil over with frustration because he won't listen to me. He still thinks he knows what's best for me, just like he always has. You see, after Mum died, we threw ourselves into my rugby and that meant . . .'

His words trailed off as the back door opened and Kate and Luke rushed in out of the rain.

'Have you talked to Luke about this?' I asked urgently.

'Not really. Not all of it anyway, but it's fine. I can handle it. I can deal with Dad, and I promise I won't do any more scrolling online.'

He seemed to think that was a suitable tactic for dealing with what he was going through and clearly didn't want to carry the conversation on in front of the others, so I took the hint and piled our plates together.

'Here she is!' Kate said. 'The saviour of our celebration.'

'Everyone had the best time, Skylar,' Luke added.

'I'm so pleased,' I smiled. 'I really enjoyed helping, and now, having pinched some of your leftovers, I'm going to clear up the dining room and sort the pots, if that's all right?'

'You're a star,' Kate said. 'But don't rush off after you're finished, because there's something we want to talk to you about.'

'And you won't need to take the pots over to the bothy because Freya and Finn collected them earlier,' Luke told me. 'They thought it would save you having to do it.'

I was pleased about that, not only because it was still raining, but because I wasn't sure where the pots would be best positioned but I knew Freya would. I'd thank her later. And check the WhatsApp group messages. I had a feeling, given how much everyone had enjoyed the party, I might have some catching up to do there and some thanks of my own to send because the feast had been spectacular.

With Erik acting as my right-hand helper, it didn't take long to repack the decorations ready for putting up at home, sweep away the spilt compost and give the dining table a polish. He didn't return to the conversation we hadn't finish and I didn't either because if he'd wanted to tell me more, he would have done.

'I think that's it,' I said as I stood back to give the room one final check. 'This is how it was before, isn't it?'

'Looks good to me,' he agreed. 'And I don't mind helping you carry this lot back to the square, but it might be quicker for you to go and get your car to ferry it.'

'You're right,' I puffed. 'I don't fancy carrying it, so I'll talk to Kate and Luke and then go and get the car. Are you coming back to the kitchen?'

'Only to help you get this stuff that far, then I need to head outside to check some guttering that I've got a horrible feeling might be blocked.'

'Make sure you wear your wet weather gear,' I smiled. 'You don't want to end up looking like a drowned rat.'

'You're not going to let me forget that comment, are you?' he laughed.

'Not in a hurry.'

I found Kate and Luke in the kitchen with mugs of tea and a plate of biscuits which they offered to share with us. Once Luke had heard what Erik was going to do, he decided to go with him.

'Do you mind?' he asked Kate. 'You can talk to Skylar, can't you? And we won't be long.'

Decked out in raincoats, the guys went off and Kate told me that she and Luke had something to ask me but that there was absolutely no pressure for me to say yes.

'The thing is,' she began, 'Luke and I want to host a fund-raising Halloween ball.'

'Oh wow.'

'Not a huge one, but it would be the biggest event we'd ever held here and for an amazing cause,' she continued. 'But we appreciate it is short notice.'

'You want to put it on this year?' I gasped. 'That's just, what . . . five weeks away.'

'I know,' she grimaced. 'We were all guns blazing, but then we started to list everything we'd have to organise,' she reeled a few things off, 'and realised we'd probably bitten off more than we could chew, especially in such a tight timescale.'

'Well, maybe you could scale it back at bit,' I suggested. 'Make it an exclusive party rather than a ball and with limited tickets. That always creates demand.'

'Yes,' she nodded. 'I like the sound of that.'

'What is it you want to raise funds for?'

'The Chapel. It's not far from here. Have you heard of it?' I hadn't. 'It's a creative community space for youngsters who want to sing, dance, act, be creative and perform. Eli's the manager and pretty much all of us have played a part in keeping it open during the last couple of years, but now it's hit a snag.'

'Don't tell me,' I guessed, 'the money's run out.'

I knew so many of these sorts of ventures ran on goodwill, volunteering, endless form filling and an ever-stretched shoestring.

'Not completely run out,' Kate explained, 'but there's a shortfall between one pot of funding coming to an end and the next kicking in and it's that gap that we were hoping to help fill.'

'I see. And where do I come in?'

'Well, we were wondering,' she continued, 'that as you have so much experience and did such a great job with the equinox party with practically no notice, if you'd help us work out if it really is doable. We haven't mentioned anything about it to Eli in case we can't pull it off. If nothing else, it would be helpful to pick your brains to see if we can come up with something in the time available.'

'So, really, all you need at this point is some advice?'

'That's it,' she nodded. 'But then,' she added, 'if you thought we could do something, perhaps you might consider offering a sort of guiding hand.'

None of it sounded too onerous, apart from the limited time aspect, but the prospect of a Halloween celebration to raise money for a cause surprisingly close to my heart, and happening right on the doorstep, would be the best fun. However, what Kate said next was the real clincher to get me on board.

'And between you and me, Luke and I don't think it would be a bad thing if Erik had something else to keep him occupied at the moment, so we'd like him to help out too if we do go ahead. I think he's having family issues, and this time of year is bound to be tough, what with the rugby season getting underway.'

She stopped talking as the back door opened and slammed shut and the two friends, looking saturated right through, squelched into the kitchen.

'Boot room,' Kate commanded and they traipsed off again.

'Is the event a secret from everyone?' I asked with a nod to where Erik and Luke had gone to get out of their wet clobber.

'Erik knows we've been mulling over the idea of hosting some sort of party,' she told me. 'But we haven't mentioned it to anyone else because they'll all be thrilled, tell us to go for it and then we'll be under even more pressure than just time constraints.'

'That gutter is blocked,' Luke huffed as he came back into the kitchen.

'And even though I'm the maintenance guy,' Erik grumbled, 'I can't clear it because I'm not suited to climbing ladders thanks to this.'

He gave his knee a prod and sounded thoroughly fed up.

'We'll get that specialist firm in to check the lot,' Luke told him. 'Don't worry about it. We've already looked at some quotes, and it wouldn't be a bad idea to make sure all's well ahead of the winter.'

'I suppose,' Erik said morosely as he pulled his jumper, which was soaked on the shoulders and neck, up and off. 'Shall we go and get your car, Skylar?'

The answer lodged in my throat as his T-shirt rode right up and I took in his toned torso. It looked every bit as firm as it had felt when I'd hugged him at the garden centre.

'Skylar?' Kate said as Erik rearranged his top.

'Er . . . yeah,' I said and looked at her, 'if we're finished here.'

'We are but think it over,' she said. 'And let us know when you can.'

'Oh, I already have,' I nodded, looking at Erik again.

Given that he was going to help me load the decorations into my car he should have kept his jumper on, but I was pleased he hadn't, which was an inappropriate thing to think. However, I was also thinking that helping with the ball, party or whatever was decided on, could be my way of pulling him out of the fug he'd fallen into and that was a more acceptable train of thought which cancelled out the other one.

'Really?' Kate gasped and crossed her fingers.

'Really,' I smiled, 'and the answer is yes. If I can help in any way, I will.'

'*Really*?' Luke gasped. 'You think it's possible?'

'I can't say for certain until we've talked it over properly,' I said in a bid to temper his enthusiasm, 'but I'm sure we can come up with something.'

'What's this?' Erik frowned.

'We're having a Halloween ball,' Luke said and clapped Erik on the back. 'And you and Skylar are going to help us organise it.'

That wasn't quite what I wanted him to have his heart set on or how Kate had framed her request for me to help, but the sudden look of surprise and delight on Erik's face left me in no doubt that I would support them in making some sort of spooky celebration a success, no matter how hard I had to work and in the process hopefully make a mint for The Chapel.

The day was getting on by the time I'd moved my car, Erik had found a dry coat to wear and helped me fill the boot which I'd then unloaded at the house. I was excited to decorate the house over the weekend, and I was excited about the prospect of the Prosperous Place event now, too. My mind was already full of ideas as to how I could help and with just five weeks left to organise it there wasn't any time to lose. Kate and Luke had a busy weekend ahead, but we'd set a time to go through everything on Monday.

'Have you finished for the day?' I asked Rafe, when I found him reading in his sitting room with the cats for company.

'Yes,' he said. 'It's felt like wading through treacle today, so I called time about an hour ago.'

'I'm sorry to hear that.'

'That's just how it is sometimes,' he shrugged.

'Given that it's been going so well so far, I'm sure you'll soon get back in the swing of it,' I encouraged. 'Maybe you're tired after the party?'

'Perhaps,' he said and went to go back to his book.

'I'll leave you to it,' I said, 'but before I do, there's something I have to tell you.'

He picked up a leather bookmark and, having marked his page, put the book down. I joined him on the other end of the sofa.

'I know you have,' he said. 'I know you have something to tell me.'

'You do?'

'Yes.'

'How do you know?'

Given what Kate had said, I was certain no one else knew about the potential fundraiser.

'I know,' he said, 'because the wind blew over the recycling bin and among the empty egg cartons and loo roll tubes, I picked up the piece of paper with your new job details on.'

'Oh, no—' I started to protest.

'It's all right,' he cut in. 'You're moving to Devon and even though I wish with the whole of my heart that it wasn't so far away, I also know you're a grown woman who knows her own mind and if this is what you've decided to do, then—'

'It isn't what I've decided to do!'

'It isn't?'

'No.'

'So, you haven't already been applying for jobs then?'

'Not a single one,' I responded, feeling devastated that he'd thought that.

'But the sheet? The job offer . . .'

'Arrived completely out of the blue, unlooked for and even though it was a very attractive package, it wasn't the right fit for me. After a bit of time thinking it over, I realised it would be an out of the frying pan situation.'

Given that I had now accepted that I needed a rest, the idiom wasn't an exaggeration, though I never would have told Madeline and Tobias how worn out I had become. They would have been mortified to think I'd been working too hard for too long even though much of it had been self-inflicted.

'Do you mean it?' Rafe sniffed.

His eyes were full of tears.

'I do.'

'Oh god Skylar,' he swallowed. 'Last night I was so desperate to beg you not to do it, I wanted to plead with you not to go, but I knew it was none of my business, so I kept quiet. Then I nearly got into it this morning, but you were in such a rush.'

'So, this is why you've been out of sorts,' I said. 'You should have said something straightaway, and I would have told you then. No,' I tutted and reached for his hand, '*I* should have told *you* about it as soon as I'd decided to turn it down.'

I had previously thought there would be no point in mentioning it, but I hadn't reckoned on this horrid muddle happening.

'You didn't have to tell me anything,' Rafe choked and squeezed my hand.

'All right, I should have hidden the evidence better then,' I joked.

He looked at me and shook his head.

'So, you're really not job hunting and you're not going to leave?'

'Leave!' I laughed. 'How can I leave when I've just agreed to support Kate and Luke who will soon be hosting the biggest event they've ever put on at Prosperous Place?'

'An event happening just over the road!' Rafe gasped, his eyes widening in delight and surprise, before narrowing. 'But it won't be like a Highfell event, will it?'

'Nothing like,' I promised.

'In that case,' he said, 'that you can tell me about!'

There wasn't much I could tell Rafe yet about the celebration Kate and Luke were hoping to put on, but having explained about The Chapel and them not wanting to get anyone's hopes up, I did make him swear to keep it a secret. Had it not been for the muddle over the job I'd turned down I wouldn't have told him anything, but I knew he would keep it to himself.

Chapter 18

On Saturday, my father and I had the best time as we each described in detail what our fantasy spooky celebration would be like while we festooned every room in the house with autumn decorations. It soon became obvious that daydreaming wasn't the only thing we had got carried away with!

'And there was me thinking I'd gone a bit overboard on my shopping trip,' I said to Rafe as he added leaf and pumpkin patterned cushions to his sofa and offered a spare couple to me to put in my sitting room.

'You should know me by now, Skylar,' he grinned. 'If something's worth doing—'

'It's worth doing with flamboyance and flair.'

'Exactly,' he chuckled as I recited one of his mantras. 'Now, where are those little fabric pumpkins you had a stack of? They'd look ideal on your mantel and hearth.'

The fireplace in my room was already embellished with a silk leaf garland and fairy lights, as were the bannisters.

'Are you sure the cats will ignore all of this?' I asked as I looked around at the many additions to the décor.

The whole house was transformed, Rafe even had bed linen

and towels in autumnal hues, and I adored it all, but it wouldn't look anywhere near as impressive if Socrates and Plato had an attack of the zoomies and shredded everything.

'Trust me,' Rafe said. 'They'll be utterly indifferent.'

By the end of the day, I realised he was right. They'd taken it all in their stride and I was grateful for that because I would have hated to see it spoiled.

'I told you,' Rafe said rather smugly as the cats stalked around us to check their food bowls hadn't magically refilled even though it wasn't anywhere near their dinner time. 'Now, go and find something to do while I make us some dinner.'

'Don't you need a hand?'

'Not for what I have in mind. Go and have a bath or read a book or something and I'll call you when it's ready. It will be an hour or so.'

I didn't need telling twice and, once I'd drawn my sitting room curtains, turned on all the fairy lights and the flame setting on the faux fire, I curled up in my armchair and let my thoughts drift.

Rafe and I had had such a wonderful day. He was far happier now he knew I was completely committed to doing what he'd invited me to Nightingale Square to do. There had been a moment when we'd been having our heart to heart the evening before, that I wondered whether I should mention that I *might* not be staying for ever, but I'd kept it to myself. What would have been the point in putting the thought in his head when neither of us knew what the future might hold . . .

'Skylar!' he called after rather less than an hour. 'We forgot the wreath!'

I had been drowsing in my chair, but as I came to, I breathed in the most delicious aroma.

'What are you cooking?' I asked, as he came in holding a huge wreath for the front door and handed it to me.

It was quite heavy, but so beautiful. Red, orange and gold leaves formed the base and there were tiny pumpkins and gourds, orange sunflowers, ribbons tied into bows and of course, more golden fairy lights, filling every available space.

'Just a traybake,' he said as if the aromas he'd conjured were nothing out of the ordinary. 'Chicken, herbs, sweet potato, lardons, sprouts, garlic and apples,' he reeled off. 'It's an autumn staple of mine.'

'Well,' I said as I breathed in deeply, 'it smells sublime. I didn't think I'd eat again after the equinox feast, but I can't wait for this.'

'It won't be long,' he smiled, appreciating the praise. 'Though it will probably feed eight rather than two. Hang that up, will you?' he requested, just as someone knocked on the front door. 'And if that's anyone we like,' he added as he went back to the kitchen, 'invite them in to eat with us!'

Still holding the wreath, I opened the door to find Erik, Freya and Finn on the step. They were crowded together because it was just starting to rain again.

'Hi,' Erik smiled, as he turned up the collar on his jacket. 'Pub?'

'What he means is,' Freya said, as Finn leant forward, took the wreath from me and hung it from a perfectly positioned hook on the door that I'd never noticed before, 'would you like to come with us for a pint in The Dragon, Skylar?'

'That's a beauty,' Finn said in praise of the wreath before I could answer her.

'It is,' I agreed. 'It's Rafe's. Though how he safely shipped that from the US when he moved, I have no idea.'

'I didn't,' my father said behind me. 'I had it delivered from a local maker last week. Are you going to ask our friends in, Skylar or leave them getting slowly soaked on the doorstep?'

'Sorry,' I stepped back to make room. 'Come in.'

'We were just on our way to the pub,' Erik said, without moving.

'Well, you're very welcome to eat with us before you go,' Rafe offered and the three of them quickly bundled in. 'It's nothing fancy, but there'll be plenty to go around.'

'It smells amazing,' Freya smiled as I took her jacket and hung it up while she looked about her. 'And I love your decorations.'

'Come on,' I said to our unexpected guests. 'I'll show you around. This is just the tip of the iceberg!'

No one made it to the pub that evening. Our impromptu supper party was a total triumph, and we all sat in the kitchen that was made for entertaining. We devoured Rafe's delicious traybake, drank wine and talked for hours, with music quietly playing in the background and candles adding another layer of comfort to the ambience.

My father had always been a laidback host and as I watched him, I could see he was in his element and his cats were, too. They'd made a beeline for Finn, even Plato who tended to be shy of newcomers, and he'd fussed them until their purrs were almost as loud as our conversation.

'I've been thinking about this Halloween ball idea,' Erik said quietly to me, when we found ourselves next to each other on the sofa while the others were still talking at the table.

'Me too,' I said back. 'I'm really looking forward to talking to Kate and Luke about it all on Monday.'

'So, you really think it's going to be possible to pull it off?' he asked, sounding doubtful.

'Well,' I hedged, 'I think it's going to be possible to pull *something* off for sure. I know they were thinking of a ball, but that suggests a hundred guests or more which would be tricky to set up in five weeks. Selling all those tickets for a start, then securing the right size marquee, catering, luxury outdoor loos and that's just for starters.'

'Oh crikey,' Erik said as he puffed out his cheeks. 'I was so worried about where everyone would park, I hadn't thought about fancy loos.'

'Kate was open to the idea of scaling back a bit,' I told him, 'so hopefully Luke will be too when he realises just how much would be involved.'

'At least he has decent contacts for promotion purposes.'

'He does?' I frowned.

Had I not known Erik as well as I now did, I might have encouraged him to put himself forward as the star attraction for the event. His celebrity – for want of a better word – status would have made him a huge draw, but given his current circumstances, that sort of pressure was the last thing he needed. I still wanted him to elaborate on the conversation we'd been having about his dad but knew it should happen on his terms.

'Do you not know what Luke's famous for?' he asked me, looking amused.

'Famous,' I frowned. 'No, should I?'

'Most people know at first sight,' Erik laughed, no longer

keeping our conversation quiet. 'Google him while I refill our glasses.'

'No more wine for me, but thanks,' I said and reached for my phone.

'Find him?' Erik asked when he came back with his glass and a lemonade for me.

'Er, yeah,' I said and turned my phone around. 'I had no idea. I mean, I knew he was a good-looking guy but . . .'

The image was of the philanthropic man I knew, wearing very little while reclining provocatively on a speedboat and ostensibly advertising expensive aftershave while no doubt also raising pulses.

'Nothing to write home about though really, is he?' Erik grinned.

'I've seen better,' I shrugged. 'And according to this, it was literally years ago that he was named the most desirable male model in the world. He's *really* let himself go since then.'

We looked at each other and laughed.

'I can't believe you didn't know,' Erik grinned.

'I didn't have a clue,' I said and shook my head, 'but now I do, I'll be making the most of him to help pull this party off!'

'What's so funny?' Rafe asked as he, Freya and Finn, who was carrying both cats, came to join us.

'Skylar didn't know about Luke's former career,' Erik said on my behalf.

'You're joking?' my father was agog.

'You knew?' I gasped.

'Of course, I knew!'

The other three laughed.

'Why didn't you say anything?'

'I assumed it was a given and that everyone knew,' Rafe shrugged. 'Luke was top torso for five years running among my closest circle of friends in LA. An achievement unsurpassed to this day.'

'Now that, you could have kept to yourself,' I said, making the others laugh again.

I didn't mention that Erik could have given Luke a run for his money.

'Fair enough,' Rafe grinned.

It was close to midnight before Freya said she and Finn should get back to see to Nell.

'And I should go, too,' Erik said.

'I'll show you out,' I offered. 'I'm sorry you didn't make it to the pub.'

'Don't be,' Erik smiled. 'None of us are. We've had a lovely evening. Thank you both.'

'And thank you Plato and Socks,' beamed Finn who was covered in cat hair but didn't care.

I wondered if Nell would!

'See you tomorrow, Skylar,' Freya said as soon as I'd opened the front door and as she and Finn headed for home.

'What are you up to tomorrow?' asked Erik who was still standing on the doorstep.

'I'm going over to the Grow-Well in the morning,' I told him. 'Then Grandad George is coming here to have a tour of the house. Or the ground floor at least. And Rafe is cooking his famous roast beef with all the trimmings for a late lunch.'

'Will you have room for it?' Erik grinned.

'I'll manage a bite or two if I work hard enough in the morning,' I smiled back.

I found myself looking up into his blue eyes and was suddenly transfixed.

'Well,' he swallowed, 'night, Skylar.'

He bent to kiss my cheek and my breath caught.

'Jacket!' Rafe suddenly shouted from the kitchen. 'Have they gone? Someone's left a jacket! I think it's Erik's.'

'Just a sec,' I called over my shoulder and when I turned back, I found Erik hadn't moved, and rather than kissing my cheek, it was our lips that connected.

The surge of electricity that raced through my veins could have lit up the whole of the city and rather than pull away I found myself compelled to move closer and increase the pressure. Erik didn't pull away either and had it not been for the sound of footsteps behind me, I don't know what would have happened. We sprang apart just as Rafe appeared in the hall holding Erik's jacket.

'It is yours Erik, isn't it?' he asked, thankfully not seeming to notice the sparks or feel the crackle of current that had sent a jolt through me like nothing I'd experienced before.

'It is,' Erik answered rather huskily. 'Thanks Rafe. I'll see you Monday, Skylar,' he added. 'If not before. Thanks for a great night.'

I watched him walk down the path, shrugging on the jacket as he went.

'Close the door then,' tutted my father. 'You're letting all the heat out.'

Given how hot I was still feeling, I didn't think that was any bad thing.

After a restless night, I felt apprehensive about my trip to the Grow-Well on Sunday morning. A peck on the cheek would have been perfectly acceptable between friends who were also acting as a PPO for each other, but a lingering kiss on the lips was a different matter altogether. And it hadn't been just any old kiss. Not for me anyway. But perhaps I was making too much of it . . . my next conversation with Erik would let me know, but I wasn't ready to have it just yet.

I had felt that intimate moment deeply and needed more time to compose my thoughts and feelings. The one thing I did already know, and it wasn't helpful at all, was that my heart wouldn't have been averse to repeating the experience. While my head was trying to quash the desire with dire warnings that a re-run could lead to a lost friendship and awkward moments, my heart was telling me to throw caution to the wind!

As it turned out, I was in no danger of compromising either my head or my heart, because Freya, who was also working in the garden, told me Erik had gone to the gym and taken Finn with him.

'I didn't have Finn down as a gym kind of guy,' I said as I tried to imagine him on a treadmill and lifting weights.

Though not at the same time, obviously. How Erik would look doing both, however, was an image that was far too tempting to conjure . . .

'He's not,' Freya said, cutting through my daydream. 'But it was either that or I was going to crown him.'

'Why?' I laughed. 'What's he done?'

'Spent the whole time since we got back from yours trying to convince me that we should get a cat,' she said and rolled her eyes. 'He's perused every puss rehoming website within a fifty-mile radius and reckons Nell would soon get used to having a feline around the house.'

She sounded doubtful that Nell would adapt and I gave the lovely dog sitting next to her a fuss. Nell was getting used to me now, but I didn't think Finn had a hope of convincing her to accept a cat companion at her stage in life. She was getting on in doggy years.

'Oh dear,' I sympathised. 'If it would be any help, you can tell Finn he's always welcome to come and fuss Rafe's two. Socks loves attention, and from what I witnessed last night, Plato loves it too *if* it's Finn giving it.'

'Thanks,' Freya said. 'I'll tell him that. Now come on, let's get these empty beds mulched. It'll be much quicker if we do it together.'

As well as the mulching there were courgettes to pick before they got too big and plenty of runner beans, too. We put the harvest in wooden crates on the bench in the bothy, so anyone could help themselves. And the pots of Christmas flowering bulbs were lined up in there, ready to spring into life during the next couple of months.

'I'll take a handful or two of the runner beans,' I told Freya. 'Rafe's cooking a late roast lunch and he'll love using these.'

'Take some courgettes, too,' she practically begged. 'We're almost overrun!'

'All right,' I laughed. 'And now I'd better get back so there's time to prep them.'

Grandad George arrived while I was in the shower and Rafe had already given him the ground floor tour before I came down.

'Skylar,' he beamed, 'you look the picture of health!'

'That's down to working in the Grow-Well this morning,' I told him as I kissed his cheek. 'It's given me a rosy glow.'

'It's put roses in your cheeks for sure,' he said approvingly.

'That's not an expression I've heard before,' Rafe said.

'Me neither. I like it though. What do you think of the house Grandad?'

'I love it,' he enthused. 'What I've seen of it anyway. It's a shame I can't get upstairs.'

'I was thinking the same thing myself,' I said, as I pulled up a chair to sit next to him. 'So, before I came down, I filmed this on my phone.'

Rafe came to look over my shoulder. He was wearing a pinny and had a tea towel slung over one arm. He really was in his element, and I felt another hankering for all the years we'd missed. At least we were making up for them now. No matter how long this halcyon time lasted, I felt even more determined to make the most of it.

'Beautiful!' Grandad George clapped, once the virtual upstairs tour came to an end. 'It's an absolute treat to see so many of the original features still in situ.'

'And taking that video was a very clever idea,' Rafe said as he kissed the top of my head and went to check something on the hob.

'That's because she's a very clever woman,' Grandad George praised. 'And all thanks to good genes, of course.'

'Mum would be so happy to hear you say that,' I laughed.

'Um, well,' he teased rather ungenerously. 'I wasn't thinking of Faye.'

Rafe and I laughed and then I set the table.

'Sherry, Dad?' Rafe asked.

'Oh, yes, please,' Grandad George said and rubbed his hands together. 'Just a large one.'

How any of us had the ability to move after the platefuls of succulent roast beef, crispy roast potatoes, huge Yorkshire puddings, medley of fresh, seasonal veg, flavoursome gravy and hot horseradish from Poppy's kitchen, I had no idea.

'I've made an autumn pudding for dessert,' Rafe said, once we'd cleared the table and sat back down again, 'but shall we wait to have it later with a cup of tea?'

'I think we'd better,' Grandad George agreed. 'Otherwise, you'll have to roll me back to Cavell when it's time to see me off the premises.'

'What do you think, Skylar?' my father asked me.

I'd only had half an ear on the conversation, so the question didn't register immediately.

'Earth to Skylar,' Grandad George said, clicking his fingers.

'Earth to what?' I said vaguely.

'Where did you just go?' my father laughed.

'Yes, penny for them,' Grandad George said.

I felt the roses come back into my cheeks because I'd been thinking about the last person I'd seen off the premises and what had happened seconds before his departure.

'Oh,' I said, 'they're worth much more than that. Now, who wants dessert?'

Chapter 19

Rafe had rather indiscreetly mentioned to Grandad George that I was going to be helping Kate and Luke plan a big party, and despite my initial admonishment, seeing Grandad's excitement, I was pleased he had. He promised to keep it under his hat until decisions had been made and plans were underway and seeing how delighted he was about it, I felt even more determined that the event would happen and be a huge success.

Consequently, the next morning, I dressed rather more smartly than I had of late and headed over to Prosperous Place at the allocated time with my professional head on and feeling resolute not to let my kiss with Erik have even the slightest impact on our meeting.

I was still feeling grateful to my father and Grandad George for their enthusiasm because it helped me get my game face on. Even if the mood lasted just the time it took for me to walk from the square to the garden gate.

'Woah!' I screeched, the moment I was through it. 'What the fluff?'

I had immediately collided with Erik. My hands had shot up in an attempt at a defensive gesture, which would have been wholly inadequate if he'd been an intruder intent on causing me harm. I was certain my feet had left the ground because I'd jumped so high.

'Sorry,' he said, but he didn't sound it. 'I wanted to catch you before you went to the house.'

'Why are you smirking if you're sorry?' I scowled at him.

My heart was beating wildly, and I felt embarrassed as well as shocked and the look of amusement on his face did nothing to repair either my former buoyant mood or my dignity.

'Nothing,' he said and bit his lip.

I supposed I must have looked hilarious as I leapt out of my skin, and I could only imagine the horrified expression my face had pulled.

'Good,' I huffed.

Perhaps pretending that kiss hadn't happened wasn't going to be so hard after all.

'Did you really say "what the fluff"?' he smiled.

'Well,' I said, drawing myself up, 'it's better than the alternative, isn't it? What did you want to see me about?'

The change on his face made me regret asking.

'To apologise for Saturday night, of course,' he said and raked a hand through his hair.

'I thought you enjoyed the evening. We all did. Rafe's a fabulous host, and—'

'Skylar,' he cut across me. 'Stop.'

I looked everywhere but at him.

'You know I'm not talking about your father's hospitality skills,' he said and shoved his hands in his jean's pockets. 'I wanted to apologise for that kiss.'

So, it was going to get a mention then.

'I don't know what came over me,' he said. 'It was absolutely not acceptable behaviour for a PPO, was it? And I've been thinking about it ever since.'

I wondered if he'd been thinking about it in the same way that I had. Possibly not given the sincerity and regret in his tone.

'Well,' I said, because I couldn't really let him shoulder the blame when I'd been the one who had leant properly in and carried the kiss on, 'it wasn't all you, was it? My lips were as badly behaved as yours.'

He smiled again. 'So, we can put it behind us?' he asked.

'Already have,' I lied. 'In fact,' I continued to fib, 'if you hadn't been here and scared me half to death, I would have sought you out and apologised first.'

'You would?'

'I would.' I still couldn't look at him properly. 'Personally, I blame the wine.'

'We had drunk quite a lot.'

'We had and that doubtless lowered our inhibitions.' The word sounded elicit on my lips.

'So, we can go back to our former PPO status then?'

'I don't see why not,' I shrugged and found his eyes were focused on my face. 'Now, come on,' I said briskly. 'I'm in work mode and work mode me would never be late for a planning meeting, even if I had been accosted en route.'

Erik took the seat next to mine at the kitchen table and though initially I struggled with his proximity I soon realised it was better than having him opposite me where I wouldn't be able to avoid the intensity of his blue gaze. As it was, I just had to keep my breathing shallow so as not to draw in the smell of his aftershave and . . . him.

During the walk from the gate to the house, I'd recalled our early conversation where we'd touched upon our single status and reminded myself that Erik and I were both still processing the changes in our lives and that he wasn't looking for love and I was only interested in Big Love but not right now. The memory of that fortified me just enough to be able to competently carry on.

'So,' I said, once Luke had poured us all coffee and sat next to Kate, 'in view of our conversation last week Kate, I've had a quick look at some options online and some of them are rather limited and going to be expensive if you're set on going ahead with hosting a ball.'

'I had a feeling that might be the case,' she frowned. 'A marquee doesn't come cheap, does it?'

'It doesn't,' I confirmed. 'You're looking at anything from at least a thousand upwards, depending on size.'

'And those posh loos you mentioned weren't much less, Skylar,' Erik said. 'I've been having a look online, too,' he added by way of explanation. 'And you know my concerns about parking guys.'

'All in all,' I said, 'and this is only my opinion, but with the time constraints and the overheads, I'm not convinced that such a large event happening on just one night is the best way to go on this occasion.'

Kate let out a breath, but Luke looked less disappointed than I had expected. Perhaps he'd started to come to that conclusion already.

'I agree,' Erik said. 'Though it would have been fun.'

'So, it's back to the drawing board,' Luke said. 'We have to do something to help. Poor Eli was frantic when I spoke to him last week.'

'So many kids will be disappointed if The Chapel has to close,' Kate sighed, 'even for a short time, and it will seriously impact their preparations for the Christmas performances if they can't access the building and all the kit in there to rehearse.'

'I do have one idea,' I said. 'But it's nothing like you were hoping to do.'

'Go on,' Luke encouraged.

'How would you feel about getting the house and grounds directly involved instead of hiring a marquee or something?'

'That would depend on what it was for,' Kate said. 'The grounds definitely, but the house isn't really big enough to host a huge party, is it?'

'It's not a party I'm thinking of now,' I told her. 'If I'm right, half term falls during the last week of October, doesn't it?'

'Yes,' Luke confirmed.

'That's perfect,' I nodded. 'Because I think you could really use that to your advantage.'

'How?' Kate frowned.

'Well, The Chapel is primarily for under eighteens isn't it?' I continued. 'So, you could get the youngsters, as well as adults, in on the fundraising fun and for much longer than one night if you set up say . . . a haunted house extravaganza inside and a trick or treat scavenger hunt in the grounds. It could run all week.'

Neither Kate nor Luke said anything.

'So, the parents would bring their kids along?' Erik asked.

'With pre-booked, timed tickets so you could control the number of people on-site,' I nodded. 'It could be set up as spooky fun during the day and then in the evenings, make it over eighteens only and crank up the haunted house tour element. And maybe offer an exclusive banquet or something on Halloween night as a grand finale.'

'Everyone could come in costume,' Erik joined in. 'And we could get people to dress up and haunt the rooms and spin scary tales! That would help with the security element, too.' He was obviously as keen on the idea as I was, but mindful of his role as volunteer property manager. 'You've told me yourself that this place is haunted, Luke, so why not make the most of it? Even play it up a bit.'

'It would be a lot of work to get the place set up and dressed but the overheads would ultimately be less,' I pressed on. 'And the fundraising would go on for far longer than just the one night. You'd need insurance though.'

'We've already got that,' Kate said.

'And what about some volunteers who can act a bit?' I asked.

'May Madison,' Luke and Kate said together.

I didn't know who that was.

'Oh, yes,' Erik said. 'She'd love this idea and she's involved with The Chapel, isn't she? I bet she could get Freddie Fanshawe in ghostly attire to play some spooky tunes on your piano.'

I did know who that was, but I was surprised Erik did!

'I might even be able to convince Rafe to read a ghost story or two,' I added, roping my father in before I'd asked him.

'Brilliant,' grinned Erik.

'So,' I ventured, 'what do you think?'

'I think,' Luke said, having looked at Kate who nodded enthusiastically, 'that someone needs to go to Blossom's and pick up some sustaining baked goods because we've got a lot of planning to do!'

We spent the whole of that day writing down every idea

we had, who had specific areas of expertise we could utilise – such as Luke with his press and media contacts – which rooms and parts of the garden would be the spookiest, how many tickets we would need to sell and at what price to make a profit which would go to The Chapel. You name it, we thought of it, and by the time we'd eaten the takeaway we'd had delivered and the children who Kate had only just remembered to collect from friends after school were yawning at the table, we each had a list of things to work on.

'So,' Luke said, 'we're all agreed to meet the day after tomorrow? I know that's not long, but if we're planning to launch on the twenty-sixth then we have a week less than we had for the ball idea.'

'I think that's going to be fine,' I told him. 'We have a lot to source and plenty of people to tell and hopefully recruit, though May Madison sounds ideal for that, but I'm certain we can do it.'

I'd now discovered she was a retired actress who still had huge appeal and someone you couldn't say no to which was also just what we needed.

'She'll rally the troops,' Kate said with conviction.

'And we're all happy with our lists?' Luke asked.

'Yep,' we confirmed in unison.

'Let's get cracking then,' Erik said as he stood up. 'Come on Skylar, I'll walk back to the square with you.'

'Thanks,' I smiled, and got to my feet, too, 'but there's no need. It's not dark and I don't think I could be more scared of anything than I was when I arrived this morning.'

'Oh?' Kate questioned.

'Don't ask,' I said and rolled my eyes.

'I scared the fluff out of her,' Erik grinned.

I put a hand on his chest to give him a shove but pulled it away after the briefest contact. The muscles beneath my palm had felt as firm as they'd looked the day I'd glimpsed his torso and the sensation the touch triggered deep in my belly was far from appropriate.

'I'll see you all on Wednesday,' I gabbled and made a quick getaway.

Chapter 20

It had been apparent the moment my hand made fleeting contact with Erik's broad, firm chest that I still wasn't over our doorstep kiss. Fortunately, however, the Halloween event, the endless sourcing, planning, prepping and coordinating, along with my stints in the Grow-Well, volunteering sessions and regular visits to Grandad George, kept my mind occupied.

Even when Erik and I were together in the run up to the October half term holiday, we were rarely alone, and that ensured I didn't have the opportunity to start mooning over him and remembering the glimpse of his bare body, the pressure of his lips against mine and how that had made me feel along with the stirring sensation the recent contact with his chest had aroused . . . well, it was working most of the time . . .

'Before you head off,' Rafe said that Wednesday morning and just as I was getting ready to walk across to Prosperous Place, 'can you spare a minute?'

'Not really,' I said with a look at the kitchen clock. 'I need to get on. We haven't had a decision about the smoke machine yet and I need to book it.' Rafe didn't say anything, but his frown spoke volumes. 'What?'

'Nothing,' he shrugged and looked away. 'I just hope Kate and Luke appreciate how many hours you've been putting in to make this work. You've barely stopped since they decided to go ahead.'

'I'm sure they do,' I said rather defensively. 'Though they never asked me to go all in, so really there's no reason why they should appreciate the trouble I'm going to, is there?'

When I thought back, I realised it was a guiding hand and some support that Kate had originally asked for, but I was practically project managing the entire thing single-handed now and constantly checking anyone else involved was on top of what they were supposed to be doing. I did have Erik, the sidekick I was doing my best to avoid, to help with anything extra, but I hadn't called on him yet. Still, no one had complained about my involvement, and it was keeping my mind almost tipsy-doorstep-kiss free, so where was the harm?

'Why are you going to so much trouble?' Rafe asked interestedly.

Obviously I wasn't going to say that it was to stop me obsessing over a kiss Erik and I had succumbed to, but I could tell him the other reason which was both true and a handy diversion from that other motive.

'Well,' I explained, 'as I know you're aware, Mum never kept me in one place for long when I was growing up, but when I was in my first year at high school, we did stay somewhere for a while.'

The memory of that unusually settled time caused a lump to form in my throat. It was about the only time growing up that I'd felt like I'd belonged anywhere and my friendship with fellow wanderer, Alisha, had further compounded that.

'Go on,' Rafe said softly.

'In that time,' I told him, 'I joined a centre very similar to The Chapel. I was never going to be nominated for an Oscar for my acting, but I was encouraged there in a way that I wasn't at school. I was never made to feel out of place or like I was doing a bad job.'

'Ah,' Rafe said understandingly. 'So, when you visited The Chapel . . .'

'When I visited The Chapel,' I said, picking up the thread, 'and saw for myself how the kids' enthusiasms and passions were being encouraged, it really struck a chord. It didn't matter if they were the best at something, they were encouraged to have a go with no pressure or judgement from their peers or the adults supporting them, and when you're at a tender age and want to try things on for size to see if they might fit, those kinds of opportunities are worth more than their weight in gold.'

Rafe looked rather taken aback by the passionate statement which had tumbled out in a rush, and to be honest, it had taken me by surprise, too.

'Have you said any of that to Kate or Luke?' he asked.

'No,' I said, as I cleared the emotion from my throat. 'It's not a time I generally like to talk about because being uprooted again was so painful. I'd made a friend at that school who was having a similar upbringing to mine, so it felt like even more of a wrench than usual.'

'Oh Skylar,' he said sadly. 'I should have been around more, shouldn't I?'

'You're around now,' I smiled. 'And right when I need you the most.'

Mindful that I was now running late, I gave him a hug then rushed off having not heard what it was that he had originally wanted to talk to me about, but there'd be plenty of time for longer chats again once November landed.

'Kate!' I called as I spotted her walking back along the road after the school run, 'Have you got a minute?'

'Absolutely,' she said. 'What do you need? We're nearly ready to begin setting up now, aren't we? And Luke has said we've practically sold all the tickets, which is amazing.'

'And he's got that radio slot later today, hasn't he?' I asked, looking down at my checklist, which was never out of reach when I was in event planner mode.

'Yes,' Kate confirmed. 'That's bound to ensure a sell out when he gives his "last few tickets remaining" spiel.'

'And May has confirmed overnight that she's rallied enough local am dram chums to put someone in every room that you're opening,' I was delighted to say.

'Excellent!' Kate clapped, then unlocked the gate. 'So, what do you need from me? If anything.'

'An answer about this fog machine,' I told her. 'Today is the last chance we'll have to book it, and I know it's not the cost that's delaying a decision because we've sourced a really good price on hiring for the week.'

'You're right,' she said, 'it hasn't been a cost issue, and we know it will create a really spooky atmosphere, but we've talked it over and we don't want to have it in the house.'

'Why not?'

'We've had a look online,' she explained, 'and even though everything says they're safe, we're a bit concerned about having it running indoors for so long. We're keeping windows and curtains shut so it will be dark inside, and consequently, it could build up a bit. The last thing we need is to aggravate Abigail's asthma or anyone else's for that matter.'

'Of course,' I nodded and quickly came up with an alternative idea. 'I understand that. How about if I ask the company if they have an outdoor model instead? We could put it in the fern garden as that's a part of the spooky outdoor trail, couldn't we?'

'Oh yes,' Kate said, 'that's a brilliant compromise. Let's go for that, if they've got one. The weather looks like it will be okay, not windy or anything. Will it need electric though?'

'I'll find out,' I said and made a note on my list.

'Is there anything else I can do?'

'I don't think so. Erik and I are going to look over the decorations this morning, to make sure we've got enough and then allocate them room by room.'

It was the only thing we would be tackling alone, and I had given myself a stern talking to earlier about how it wouldn't be an issue because there was so much to focus on.

'In that case, I'll double check everything's all set for the Beastly Banquet,' Kate said. 'Now, there's a sentence I never thought I'd hear myself say!'

We were laughing as we arrived in the kitchen and Luke and Erik were sitting at the table drinking coffee and chatting. They looked up as we walked in. Erik was wearing that wretched ruby coloured henley shirt – I say wretched because I adored the way he looked in it – and his hair was tied back, which made the most of his bone structure. Given that his sports career had involved getting knocked about on a rugby pitch, he looked good for it!

'With an event to launch here in a few days,' Luke grinned, 'laughter is something I wouldn't have expected to hear.'

'That's because you've never had me organise one for you, isn't it?' I smiled at him.

'Good point,' Kate said. 'Would you like a coffee, Skylar?'

'Yes, please.'

I noticed Erik was the only one of us who wasn't smiling, but he was looking at me. I wished he wouldn't, especially with his hair pulled back from his face so I could see the whole of it. Why was he looking so tense?

'Shall we get on?' I suggested, once I had my coffee to look at rather than him.

'Yep,' he said and stood up. 'Lead the way.'

The dining room looked completely different to how it had been on the evening of the autumn equinox. It was stuffed full with boxes overflowing with Halloween decorations, a large and eclectic mix to switch between the day and evening tours, along with spooky polystyrene statues and even a couple of paintings with moving eyes which I didn't like at all and turned straight to the wall.

'Idiot,' Erik smiled.

'What?' I objected. Ordinarily I would have been pleased to see his mood lift but not when it was at my expense again. 'They freak me out.'

'Mission accomplished then.'

'I'm not sure we should have them up during the day when the kids will be going round,' I said, with a shiver. 'They'll be terrified.'

'Isn't that the point?'

'Um,' I said, 'let's vote on it when we decorate the rooms.

We're going to set things up so it's easy to switch between day and evening tours so they could be added to the changeover list.'

May Madison herself had offered to be the guide on the evening tours which were for adults only and had a gothic, rather more sophisticated theme in keeping with the house. She, Luke and Rafe - who had decided not to play storyteller - had come up with a blood curdling script featuring ghosts and ghouls which was a blend of fantasy and fact.

The most spine-chilling parts for me were the facts, such as the retelling of how one of Luke's ancestors had hung himself from a tree in the garden as a result of having his heart broken. Now I knew which tree it was I'd been giving it a wide berth since listening to May read that part.

'I've no idea where half of this has come from,' Erik said as he looked around the room. 'And I'm sure it's multiplying just like you said your decorations were before the equinox party.'

'Now that would be scary,' I said. 'I think May has called in a few favours from some prop people she knows and I've sourced quite a bit online as well as scouring the local charity shops and discount stores.'

'You have an eye for a bargain, Skylar,' Erik praised. 'And it's no wonder I haven't been able to tempt you to a trip to The Dragon for ages, you've completely thrown yourself into this, haven't you?'

'Oh, don't you start, too,' I huffed crossly and he looked surprised.

'Sorry,' he said, looking shocked. 'I didn't mean to—'

'Have Kate and Luke said something?' I interrupted. 'Are they fed up because I've taken over? Because I can always—'

'No,' Erik cut in. 'God no. If anything, I'm sure they're thrilled that you're so on the case. I just meant that . . . you know what, never mind. Where shall we start?'

With hindsight, that would have been the ideal opportunity for me to explain that I was so invested because of my own youthful experience with somewhere like The Chapel, but at the time, I was in no mood to.

I was angrier with Erik than I should have been and all because I was trying not to think about my feelings for him and the kiss we'd shared. They were perhaps the biggest part of my helping agenda, but he had no clue about that. The poor bloke looked like I'd just kicked him, but I couldn't seem to recover my temper enough to make amends.

'So, we need to decide what will work where,' I said efficiently and took a lengthy list out of the folder I'd put together. 'And then assign the things to a labelled box for each of the rooms so nothing gets muddled up.'

Each room that was going to be included on the tour now also had one of May's actor friends allocated to it. We also knew what they were going to wear and how they were going to 'haunt' the space they'd been assigned – some would talk, while others would moan scarily or be ominously silent – and we were going to set the theme of the room and decorations to marry up with what they'd be doing. The boxes of what would be going in the garden were arranged in a different corner of the room.

We didn't talk much as we got to work and not at all about anything other than what we were there to do. By the time my tummy grumbled around lunchtime, I was ready for a break, and not just from the task in hand.

'Darling!' May greeted me when Erik and I returned to the kitchen. 'Kate has just been telling me how hard you've been working. You're an absolute star.'

'I think that title should be awarded to you, May,' I insisted as I bent to fuss her diminutive dachshund, Monty, who was wearing a coat made of pumpkin patterned fabric. The friendly dog had a more diverse wardrobe than most humans. 'Your friends are going to make this event a triumph and the costumes you've got for them are amazing.'

'Well,' she said, 'The Chapel is a cause close to my heart.'

'And mine,' said Lisa who then walked in with Luke. 'I was hoping to see you May because I wanted to talk about the Christmas rehearsal schedule. If we do have to close for a while—'

'We won't have to close,' May interrupted as if the suggestion was preposterous. 'This time next week we'll be solvent again and the doors will be open.'

'But shouldn't we have a back-up plan, just in case?' Lisa said reasonably.

May wouldn't even entertain the idea.

'I'll be back in a bit,' I said quietly to Kate, and went to duck out before the conversation between Lisa and May turned querulous.

With two such big personalities thrashing it out I sensed it had the potential to do just that.

'You're welcome to stay,' Kate told me. 'I've got soup on the go and some of Mark's sourdough to go with it.'

'Thank you,' I smiled. 'But there's something I need to do. I'll be back in about an hour.'

It was a relief to get outside, and I breathed in the crisp autumn air as I walked back to the square hoping Rafe would be writing or out and I could decompress in peace. I needed to rid myself of the tension in my shoulders and enjoy a few minutes of quiet after the uncomfortable conversation with Erik that had neither been finished nor resolved.

The house was blissfully empty, but the peaceful feeling only lasted long enough for me to heat a bowl of Rafe's delicious leftover risotto before the doorbell rang. I toyed with the idea of ignoring it, but when it rang a second time I went to see who it was. I had my hopes pinned on the postie delivering something that wouldn't fit through the letterbox, but it wasn't her. It was Erik.

'Erik,' I said with a sigh that I didn't disguise. 'What's up?'

'I'm not sure,' he shrugged. 'That's why I've walked over to check you're okay. That and the fact that the kitchen over there now feels packed to the gunnels ahead of Luke's radio interview this afternoon.'

'I'll be back to listen to that,' I told him. 'I'm just having some lunch.'

I had one ear on the kitchen because I knew Socks had a fondness for Rafe's risotto too and I'd left my bowl unattended.

'Fair enough,' Erik nodded. 'I'll see you in a bit.'

I noticed it was just starting to rain.

'Unless you want to come in,' I suggested hesitantly, thinking about the 'don't be alone with Erik' pact I'd made with myself, which accounted for the caution I felt about inviting him over the threshold, as well as the fear of losing my lunch to the cats.

'I'm not sure,' he faltered, obviously aware of the reluctance behind the invitation.

'There's leftover risotto,' I said.

If I fed him as well as myself we'd both be occupied and I wouldn't have to look at him or be tempted to fling myself at him. Though I might be tempted to watch him eat . . . damn.

'Did Rafe make the risotto?' he asked.

'He did,' I confirmed and Erik walked in.

'Not that there would be anything amiss with it if you'd made it,' he said hastily as he hung up his jacket.

'But my father does have a knack with ingredients,' I allowed. 'Even the simplest ones.'

My meal was thankfully untouched, and Erik and I sat opposite one another with the steaming bowls topped with a handful of grated pecorino cheese. Had we not had more work to do, I would have suggested wine. But then again, after what happened the last time we'd drunk wine in the kitchen, perhaps it was best that we did have work to do.

'At the risk of ruining this serene moment,' Erik said, once he'd eaten a good amount of his risotto, 'can we clear the air? I don't like the mood between us.'

'Me neither,' I swallowed. 'I'm sorry we had cross words this morning.'

'I'm sorry, too. But I know it wasn't just this morning that's felt a bit . . . off. Was it?'

'No?' I asked innocently.

'You must know it wasn't,' he said. 'And the only thing I can think of that might account for the awkwardness, which seems to be growing, is that kiss. It feels like it's changed things between us and that's the last thing I want. I've loved you being my PPO, but more than that, I thought we were shaping up to be really good friends.'

His words were so heartfelt and the expression on his face

so intent that I knew that I couldn't tell him the truth. I couldn't bring myself to tell him that the kiss *had* changed things for me because all I could think of was the desire to repeat it. I couldn't tell him that when he so obviously wanted me to be his friend and especially as I wanted to be his friend, too. If it was going to be a platonic relationship or nothing, then I'd be his friend any day.

'We are really good friends,' I said on an out breath. 'I suppose I've immersed myself in planning this event so much that I've let other things, such as spending time with you, slide. I've probably taken over far too much—'

'No, you haven't,' he cut in. 'No one's so much as hinted at that, and I didn't mean to imply it this morning. It's just that I've noticed how much you've taken on, and I suppose I've been worried about you as well as concerned about the consequences of the kiss on our friendship.'

'Worried about me?' I frowned. 'Why?'

I had just been going to tell him why I felt so passionately about helping to increase The Chapel funds, but his concern cut the explanation off.

'Because,' he said, 'old habits die hard.'

'Old habits?'

'Your work ethic,' he elaborated. 'Getting so stuck in with the details, making an event the very best you can, taking it all on yourself,' he incisively reeled off. 'Not in a controlling way, but in a . . .' he cocked his head, 'you can totally count on me kind of way.'

'I see.'

'To put it plainly, I'm worried that because of the hours you're giving to this event, you're going to end up as exhausted as you were when you arrived,' he said. 'You literally haven't taken a breather since this idea was settled on, have you? And before you contradict me, I know I'm right because I've walked the big change path myself, still am, and I know how easy it is to regress and revert to old patterns when the opportunity arises and before you've realised it.'

I might have been using the event as a diversion tactic, but I realised there was also a lot of truth in what he said, and I wondered if Rafe had been planning to say something similar. I had been trying to distract myself, but in doing so, I had reverted to type. I had morphed into the event organiser I'd previously been, rather than considered ways I could get the job done differently if I hadn't shouldered practically all the responsibility for it myself.

'I have to say,' I tutted and Erik winced in obvious anticipation of a negative reaction, 'I'm feeling a bit fed up that I haven't picked up on what I've done. I should be fixing myself rather than looking for someone else to do it, shouldn't I?'

'You weren't looking for me to do it though, were you?'

'I suppose.'

'And I haven't fixed anything. I've just pointed something out in you that it took me a lot of mental turmoil and physical pain to recognise in myself. Consider it my gift to you. What you do with it is entirely up to you.'

I smiled at that, and encouraged by my reaction, Erik carried on.

'You might take it back to the store for a refund,' he shrugged. 'Or you might decide to try it on for a while. After all, you did come here with a view to potentially making changes to your life and the way you work, didn't you?'

'I did,' I confirmed, realising how his words about trying something on echoed those I'd said to my father earlier.

'There you are then.'

'I think,' I said after I'd thought the situation through further, 'I'll hand over to Kate and Luke, now. I could be a helper rather than the coordinator, couldn't I?'

'You could and that way you'll have the opportunity to step back and enjoy what it is you've achieved,' Erik suggested, and I did like the sound of that.

'I suppose I am one day away from unpacking the headset and intercom, striding about and strictly issuing commands . . .' I joked.

'And no one wants that,' Erik said as he reached across the table to squeeze my hand. 'They're not the actions of the Skylar we've come to know and love.'

'Don't be ridiculous,' I blushed and batted him away.

'Come on then,' he laughed. 'I'm still looking forward to working out where those moving eye pictures can create the most havoc.'

I shivered, but it wasn't the thought of hanging the paintings that made me do it.

Chapter 21

That evening, having avoided those unsettling paintings, listened to Luke on the radio and handed the fictional headset over to Kate with details of which smoke machine to order, I sat down with my father for a proper catch up. He didn't materialise from his writing room until almost seven, but when he did there was a delicious Spanish tapas platter waiting for him along with a glass of his favourite wine.

'What's all this?' he asked, when he walked in yawning and stretching.

'Well,' I said, 'neither of us had a holiday this year, so—'

'You haven't had a holiday in *many* years,' he countered.

'So,' I continued, glossing over his comment, even though he was right, 'I thought I'd treat us to a taste of Spain and some father–daughter time.'

'I'm all for that,' he smiled. 'What's to drink?'

'Your favourite wine,' I said and handed him a glass before picking up my own. 'But before we toast, I'd like to apologise.'

'Me too,' he sighed. 'And can I go first, because you'll probably find that you don't need to when you hear what I've got to say.'

'Age before beauty,' I teased and he pretended to scowl.

'That's hardly fair,' he said, 'when I have both.'

We sat at the table with the delicious food between us.

'In that case,' I said, helping myself to a glossy olive, 'you had better go first.'

'I want to say sorry for an assumption I made,' he said sincerely, 'and which I would have made you aware of this morning had you not taken the wind out of my sails by telling me about your experience at that arts centre. I had no idea you aspired to act, Skylar.'

'It wasn't my life's dream or anything,' I told him. 'Just something I wanted to have a go at, and school wasn't the right environment to stick my head above the parapet.'

'School isn't the right place for a lot of things,' he said and then continued with his apology. 'However, your explanation made me realise that I'd got the wrong end of the stick. I had assumed that you'd been working so hard on the fundraiser because you'd slipped back into event planner mode. I was worried you were putting in so many hours because that was what you had done in the past. However, your experience of trying out acting somewhere supportive and having to leave it added a different dimension to what you've been doing, and I know I was wrong.'

'Not entirely,' I felt duty bound to admit.

'But you want to ensure the event is a success and makes a packet for The Chapel because of your memories, don't you?'

'For the most part,' I confirmed. 'But you were also right in that I had fallen back into working the way I always have in order to give it the strongest chance.'

'Oh.'

'I'd taken almost all of it on,' I said, baring my soul, 'and delegated only the tiniest amount . And even that was a struggle because I'd never shared the load before. The thing is, if you're an event planner, you're an event planner, the buck stops with you and you are, or at least I always have been, responsible for absolutely everything, right down to the tiniest details that no one else will have thought of.'

'I see.'

'But I've had a proper think about it now,' I said, 'and remembered that's not what Kate and Luke asked of me when they first mentioned the idea.'

'What did they want you to do?'

'They did ask for my help, assuming I thought it was feasible to set up in the limited time, but they weren't expecting me to micromanage the entire thing.'

'I don't think that's what you've done—'

'Well, not far off,' I interrupted. 'But I've taken a step back today and I'm just going to be a general volunteer now, mucking in with everyone else. I've handed over my clipboard to Kate.'

Rafe heartily approved of that and clinked his glass against mine as we filled our plates with the tapas and began to eat. I could feel one of the cats weaving their way around my legs, doubtless enticed by the smell of the chorizo.

'I'm proud of you, Skylar,' Rafe smiled, his expression happy again. 'And relieved you were able to take a step back and work it out. Perhaps it was a timely lesson? An opportunity to have a think about what you won't want to do when you look for another job.'

It was the first time he'd mentioned me returning to work since the muddle over the job offer from Mr Fuller.

'I think you're right,' I agreed. 'I already know I won't want to live on-site again because it's too easy to never stop working. Ideally I'd love to find something local to here, but that might mean going freelance, which could end up being even more full on.'

Even the thought of travelling between venues and constantly working with different caterers, venue owners etc made my heart race. Was that really what I wanted? If I didn't want to move to somewhere with a need for a full-time event organiser, then it might be the only alternative. It would be another huge change, but perhaps one I'd get used to . . .

'Well, there's no rush to think about it yet, is there?' Rafe reminded me. 'Just add this lesson to your thoughts and let it settle there.'

'Um.'

'You look stressed now.'

'Sorry.'

'Don't be sorry,' he insisted. 'Just know you've got as long as you need before finding something that's going to work for *you*. I know you loved working at Highfell, but you can also see now how intense it was. It's time you put yourself first.'

I knew I'd always resisted doing that in the past because it was exactly what Mum had always done and with negative consequences that impacted on both me and those who had got close to her. Subsequently, even just the thought of putting myself first felt selfish, so putting it into action was going to require a total change in mindset.

'I know what you're thinking,' Rafe said astutely.

'Do you?' I asked with a smile, because I knew he did.

'Of course. Have you heard from her?'

'Nope. She's someone else who's reverted to type.'

'I don't honestly think she has it in her to change.'

'Isn't that the truth?' I agreed. 'And while we are truth telling, it wouldn't be right for me to let you believe that it was a blinding moment of independent enlightenment on my part that made me realise what I've been doing, because it wasn't.'

'Oh. How did you work it out then? Did someone give you a helping hand?'

'Erik did,' I confessed. 'He explained this afternoon that he had recognised in me something that he'd done himself in the past, i.e., fallen back into old habits because they're the ones he was used to and felt comfortable with.'

'Good old, Erik,' Rafe nodded. 'It sounds like he's done some thinking and I daresay he knows how to put himself first as a result.'

'I'm sure he does,' I agreed. 'Not that he's self-centred. Far from it.'

'Um,' Rafe frowned. 'If that's what you think putting yourself first truly means, then perhaps we need to have a conversation about putting your own oxygen mask on first.'

'No, we don't,' I said. 'I know what it means, I've just had my opinion about it skewed by Mum.'

'In that case, perhaps I'll ask Erik to give you a pep talk,' Rafe suggested. 'Apparently, you'll listen to him.'

I wasn't sure I liked the turn the conversation was taking and I liked even less the rosy colour I could feel blooming in my cheeks.

'I've forgotten the dip,' I said, and stood up. 'It's still in the fridge. Do you want some? I do.'

'Go on then,' my father said, sounding amused.

I hoped he hadn't guessed that my feelings for Erik were more than they should be. Especially now I was determined to pack them away and become the friend Erik wanted me to be. I knew Luke and Finn were part of his inner circle, but it was us two who had most recently arrived and were going through some big life stuff. That gave us a solidarity of sorts, and given his perfect earlier summing up of what I'd fallen foul of doing, I could do a lot worse than make the most of his observations and the wisdom he'd accumulated as a result of doing something like what I'd arrived in Nightingale Square to do.

'So,' I said, when I sat back down with the dip, 'what are your plans for the rest of tonight? More writing?'

'No, not this evening,' Rafe said as he swiped a chunk of bread through the rich tomato and smoky paprika dip. 'I'm meeting Hugh in the city.'

'Hugh,' I smiled. 'It's getting serious if you're happy to tell me his name.'

'That's enough of that,' Rafe tutted, but with a smile. 'If I'm not going to tease you about Erik, then you can let a name drop pass, can't you?'

'Yep,' I said quickly before I blushed again. 'I won't say another word.'

Having checked in with Kate that all was well at Prosperous Place on Thursday morning I then walked to Cavell Care to catch up with Mabel and also Grandad George. Both were delighted to see me and Mabel had made a new friend, Bill. He'd only arrived at the beginning of the week but was feeling a bit out on a limb, so Mabel was making it her mission to gently help him settle in.

'I thought I'd show Bill around the garden while the sun's shining,' Mabel said, after she'd introduced me to Bill. 'Do you mind, Skylar? I know this is our usual time to chat.'

'Not at all,' I smiled. 'Make the most of the sunshine and we'll catch up another day.'

I was thrilled that Mabel felt settled enough to make someone else feel at home and then, having watched the pair through the window, I chatted to everyone in the day room and helped Beth set up a crafting session. I also filled her in on how things were shaping up for Halloween.

'That all sounds perfect,' Grandad George said, listening in. 'I thought Freddie was exaggerating when he told me the scale of the thing, but apparently not.'

'Honestly, dear boy,' Freddie, who was sitting next to him, said haughtily, 'when have you ever known me to exaggerate?'

Beth rolled her eyes and left us to it.

'How long have you got?' Grandad George fired at Freddie.

I stepped in before the spat escalated.

'I was talking to Rafe last night,' I said, 'before he went off to meet this guy he's seeing. Do you happen to know what he's called?'

'I might,' Grandad George shrugged.

'Of course, he does,' Freddie butted in. 'Your grandfather set them up.'

'He did what?' I gasped, looking between the two men.

'Freddie Fanshawe!' Grandad George admonished. 'Secretly set them up,' he scowled. 'The emphasis being on the word *secretly*, you blasted fool.'

So much for me acting as a peacekeeper. Freddie had just shot himself in the foot.

'Oh yes,' Freddie said, looking chastened for once. 'I forgot that part. You won't let on will you, Skylar?'

'I will not,' I said. 'I'm keeping out of it, even though I'm dying to know how you managed it.'

'You might as well tell her,' encouraged Freddie. 'Now I've let the cat out of the bag, there's not much point in carrying on with the cloak and dagger, is there?'

'But Rafe doesn't know, does he?' Grandad George pointed out.

'Well, I won't tell him,' I promised again. 'But given that he seems so happy, I'm sure he wouldn't be upset even if he did find out.'

It turned out that Hugh's mother, Ottilie, was also a Cavell Care resident. She lived in one of the on-site assisted living apartments but often came along to Beth's activities.

'One day she had her son with her,' Grandad George smiled, 'and I just knew. Handsome, the right age, a lit lecturer at the university and single. He was perfect for Rafe.'

'So, your grandfather and Ottilie made arrangements for Hugh and Rafe to be here at the same time and bump into each other,' Freddie chimed in, putting air quotes around the last four words.

'And it worked like a charm,' Grandad George said proudly. 'Love at first sight, I reckon.'

'So, is that what you were up to the day you wouldn't say what you'd been doing?' I laughed. 'Were you scheming?'

'I might have been,' Grandad George said with pride.

'My goodness,' I sighed. 'How romantic. Is Hugh a bit of a silver fox by any chance?'

'Hugh is a lot of a silver fox,' Freddie winked.

'In that case,' I shared, 'I think I've seen him. He and Rafe were walking together one day and I spotted them. I didn't call out because I didn't want to engineer an introduction neither of them were ready to make. He looked very handsome.'

'Fingers crossed for a happy ever after,' Grandad George twinkled and Freddie agreed.

'Fancy falling in love within weeks of arriving in Nightingale Square,' I said rather dreamily.

'Don't you worry, my dear,' Freddie said consolingly. 'There's plenty of time for you to fall in love, too.'

I snapped out of my daydream faster than my heart had started to race.

'But there's not much time to get Prosperous Place ready for Halloween,' I said quickly, 'so I'd better get going. I'll see you Monday, Freddie if not before.'

'I'll be there,' he called after me. 'I've been spending hours on the piano brushing up on "The Phantom of the Opera". I thought I might kick things off with that!'

'Perfect!' I called back and gave him a thumbs up.

The following week was going to be interesting.

Chapter 22

I didn't have to be at Prosperous Place until the following morning, but I would have used whatever excuse I could have dreamt up to leave Cavell Care when Freddie had started talking about the possibility of me, rather than my father, falling in love. That brief conversation combined with Rafe's knowing comment about Erik was enough to give me palpitations without the assistance of those moving eye paintings I was becoming borderline paranoid about!

'Just a heads up,' I said to everyone I found in the Prosperous Place kitchen early on Friday, 'I saw Freddie yesterday and he's planning to open the event on Monday with a rendition of "The Phantom of the Opera". You have been warned.'

A cheer went up and I realised that everyone assembled was more excited about that than I was.

'I did know that was his plan,' smiled Luke. 'Freddie emailed me his playlist last night and that was billed as the opening tune. We're going to rig up a speaker or two outside, so his playing will eerily drift over the grounds.'

I wondered what else we were in store for from Freddie's repertoire but didn't ask. It could be a surprise.

'So,' I said instead, 'where do you want us this morning Kate?'

Along with her and Luke, Erik was also there and so were Freya and Finn. More of the neighbours would be forgoing their stints in the Grow-Well to help in the house and grounds over the weekend if needs be and it felt strange for me not to be checking the schedule of what needed to be done but instead waiting to be assigned a task.

'Erik and Finn are installing the speakers in the garden,' Kate reeled off. 'The fog machines are coming today, so they'll also be dealing with those, and they've got some lighting to rig up, too.'

'Machines plural?' I questioned.

'Yes,' Kate confirmed. 'When I phoned to book and confirmed the delivery address, the chap I was talking to said he'd heard Luke on the radio and that his nephew loves his sessions at The Chapel.'

'What a coincidence,' I smiled.

'And a money saver for us, too,' she added thrillingly, 'because he offered the fog machines for free and heavily discounted some lighting that's going to add some real drama to the end of the day trail explorers along with the evening tours.'

'He's coming himself to help set everything up,' Erik told me. 'So, we'd better get out there, Finn, and open the gate so he can get his van in.'

'See you later,' I said as he and Finn rushed off.

'And a couple of other suppliers have also been in touch to say they're happy to discount their bills if I mention them in the interview I've been asked to give the local paper following the event,' Luke added excitingly.

'At this rate we'll make a fortune for The Chapel,' Freya said, handing me a mug of coffee. 'Isn't it great?'

'It certainly is,' I agreed.

'This is the sort of thing that happens when we all pull together,' Luke cheered and raised his mug.

It was yet another poignant reminder that working as a team could have even bigger and better results than when you took everything on yourself . . . like I previously had for this event. It was a total change when compared to what I was used to being responsible for but sharing the load certainly had its benefits. Perhaps if I did go freelance, I might consider taking on a partner.

'So,' I said, before I got further sidetracked, 'what needs doing first? I'll do anything that doesn't involve finding a spot for those moving eye paintings.'

'Erik mentioned you weren't keen,' Kate grinned.

'Which is a shame because I've got two more being delivered today,' Luke said and I gave a groan loud enough to rival the most miserable ghost, which made everyone else laugh.

By the end of the day, most of the rooms that were going to be open were transformed and we'd had a run through in those to check how long it would take to switch out the decorations that needed changing between the daytime spooky trail and the more sophisticated and scarier evening tours.

'As long as there are half a dozen of us here every day to do it, an hour will be plenty long enough,' I said, checking the timer on my phone. 'And we're bound to get faster as the week goes on.'

'We're almost done in the house now, aren't we?' Freya asked.

'We're getting there,' Kate said. 'There's another bedroom to sort and the dining room. That's the room that will take longest.'

'Count me in for that,' I said. 'I can't wait to see it banquet ready.'

Even though the grand finale wasn't until Halloween, which was a week and a day away, we'd worked out there wouldn't be enough time during the week to really be able to do the decorations justice, and as the tickets to attend had been pricey, it needed to be spectacular.

'And if a little dust settles between tomorrow and Halloween,' Luke shrugged. 'Even better because it will add to the ambience.'

'True,' I agreed.

'So, I'll rally the troops to help in the garden tomorrow and Sunday, shall I?' Freya asked. 'I know there's a lot to do out there and with you three and Erik in here, assuming he's finished with the lighting and so on, the rest of us could get on outside.'

'That sounds like a plan,' Kate said.

'And we've got the volunteer room hosts coming on Sunday for a dress rehearsal,' Luke reminded us.

'I'm going to stay away for that, if you don't mind?' I asked. 'I want to have the full experience on Monday when you open to the public.'

'Of course,' Luke said. 'You deserve a day off, Skylar! You've been flat out for weeks.'

Even though I hadn't needed to be as Erik had gently pointed out, but I wasn't going to highlight that.

'And I'm going to get Lisa and John to round up their kids and perhaps a cousin or two, along with our girls for a trial run,' Kate informed us. 'They've got a good age range of youngsters in their family.'

'That's a brilliant idea,' Freya said.

'Even if they just walk around the house we should be able to get a feel for how the ticket holders will react and we can tweak anything that doesn't have the desired effect,' Kate continued.

'We'll need to see the full range of human emotions,' grinned Luke. 'Terror, tears, tantrums and laughs.'

'No tantrums!' Kate objected.

We all jumped as someone thudded on the back door.

'That's a good start,' Luke laughed. 'And that'll be the paintings. Stay there, Skylar, I want to see if you're terrified, tearful or both when I unwrap them.'

'No chance,' I told him. 'I'm off to the pub. Anyone else coming?'

With no takers, I rushed ahead of Luke and collided with Erik, who was holding the parcel, at the back door.

'Keep that away from me,' I said warningly, and given how broad his smile was, I guessed he knew what was inside.

'Did I hear you mention the pub?'

'You did,' I confirmed as he handed Luke the package. 'But it's just me going.'

'I'll come with you,' Erik said, 'that is, if you don't mind.'

'Of course I don't mind,' I told him. 'Why don't you get washed up here then meet me over the road in half an hour?'

'Are you suggesting I need a wash?' he laughed, threatening me with his mucky hands.

'Don't!' I squealed and ducked out of the way.

'What's going on out there?' called Kate, who was getting ready to pick the girls up.

She sounded very much like a cross mum.

'Nothing!' Erik and I chorused and grinned at one another.

'I'll see you in thirty minutes,' Erik said and I let myself out, shrugging off how much I'd enjoyed our playful moment.

Once home, I had a wash, changed my clothes and brushed my hair which had been tied up all day. It didn't look too bad considering. Not that it really mattered because it was only a drink in the pub. A drink in the pub *and* the perfect opportunity to launch my renewed determination to be a good friend to Erik.

And as it turned out, it couldn't have come at a better time because when he came to meet me, his former bright mood seemed rather dimmed.

'I don't suppose you had a chance to look at what we'd done in the house, did you?' I asked, to kick our conversation off.

'Not yet,' he said as I struggled to keep up with him as he strode along.

'Could you slow down a bit, Erik?' I puffed. 'For someone with a knee problem, you do walk fast.'

'Sorry,' he said and slackened his pace.

I had been hoping for a wry smile or being teased about being so unfit but neither the change of expression nor a dig about my fitness was forthcoming.

'You grab a table,' I said, when we arrived at The Dragon, which was already quite busy, 'and I'll get us a drink.'

'And some chips,' Erik requested. 'Just a bowl to share will do.'

I was hungrier than I realised so I ordered us a bowl each and carried our pints to the table while the food was being prepared.

'Cheers,' I smiled and clinked my glass against his.

'Cheers,' he responded.

'I'm pleased you said you'd come with me tonight,' I forged ahead rather than starting to fret over why he looked so glum when less than an hour ago we'd been laughing and messing about.

'You are?

'Yes,' I smiled, 'because I wanted to thank you and preferably not in earshot of anyone else.'

'Oh? What have I done to warrant that?'

'The gift you gave me.'

'The gift?'

'The nudge I needed to realise that I'd taken over the fund-raiser and had fallen back into old habits. You opened my eyes at just the right time.'

'You really are grateful about that?'

'So grateful,' I said sincerely. 'I might have only stepped back very recently, but working as a team has already proved to be fun *and* it's benefited the event because of the discounts Kate and Luke have secured.'

'Well,' Erik said, sounding happier, 'you've all had some skills to bring, and I'm pleased you don't think I overstepped when I said what I'd noticed you were doing.'

'Not at all, and if anything else comes up,' I told him as someone came over with our chips, 'feel free to fill me in.'

'I will,' Erik said and his smile was genuine. 'You got two bowls.'

'Of course, I did,' I laughed. 'I might be open to listening with equanimity to you offering me advice about where I'm getting things wrong in my life, but I could easily fall out with you over the biggest, crispiest chip in The Dragon.'

'Fair enough,' he laughed and pinched one from my bowl anyway. 'But from what I can see, you haven't got anything else wrong, have you?'

I put a protective arm around my bowl and ate a couple of the cooler chips from the top before answering.

'Well,' I said, having reflected, 'I'm loving the hours I'm putting in at the Grow-Well and as a volunteer at Cavell Care.'

'And you're enjoying living with Rafe?'

'Yes,' I said, 'though I did get one thing wrong where he was concerned. I had this amazing out of the blue job offer which I soon decided I didn't want.'

'Why not?' Erik asked while fanning his mouth because the chips were still hot and his hunger had made him greedy.

'Because it was almost identical to what I was doing before,' I explained, 'and, as much as I loved my years at Highfell, I've decided I don't want to live where I work again. It's too intense.'

And since then, I'd also decided that I might not want to work alone either, but that wasn't relevant to what had happened with Rafe, so I didn't include it.

'I think it's every bit as valuable to know what you don't want in life as well as what you do,' Erik said wisely. 'But where does your father come in?'

'I'd printed the job details off and he found them,' Erik winced. 'I'd put them in the recycling bin, but it blew over and Rafe retrieved the sheet and read it.'

'And jumped to the wrong conclusion.'

'Yes,' I sighed. 'If I'd told him about the job and that I'd turned it down, he wouldn't have been upset about me moving to Devon when I wasn't even considering it. I should have talked to him.'

'Or shredded the paper,' Erik suggested sardonically.

'Or that,' I nodded. 'But on reflection, I think talking to him would have been better and that's what I'm resolved to do going forward.'

'Well, for what it's worth,' Erik said, 'given that you've only very recently moved in together and had to completely recalibrate your relationship as a result, I think you're both doing brilliantly. That job situation is hardly a hiccup at all.'

Having thanked Erik for that, I fell to wondering whether in the spirit of talking openly and being transparent, I should come clean about the true impact the doorstep kiss had had on me, but I decided not to for two reasons. Firstly, my head was muttering something about sleeping dogs and secondly, Erik then started talking about his own dad.

He hadn't said much about him before, but from the little I'd gleaned, I'd guessed enough to assume that there was a complicated father–son relationship, so sat back and gave him my full attention.

'If I had to live with my dad again there'd be endless hiccups,' he said. 'And I don't think we'd overcome any of them.'

'I'm sorry to hear you say that.'

'We never used to be at loggerheads,' he sighed. 'Not when I was much younger.'

'So, what changed?'

He took a moment to marshal his thoughts.

'It's a long story.'

'Well, I'm not going anywhere.'

'It goes right back to my childhood,' he began. 'With Dad's encouragement, I'd already shown an aptitude for rugby before Mum died. And when we lost her, we threw ourselves completely into it. It gave us something to focus on other than the nightmare we were going through. The two of us were on the same page back then.'

'That makes sense.'

'Looking back,' he continued, 'I'm not sure it was helpful because the training schedule we devised ensured we both had something to constantly keep busy with. We didn't allow ourselves to grieve because we never stopped long enough to let it happen.'

'I can appreciate the appeal of wanting to block it all out though.'

'Dad has always been my biggest cheerleader,' Erik carried on. 'Whatever else was going on, he was always on the touchline or in the gym with me. He'd had quite a successful career in the sport himself, so took on the role of being my coach in the early years. He worked both of us relentlessly.'

It sounded to me as though Erik's father was the total opposite of my mother. His dad had been hands-on and ambitious whereas my mum had shown no interest in my aspirations and left me entirely to my own devices. Thinking about it, I wondered if a happy parenting medium would have been more beneficial to both Erik and me. Interested and encouraging rather than completely dispassionate or totally smothering.

'He must have been so proud to see you reach the top of your game.'

'He was,' Erik confirmed.

'And as devastated as you were when you had to retire.'

'He was,' Erik said again. 'But whereas I've accepted that it's over and am coming to terms with it, he still can't let it go. Here's me, enjoying doing something completely different while

I discover who I am, for the first time in my life, without the game shaping my every second, and he's still stubbornly clinging on to it.'

'You mean, he thinks you can play again?'

'Not play,' he said, 'but have some sort of connection to the sport.'

'Have you talked to him about it?' Erik gave me a look. 'Sorry.'

'I've talked to him until I'm blue in the face,' he said, sounding frustrated. 'But he reckons I'm giving up too easily. That there's more I could do.'

'And perhaps there would be,' I said, 'if you wanted more, but you don't, do you?'

'No,' he said, 'I don't want any part of it. Like you, Skylar, I know what I don't want now and I'm taking my time to work out what I do.'

'We really do have a lot in common, don't we?' I smiled.

'We've certainly arrived here with similar challenges,' he agreed. 'And I know I can talk to the others about it, but it's a comfort talking to someone who's still floundering, too.'

'Oh, thanks,' I laughed and gave him a shove but of course, being so solid, he didn't move an inch. 'So, what is it that your dad's suggesting you could do?'

'I'm waiting to find out the current idea. I had a phone call with my agent earlier and he said Dad's gone quiet which isn't a good sign. If he's quiet, he's brewing something. Some crazy scheme that he'll be furious with me for not wanting to go along with.'

That explained the downturn in Erik's mood on the walk to the pub.

'What you need is a shock tactic,' I proposed. 'Something to help him see the situation from your point of view. It might cause some damage in the short term but then go on to save your relationship in the long run.'

Erik took a moment to mull the idea over.

'You might be right,' he said. 'I've probably spent far too long trying to factor in his feelings and letting him interfere. A bomb going off might be the only way to get through to him now. What do you suggest?'

We didn't have time to cook anything up because Freya, Finn, Mark and Neil arrived then and I felt relieved that I hadn't broached the subject of mine and Erik's kiss. Spending the rest of the evening with our friends and acting as each other's PPO again put us right back where we needed to be and I felt happy about that.

Chapter 23

Setting up the finishing touches was hectic but everyone, at some point, pitched in to help with further decorating the house and embellishing the garden. I'd never seen so many pumpkins and weirdly shaped gourds! If there was a gap to fill, an orange orb or knobbly gourd filled it.

As well as Freddie's playing, Luke had also downloaded a spooky sounds playlist to add an extra sensory element. While he decided what to use to set the scene, we carried on about our work, becoming increasingly familiar with the sound of creaking doors, manic laughter and raging thunderstorms.

'Shut the door, will you, Skylar?' Rafe said to me on Sunday morning. 'If I hear that hysterical laugh once more, I'll turn into a screaming banshee myself!'

Kate had asked Rafe to assist with decorating the dining room because she'd heard from Lisa that he had a flair for seasonal interior decoration, and when he'd shown Kate the camera roll on his phone, she knew he was just who was needed to get the tone just right.

'You and me both,' I grinned. 'It's a bit much, isn't it?'

'I'll say. Now, show me what we've got and we'll get started.'

Rafe was very organised and we began by draping the cotton cobwebs around the top of the room, including the elaborate light fitting above the table and worked our way down. The cobwebs were banned from the garden because Freya had told us how many garden birds died after being caught up in them every year. Unfortunately, they looked like the real thing to our feathered friends who flew into them looking for insects and became entangled.

'There,' Rafe said as he stood back to admire the dramatic effect of them festooned about. 'Much better in here than out. And safer, too. What's next?'

It took the two of us, with Luke and Kate popping in and out and bringing with them the spooky sounds every time the door was opened as well as drinks and snacks, until lunchtime, to complete the room.

'It's dark, macabre, pure Victorian gothic!' Kate clapped. 'And I love it.'

'Me too,' I agreed. 'Sticking to a predominantly black colour palette and adding the odd pop of crimson is perfect.'

'That was your dad's idea,' Kate said as she squeezed his arm. 'It feels like it has a spooky Satis House vibe. I can just imagine a wailing Miss Havisham drifting through here bemoaning her jilted status. Thank you, Rafe. It's amazing.'

'It's funny you should mention Dickens,' Rafe beamed. 'I can't wait for the banquet. I've got my costume sorted already.'

'You got a ticket?' I gasped.

The event had sold out in minutes which had taken us all by surprise. I hadn't known my father had been a part of the speedy booking frenzy.

'I got two,' he preened. 'And I'm sorry Skylar, but the spare isn't for you.'

I was about to say that Hugh was a lucky man, but didn't because I wasn't sure if anyone else, aside from Erik, knew he was seeing anyone.

'I still can't believe the tickets all sold at the price we set,' Kate said in wonder.

'They could have sold twice over,' Luke said, walking back in just as she'd said it. 'Oh my god, this looks phenomenal!'

'And all for just one night,' Kate said wistfully.

'As it's so stunning, I think we should have a party for the volunteers in here the night after,' Luke suggested.

'Oh yes,' Kate said, 'and then everyone can enjoy it.'

'That's a brilliant idea,' I agreed. 'And perhaps if this year is a success and you want to repeat it, you could have more than one banquet in the future.'

'That's a thought,' Kate nodded. 'Let's gauge how this year goes. I think it's going to be a hit, but with a whole year to plan rather than a few weeks, it could be even more spook-tacular in years to come.'

'If you say that word one more time!' Luke groaned, then tickled her and chased her out of the room.

'Oh, to be young and in love,' Rafe laughed.

'Or old and in love,' I nudged him.

'I think the word you're looking for is mature,' he sniffed and headed off towards the kitchen and lunch.

In the afternoon, everyone who could stay was given tasks to complete in the garden while the room volunteers had their dress rehearsal indoors. I hadn't really noticed before as I'd either been planning or helping in the house, but I could see now how much the garden had changed. Autumn was really making its presence felt.

It was a chilly, but thankfully dry day, and the forecast for the whole week was looking favourable, and with the smell of a bonfire which Graham was tending drifting over from the Grow-Well, the atmosphere couldn't have been better.

The leaves on the trees had reached peak colour and the borders Freya tended with such care were vibrant, too. With the protection of the old mellow brick walls, and still no threat of frost, the chrysanthemums and dahlias were putting on a spectacular display. It all looked and felt like the perfect autumn tableau, even with the strategically placed pretend gravestones and scary sculptures dotted about.

'Are you going to help or just stand there admiring the view?' Erik called and I realised I must have been gazing at it for a while, because I'd started to get properly cold.

'That rather depends on what you want me to do,' I said and walked over to where he was threading a cable through a wooden box.

'I'm only teasing,' he said. 'You've done more than your share. What were you looking at over there?'

'Everything.' I sighed dreamily. 'Isn't this the most perfect autumn day?'

'It is,' Erik agreed as he stood up and brushed his hands down his jeans. He was filthy again, but the look suited him. 'It's the perfect lead in for embracing what autumn offers us the chance to do, isn't it?'

'Which is?'

'Think about the balance in our lives,' he said. 'Slow down and accept that change can be beautiful and for the best, even when it's hard and unexpected . . .' He smiled and ducked his head. 'Do you think I'm mad?' he asked.

I'd never seen him look or sound more endearing. In that moment, I was transfixed by him rather than the garden.

'Not at all,' I said truthfully. 'You've just made me realise again that I couldn't have moved to Nightingale Square at a better time. Thank you.'

'Don't thank me, because I can't take the credit for being so enlightened,' he said referring to his words of wisdom. 'Thank Kate. She sent me a link to this brilliant wellbeing podcast. The guest on it last week was a witch from Wynbridge.'

'A witch?'

'Yes,' he smiled at my reaction. 'Someone Kate knows a little. She's called Molly and she lives in a cottage in some woods belonging to a grand hall.'

'Well, I never,' I said in amazement. 'A real, live witch. Wynbridge was Kate's childhood hometown, wasn't it?' She'd mentioned it when we were talking about the autumn festival there. 'The home of that festival celebrating fall.' As my father would say, though my attempt at his accent wasn't great.

'That's it.' Erik grinned.

I still hadn't forgotten about the dogs in Halloween themed fancy dress. May's Monty with his packed wardrobe would have fitted right in in the Fens!

'I'd love to visit one day,' I said.

'The town, the festival or the witch?' Erik asked.

'All three!' I laughed.

'Hey you two!' Luke waved at us from across the lawn. 'Time for a breather. We've got cake!'

'Just what I need,' I said and rubbed my hands, which were feeling the cold, together.

'I'm not surprised,' Luke teased. 'You've been hard at it since you got out here.'

I went to shove him, but then remembered there was no point, because he was built like a brick wall. I stuck my tongue out instead and he laughed and followed me back inside.

I was awake early Monday morning, which was launch day, and feeling a heady mix of excitement, anticipation and trepidation. It was a cocktail of feelings I'd experienced a lot in my early days as the Highfell event planner, but I hadn't succumbed to them for years as I knew my job inside out and was always confident the results would be just what the clients had ordered.

This week-long program of events however, that were being put on to support a project that was dear to so many members of the local community, felt deeply personal, and I knew how important it was that it went smoothly, and of course, raised as much money as possible to keep The Chapel open during its funding gap.

I resisted the urge to cross the road early. I might have been an integral cog in the planning wheel, but I knew Kate and Luke had everything in hand and would shout if they needed me. I bided my time, kept an eye on the growing queue outside the gate as the clock ticked down, and then went to wait in line to experience the spooktacular – as Kate had become obsessed with calling it – first-hand.

'Hey Skylar,' waved Mark as he left the grounds and walked back along the pavement carrying some empty lidded containers. 'What are you doing out here?'

'I thought I'd go in with the first wave of visitors to get the full experience,' I told him. 'How's it going in there?'

'I only went as far as the kitchen, but all very calm. Blossom asked me to drop off some extra cookies and skull and pumpkin chocolate lollies.'

The profits from the confectionery would be Blossom's generous contribution to the fundraising pot and her sweet treats were on sale along with trick or treat tin buckets and a range of sustainable craft kits I'd found online. We'd practically eliminated anything plastic, which made me feel better about what some of the decorations were made of, but I had sourced many of those second-hand.

'Is Freddie warming up?' I asked.

'He is,' Mark laughed. 'And you wait until you see him, he's—'

'Don't tell me. I want it to be a surprise.'

'Shock more like!'

Right on cue, the speakers crackled into life, the dramatic opening bars of 'The Phantom of the Opera' rang out, and the line shuffled forward in anticipation. There were as many adults as children and it didn't matter that it was a light mid-morning, everyone was ready for a good scare.

'Showtime!' laughed Mark. 'Have fun.'

The tour had been set up to take in the house first, then the garden and then back into the spacious hall to tempt the visitors to buy something. Luke had cleverly arranged the path, so it was impossible to leave without walking by what was on offer. Kate was worried that was a bit of a cheek considering the ticket prices, but he reminded her that it was standard practice in commercial venues and she acquiesced when she remembered how much they'd ended up spending in a local Sealife centre that summer.

By the time the stream of visitors had moved far enough into the house for me to spot Freddie, he'd moved on from 'The Phantom of the Opera' and was playing *The Addams Family* theme tune. Dressed as a vampire, he gave me a wink and I laughed, feeling delighted that he'd made such an effort. The sound of a creaking door led me into the first room and the tour began . . .

'So,' Kate said, when a couple of hours later, I joined her in the kitchen to help restock what was selling fastest, 'what did you think?'

'No tantrums yet,' announced Luke who rushed into the room to grab some more tin buckets, 'but we've had tears and terror!'

'Brilliant!' Kate called after him.

'It was really weird,' I told her, once he'd gone, 'because having had a hand in setting it all up, I didn't think I'd get so caught up in it, but with the lights dimmed and the music and sounds playing, not to mention the volunteers drifting eerily about, it all felt completely plausible. I loved it! I even got jump scared a couple of times and not from the paintings.'

'I'm so excited!' Kate squealed. 'Everyone's reaction has been amazing. Can you imagine what it's going to be like in the dark with May hamming it up?'

'Spooktacular!' I laughed.

'Don't,' she grinned. 'Luke's banned me from saying that now.'

Once the last lingering day visitors had left we were able to switch things about in plenty of time for May's arrival, and after a speedy bite to eat with the family and volunteers who were staying, the night tour began. Lots of the guests were in costume, which was fun, but the laughs and smiles happily didn't last.

Dressed, spookily enough given the Dickensian feel in the dining room, as the time-ravaged Miss Havisham, May drifted through the rooms ahead of us telling the tale she, Rafe and Luke had cooked up. I can't deny, I looked over my shoulder more than once, and when she reached the part about the family member who hung themselves, I felt a genuine chill course through me. The sensation increased tenfold when May drew back the curtain in the upstairs room to show us the tree, lit from below and with more than a hint of fog shrouding the lower part of the trunk.

Something or someone brushed my arm and I barely contained a shriek. After that, I made sure I was in the middle of the crowd as we completed the tour. Mission very definitely accomplished!

Chapter 24

Thanks to everyone pulling together, the week passed with barely a hitch and any hiccups we did encounter were swiftly solved because one of us had the skills to deal with it. Many of the visitors had posted about the event online saying what a fabulous time they'd had, and I couldn't for a minute imagine that it wouldn't be repeated the following year.

Saturday was finally Halloween, and in the evening, once the square had entertained its share of sugar-high trick-or-treaters, all that was left was the long anticipated Beastly Banquet. As we didn't have tickets, me, Erik and a few others had decided we deserved a trip to The Dragon as a reward for all our hard work. We were just about to walk there when my mobile rang.

'It's Kate,' I said to the others. 'So, I'd better answer.'

'Skylar?' she sounded frantic when the call connected.

'Hey,' I frowned, 'what's up?'

'We're two servers down,' she told me in a slightly breathless rush. 'And we can't manage to pull this off with a skeleton staff. No pun intended.'

'Oh, no,' I said. 'Of course, you can't. Give me two minutes and I'll be there.'

'What's happened?' Erik asked.

I explained the situation, and he kindly elected to come with me.

'Maybe we could help in the kitchen,' I suggested as we rushed off in the opposite direction to the others. 'That'll free some staff up to serve the banquet.'

However, the evening didn't pan out as simply for us as that.

'You could easily fit into it, Kate!' I protested, when Erik and I found ourselves being measured up for the costumes the wait staff should have been wearing.

'I really couldn't,' she said. 'It's too small for me and before you suggest Luke could wear the other one, Erik, it's made for someone taller than him and there's no time to alter it.'

So, that was how we ended up dressed to look like a steam-punk couple with make-up to match and, with zero experience between us, serving the super-exclusive Beastly Banquet for the dozen guests who had paid handsomely to be there.

I had always had a bit of a thing for men wearing eyeliner and the kohl lines enhancing Erik's blue eyes were too much! I was on the point of a swoon from the moment he revealed his look and hard pushed to focus on the food rather than him.

Fortunately, no one seemed to notice the less than silver service and even though I wanted to exclaim in shock when I realised that the two men dressed convincingly as Scrooge and Marley were my grandfather and Rafe, I somehow stayed in character and managed to suppress it.

'You two look incredible,' I said, however, as I inexpertly followed Erik around with the sauce boat and leant between them so they could help themselves.

Erik had a heavy platter to balance, but I thought I was worse off because the contents of what I was carrying would make a real mess if they spilt. I soon found it was best not to think too much about it for fear of manifesting a mistake!

'Are you surprised to see me?' Grandad George laughed and rattled his chains.

'Just a bit,' I confessed. Having assumed Rafe's spare ticket was for Hugh I was more than surprised. 'But delighted.'

'We're rather surprised to see you, too,' Rafe smiled.

'I hope I can pull it off,' I told him. 'Bon appétit.'

Having played our parts as best we could in the subtly lit dining room that was dressed for drama, at the end of the meal, Erik and I were finally able to leave the other two servers to deal with the decanters and so on.

'Shall we get some air?' Erik suggested as he undid the top button of his shirt.

'Yes,' I said, even though I wasn't convinced, given the whole eye liner aesthetic, that us being alone was sensible, 'I'm really warm in this get-up and could do with a breather.'

I went to unpin the tiny hat on a band that had been digging into my scalp and let down my hair, but Kate objected.

'Don't change a thing,' she insisted. 'We'll need you to see the diners off the premises later. That is, if you don't mind hanging on?' she added pleadingly.

'In for a penny,' I sighed, knowing we wouldn't get to The Dragon. 'Come on then,' I said to Erik. 'But I'm not going anywhere near that haunted tree.'

The garden was still set up and lit, so we headed off to sit in the little alcove in the fern garden which was out of sight of the house. Erik had the foresight to grab a couple of blankets and cushions which I was grateful for because I hadn't walked many steps in the chilly night air before I was feeling much cooler.

'What a week!' I declared as I sat on one of the cushions and Erik plonked himself next to me on the other.

'Tell me about it,' he said, then stood up again and draped one of the blankets around my shoulders.

As the fabric touched my skin I felt every nerve ending light up.

'Thanks,' I said, my breath catching.

'No problem.'

He sat down again, closer to me this time.

'I've hardly seen you,' I said in as normal a voice as I could muster, 'apart from when we've been helping switch everything about, but it's been worth all the effort, hasn't it?'

'Definitely,' he agreed and then produced two hip flasks from the pockets on his long coat. 'I'm sure the events must have raised loads for The Chapel.'

He offered one of the flasks to me.

'What's in this?' I asked.

'Some of the Phantom Punch Luke concocted. I thought we might need it, but—' I took a huge swig before he had time to finish explaining and started to cough. 'As I was saying,' he laughed, 'I pepped it up a bit because I thought we might need something stronger after what we've gone through tonight.'

'Well,' I gasped, my voice gruff, which made him laugh again, 'it's certainly warmed me up again.'

If I had been contemplating a moonlit seduction, I'd just blown it. Probably just as well.

'Have you got any left?'

I gave the flask a shake.

'Only a little.'

'Oh well,' Erik grinned, 'down the hatch.'

Knowing what was inside, he didn't cough like I had, but it did take his breath away.

'You were right,' I giggled, 'after tonight, we did need that. I can't believe I didn't drop anything because my hands were shaking the whole time.'

'Mine too,' he said and drained the dregs. 'And on top of the week I'd already had, I really needed something to settle my frayed nerves rather than ramp them up.'

'Oh no,' I gasped, pulling my thoughts back in a friendlier direction and thinking it was a shame we hadn't had time to catch up before. 'What's happened?'

He huffed out a breath, and it streamed ahead of him. It must have been colder than I had realised. The blanket he'd given me was keeping me warm.

'Do you remember me telling you,' he began, 'that my dad going quiet wasn't necessarily a good sign?'

'Of course,'

'Well, on this occasion, it was a *very* bad sign because he's finally shown his hand and got my agent involved and on the case, too.'

'What have they cooked up between them?' I asked. 'Something you're really not keen on, I'm guessing?'

'Not keen at all,' he confirmed. 'I heard about it through Peter, my agent, but I knew Dad must have had a big hand in it and yesterday he admitted as much.'

'So, what do they want you to do?'

Erik looked as if he couldn't believe what they were suggesting.

'Take up a television commentary position with a sports channel,' he told me. Obviously, I hadn't known what he was going to say, but I hadn't expected anything like that. 'And I do get why they're keen,' he added. 'I really do. They're both still thinking that I should be squeezing every last drop out of my career, and this is a route lots of other ex-players take, but I don't want it.'

'You're happy as you are right now, aren't you?'

'I'm very happy as I am,' he nodded. 'This quiet life, doing something completely different now that I can't play the game I loved, is really helping me process what's happened and focus on what the rest of my life could be. Without that odd-shaped ball occupying my every waking moment, there's room for so much more.'

I snorted at that and Erik smiled.

'Sorry,' I said and held up the hip flask. 'Your fault though.'

I drained the very last drop and handed the flask back. His fingers brushed mine and felt far warmer than my hand. He slipped the flask into the coat pocket again along with his.

'Here,' he said and took my hands in his and blew warmth onto them.

It felt like an intimate gesture and kicked off that stirring feeling deep in my belly again, and just when I thought I had reined it in. The sensation spread considerably further as his kohl rimmed eyes met mine and I knew I had to break the moment.

'Though you know,' I said, as I gently eased my hands from his, 'if you did take the commentary role, your continued fame could then take off in all kinds of TV directions.'

'Such as?' he asked huskily.

'Game shows. Reality TV. I could just see you in the jungle doing those mad challenges and eating, instead of playing with odd shaped . . .' I shook my head feeling embarrassed. 'I'm going to shut up now,' I blushed as Erik doubled over with laughter.

'I can always rely on you, can't I Skylar?'

'To do what? Make a fool of myself?'

'No,' he said and turned to face me. 'Make me laugh!'

'Well,' I said, 'that's what friends do, isn't it?'

'Um,' he said, his gaze flicking to my lips before resting on my eyes again, 'friends.'

'Best friends,' I whispered and swallowed.

'Friends who—' he began, but I didn't give him time to finish.

Throwing caution to the wind, I dismissed my determination to keep my distance, closed the gap between us, pulled him to me and kissed him. He didn't resist and neither of us held anything back.

'Wait,' he said, and pulled away the tiniest bit after what felt like too short a time. I leant further in to counter his move. 'Is this the impact of the punch?' he asked, between kisses. 'Because I didn't mean for this to happen when I added to it—'

'No,' I said and kissed him again. 'It's not the punch. This is all me.'

Having told him that, we carried on and I soon realised that our doorstep encounter had been just the tip of the iceberg when it came to releasing the passion I felt for him.

'Erik,' I gasped as he kissed my throat and then moved on to my collarbone before turning further so his hands could find my waist.

There was no holding back from either of us and the deeper the kisses, the more I became aware that the Big Love I'd experienced before was nothing like this. There was no doubt in my mind that we would have taken things further had Luke's voice not rung out on the speakers asking us to go back, making us spring apart.

'Crikey, Skylar,' Erik said breathlessly as I stood up and rearranged my outfit.

'I know.'

I'd never be able to visit the alcove again without blushing.

'I don't feel like I've cooled down much,' he said as he also stood up.

'Me neither,' I agreed as we made a move to leave the fern garden.

And I didn't feel like much of a friend, either.

'But I can promise you that won't happen again,' Erik continued and caught my hand to make me stop. 'That's the second time we've jeopardised our friendship and I don't want to lose you. I value you too much.'

My stomach plummeted, even though I knew he was right. The timing for both of us was rotten. He now had even more on his plate with his dad and agent nagging him to consider the television commentary role and I had no idea where my future might take me.

It was time to remind myself again how all of Mum's rash relationships had ended. There was no friendship left following the fallout of any of those and I couldn't risk mine and Erik's relationship by allowing myself to further fall for him.

Nightingale Square might end up not being where either of us settled long-term, so whatever spark there had been between us, it had to be snuffed out. I should never have kissed him again, and I only had myself to blame for the feelings I was going to have to start from scratch to battle back into their box.

'And I don't want to lose you either,' I said and gave his hand a squeeze before letting it go. 'Now, come on, before everyone thinks we've been spirited away.'

After a restless night, I was bleary eyed the next morning, but there was no time to kick November off with a Sunday lie-in because I'd promised to go back to Prosperous Place to help return the house and garden to its pre-Halloween state. Kate was cooking a big breakfast to fill us up for the task ahead, so I ignored my bruised feelings and looked forward to the fundraiser debrief as I tucked into some bacon.

I walked into the Prosperous Place kitchen with a somewhat forced smile on my face, but it vanished when I spotted Erik looking furious and Kate and Luke sporting contradictory expressions of concern and amusement.

'What's going on?' I frowned.

Luke looked at Erik.

'Show her then,' Erik said gruffly.

Luke leant across the table and slid over an open newspaper.

'It's not a paper we usually read,' he told me. 'But John was in the newsagent's first thing, and someone was talking about this, so he picked up a copy and dropped it round.'

'Is it your story about the fundraiser?' I asked naively as I forgot Erik's look of upset. 'That was quick. I didn't realise you'd been interviewed already. And this is a national.'

'Just look at it properly,' Erik said.

It took me a moment to register what exactly I was seeing.

'Oh my god!' I gasped. 'Erik, that's us!'

The photograph wasn't as crisp as it could be, but the garden lighting showed that it was unmistakably us kissing in the fern garden the evening before and the clinch looked more passionate than I would have thought possible.

'Former rugby star, Erik Svensson,' I read aloud, 'showing his softer side to mystery woman following a fundraising event in Norwich. This is outrageous!'

'I know,' tutted Luke. 'It doesn't even mention The Chapel.'

'Luke!' Kate admonished.

'You're right,' he said, amending his tone, 'it is outrageous and I can only apologise. To you both.'

'Why are you apologising?' I frowned as I turned the paper over and slapped it back down on the table.

'Because I invited a photographer here to take some snaps of the banquet,' he explained. 'With the guest's consent, of course and supposedly only for local use, too.'

'Well, this isn't very local, is it?' I choked. 'It's countrywide! And what was he doing sneaking around in the garden taking photographs without *our* consent?'

'He told me he was popping out for a cigarette,' Kate said.

'But in truth, he must have seen you two sloping off,' Luke added.

'We didn't slope off,' Erik ground out. 'And how did he even recognise me? I was wearing that ridiculous costume for pity's sake.'

'You're not exactly unknown around here, mate, and you do stand out a bit whatever you're wearing,' Luke pointed out.

'My guess is the guy was . . . surprised by what he saw and decided it was too good an opportunity to miss. He sold it on sharpish, I must say.'

'That's what they do, isn't it?' I swallowed.

I'd never been the victim of an invasion of privacy like this before and felt exposed and vulnerable even though I hadn't been identified.

'I'm so sorry, Skylar,' Erik said earnestly.

'It's not your fault,' I told him, then added. 'None of it is your fault.'

It had been me who'd kicked the kisses off, but I didn't want to admit to that in front of Kate and Luke.

'So, whose fault was it?' Luke asked, a ghost of a smile playing around his lips. 'My punch wasn't that deadly, so you can't blame me for getting you drunk.'

Kate gave him a shove.

'Look,' he carried on, 'things like this happen all the time. Heaven knows, I had my share of misleading photos in the press when I was a model. Today's gossip is tomorrow's fish and chip wrapping, remember that.'

'I don't think they wrap them like that anymore,' I huffed.

'But you know what I mean.'

'You try telling my father that,' Erik said as he held up his phone to show 'Dad' lighting up the screen. 'That's the tenth time he's rung so far this morning. I bet he and Peter are loving this.'

As far as Erik's father and agent were concerned it probably was perfect timing for Erik to be shoved back into the public arena again.

'I am sorry about that,' Luke told him with a nod to the

phone. 'Truly I am, because I know the hassle you're going to get for it, but you'll have to pick up at some point.'

'Hassle,' Erik frowned.

Talking to his father was obviously going to be more than a minor nuisance.

'You can't put it off for ever.'

'I wanted to apologise to Skylar, first,' Erik shot back at Luke. 'Like I said, I am sorry and I do blame the punch.' Luke opened his mouth to object. 'Because I added a couple of measures of brandy to ours. We needed it to steady our nerves after serving that banquet.'

'That's right,' I said, latching on to the excuse for our embrace. 'We were tipsy and we ended up having a quick kiss. No big deal,' I was seriously underplaying it. 'Obviously we didn't expect it to end up in a newspaper, but it didn't mean anything, did it Erik?'

He hesitated before answering and, given that last night he'd said it wouldn't happen again, I was shocked to see a look of upset cross his face. However, by the time Kate and Luke looked at him it had gone, so perhaps I'd misread his fleeting expression.

'No,' he said, as his phone rang again. 'It was nothing. Bloody hell! I'll speak to Dad and be back for breakfast.'

He walked out of the room, and I shoved the paper further away.

'You can light the fire with that,' I said. 'Now, which room would you like me to start in and how do you want everything packed?'

'Wouldn't you like some breakfast first?' Kate asked.

'No thank you,' I told her. 'I've lost my appetite. We can talk later about the success the fundraiser has hopefully been.'

Erik was in a foul mood after the phone call to his father. Apparently, it didn't matter how he tried to express it, his dad wouldn't believe that this hadn't been a masterstroke on his son's part. A clever way of getting his face back in the public domain ahead of accepting the commentary job. He'd even gone so far as to suggest that Erik should now take me – even though he didn't know who I was – out shopping or to a restaurant and be snapped again. Obviously, that wouldn't be happening and at lunchtime, with most things packed away, I headed straight home taking my heavy heart with me.

'How about this then?' Rafe laughed, when I went to make a sandwich and applaud him for the brilliant costumes he and Grandad George had worn for the banquet. 'I take it congratulations are in order?'

He was waving a copy of the offending red top about.

'What are doing with that?' I scowled. 'You don't read that paper.'

'Lisa brought it over,' he told me.

'Of course, she did,' I grumbled. 'I bet everyone in the square's seen it now, haven't they?'

'Probably,' he said and gave me a quizzical look. 'And I know you probably wanted to keep your relationship—'

'There is no relationship,' I snapped. 'We're not a couple. We're just friends.'

'So, this was . . .'

'A phantom punch induced snog,' I said glibly. 'The sort of moment kids go in for at the end of a school disco. Nothing more.'

'I see,' Rafe said thoughtfully. 'So, the last time it was the wine and this time it was the punch. Perhaps third time will be the charm, you'll both be sober and able to see what's so obvious to me.'

Having not known my father had been aware of our first kiss, that rather took the wind out of my sails. Were my feelings for Erik that obvious to everyone around me or just to Rafe?

'You're being absurd,' I said, trying to keep my voice steady. 'We're friends, nothing more. Friends with a lot in their lives to process, so we're helping each other through it.'

'Well,' Rafe said, with another nod to the paper. 'The pair of you certainly have an interesting technique.'

Chapter 25

I kept my head down on Monday and decided not to attend the party for the volunteers that was taking place in the still dressed dining room. I didn't want to miss it, but I'd had a message from Erik warning me that another photo of us walking back through the garden holding hands had appeared in the paper that morning and that everyone popping in and out of Prosperous Place was full of it.

I might have been a little punch-drunk, literally rather than figuratively on the walk back to the house on the night of the banquet but I knew we hadn't properly held hands. We had made very brief contact and that was obviously when the photographer had snapped us again. What a snake.

Erik also said he wasn't looking forward to the party but would stick it out. I considered inviting him over to the house while it was happening but then reckoned that if we were both absent everyone would jump to the wrong conclusion irrespective of whether we were together or not, so I didn't.

'Where were you?' Rafe asked, when he arrived back from the celebration and found me in my sitting room with the curtains closed and the cats on my lap. 'You never said you weren't coming over.'

'I had planned to but changed my mind,' I fibbed. 'I've got a bit of a headache.'

'Anything to do with the second photo that appeared this morning?' I turned to give him an anguished look. 'Erik brought it up,' my father said quickly, to reassure me that it wasn't the hottest topic of conversation.

'Why did Erik mention it then?' I frowned. 'And to whom?'

'I think he saw the party as an opportunity to talk to everyone en masse,' Rafe explained. 'He was most insistent that the photographer had made the most of what had been nothing more than a punch ignited kiss that you both immediately regretted and that you definitely weren't in any kind of romantic relationship.'

Hearing what Erik had said and imagining him saying it in front of all my neighbours and new friends, I could appreciate then how he'd felt when I'd made light of what had occurred between us in front of Kate and Luke on Sunday. Even though we were both keen to shrug the moment off, being so blunt about it, though necessary, did feel rather harsh.

'And did everyone accept that?' I asked croakily, because for some reason my throat felt tight.

'They did,' Rafe confirmed. 'Erik also said the same thing as what you'd told me about the pair of you being the two Nightingale Square newbies helping each other settle in, which is why you're sometimes together. Not that that needed justifying, of course.'

'Good,' I said. 'Well, let's hope that's an end to any gossiping and we can all get back to normal.'

I hadn't heard any gossip first-hand, but I couldn't imagine there hadn't been any. I was momentarily surprised Freya hadn't outright asked me if anything was going on but then realised she didn't strike me as the sort of person to pry. She probably thought that if I wanted to tell her something then I would, much like I'd waited for Erik to fill me in about his dad rather than push for information.

'Yes,' Rafe agreed. 'I hope that's an end to it, too. I don't like you hiding away over here when—'

'I'm not hiding away,' I butted in. 'I told you, I've got a headache.'

'Well maybe this cake Kate sent over will help get rid of it,' he suggested and held up a plastic container. 'She and Luke were hoping to talk to you and asked if you'd go over tomorrow after the school run.'

'I daresay they've totted up the total we've made for The Chapel,' I said, as I lifted the cats off my lap and followed him to the kitchen. 'I thought they might have announced the amount at the party.'

'It wasn't mentioned. Now, how big a slice of this cake would you like? Obscenely huge or the whole thing?'

Once I'd eaten an obscenely huge slice and washed it down with a massive mug of unsweetened tea to keep the resultant sugar hit under control, I messaged Erik and thanked him for putting everyone straight. I also messaged Kate and confirmed that I'd go over and see her in the morning. I set my phone aside then and opted for an early night.

I managed to make it over the road the next day, through the gate and into Prosperous Place when the square was deserted.

I was feeling a bit paranoid after being 'papped' and wondered how celebrities coped with the invasion on a daily basis. I knew some people courted it for one reason or another, but there must have been times when it became wearing.

'Morning,' I said, when Luke answered the door and I quickly stepped inside.

'Morning, Skylar. Why did you knock? You can still walk in now the event is over you know.'

'I didn't like to assume,' I told him as I pushed back the hood of my sweatshirt and slipped off my boots which were a bit muddy.

'Is it cold out?' he asked, with a nod to the hood.

'Not really, I'm just keeping my head down.'

'If you're worried about that photographer,' he said. 'Don't be. I've given him a piece of my mind and told him I won't be putting any work his way from now on.'

'So, he's not likely to be hanging around then?'

'Not around here.'

It felt as warm and welcoming in the kitchen as always and the atmosphere combined with the reassuring news pulled my shoulders back down to somewhere around where they should be.

'Morning, Skylar,' Kate smiled and held up a mug. 'Coffee?'

'Morning,' I smiled back and pulled out a chair at the table, which was covered in paperwork. 'Yes, please.'

'We missed you at the party yesterday,' she said, 'but I'm not surprised you wanted to stay away. Did Rafe tell you that Erik let everyone know that there was no truth in what they'd seen in the papers?'

'He did,' I confirmed. 'And I've thanked Erik for setting

everyone straight.' It hadn't escaped my notice that Kate had said papers, plural, but I wasn't going to get drawn into asking if more than one had picked the salacious story up. 'Now,' I said instead, 'I'm hoping you've asked me over to tell me how much last week made for The Chapel. Was it the financial success we hoped it would be?'

'We are going to discuss that,' Luke said as he and Kate also sat down, 'but it's not the only thing.'

'Okay,' I said, drawing the word out.

'But with regards to last week,' Luke continued, 'it was a huge success!'

'We haven't got a final figure yet,' Kate said excitedly, 'but it's well over double what The Chapel needed to bridge their funding gap!'

'Double!' I gasped.

'More than double,' she repeated.

'That's incredible,' I said in wonder. 'The generous contributions from local businesses and the hours the volunteers all gave for free, must have made the biggest difference.'

'Along with your bargain hunting,' Kate added.

'And do you want to know the best bit?' Luke asked.

'There's more?' I laughed.

'Everyone who supported us has already pledged to do the same next year,' Luke announced and my mouth fell open.

'So, you'll definitely be doing it again?'

'We certainly will,' Kate said. 'And with even more time to get organised, we can make it even bigger and better.'

'I have every faith in you,' I told them both. 'You'll achieve terrifying things. I'm so pleased I braved leaving the house to talk to you now!'

'So are we,' Kate laughed. 'Because we have a thank you gift for you.'

She handed me a wrapped parcel. 'And like Luke said, it's not the only thing we want to talk about.'

'You didn't have to do this,' I said as I tore off the paper, 'but thank you so much. Oh wow! These are perfect! It's about time I had my own. Rafe has a collection, but nothing like these.'

The gift was a pair of Emma Bridgewater mugs from the Halloween selection I'd seen online when I was looking for Christmas present inspiration for my father.

'You like them?' Luke asked.

'I love them! Thank you. They're perfect.' I set them in front of me so I could admire them. 'So,' I encouraged, 'what else did you want to talk about?'

I hoped it was more good news.

'Has anyone mentioned the Winterfest to you?' Luke asked and I shook my head.

'I'm not surprised,' Kate sighed, 'because it isn't happening this year. Well, not how it usually would anyway.'

Luke then went on to explain that in the past he had been diagnosed with Seasonal Affective Disorder and how he had come up with the Winterfest to offer anyone who finds the short dark days a challenge, ways of keeping creatively occupied and passing the time with a new hobby while also improving their mental health.

'There are all sorts of workshops set up here on-site,' he told me. 'And we hold as many of them outside as possible. Things like creative writing, making nature journals, nature-based crafts, cooking and preserving, even winter gardening.'

'Is this what inspired your winter garden here?'

'Yes,' Kate said. 'That was Freya's first project when she started working for us and she now runs tours and offers workshops on the subject.'

'The Winterfest first ran from November onwards but has faltered in recent years, and this year, aside from Freya's contribution, isn't scheduled to happen at all,' Luke said sadly.

'May I ask why?' It sounded perfect to me so I couldn't understand why it wasn't happening.

'We usually oversee it ourselves,' Kate said, 'but life has taken over and not just for us but for the neighbours who also help with some of the workshops, too. We had a meeting a couple of months back and decided we'd take a year off and start afresh next winter, with a view to inviting business owners and professionals to take part, rather than relying so heavily on friends and their families.'

'It sounds really special,' I said, 'and important, too, given the diagnosis that kicked it off.'

'We've had dozens of fabulous testimonials,' Luke said proudly. 'So, we never wanted to give it up. In fact, we're now considering having an outdoor classroom or studio built that will have floor-length windows to make the most of the light to host it.'

'So, you can be indoors but sort of outdoors at the same time whatever the weather.'

'Exactly,' he smiled.

'It feels even more spectacular now, given what you just said about SAD and your busy lives, that you pulled the fundraiser off at such short notice,' I praised.

With the days shortening, especially now the clocks had

changed, Luke had probably noticed the impact of that more than the rest of us.

'Ah,' Kate said, 'but we didn't, did we? That was all you, Skylar.'

I couldn't accept that. 'It was partly me,' I told her, because once Erik had talked to me, I'd stepped quite a way back. 'It was a team effort.'

'Not in the beginning,' Luke said. 'And that's why we wanted to tell you about the Winterfest.'

'You aren't going to ask me to set that up this year, are you?' I joked. 'It's November already!'

'Not this year,' Kate smiled. 'But maybe next.'

'I don't understand,' I frowned.

'We've always wanted the house and grounds of Prosperous Place to be somewhere that works for the community as well as a family home,' Luke elaborated. 'And seeing it come to life last week for both adults and youngsters during what is generally considered a dreary time of year was such a boost that it's given us the impetus to want to put on more events on a regular basis. We want to plan a proper calendar of things that people can rely on to happen, rather than having them popping up every now and then.'

'The Winterfest, and now Halloween week, could be just the start of that,' Kate joined in.

'Perhaps even another summer fair with Prosperous Place playing an even bigger part than last time,' Luke chimed in thoughtfully.

That was something else I hadn't heard about.

'But the point is, having to put off the Winterfest this year has shown us that we can't do it all ourselves,' Kate continued.

'And nor would we want to because it would take up so much of our time. It could easily become too much for us and feel like a burden.'

'What we need is someone to take on the role for us. A professional event planner who has the experience and vision to help us make a success of it all, not just the Winterfest, but the entire year,' Luke beamed. 'And working in a paid role, rather than as a volunteer.'

'Someone who can get things up and running but who is also able to work in a team because we'd still want to play a part, just not such a major one,' Kate elaborated.

'I see,' I swallowed.

'So, what we're asking, Skylar—' Luke said.

'But with no expectation of an immediate answer,' Kate insisted.

'Is if you'd like to be that event planner for us?' Luke asked. 'Would you consider taking on the role of event planner for Prosperous Place?'

My heart began to skitter, and I felt my face flood with colour. I had assumed I was coming over to hear how much we'd made for The Chapel and possibly help with the last bit of decoration dismantling, but I was being offered a job. And not just any job! A job doing what I loved, that was right on my doorstep and would potentially secure my future in Nightingale Square!

'Will you?' Kate asked. 'Will you consider it?'

'Of course I'll consider it!' I told them. 'I can't believe it.'

I was already keen to accept, in principle, but didn't get carried far enough away to say that. And I thought I would keep the offer to myself for now, because if Rafe knew he'd be as thrilled as I was and all objectivity would go out the window. I wanted long enough to weigh up the pros (many) and cons (not even one so far) for myself, just to be completely sure.

'You might be interested then?' Luke asked and Kate swatted his arm.

'Don't pressure her,' she scolded. 'But are you, Skylar?'

I laughed at the contradiction.

'Yes,' I said. 'I'm very interested indeed.'

'Feel free to fire as many or as few questions at us as you like while you're mulling it over,' Kate said.

The back door banged and we all fell silent.

'Only me!' Erik called.

'And for now,' Luke whispered, 'we won't tell a soul.'

'Agreed,' I nodded as Erik walked in bringing a blast of crisp cold smelling air with him.

'Hey Skylar,' he smiled. 'How's your head?'

I looked over at him and my heart skittered again. It was in that moment that a difficulty regarding accepting the job hit me straight in the solar plexus. Working at Prosperous Place, depending now on what Erik's plans were, might put me in constant contact with the friend I was still wrestling to think of as a platonic pal only.

Rather than seeing the change in my circumstances as a Big Love opportunity it was potentially a barrier to accepting the job because Erik had made it very clear that it was friendship that he wanted. He had ruled himself out of being interested in any kind of love. As had I when we first discussed our relationship status. But that was before I'd got to properly know him. And kissed him. Twice.

If I took the job, and if Erik didn't succumb to what his father wanted, was I going to be able to get used to living with us being just friends long-term and at such close quarters?

'My head?' I frowned.

'You had a headache?'

'Oh, yes, sorry,' I gabbled. 'It's fine, thanks. In fact, I think I'll take it for a walk around the garden and then treat it to a trip to The Dragon for lunch.'

Now I knew that the photographer had disappeared with a flea in his ear, I felt more relaxed about going out again.

'Sounds like a good idea,' Erik nodded. 'I might see you in the pub later.'

'I'll save you some chips,' I said automatically, as I carefully returned the mugs to the box they'd been packed in.

'I've heard that before,' he grinned and I looked away. 'Whatever you want to tell me you two, keep it brief,' he added, 'because I'll need to get to The Dragon before Skylar's eaten every potato in the place.'

Pretending to be offended, I left them to it and let myself out. As I walked around the grounds, it didn't take any imagination to picture the building Luke had talked about having built and it working as the ideal venue for the Winterfest and more. I could also imagine myself there, in all seasons, working alongside him, Kate and Freya to create the most exciting and inspiring calendar of events.

I tried to put the Erik conundrum to the back of my mind and almost had a spring in my step once I'd checked the bulbs in the bothy and had a walk through the Winter Garden which I hadn't taken all that much notice of before but could now see was just starting to come into its own. In something of a daze, I dropped the mugs at home and wandered down to The Dragon.

'So, have you hogged all the chips?' Erik asked, when he arrived.

He sounded perfectly friendly and I resolved to work much harder and loads faster to reassign him to the zone he'd obviously had no struggle sending me back to. Ultimately, and with my common-sense cap on, I was grateful for that because no matter how long we were both in Norwich for, it would mean no crossed wires going forward.

'No,' I said, putting on my brightest smile while also pretending to be offended. 'I haven't hogged all the chips. I haven't even ordered any food yet.'

'There's hope for me yet then,' he commented, then pulled off the beanie he was wearing and ran a hand through his hair.

I ignored my traitorous quickening pulse and nodded to the chalkboard above the bar.

'I thought I might go for something other than a spud today,' I told him.

'Such as?'

'The Brancaster mussels seem to be calling me,' I said and my tummy rumbled. 'Served in a white wine and garlic sauce and with Blossom's crusty wholemeal baguette.'

'That does sound good,' Erik agreed. 'And if you're having garlic, maybe I should, too.'

'Why?' I laughed. 'Are you thinking of kissing me again?'

'No,' Erik blushed. 'And as I recall it was you—'

'I know,' I said as I jumped up. 'It was all me. Right, I'll go and order.'

By the time I got back from the bar he was in a pensive

mood, and I hoped my stupid kiss related question hadn't impacted on his previous bright one. How ridiculous that I'd just pledged to keep a grip on my feelings and then blurted something so inappropriate!

'Our food will only be a minute,' I told him and gave him the glass of Coke he'd also asked for. I'd gone for white wine to match the sauce, and I intended to make it last, so I wouldn't lose my inhibitions and end up saying or doing something else I'd regret. 'You weren't long talking to Kate and Luke.'

'I know,' he said and seemed to perk up a bit.

'Did they tell you how much the events made last week?' I asked, as he took a swig of his drink.

'They did. I couldn't believe it.'

'Me neither,' I said and shook my head. 'I'm thrilled though.'

'Me too,' he said and clinked his glass against mine. 'And you should be. Your hard work certainly paid off.'

'Our hard work,' I corrected. 'Everyone got a look-in once you'd told me to back off.'

'Oh, is that how I put it?' he laughed.

'As I recall,' I stated, then turned bright red because that's what he'd said in response to my stupid kiss question! 'So,' I said, 'what else did you talk about?'

'I'd love to tell you,' he said, 'but the three of us agreed that we'd keep it to ourselves for now.'

That sounded very much like what Kate, Luke and I had also agreed.

'Fair,' I said. 'But funnily enough, I'm keeping a secret following my chat with them earlier, too.'

Erik's eyes widened. 'You are?'

'I am.'

We stopped talking then as our lunch arrived. It looked, smelt and tasted delicious. We both slathered salted butter on to the warm baguettes and then dipped them into the sauce.

'I do love a chip,' I said in something akin to ecstasy, 'but this is next level.'

'A very good call,' Erik agreed. 'It's divine.'

Once we'd finished eating, I tracked back to where we'd left the conversation off.

'So,' I said, when the table had been cleared and I'd drunk practically the whole glass of wine, 'how can I convince you to give me a clue about your Prosperous Place secret?'

'You can't!' Erik laughed. 'It's a *secret* remember?'

'Fair enough,' I shrugged. 'That was a test. You passed.'

'Are you going to drop a hint about yours?'

'I can't believe you'd even ask!' I gasped and Erik laughed.

A few seconds of silence passed, and it was Erik who broke it.

'Mine's potentially to do with my future,' he blurted.

'And mine's related to last week,' I divulged, then clapped a hand over my mouth.

'Perhaps,' Erik said and moved to sit in the seat next to me, 'we could share.'

'I suppose,' I swallowed. 'After all, that's what friends do, isn't it? Share secrets?'

'Exactly,' he agreed.

'You go first then,' I nudged.

'You promise you'll tell me what you talked about if I do?'

'Cross my heart,' I said seriously and made the gesture.

'They offered me a full-time paid position working as the property and grounds manager at Prosperous Place,' Erik confided. 'It's similar to what I'm doing at the moment, but this would be an official role, with more responsibility and a salary.'

'So, you'd be staying in Norwich for good, rather than for as long as it takes you to get your head around your life not revolving around that odd-shaped ball?' I swallowed.

Suddenly it didn't feel like the wine had relaxed me at all.

'If I accepted it, then yes,' he looked troubled for a moment. 'Though heaven knows what Dad would make of that . . .'

He clearly wanted to take the job but still felt beholden to his father.

'Well,' I said, 'he'd get used to it eventually. And it's not as if you live in the same country, so at least he wouldn't be berating you in person day in, day out.'

'That's a very good point,' Erik agreed. 'But it's going to be hard for him if I do take it on. Rugby has been the glue that holds him together for so long and I'm worried that without it, he might fall apart.'

'But that can't be the reason that you don't pursue your own happiness, Erik,' I pointed out.

'I know,' he swallowed. 'I do know that really. Now, tell me,' he added, shifting the focus to me, 'what was it that Kate and Luke wanted with you?

I took a deep breath.

'They offered me a job too, working as an event organiser. They've got plans to host a whole calendar of workshops as well as the Spooktacular, and have asked if I'll take the bulk of it on. And, like you, it would be in an official capacity.'

Erik looked surprised. 'Right,' he said. 'And how do you feel about that?'

'Over the moon,' I told him, while my head chanted *friend, friend, friend*.

'You'll accept it then?'

'Yes. I think I will.'

'So, we'll be working together?'

'I suppose we will sometimes, to a certain extent.'

'In that case,' he said and clinked his glass against my almost empty one, 'here's to a successful working relationship.'

'I'll drink to that.'

It didn't strike me until much later that neither of us had sounded particularly enthusiastic about the prospect.

Chapter 26

'Here she is!' Freddie declared when I walked a little stiffly into the Cavell Care day room on November 5th. 'The not so mysterious woman still making headlines! We didn't know if you'd show up today. Thought you might have a photoshoot somewhere.'

I really wasn't in the mood for Freddie's teasing. My arms and legs ached from hours working in the Grow-Well the day before and my resultant slower walk to the care home meant I was chilled right through, too. At least the sun was shining though.

It was the perfect weather for the film and sparkler night happening later in the garden. Having had the equinox celebration indoors, everyone was keen to party outside before winter arrived and thanks to a concerted effort everything was set up and ready. Other than providing some muscle, I hadn't had anything to prepare or contribute for this regular event as it followed a tried and tested format, and with my mind still full of thoughts about the job offer, I was otherwise happily occupied.

'What do you mean *still* making headlines?' I frowned at

Freddie, once I'd shrugged off my coat, hat and gloves and his words had sunk in.

'Never mind,' said Grandad George, who walked in behind me. 'Ignore him. It's most likely an old paper.'

'You know it isn't, George,' Freddie said, as he held up the offending page. 'This was hot off the press today.'

'Let me see that,' I demanded.

It was yet another photo of Erik and me. This time we were walking along the street following our lunch in The Dragon. When we'd got ready to leave I'd almost suggested setting off separately but knowing that Luke had had words with the photographer, I didn't. By the looks of it, I should have stuck to being paranoid, after all.

'I don't believe it,' I said and slapped the paper back down on the table Freddie was sitting at.

'Did you read the copy?' he asked.

'No,' I said. 'And I don't want you to tell me what it says, either.'

After that, I wasn't in the right frame of mind for idle chat, but that wasn't what Mabel had in mind anyway.

'You make a handsome couple,' she said, when I went and sat on the chair next to hers.

'Sorry?'

'You and the fella in the paper.'

'It's not the best picture,' I said brusquely. 'And we're certainly not a couple.'

'He's been here recently, so I know what he looks like and he's a handsome chap.'

I couldn't argue with that, but I was surprised he'd been to Cavell Care.

'Erik has visited someone in the care home?'

'The manager,' Mabel said. I wondered what that was about. 'He was with her a while.'

'Right. How's the tai chi coming along?'

'Do you remember what I told you about my heart speeding up whenever I saw my Arthur?'

I wished she'd change the subject.

'Of course.'

'Does yours do that when you see Erik?' I didn't tell her that sometimes it felt like it was going to burst out of my ribcage. 'Because if it does, you should be mindful of that. Follow your heart and you won't go wrong.'

She patted my hand and for a horrible moment I thought I was going to cry. Fortunately, another resident, Violet, came to my rescue with a request to help her with a jigsaw she was struggling with.

'You mind what I've said,' Mabel persisted, as I gave up my seat for Bill who had just walked in.

I did mind. I minded very much.

'Don't let it get to you, love,' Grandad George said after we'd had a chat and as I got ready to leave. Clearly, he had picked up on the mood I harboured beneath the sham sunny surface. 'I would imagine Erik's dad is feeling as surprised as you.'

'Erik's dad?' I frowned as I pulled up my hood. I had been recognisable in the most recent photo so would be walking back to the square incognito. 'What's he got to do with it?'

'The article accompanying that photo has a quote from him in it,' Grandad George told me and I felt my heart sink. 'He said he hadn't been introduced to you yet, but Erik had talked about you a lot and that he was looking forward to meeting you.'

'I didn't know that. I wish he hadn't said anything.'

Erik's father had already suggested that Erik should set something up featuring the two of us, so he was no doubt thrilled to see us in the paper again. I hoped he wasn't thinking it was a moment that we'd manipulated because I wanted no part of it and I was certain that Erik didn't either.

'He made it sound like the two of you are a couple and also that Erik was in Norwich on holiday, but then the journalist could have twisted his words to suggest that because I got the impression when I talked to Erik at the banquet that he was quite settled here . . .'

'My guess is, the quote wasn't even from his dad,' I shrugged, even though I was certain it would have been. It must have made his day when he was asked to comment, and he realised he could say something to add further interest to the made-up situation. 'Now, are you coming tonight?'

Grandad George and Freddie had both been invited to the bonfire party. Which was really a brazier party in lieu of an actual bonfire, but I supposed that didn't sound as exciting.

'No,' Grandad George said. 'And Freddie's not either. It's too cold for us.'

'Fair enough,' I smiled and gave him a hug. 'You stay indoors and keep warm.'

'I intend to.'

'Oh, Skylar,' Rafe laughed, as we got ready for the party, 'it's not that cold, whatever Dad reckons.'

'I'm well aware of that,' I said as I pulled my scarf right up over my mouth and nose, so my voice became muffled. 'I'm in disguise remember.'

The only part of me that was visible was my eyes though I wasn't sure I'd be able to properly see where I was going with limited peripheral vision, so Rafe's guiding hand out of the square and across the road was going to be essential.

'I'm sure that photographer won't be hanging about now,' he tried to reassure me, but I was beyond being placated.

I hadn't heard from Erik so I could only assume that he wasn't aware of this latest invasion of his, and my, privacy. I had thought about letting him know but with the situation with his dad already precarious, I didn't want to potentially be the person responsible for estranging them for good.

'Well,' I said, 'I'm not taking any chances. Come on.'

Once safely through the garden gate, I pulled my scarf back down, pushed back my hood and took a big breath.

'Did you see anyone?' I asked Rafe.

'Not a soul,' he said. 'You mustn't get paranoid about this, Skylar. With no story to go on, they'll soon get bored.'

'But they do have a story now, don't they?' I muttered under my breath. 'Courtesy of Erik's father and the clearer photo of us walking back from the pub.'

The gate opened behind us before Rafe could answer and we moved along the path. It was Freya and Finn.

'Hey, you two,' I said, forcing myself to get into the swing of things. 'Are you heading to party central, too?'

'We are,' Freya smiled.

'I want to check the braziers before it gets too busy,' Finn said, and he and Rafe went ahead.

'No Nell?' I asked Freya. 'This is a firework free party, isn't it?'

'It is,' she confirmed. 'But there'll probably be others going off elsewhere and she's not a fan. She doesn't mind sparklers, but she's better off at home.'

'Bless her heart,' I said sympathetically. 'I adore sparklers myself. It's the smell as much as the sight.'

'Yes,' Freya said, 'they do smell good, don't they? How's your week been? It feels like ages since I saw you.'

'Interesting,' I told her, as we arrived at the Grow-Well where quite a crowd was already gathered. 'A bit of a mixed bag.'

'Such is life,' she sighed. 'Tonight will be a highlight though. Look, John's already made some pizzas.'

'Finally!' I applauded.

With everyone assembled and the trestle tables groaning with food, it was time to get ready for the film, which would be followed by sparklers. We all filled a plate before picking where we wanted to sit. The kids nabbed the beanbags which the adults joked they wouldn't have been able to get out of anyway and most of us sat at the back of the table facing the home-made cinema screen, which made it easier to eat. Carole and Graham sat snuggled under a blanket on a bench to one side while Luke and Finn were sorting the projector.

'John, this is amazing,' I said, as I tucked into the goat's cheese, beetroot, balsamic and honey dressed slice.

I had started to properly relax since no one had mentioned my third appearance in the newspaper, and as the company was made up of neighbours who had become friends inside the sanctuary of the Prosperous Place gates, the feeling deepened.

'Worth the wait?' John beamed, looking chuffed.

'Totally,' I nodded and wiped some dressing from my chin.

As well as a variety of pizzas, there were also hotdogs with all the usual accompaniments, a huge vegetarian pasta bake, twice baked jacket potatoes, autumn slaw and the stars of the feast, Mark's edible glitter covered toffee apples. Some had been left as the traditional apple and crunch formula, while others were coated in salted caramel. Whatever the flavour, they all looked sparkly and enticing.

'Do you know what the film is?' Rafe asked the table in general.

'The kids voted for *Fantastic Mr Fox*,' Lisa told him.

'Perfect autumn viewing,' Rafe smiled and settled back in his chair.

He'd eaten his pizza in record time but declined a toffee apple. The plates and bowls were emptying fast, and I realised then that Erik still wasn't with us.

'Is Erik not coming?' I asked Kate, who was sitting next to me.

'He's supposed to be,' she said and looked towards the gate which he suddenly strode through looking grim. 'Here he is. Oh, dear. He was on the phone when we left the house.'

'I think I might know why,' I sighed. 'But I hope I'm wrong.'

Kate turned to look at me. 'You saw it then?' she asked and I nodded. 'Damn, we were hoping you hadn't and we'd all agreed not to mention it in the hope it had passed you by.'

'Everyone here knows?'

'They do,' she confirmed. 'But no one's taken any notice of it since Erik explained the situation at the volunteers' party, so please don't let it spoil your evening.'

'I'll try not to,' I sighed and dropped the last of the pizza slice back onto my plate.

My appetite had headed for the hills.

'Erik says can he have a word?' Luke came and whispered in my ear a minute or so later. 'He's in the bothy.'

'Hi,' I said, when I walked over. 'Are you okay?'

'I'm all right,' he said with a shrug.

'No, you're not. And neither am I, not really.'

'So, you saw it then?' he groaned. 'I was hedging in the hope that you hadn't.'

'It was hard to miss with Freddie waving it under my nose at Cavell Care this morning,' I tutted and then unfairly added, 'and now your father's stuck his oar in, assuming that quote was really from him, it feels even worse.'

'I'm so sorry, Skylar.'

I'd instantly regretted the dig because it was hardly fair to take it out on him, was it? Erik was as much a victim as I was.

'It's not your fault,' I sighed. 'I know it's not. I'm just fed up.'

'Me too,' he said grimly. 'Dad has just told me that he'll do anything he can to keep the story running until I've made up my mind about the commentary job because it's all good publicity . . . What?' he then frowned as my expression must have changed.

'Nothing,' I shrugged. 'Well, I mean, I'd kind of assumed that the decision had been made and you were going to take the job here. I shouldn't have jumped to that conclusion though. Sorry.'

'It's okay,' he said and ran a hand through his hair. 'I don't think I'm really wavering, but it doesn't help that I haven't been able to convince him that TV isn't the place for me. He's so pig-headed. If I'm not saying what he wants to hear he just tunes out.'

'Given what you've told me about you both latching on to the sport when your mum died, it must be hard for him to give it up. And I know you appreciate that,' I added, so Erik didn't think I was judging his reaction to his father's behaviour.

Given that I could have happily throttled him myself that wouldn't have been fair.

'I do know that,' he sighed and shoved his hands in the pockets of his jeans.

He looked utterly dejected.

'Have you told Kate and Luke what you're thinking about the job they've offered?' I asked him.

'Not yet. Have you?'

'No. They asked me not to hurry my decision and even though I'm certain I want it, I don't want them thinking I've rushed. Though if I had my way, I'd start tomorrow.'

'They'll be thrilled that you're so keen,' Erik smiled.

'And I'm thrilled, too and I will tell them once this newspaper situation dies down. For now, I think it's better to keep a low profile.'

'I'm feeling the same way myself,' he empathised. 'Though it's worse for you because you're an innocent friend who has been caught up in it.'

He wouldn't have thought I was innocent if he'd been privy to some of my former more than friendly thoughts!

'We're both victims, and we'll just have to wait it out.'

'Yes, that's all we can do, but how about if we don't do it here?'

'What do you mean?'

'Well, I've been thinking,' he said rather wickedly. 'If we're not here, there won't be anyone to photograph, will there? And no one here would talk to any journalists about us, so that would kill the story dead, wouldn't it?'

'I suppose. As long as your dad doesn't make something else up.'

'With no more photos to go with a quote, it wouldn't be worth it.'

'So, what are you suggesting?' I asked. 'That we should leave?'

'Just for a couple of days.'

'Where are you planning to go?'

'The same place as you, I hope,' he said unexpectedly. 'I want to take you to Wynbridge.'

'What?'

'That autumn festival you were so keen on is in full swing and I thought we could head there on a glorified research trip.' I couldn't believe my ears. 'It might give you some ideas for the Spooktacular or the Winterfest next year.'

'You're really suggesting we go together?'

'Why not? I'll keep my head down and my hat on and you don't know anyone there, do you?'

'No.'

'So, we should be fine, shouldn't we?'

'But where will we stay?'

'I've found an Airbnb which had a last-minute cancellation, so I've booked it from tomorrow afternoon until Sunday night,' he seemed to have it all worked out. 'We can have the whole weekend at the festival if you fancy it.'

I was flabbergasted.

'Of course, you don't have to come,' he carried on when I didn't say anything. 'I do appreciate that I've sprung the idea on you, but I thought it was a good one, so I forged ahead when I found somewhere available. I thought it might be fun. We're due some fun.'

'It is a good idea,' I said. 'And I'm sure it would be.'

However, I wasn't entirely sure that spending a whole weekend living with Erik was going to help contain my feelings for him, but I supposed it would be the perfect opportunity to find out how we might get along working together if we accepted the jobs we'd been offered. If I found the proximity a total nightmare, then I'd still have the chance to turn the job down.

And you never know, perhaps some Prolonged Exposure Therapy might cure me of my Erik crush for good and put him back on a friendly footing once and for all. Maybe he'd have some annoying and horrible habits that would put me off fancying him for life . . .

'So, will you come?' he asked hopefully.

Clearly, he had no qualms about spending so long alone with me.

'Yes,' I swallowed, feeling unsure as to whether I was relieved or offended about that. 'Yes, I'll come.'

Having agreed on a time to meet the next day, we slipped back to the bonfire party. We'd missed the start of the film but as Rafe, who I had been sitting next to, had nodded off, I didn't think I'd been missed.

Feeling peckish again, I tucked into the slice of now cold pizza that I'd previously abandoned and later had fun making shapes in the air with the sparklers and eating s'mores made using the flaming braziers.

By the end of the party, the youngsters were ready for bed and the Nightingale Square contingent all trooped back across the road in a group. Eli, who had earlier thanked me profusely for my involvement with the fundraiser for The Chapel, had reckoned that I would be harder to pick out in a crowd, and when everyone agreed, I felt loved and supported, which was a comforting sensation given the vulnerability I'd experienced when I saw myself plastered across the paper again courtesy of Freddie indiscreet Fanshawe.

I went to bed feeling a whole mix of emotions tangled up with the prospect of spending a weekend in the Fens, which was somewhere I'd never visited before. I refused to stress over the bathroom and sleeping arrangements. Erik was responsible for sorting all that and I was just going along for the ride.

Chapter 27

Had any doubts that our weekend trip to Wynbridge wasn't a good idea made their presence felt overnight, a message from Erik the next day banished them to the back of my mind. The poor guy was at his wits' end following a further conversation with his dad and as his friend, and with the getaway already planned, the least I could do was support him through it and hopefully veer him away from breaking all ties with his father.

'What's all this?' Rafe asked, when he came down from his writing room where he'd been typing away for hours and spotted my overnight bag in the hall.

He looked tired but that was no surprise given the hours he'd been putting in. Having not lived with him before I didn't know if his current time at the keyboard was the norm when the muse struck or a new development. As he seemed happy enough, I hadn't asked.

'I know it's short notice,' I told him, 'but I'm going away for the weekend.'

'Oh,' he said, sounding surprised. 'When was this decided?'

'Just last night. At the party.'

'Any particular reason?' he frowned. 'My typing isn't getting on your nerves, is it?'

'No. It's nothing like that. I hardly hear you. I've promised to go away with a friend who needs some . . . support.'

He looked at me for a moment.

'Not Erik?'

'Why *not Erik*?' I swallowed.

'It is him then?'

'Yes.'

'Oh, Skylar. Are you sure that's a good idea?'

I wasn't sure, but I wasn't about to admit that.

'I am,' I said instead. 'He's really struggling and I want to help him, and besides, the trip isn't only about that. We're going to Wynbridge. It's a town in the Fens which hosts an autumn festival and we're going to see if we can get some ideas for next year's Prosperous Place Halloween events.'

Rafe's eyes widened at that, and I realised I'd inferred more than I'd meant to in my bid to stop him talking about Erik.

'Does that mean you're certain that you'll be here next autumn?' he asked hopefully.

'Well, I haven't got a crystal ball,' I said evasively, 'but you never know and even if I'm not, I can still pass on anything that looks promising to Kate and Luke, can't I?'

My father looked disappointed that I hadn't promised I was staying put, but I knew it was better to get this weekend under my belt before I made any declarations about my future.

'I suppose,' Rafe agreed. 'But I'm still not sure this is a good idea. What if you're both spotted and end up in the paper again? Won't that make the situation worse?'

'I hardly think the photographer is going to tail us all the way to Wynbridge,' I joked lamely. 'And besides, Erik is planning on keeping a low profile and I'm sure not everyone in the world knows who he is.'

'It would only take one,' my father pointed out. That was completely true and also extremely annoying. 'But never mind the press, I don't want to see you get hurt, my darling.'

I shook my head at that.

'Why would you think I was going to be hurt?' I frowned as my phone buzzed.

'You know why,' he said softly. 'I know you're insisting that you and Erik are just good friends, but you can't deny that the lines around your relationship with this lovely guy have been blurred on more than one occasion.'

My father thought Erik was a lovely guy . . .

'You're right, I can't deny that,' I concurred. 'But I can assure you that they won't be blurred again and now, I have to go. Erik's waiting for me. I'm going to drive over to Prosperous Place and then we're leaving in a hire car. Luke will drive my car back and park it on the drive later.' I swiftly kissed Rafe on the cheek and picked up my bags. 'I'll be back Sunday night. Don't work too hard.'

I felt bad about leaving in such a rush, but my resolve to provide a shoulder for Erik to lean on wouldn't be further strengthened by listening to my father's doubts.

The big garden gate was already open and, as soon as I'd driven through it, it closed again.

'Hey Erik,' I smiled when I climbed out and saw it was him who'd shut it. 'All set?'

'I am,' he nodded.

He sounded tired and I felt annoyed with his dad again. I

wished he could understand how hard he was making life for his son who neither wanted to be governed by his advice anymore, nor hurt him by yelling at him to back off.

I'd been frustrated by my mother's lack of interest in me in the past, but I couldn't now help thinking that I preferred her role, or lack of it, in my life when compared to the suffocating nightmare Erik was dealing with. It felt absurd given that he was a grown man but knowing the circumstances about the importance of rugby in his father's life made the situation look less bizarre.

'We're not taking a car now,' Erik said. 'Finn has offered to lend us his truck. My stuff's already inside.' I looked over to where it was parked. 'It's comfier than it looks.' Erik laughed and I felt pleased that my doubtful expression had amused him.

'As long as it has a working heater,' I said as I gathered my bags. 'That's all I care about.'

I noticed Erik was constantly checking the rear-view mirror when we set off and it had nothing to do with him getting used to driving the bulky truck.

'You don't really think that we're newsworthy enough to warrant being followed, do you?' I frowned as I also checked the vehicle behind us.

'No,' he sighed. 'Not really, but my paranoia might take some convincing.'

'Let's hope this weekend in Wynbridge will alleviate that,' I said and unlocked my phone. 'I know you want to keep your head down a bit, but there's still loads we can do while we're playing it safe.'

I then proceeded to give him a rundown of everything that was happening in the town over the next couple of days and the further he drove, the more he seemed to relax. By the time we pulled up outside the large house he'd booked a part of for us to stay in, his frown lines had disappeared completely, and he was sounding as excited about it all as I was feeling.

'I've never seen such a flat landscape,' he said in wonder as he recalled the scenery we'd driven through before reaching the outskirts of the town. 'You could see right to the horizon before it got dark.'

'And if we head to the pumpkin patch at some point, we'll see even more of it,' I reminded him. 'Lucky for us the weather in the summer made for a lengthier harvest.'

'Have you not had your fill of pumpkins yet?' Erik laughed as he cut the engine. 'We put them everywhere for the Spooktacular and now Kate and Luke's freezer is groaning with soup and pies.'

'But we didn't pick our own, did we? Oh, look. Do you think that's the owner of the house?'

The front door had opened, and a woman was standing on the doorstep with the cutest King Charles spaniel sitting at her feet.

'Could be,' Erik nodded. 'Will you go and talk to her?'

'But you made the booking.'

'Please.'

'All right,' I relented. 'Did you book in your real name, or do you have an alias?'

'I booked in my name,' he tutted at my teasing. I was determined to keep the tone light now it had lifted. 'I'll grab our bags.'

Once I'd procured the key from Bella, the homeowner, and fussed her friendly dog, Tink, I went to help Erik.

'Bella said she'll leave us to settle in,' I told him. 'But if there's anything we're not sure about we're to go and ask. There's a separate entrance around the side for us.'

Once inside and up the stairs to the tiny and immaculate apartment I immediately spotted something I wasn't sure about.

'There's only one bedroom,' I frowned.

'I know,' Erik shrugged. 'It doesn't matter.' It mattered to me because there was only one bed. 'The sofa's a pull out and there's linen for it in the chest which doubles as a coffee table.'

I was relieved about that. Wasn't I?

'Ah, right,' I said. 'Well, I'll take that then.'

'No, you won't,' Erik insisted. 'You're having the bedroom.'

'But you can't sleep on a sofa. Your knee would never forgive you.'

'It looks comfy enough,' he shrugged.

In the end, we decided to flip for it and because I won the toss, I stipulated having one night in the bed and the second on the couch rather than both on the divan. Erik took some convincing, but I wasn't going to back down.

'You're a wilful woman, Skylar Shawe,' he grumbled.

'Not wilful,' I responded as I flicked on the kettle and arranged mugs. 'I just know my own mind.'

Erik accepted that. 'So, tell me then,' he said as he leant on the kitchen counter, 'do you know what you want for dinner tonight?'

I looked over at him and realised he was eye to eye with me.

'Are we staying in or going out?' I asked and hoped I sounded unaffected by the proximity of his piercing blue gaze. 'There's some things in the fridge that are probably meant for breakfast, but we could have them tonight.'

'I'd love to stay in,' he said. 'I could do with an early night and a decent sleep.' I didn't bother offering him the bed again because it had taken us long enough to settle on the compromise we'd only just reached. 'Though I'm not sure I fancy a cooked breakfast for dinner. Do you?'

'Not really, though the ingredients for it look great.'

'Let's save them then and I'll have a look in this folder for takeaways. There's bound to be someone around here who delivers.'

'Good idea and while you're doing that, I'll go and unpack.'

I didn't have anything besides my clothes, bedtime read and washbag to organise but getting out of the room gave me a minute to compose myself. I had known that we were going to be staying in the same place together for the weekend and that was some of the point for me, but I hadn't realised just how close we'd be. The apartment was beautiful, but really tiny and Erik took up a lot of space in it. The next couple of days were going to offer Over Exposure Therapy to the max and so far without an annoying habit in sight!

With my father's concerned words ringing in my ears, I pledged to get Erik up and out first thing in the morning and we'd stay out the entire day and the next to balance out the time we were confined to four walls. That would surely put my head back in the PPO post Erik had recruited me for, wouldn't it?

'How are you finding them?' he later asked as we tucked into the fish and chips we'd had delivered and had a bit of a wait for.

'Delicious,' I said and dunked a chip in the mushy peas. 'Totally worth the wait.'

'I cannot believe you're a mushy pea fan,' he said and wrinkled his nose.

'Well, you're no better with that curry sauce,' I laughed. 'I hope Grandad George enjoys his dinner tomorrow as much as we're loving this.'

I then proceeded to tell Erik about Saturday being fish and chip night at the care home along with some of the activities that went on there and how much I was enjoying my role as a volunteer befriender.

'And the brilliant thing is,' I finished up, 'if I take the Prosperous Place job, I'll be able to carry on with the volunteering.'

I had wondered if he might tell me why he'd visited the home, but he didn't, and given the situation with the photos in the newspapers, I wasn't going to mention that Mabel had spotted him there.

'That is a brilliant thing,' Erik frowned. 'But you just said *if* you take the job. I thought your mind was already made up and you were just hanging back before accepting so Kate and Luke didn't think you'd rushed into it. What's changed?'

I could hardly blurt out that I was using this weekend as some sort of litmus paper to help me decide if I could work in the same place as him without my heart wanting to beat out of my chest, could I?

'Nothing's changed,' I shrugged, putting what Mabel had said about hearts and their reactions to the back of my mind. 'Slip of the tongue. I meant to say when. And what about you? Are you still thinking about what you're going to do or have you made up your mind?'

He took a moment before answering and I remembered the

change in him after he'd first told me about the offer he'd received, and I'd then gone on to share the details of mine. I didn't think it had been my imagination that he'd suddenly been less enthusiastic, and I didn't reckon it was all a result of what his dad was trying to pressure him into doing, either.

'I'm still thinking about it,' he said and pinned me with one of his most intense stares. 'I'm almost decided but I'm just waiting to see how something else plays out first.'

His cheeks flushed and I got the impression he'd inadvertently said exactly what he was thinking and then regretted it, even though I didn't know what the something else he wanted to get the measure of was.

'Is that the situation with your dad, by any chance?'

'Yes,' he said and jumped up. 'That's exactly it. Now, I'll get rid of this rubbish, so the smell doesn't linger and there's more beer if you fancy it?'

'No,' I said, 'I won't have more, but thanks. I think I'll go and have a shower unless you want to get in the bathroom first?'

The last thing I needed was the impact of alcohol working its magic on our first night away. In fact, I probably should have opted to stay teetotal for the whole three days. I'd begin tomorrow.

'You carry on,' he said and began clearing away.

I didn't spend all that long in the bathroom, but by the time I came out again, Erik was already looking at how the sofa pulled out in preparation for the early night he was craving.

'Are you ready for bed?' I asked him. 'I don't mind if you are.'

'Pretty much,' he said and yawned. 'I know it's still early, but we'll want to get a decent start tomorrow, won't we?'

'Great minds think alike,' I nodded. 'I'm happy to turn in now, but I wouldn't mind making a hot drink to take with me, if that's all right.'

'Of course. Good idea.'

We both chose cocoa, which I hadn't had in years, and then said a quick goodnight with zero eye contact. I'd offered to help with the sofa, but Erik insisted he could manage and a few minutes after I'd closed the door, I heard him setting it up and then getting comfy. I expected to fall asleep within minutes, but I didn't nod off once while reading like I usually did and I had feeling it was going to be a long night . . .

Chapter 28

I knew, even before I'd opened my eyes, that it was later than I wanted it to be. Having taken ages to nod off, I'd then slept like the dead and our trip into town to check out the autumn market was going to be delayed as a result.

Rather than lingering to see if I could hear Erik moving about, I quickly opened the bedroom door and found him sleeping at a diagonal angle across the sofa bed. He was on his front, with one leg bent and one arm above his head. I was grateful that he was wearing pyjama bottoms, because the sight of his bare tanned back and arms was enough to cause my heart to race again and now I had a dilemma. Should I wake him or leave him be?

Given what he'd said about not sleeping I decided to leave him and crept into the bathroom. When I came out he was still asleep but now on his back, the same arm stretched over his head and his hair mussed up and covering half his face. He looked so peaceful, not to mention hot but I didn't stand and stare because that would have been creepy!

Feeling desperate for a drink but mindful of the noise the kettle would make, I went back into the bedroom and quietly closed the door. I snuggled back under the duvet and checked the forecast. Both days were looking fine so we wouldn't have to cram everything in in a rush and I thought the pumpkin patch and a walk around the nature trail on the farm belonging to it, which was called Skylark Farm, could be the Sunday highlight ahead of finding a pub somewhere for a traditional roast before driving back to Nightingale Square.

I was just beginning to doze off when there was a soft knock on the bedroom door.

'You can come in sleepyhead,' I called and the door opened.

Erik, still half naked and with his hair now in a total state, stood looking sheepish.

'I overslept,' he croaked.

'No, you didn't. You slept for as long as you needed to.'

'In that case,' he said as he gingerly lowered himself to sit on the bed, 'would you mind telling my knee that because it's a bit stiff this morning. I must have slept in the same position all night.'

'Oh Erik,' I winced. 'Is it really? I told you I should have slept on the sofa.'

'I don't think it was the sleeping arrangements themselves that were the problem,' he grimaced as he bent and straightened his left leg. 'More like me not moving while I was asleep on top of using a manual gearbox for the first time in so long.'

'Oh, crikey,' I said. 'You're used to an automatic?'

'Yep,' he grimaced. 'And it was stop start for a while in Norwich, wasn't it?'

'It was a bit. We should have come in my car.'

Our conversation was interrupted by a knock on the apartment door.

'I'll get it,' I said as I pushed back the duvet and edged around him.

'I'm sorry to bother you,' Bella said, when I opened the door, 'but I've just had to pop back from town and wanted to check everything was okay before I head off again.'

'Yes,' I said, 'thank you. The apartment is lovely, and we've got everything we need.'

'That's all right then,' she smiled. 'I won't keep you.'

She turned to walk away just as I did then think of something that might be useful.

'Actually, there is something. Do you, by any chance, know of a taxi firm local to here?' I asked. 'We were thinking of booking one to take us to town this morning. I'm so excited to visit the autumn market.'

'Oh, fantastic,' she said. 'You'll love it and there's a number listed in the welcome folder, but my partner, Jude, will be driving into town in about an hour. I can ask him to give you a lift if you like?'

'Oh yes please,' I smiled. 'As long as it wouldn't be a bother?'

'No bother at all,' she smiled back. 'I'll tell him now and I'll see you at the market.'

She didn't say why she'd be there.

'Thank you,' I said as she headed off. 'We'll be waiting outside in an hour.'

I found Erik still sitting on the bed.

'I didn't want to appear half-dressed,' he explained.

'Did you hear Bella offering us a lift with her partner?' I asked. 'I hope that was okay. I thought it might be easier on your knee if you didn't have to drive today.'

'More than okay,' he said and awkwardly stood up. 'I'll

jump in the shower now if that's all right? The hot water will help.'

'Yes,' I nodded. 'You go for it. Though I don't recommend you jump anywhere for the time being.' Erik rolled his eyes. 'We'll find somewhere to have breakfast in town so we can get straight on.'

'Good idea.'

By the time Jude, who was as lovely as Bella, had dropped us off next to the market, Erik's knee was feeling much better and we made an attempt at a beeline towards The Cherry Tree Café that I'd read about online for some breakfast and to get our bearings.

I say *attempted* to make a beeline because it was a struggle not to become distracted. With the whole market square decorated for autumn, including all the shop windows and market stalls, it was a miracle we arrived at all.

'Come on,' Erik encouraged, more than once as I veered off to admire something, 'I'm fading away here and you read online that this café is always packed out.'

Taking pity on him, with his hat pulled down and his collar right up to hopefully avoid being recognised, I put my blinkers on and made for the café door.

'Oh wow,' I gasped as the bell melodiously chimed our arrival and my senses were hit with a full-on autumnal tableau.

The entire aesthetic was seasonal perfection and the smell was spot-on, too. There were lengths of autumn leaf and pumpkin fabric bunting strung about, patterned oilcloth on every table and the cake counter was practically glowing orange, red and gold and filling the room with a hunger inducing waft of what smelt like cooked apples and cinnamon.

'This place is amazing,' I said as I took it all in.

'And busy,' Erik said as he nudged me further inside. 'Look, there's a table over there. Let's nab it quick.'

The table was just big enough for two and Erik manoeuvred his chair so he could face me. It only gave him a view of the wall behind me, but he didn't mind that. We both ordered the same thing – autumn harvest pancakes and coffee – and I spent as much time looking around and out of the window as I did talking. I had wanted to engage the woman serving us, who introduced herself as Jemma, in conversation about the town, but knowing Erik didn't want to draw anyone's attention, I didn't.

'That must be the Jemma, who's married to Kate's brother, Tom,' I said quietly. 'No wonder Kate and Luke love visiting. I'd be the size of the house if I had someone in my family who could bake like she can!'

'Don't let Mark hear you say that.' Erik smiled. 'His are the only buns any of us are supposed to be interested in.'

That made me laugh.

'Here we are then,' Jemma said. 'Two coffees and your pancakes. Just wave at me if you'd like a refill.'

'Oh, my goodness, these look delicious,' I praised. 'Thank you.'

'I hope you enjoy them,' she said, before rushing back to the counter where a queue was forming.

The stacked pancakes were light and fluffy and tasted of apple, pumpkin and cinnamon and they were topped with maple syrup, whipped cream and chopped pecans.

'Oh my god,' Erik groaned after his first mouthful. 'How sublime are these?'

'Definitely not something to discuss in front of Mark,' I grinned and Erik nodded in agreement.

Once we'd devoured the lot and enjoyed a second cup of coffee we paid and reluctantly left. I think we both could have spent the entire day ensconced in the café, but with people waiting that wouldn't have been fair, and now the sky had cleared and the sun was shining, the market beckoned.

'Don't forget we're supposed to be looking for inspiration,' Erik reminded me as we walked around and made a few purchases.

There were lots of autumn themed stalls, and I could have easily been tempted to buy something from each of them.

'Hello,' smiled Bella, who was standing behind a stunning display of handmade fairies. 'How are you enjoying the town?'

'It's so lovely,' I gushed. 'And these are exquisite.'

'Thank you,' she blushed.

'Did you make them?' Erik asked.

It didn't escape my notice that she gave him a double take but if she recognised him, she didn't say so.

'I did,' she confirmed. 'My business is called Away with the Fairies. I sell mostly online, but the Wynbridge markets are such fun I make enough stock to come here, too.'

I'd never seen anything like the fairies she created. They were so detailed and each one had a slightly different character and outfit. They came in a range of sizes which, Bella smilingly informed us, was true to real-life fairies.

'I'm going to buy two,' Erik said to me while Bella served someone else and I noticed she was wearing a set of glittery wings over her coat. 'Jasmine and Abigail will love them, and I can wrap them up for Christmas. What do you think?'

'I think Jasmine and Abigail are two very lucky girls,' I smiled dreamily up at him.

'No,' he laughed. 'I meant which two do you think I should get?'

I still thought they were lucky, but I helped him look through the fairies on offer. He had the final say though because he knew the girls so well.

'Have you seen anything else you might like?' I asked him as we explored further.

'I did see something on a stall further back,' he told me. 'And now I wish I'd got it.'

'Let's go back then,' I said. 'Which way was it?'

'I can find it,' he insisted. 'Why don't you start checking out the shop window displays? I heard someone say the first-place prize for the best dressed is highly coveted.'

We spent quite a while admiring the windows and then, sitting on a bench in the square, shared the most amazing bowl of jacket potato halves which had been twice baked and stuffed with lardons and raclette. Washed down with warm apple cider made from local apples, it was the ultimate autumn feast. In fact, everything about the day had felt like the ultimate autumn experience.

'Can I just say,' I said to Erik before we decided what to do next, 'how pleased I am that you suggested this trip, even if it was inspired by something that neither of us wanted to be caught up in.'

He shifted to look at me, and I confidently returned his gaze as any friend would.

'You're enjoying yourself?'

'Immensely,' I sighed contentedly. 'And I hope you're feeling better, too. Are you?'

'Immensely,' he echoed with a grin. 'A bit of distance and a distraction was just what I needed and you're a total distraction, Skylar.'

His smile faltered and his gaze dipped to my mouth and then back to my eyes.

'Well,' I swallowed, determinedly not looking away, 'I'm delighted to hear it.'

I refused to allow myself to be seduced, especially when such progress was being made. The day had been a tonic for us both and I wasn't going to do anything that might jeopardise the headway we'd made with regards to thinking about the photos in the press *and* my own personal quest to friend-zone Erik again. Even if the look on his face, to my mind at least, hinted that I wasn't quite the kind of distraction I'd been striving to be . . .

'What do you fancy doing next?' I asked as I quickly distracted myself by sorting our rubbish into recyclable or not. 'I think there's a little close nearby with more shops or we could try The Mermaid? We haven't been in there yet.'

'The pub looks packed,' he said with a nod to the door, which was constantly being opened to let people in, but no one seemed to be coming out.

'You're right. And to be honest, I'm not sure we do need to visit more shops.'

There was an array of bags at our feet now. I'd been particularly tempted by a stall organised by a woman called Lizzie Dixon who ran the café with Jemma and sold the most exquisite handmade crafted items and fabric decorations. Knowing my father's fondness for fall decorating, I knew he wouldn't mind me adding a few more to our already impressive collection so had rather gone to town.

'We could always go back to get the truck and then drive out to the farm with the pumpkin patch,' Erik suggested. 'Didn't you say there was a nature trail there, too?'

'I did,' I confirmed. 'But what about your knee? You don't want to have another flare up ahead of the drive back to Norwich tomorrow, so maybe you should rest it for the remainder of today.' I still hoped to at least visit the pumpkin patch, but that would depend on how Erik was feeling in the morning. The truck was so big, I didn't dare offer to get behind the wheel myself. 'And besides,' I added, not wanting him to feel bad about calling it a day, 'it is quite late. It would be getting dark by the time we got to the farm.'

'Would you mind if we just went back to the apartment then?' Erik asked, having mulled over what I'd said. 'I'm pretty certain no one has recognised me today but perhaps I shouldn't push my luck.'

I was sure he had been spotted but didn't want to worry him by mentioning it.

'Not at all,' I responded. 'I've had a few ideas about the Spooktacular, and it would be good to make a note of them while they're still fresh in my mind.'

'Have you got a notebook?'

'No, I'll just send myself an email with it all written in.'

'That's a good idea,' Erik laughed. 'Come on then. Let's go and ask Bella if she knows where we'll find a taxi.'

We were starting to feel the cold by the time we arrived back at the apartment, so I turned the heating thermostat up a few degrees while Erik turned the sofa bed back into a sofa so we could sit on it for the evening.

'Don't forget I'm on there tonight,' I told him as I unpacked the bags of snacks we'd picked up to see us through the rest of the day. 'No arguments. Your knee will need some decent support ahead of driving tomorrow and the bed is ever so comfy.'

'Fair enough,' he accepted surprisingly. 'You don't fancy driving the truck then?'

'Er, that'll be a hard no,' I said and he laughed at the look of horror on my face. 'Unless you're really struggling, of course.'

'I'm sure I'll be fine,' he grinned. 'Would you like something to drink?'

'I could go for a tea.'

'Nothing alcoholic?' he asked. 'Bella has put a couple of miniatures from a local distillery called Brambles in the cupboard above the fridge.'

'No thanks,' I said. 'I'm not drinking alcohol at the moment.'

'Why not?'

So I don't run the risk of flinging myself at you again was the honest response to that question.

'I guess I'm just not in the mood,' I said in lieu of the truth. 'But don't let me stop you. If they're only miniatures, they'll be well out of your system by the morning.'

'No, they can stay where they are,' he said as he plumped the sofa cushions. 'I told myself I'd keep a clear head this weekend.'

My head snapped up and I found he was looking at me.

'Any particular reason why?' I swallowed.

'You know part of the reason why,' he said softly. 'You, me and alcohol is a recipe for disaster where our friendship is concerned, isn't it?'

'I don't think there are any paparazzi lurking here to record any mishaps,' I said and made a show of looking around, while admiring his ability to be honest about the situation out loud, unlike me, 'but you're right, booze has caused us some bother in recent weeks.'

Not that alcohol was entirely to blame.

'Exactly, and because of that, I want to keep a clear head.'

'Me, too.'

'I want this weekend to be the best it can be. No bother allowed.'

'Agreed.'

'Because the truth is, Skylar,' he carried on even more honestly, 'I had to think hard before suggesting you should come with me on this trip. I knew the apartment was going to be tiny and I wasn't sure if I was going to be able to . . .'

'Go on,' I encouraged and moved next to the sofa, so I was standing in front of him. The air between us seemed to positively crackle. 'Tell me what it was that you weren't sure you were going to be able to do.'

Part of my brain was screaming at me not to pursue the topic but the tone of Erik's voice had ignited another sudden fire in my belly, and encouraged the other part of my mind to do its utmost to convince me that sticking to my Big Love ethos could mean I would never get to feel the exquisite pressure and pleasure of Erik's lips on mine again, and that if the opportunity arose then I should just go for it.

So much for the friend zone I'd been working my way back towards, but in that moment, missing out felt like it would be a tragedy, whatever the resultant consequences.

'I was worried,' Erik said so quietly that I had to lean in to hear him, 'that I'd struggle to keep my feelings for you in check and end up doing something which could jeopardise our friendship for a third time.'

Rafe had said to me that the third time might be the charm. Was this a sign from the universe that no harm would come from giving in to temptation?

'Your feelings for me?' I breathed.

I knew I wasn't being fair encouraging him to say more, but I wanted all the information I could get before I responded.

'Yes,' he blurted, 'my feelings for you, Skylar. You must know I have some and even though I told you right at the beginning of our friendship that I was happily single and you told me you were the same and we both agreed that processing the changes in our lives left no room for romance, I haven't been able to stop myself thinking about you . . . and not just in a . . . friendly way.'

After the words had tumbled out, he ran a hand through his hair and huffed out a breath. I didn't know if the declaration had felt uncomfortable or cathartic for him, but I had enjoyed it.

'I see,' I said. 'So, all the while we've been acting as a PPO for each other, we've both secretly been wanting more.'

'You feel the same?' Erik gasped, and his gaze snapped back to mine.

'I certainly feel something,' I confirmed. 'But I'm not sure exactly what. I've only ever gone in for serious relationships, but I keep thinking about you too, and not just in a friendly way.' Erik smiled at that. 'You're beginning to feel very much like an itch that I need to scratch but the last thing I want is to ruin our friendship as a result of you thinking I'd expect a committed relationship to be the outcome of us getting together.'

'This is exactly why we need clear heads,' Erik said firmly. 'If we're going to consider acting on our feelings then we need to be certain we're doing the right thing.'

'Is that what we're doing?' I whispered. 'Contemplating acting on our feelings.'

'Well, I know I am.'

'Me too,' I swallowed. 'Though I need to be certain that we're both on the same page and in agreement that whatever happens won't go any further than this weekend.'

I could scarcely believe the words coming out of my mouth! Who even was I? I'd never suggested anything like this before, but I'd never experienced such desire either. If it was a one-off or nothing, sorry Mabel, but my libido was determined not to miss out even if it meant denying what I truly felt in my heart.

'We are on the same page,' he nodded. 'We're both still coming to terms with other things, and neither of us has the headspace to nurture a new relationship. Do we?'

'We don't,' I said after the briefest hesitation. 'I'm not looking for any kind of commitment.'

'I mean,' he babbled, 'we're both at major crossroads in our lives and as we only live a stone's throw apart and might end up working at the same place, we must—'

'Erik—'

'And I don't want you to think I invited you here in the hope that anything would happen, because it genuinely was about the papers and those photos and my dad—'

'Erik,' I cut in again. 'We are definitely on the same page.'

'We are?'

'We are.'

I reached for his hand, laced my fingers through his and

pulled him close. Having had such a lengthy run-up, setting out the 'what happens in Wynbridge, stays in Wynbridge' ground rules, what happened next could have felt stilted, but it wasn't. With so much pent-up passion on both sides, we were immediately lost in the moment, and unlike in the fern garden, there was no one to interrupt us.

Our previous kisses had been intense, but these were searing and the way we tore at each other's clothes it was a miracle they stayed in one piece. The second Erik's fingers touched my bare skin I was desperate to feel more of him, the whole of him. I wanted to feel his firm body pressed against mine and rushed towards the bedroom, pulling him along with me, all inhibitions lost.

'Are you sure?' he whispered as we fell onto the bed and began to explore the parts of us that had been hidden from each other for what felt like far too long.

In response, I ran my hands across his back and pulled him down on to me. The weight of him made me yearn to complete the connection.

'Yes,' I gasped, as his kisses ranged far and wide. 'Yes.'

In the next moment we both gasped and I was swept away on a rapidly building journey of the most intense pleasure. It was repeated more than once and exhilaratingly lasted until the early hours. Feeling satiated in every way, we finally fell asleep with our limbs entwined and ended up missing what Sunday morning in Wynbridge had to offer.

Chapter 29

I woke first, and once I had pulled on my dressing gown, I sat on the edge of the bed and watched the steady rise and fall of Erik's chest. The ache in my body was an indicator of a night thrillingly spent. The best night I'd ever spent in fact, but one that I had known had been a mistake the second I opened my eyes.

What a lust-led fool I had been to think that I would be able to friend-zone Erik again after hours of such pleasure and connection. He had fulfilled me in ways I had never before dreamed of and I knew he'd been satisfied, too, but now I had to somehow flick a switch and pick up where my head had been aiming for twenty-four hours ago.

Rather than wait for Erik to wake, I made us both a coffee and took a long, hot shower. As I lathered and rinsed, I imagined the water washing away my feelings and I wondered how Mum managed to breeze through life with nothing more than the briefest bedroom encounters. I could only suppose she'd never had the same experience that I'd just had. One that had felt meaningful on every level and threw what I had once thought had been a Big Love with Reuben right out of the window.

'Good morning,' I smiled brightly when I went back into the bedroom and found Erik sitting up and drinking his coffee. 'How's your knee?'

'It's good,' he said. Bending and straightening it under the duvet. 'The rest of me is a bit—'

I didn't need to know that what we'd intimately shared had physically impacted on him in the same way that it had me.

'So, you'll be okay to drive?' I cut in.

'Yes, but—'

'Great.'

I turned the hairdryer on before he had a chance to say thanks for the memories or something similar. It was going to be hard enough being just friends again, so I certainly didn't want to talk about our night of passion. Or anything really.

'Sorry,' I mouthed, because of the noise.

'I'll go and get showered,' he said loudly. 'We've got to be out of here soon.'

There was just enough time for the cooked breakfast Bella had supplied the components of, so I busied myself making that while Erik used the bathroom. Rafe's 'third time being a charm' prediction came to mind again and I almost wished I could tell him that he couldn't have been more wrong, but I wouldn't be confiding in him. Or anyone.

'This looks good,' Erik said in a similar cheery tone to the one I'd previously treated him to. 'I'm famished.'

I couldn't look at him then and shoved more bread in the toaster.

'What time do we need to leave by?' I asked.

'Twelve. And Bella would like us to put the towels we've used in the shower.'

'I'll strip the bed, too,' I said, as I added a poached egg to my plate along with the grilled bacon and tomatoes.

I'd just started to eat when the toast popped up.

'I'll get it,' Erik insisted when I went to retrieve it.

'Thanks.'

'Bugger,' he winced when he was on his feet. 'My knee is much better than yesterday but I'm not sure it's up to walking around that nature trail. Would you mind doing it alone?'

'It's fine,' I told him. 'I'm happy to miss it, but I would still like to go and pick a pumpkin or two. I don't think it will take us too far out of our way, and you can wait in the truck if you don't want to risk walking around a slippery, muddy field.'

'And lunch?'

'I don't think we'll need it after this, will we?' I smiled.

'Skylar,' he began and I felt myself go hot. 'Can I just say—'

'If it's anything about last night,' I pretended to tell him off, 'then no, you may not. We had a rule, remember, and now we need to stick to it. No further words necessary.'

'Right,' he sighed. 'Well, I was just going to say that I spent the night with the most amazing woman and had the best time.'

'I see,' I said, 'well funnily enough, as you're my friend, I suppose I can share with you that I spent the night with a gorgeous guy, and I had a phenomenal time, too.'

I did look at him then but not for long.

'How lucky are we?' he smiled falteringly.

'So lucky,' I nodded vigorously. 'And even luckier to have such a fabulous friend to be able to say that to. And not only that, they're also the perfect PPO. Double prizes!'

Double prizes? I'd never said that before in my life! I was really going overboard with the enthusiasm.

'You're right,' Erik said. 'We're both very lucky indeed.'

The rest of the day didn't pan out as I had previously imagined. There was no nature walk or Sunday lunch, but I did pick some pumpkins from the huge flat field that must have looked spectacular when it was full. I considered the possibility of returning ahead of the harvest the following year but wasn't sure I'd want to. Wynbridge was idyllic but given what had occurred after the perfect autumn adventure the day before, I wasn't sure I would want to relive the memory, and given that it had touched me so deeply I knew I wouldn't be able to not recall it.

On the drive back to Norwich, Erik and I didn't talk all that much and as I stared out of the window at the subtly shifting landscape I struggled to stop going over what had occurred, despite my best efforts. Truth be told, it was a relief to arrive back in the square.

'We've come back with a lot more than we took,' I commented, once we'd unloaded my things from the truck.

In the spirit of a speedy farewell, on my part at least, I asked Erik to drop me off right at the house. So much had happened during our brief time away that the photos in the paper, which were the things that sent us away in the first place, along with the risk of more appearing should we be seen together again, had been pushed right to the back of my mind.

'It was a good trip, wasn't it?' Erik asked.

'It was fantastic,' I enthused, because he didn't sound sure. 'I've got loads of suggestions for Kate and Luke and I really enjoyed seeing the whole town dressed up for autumn. It was brilliant.'

'I'm sorry we weren't there for the canine fancy dress competition,' he smiled. It was his first in a while. 'Maybe next year.'

'Maybe,' I echoed evasively as the house door opened behind me.

I felt immensely grateful for my father's timely arrival.

'What's all this?' he laughed when he caught sight of the pumpkins and bags. 'Did you have a good time?'

'A super time,' I said.

'Brilliant,' Erik chipped in.

'Are you coming in, Erik?' Rafe asked. 'I've got a lovely joint of pork crackling nicely in the oven.'

'As tempting as that sounds,' Erik said, 'I'd better head off. Finn will be wanting his truck back.'

I put a hand on my father's arm and gave it a light squeeze, hoping it would indicate that he should resist asking Erik to walk back over later.

'Another time then,' he said, thankfully. 'Are all these pumpkins for us? I like that white one.'

I thanked Erik again, avoiding eye contact, and picked up a pumpkin to put paid to the possibility of a goodbye hug.

'I'll see you next week,' I smiled.

'Yes,' Erik said as he climbed back into the truck. 'See you next week.'

I didn't watch him drive away and when Rafe started firing questions I handed over the pumpkin and told him I was bursting for the loo. Shut in the bathroom, I pulled out my phone and decided to send Erik a message, just to reiterate that I had no qualms about putting us back on a friendly footing. I was too slow though because he'd already messaged me.

'You don't think we made a mistake, do you?' I read aloud and felt my stomach twist.

I most certainly did because the night had left me aching for more, but I was determined that I would continue with the cheery attitude I'd displayed right from the moment I'd greeted Erik that morning. I wasn't going to let anything ruin our friendship or our potential future working relationship. There was too much at stake for us to let any doubts about whether we'd made the wrong decision linger. I took a deep breath and then replied.

'Absolutely not!' I read as I typed. 'I had the best time. Itch scratched!'

I pressed send before I had time to overthink it and watched the screen, waiting for Erik's response. He immediately read what I'd sent but didn't reply. In fact, it looked like he'd gone offline.

'Dinner will be in about an hour,' Rafe said, when I joined him again. 'So, you've got time for a nap if you need one. You do look a bit tired.'

'We had a jam-packed itinerary,' I told him. 'There was so much to see.'

'Yet you're back quite early,' he commented with a nod to the clock.

I explained about Erik's knee playing him up because of the change of vehicle, so we'd cut the day a little short to make sure he didn't have too much pain on the drive back.

'You know, I think I will have a nap,' I yawned. 'Unless there's anything I can do?'

'No,' Rafe said. 'I'm all set down here. And I hope you don't mind, but I've invited Hugh for dinner. Is that all right?'

'Of course, it is,' I smiled. 'It's about time we met.'

I really wasn't in the right frame of mind to meet my father's partner that evening, but I'd rise to the occasion, and at least having someone else in the house might distract Rafe from asking me more about my weekend in Wynbridge.

Hugh was a total tonic. I had hung back as he and Rafe greeted one another in the hallway, and when they walked into the kitchen together, I could see straightaway that the new man in my father's life was the perfect fit.

'Skylar,' Hugh beamed as he unwound the voluminous knitted scarf he was wearing and handed it to Rafe, 'I'm so pleased to meet you at last.'

'Likewise,' I smiled back. I was grateful to feel my mood lift thanks to his warm words. 'Rafe's told me nothing about you, so I'm looking forward to getting to know you. I think my father's been wanting to keep you to himself.'

I didn't mention that Grandad George had told me a couple of things.

'And who can blame me?' my father laughed.

'Me,' I said. 'We're living together now, so you must learn to share secrets.'

Rafe gave me a look which inferred that I was the pot and he was the kettle.

'I have met your grandfather,' Hugh then said. 'My mother, Ottilie, knows him and I'm convinced they contrived our first meeting, but no matter. I'm just very grateful that we met, however it came about.'

'As am I,' Rafe agreed sincerely.

The two of them were clearly very much attached, and I felt happy for my father. It suited him, being in a relationship, and I wondered if his writing output was as much related to being content in his love life as it was connected to the return of his muse . . .

'Now,' Hugh said. 'Where are these cats I've heard so much about?'

With the introductions over, I sat on the sofa and watched the two men work around one another in the kitchen. Hugh organised the drinks while Rafe continued to perfect the roast dinner that had filled the house with the most delicious smell and made my tummy rumble. The eggs and bacon Erik and I had eaten felt a long way off. Not that I was thinking about the start of our day or anything else that had happened ahead of it.

'Now,' Rafe said, once the dinner was served and we'd enjoyed enough of it to satisfy the first pangs of hunger, 'tell us about your trip Skylar. What did you make of Wynbridge?'

I should have known I wouldn't get away with it completely. I immersed us in the plethora of glorious autumn details that the visit had bestowed upon Erik and me and I was quite proud of the façade I managed to present when all the while my head was wondering if there was a response to my message waiting on my phone. I'd had to take it right out of the room to stop the itch in my fingers which was tempting me to keep checking.

'So, Kate's description of The Cherry Tree Café was accurate,' Rafe said when I'd finished telling them how perfect it was.

'Entirely accurate,' I confirmed.

'I wish you'd come back with a bake or two,' Hugh said.

'I did think of that,' I told him. 'But Erik was mindful of putting our friend Mark's nose out of joint. He's a baker at Blossom's, you see.'

'In that case, I'll let you off,' Hugh smiled. 'I'm sure I've gained at least half a stone since I started seeing your father and have become more acquainted with the area.'

'You don't have to call in at Blossom's every time we meet,' Rafe teased.

'Like you can resist!' Hugh batted back and we all laughed.

'It is tempting,' I agreed.

'Can I hear a phone?' Rafe frowned and cocked his head.

I jumped up and shot out of the kitchen, which probably looked a little suss but given what happened next, my sprint from the room was forgotten.

'It's yours,' I said to my father as I rushed back in again with it in my hand. 'It's the Cavell Care number.'

Rafe quickly answered and I listened in concern to his side of the conversation.

'No,' he finally finished up. 'You were right to call. Thank you. I'll be with you as soon as I can.'

Hugh pulled his phone out of his shirt pocket.

'Uber?' he asked as my father said goodbye to whoever had rung from the care home.

'Yes, please,' he said. 'It's nothing to panic about,' he added for my benefit. 'Dad's just a bit under the weather. He's got a cold that's taken a bit of a hold.'

'That could turn to pneumonia,' I panicked.

'It could,' he said calmly, 'but I don't think it will. A doctor has been to see him and said he's happy for him to stay at the Cavell and another GP will check on him in the morning. Any change overnight and the staff will call someone again but I'm going over now to tell him to behave while he's bed-bound.'

'I'll come with you,' I said.

'The Uber will be seven minutes,' Hugh said softly.

'I'd rather you went tomorrow, Skylar, if that's all right? Dad might worry if the two of us go piling in.'

I wanted to see Grandad George, but knew what Rafe said made sense.

'All right,' I agreed. 'I'll go first thing in the morning.'

'What would you like me to do?' Hugh asked. 'I can stay here, come with you as far as the Cavell or leave you both to it? I don't mind what I do as long as I won't be in the way.'

I noticed my father looked a little pale despite his calm response to the situation.

'I think Rafe would appreciate the company on the drive over,' I took charge and said. 'As long as it won't take you too far out of your way.'

We all knew that walking was quicker, but the weather had turned to rain and hopefully this time on a Sunday evening, the roads wouldn't be too busy.

'Not at all,' Hugh agreed. 'I'll pop to Mum's apartment and then I can be around for the drive back, if I'm needed. Come on then, Rafe. Grab your coat and we'll be ready at the door. I'll see you very soon, Skylar.'

Rafe did as he was directed and Hugh gave me a kiss on the cheek before they left. I felt soothed that my father had such comforting company. I had warmed to Hugh immediately and hoped that their relationship was going to last. I had a feeling it might.

Chapter 30

I didn't hear anything from Erik that evening but given how worried I was about Grandad George, Erik's lack of response wasn't something I fretted over. It wasn't all that late when Rafe, along with Hugh, arrived back from Cavell Care, but I felt like I'd been waiting for hours, so had kept myself occupied by tidying up after our interrupted dinner and finding the perfect spots for the extra decorations and pumpkins I'd come back from Wynbridge with.

'So,' I asked, the second the front door opened. 'How is he? Really.'

'Fed up,' Rafe smiled. 'He's insisting everyone's overreacting, but he isn't really on top form.'

I puffed out my cheeks and blinked away the tears that were threatening.

'If he rests up with a little more grace he'll recover all the quicker,' my father continued. 'Perhaps you could find a way to convince him of that tomorrow, Skylar.'

'I'll make it my top priority,' I promised.

'Tell him we didn't move here one season for him to pop his clogs the next,' Rafe then suggested mischievously.

'Rafe!' Hugh gasped and tapped him on the arm. 'That's not helpful.'

'But it is a demonstration of his humour,' I told Hugh. 'If you're here for the long haul then you'll need to get used to it. I find phasing him out or ignoring him from the off helps.'

'Hey!' Rafe objected.

'Thanks for the tip,' Hugh smiled. 'And now I'm going to go. The Uber is waiting.'

'And I'm going to bed,' I said. 'I've really enjoyed meeting you, Hugh.'

'Likewise, my lovely. I hope I'll see you again soon.'

'I wouldn't count on it if you're going to gang up on me,' Rafe huffed and Hugh and I both laughed.

I arrived at Cavell Care the next morning and sat in the chair next to Grandad George's bed. He was fast asleep, his breath slightly laboured, but the carer I had spoken to when I arrived promised that he'd had a comfortable night and seemed quite his usual self when he was given his breakfast. I couldn't help thinking he looked tiny in the bed, frail and pale too, but then the linen was white so that didn't show him at his best.

'Well, this is a fine to do,' I heard him say and I jerked awake. 'Who's visiting who here? Would you like my bed?'

It took a moment for me to get my bearings and the crick in my neck suggested I'd been out for a while.

'Sorry,' I croaked and sat up straighter.

'How long have you been here?'

'All night,' I fibbed. 'I've been keeping a vigil.'

'That's a tall tale if ever I heard one because I breakfasted alone.'

'A couple of hours,' I said truthfully.

A glance at the bedside clock showed a time I wouldn't have believed possible, because it felt like no time since I'd arrived. I guessed the weekend had caught up with me.

'I daresay you're catching up following your trip away,' Grandad George said, echoing my thoughts. 'Did you have fun?'

'Never mind my weekend,' I tutted. I was sure I hadn't told him I was going away, so Rafe must have mentioned it. 'I want to know how you are?'

'A lot of fuss over nothing,' Grandad George sniffed, then proceeded to bark out a cough. I gave him a look. 'Still coughing up a lung,' he conceded, 'but sound as a pound otherwise. Help me sit up a bit, will you? That'll help.'

'Better?' I asked, once his pillows were plumped up and he was more upright.

'Much. Parched though.'

'I'll go and make us some tea, shall I?' I suggested.

'Good idea. Then you can tell me where you've been.'

By the time I returned, the door was closed because the doctor had arrived. He wasn't long and when he came out, and once I had told him who I was, he was happy to report that Mr Harding was much improved and could stay out of hospital as long as he remained in bed for a few days and followed the carers' instructions.

'I'll make sure he does,' I pledged.

'And when Skylar isn't here,' said a voice behind me. 'I'll keep him on the straight and narrow.'

'Thank you, Freddie,' I said as the doctor went to check on someone else.

'Can't have the only decent chess opponent in the place shuffling off,' he smiled. 'What would I do for kicks then?'

'I can hear you out there, Fanshawe!' Grandad George called.

'Nothing wrong with his hearing then,' Freddie laughed.

'I've just made tea,' I said and picked the tray back up from the trolley I'd rested it on. 'Would you like to join us?'

'No,' he said, 'I'll leave you to it, but I'll be straight in when you go. See you later, Harding!'

'That sounds like a threat!' Grandad George called back.

Poorly or not, the banter never stopped and I was very happy about that.

'Now, come on,' I said. 'Drink this before you talk yourself hoarse.'

While we shared the tea, I told Grandad George that he had to take heed of what the doctor had said.

'It's the Nightingale Square Christmas lights switch on soon,' I told him. 'And Rafe and I would love you to be with us for it, but there'll be no chance of being granted a night-time trip out if you're not completely better.'

That seemed to do the trick.

'Now, tell me about your weekend away,' he requested after he'd promised he would do as he was asked. 'Rafe said you went with a friend.'

I rolled my eyes and felt a pang of frustration which I didn't try to hide.

'Yes,' I huffed, and carried on in a sing-song tone. 'That's right. I went with Erik and no matter what Rafe thinks, there's no romance between us. We really are just friends.'

Grandad George looked rather taken aback.

'Your father didn't specify who you'd gone with,' he told me. 'And I've no idea what he thinks about the parameters of your relationship with Erik.'

'Oh,' I swallowed as my cheeks flushed crimson. 'Right. Sorry.'

'I take it you and Erik didn't get on while you were away?'

'Why would you say that?'

'Because your mention of him seems to have put you in a rather grumpy mood.'

'That really is Rafe's fault,' I tutted. 'Because he keeps inferring that Erik and I are, or have the potential to be, more than friends.'

'I suppose those photos in the newspaper have helped him jump to that conclusion.'

I blushed even brighter. 'I appreciate that, but they were deceiving and not at all reflective of what was really going on. Do you mind if we change the subject?'

'Not in the slightest. So, tell me, now you've met him, what do you make of Hugh?'

Once we'd exhausted the topic of how lovely we both thought Hugh was and Grandad George had eaten most of his lunch, his conversation trailed off and he began to look drowsy. I didn't want to leave while he was asleep, so I said farewell before he properly dozed off.

'I'll come back tomorrow,' I told him, but he said Rafe was visiting then.

'And don't worry about Wednesday either. You'll be here on Thursday anyway, so let's leave it until then.'

'But that's a couple of days away,' I said uncertainly.

'Exactly,' he smiled. 'You'll notice a real change in me by then and you'll be able to congratulate me on the progress I've made.'

'All right,' I agreed reluctantly. 'Behave yourself and I'll see you Thursday.'

He was asleep before I'd left the room and I felt, despite my earlier annoyance with my father, a rush of gratitude for Rafe who had not only offered me a wonderful home but also provided a base that ensured I could visit my much-loved grandfather on a regular basis.

Having still heard nothing from Erik, I decided to head over to Prosperous Place early the next day. There were a couple of things I wanted to do that cold and sunny Tuesday morning. The first was tell Kate and Luke that I was going to accept their job offer.

Having been certain I would take the position the moment they offered it, my weekend with Erik, more specifically the passionate night with Erik and his subsequent radio silence, had made me doubt my decision because something was obviously off. However, Grandad George's illness had been a jolt and made me determined to stay close to both him and Rafe and this job would facilitate that. Hopefully a straightforward conversation with Erik would set us properly back on the friendship path, so I planned to get on with that, too.

The other item on my agenda was spending some time in the Grow-Well. I hadn't worked there for a while and wanted to catch up on the hours I'd missed. Graham had said there would be less to do now November was in full swing, but I knew there would be something I could help with. And I'd also check on the bulbs. It wouldn't be long before they'd be distributed and hopefully once inside in the warmth and light of everyone's homes they'd start to grow in earnest and be blooming around Christmas day. What a happy thought that was. Definitely one of my more inspired ideas.

'Anyone home?' I called when I arrived at Prosperous Place.

It struck me then, that if it was just Erik in the kitchen our conversation would happen sooner rather than later. I hoped I could find the words. Perhaps telling him about Grandad George's illness would smooth any awkwardness way . . .

'Yes,' Kate called. 'We're here. Come on through.'

I found her and Luke sat at the table with Freya. There was no sign of Erik.

'Am I interrupting?' I asked. 'I can come back.'

'No,' Luke said, 'you're fine. We were just going through the dates when Freya will be giving guided tours of the Winter Garden.'

'Are there many?' I enquired. 'I wouldn't mind joining one myself. I love looking around the garden on my own, but my plant knowledge is woefully lacking, and I'd love to know what's there so I could dazzle Rafe with some Latin.'

Freya laughed at that. 'The tours get booked up pretty quickly but there's a list of dates here,' she said and pointed at a sheet of paper, 'and you're more than welcome to come along to any one of them. Just follow on from where we all gather at the gate.'

'That's great. Thank you.'

'And now I'd better get on,' she said as she stood up. 'I want to make the most of the sunshine and I'm going to check the tree ferns today. It won't be long until they'll need their winter coats putting on.'

'And before you make a start,' Luke said and he also stood up, 'I just want to ask you about that tree limb I mentioned. I'll be back in a minute,' he said to Kate. 'You haven't got to rush off, have you, Skylar?'

'No, I can wait.'

I accepted the coffee Kate offered me and while she was pouring it I took a photo of the list of garden tour dates Freya had left on the table.

'It's good to know the tours are so popular,' I said. 'It's not always easy is it, wanting to spend time outside when the short dark days arrive?'

'You're right,' Kate agreed. 'And that was why we wanted to set them up. That and the Winterfest have helped so many people impacted by SAD. And talking of the Winterfest,' she wheedled, 'have you given any further thought to our job offer?'

'Of course, I have,' I laughed. 'But I'll wait until Luke's back . . .' my words trailed off as we heard the back door open and slam shut.

'You were quick,' Kate said as he rushed in, rubbing his hands together and blowing on them.

It might have been sunny, but it was chilly, too.

'I pointed out the tree needing Freya's attention from the edge of the lawn and came straight back in,' he told her. 'What have I missed?'

'I was just telling Kate that I wanted to wait until you came back before I said that I've decided to accept your job offer,' I grinned. 'I would love to work with you here at Prosperous Place.'

'Oh, Skylar!' exclaimed Kate. 'That's the best news!'

'It certainly is,' Luke added. 'Wow, I'm thrilled and excited, too.'

'We're going to have the most amazing time!' Kate clapped. 'What did Rafe say about it?'

'I haven't told him yet,' I confessed. 'I didn't want his opinion to impact on my decision, so I thought I'd wait until I'd made up my own mind.'

I didn't add that I also hadn't mentioned it because I was still waiting to see if I could curb my feelings for Erik. I hadn't kept them in check so far but hoped that would improve in time. If he kept avoiding me it might end up being easier than I thought!

'Well, we'll keep it to ourselves until you've had time to tell your father,' Kate promised.

'And Grandad George,' I said.

'And him too,' Luke smiled. 'I'm going to have another coffee to celebrate. Anyone else want more?'

'Not for me, thanks,' I said. 'Mine's still half-full.'

I remembered the delicious coffee I'd enjoyed in The Cherry Tree Café and also that I hadn't yet had the opportunity to talk with them about the Wynbridge Autumn Festival.

'And I daresay Erik has mentioned all of this already,' I said once we'd toasted my acceptance of the job. 'But we saw a few things in Wynbridge that might come in handy for the Spooktacular next year.'

'I can't believe my silly name for it has stuck,' Kate laughed.

'I think it's perfect,' I laughed, too. 'And The Cherry Tree Café was also perfect. Your sister-in-law makes the best harvest pancakes. Did Erik tell you?'

'She's a culinary genius, isn't she?' Kate smiled, but then her expression changed. 'But Erik hasn't told us anything because he isn't here.'

'Oh?' I frowned.

'Did he not tell you that he was going away?' Luke questioned.

I felt like I'd had the breath knocked out of me.

'Going away?' I swallowed. 'When?'

'He left first thing yesterday morning,' Kate filled me in. 'And I can't believe I forgot to say as soon as you arrived, but he left you something. I'm sorry I haven't had time to deliver it.'

She searched on the worktop and found a tiny box with an even tinier red ribbon wrapped around it and tied in a bow. I knew what was inside even before I opened it and felt a lump form in my throat.

'Skylar?'

'Sorry,' I swallowed. 'What did you say?'

'I was just apologising for not bringing it over,' Kate said again. 'Though why Erik couldn't deliver it, I don't know because it would have easily slipped through your letterbox if you hadn't been in. Do you know what's inside?'

'Yes,' I said. 'I think so.' I made no move to open it. 'Do you know where Erik's gone?'

'London,' Luke said. 'He's going to be away all week.'

There was only one reason I could think of that warranted a trip to London, but I hoped there was something else I didn't know about.

'Did he say what he was going to be doing there?' I asked.

'Not specifically but he did say he'd be seeing his agent,' Kate told me. 'And that his dad was planning to fly over from Sweden to spend some time with him, too.'

'Right,' I said and looked at the package on the table.

'I'm surprised he didn't tell you,' Luke commented.

I had been initially too, but the more I thought about it, the more sense it made. Erik had moved on. Granted a lot further and faster than I had and in a way I hadn't in the least expected, but he was sticking to what we'd agreed.

Despite my former misgivings, I was clearly back to being his friend, granted one he wasn't currently maintaining contact with but a pal, nonetheless. I guessed that having mulled everything over he had decided to take the TV job.

I hadn't ever thought he was seriously considering it, especially when Kate and Luke were offering him a settled future at Prosperous Place but perhaps it did make sense for him to make hay while the sun still shone on his success on the rugby pitch. I supposed time would tell and he'd let me know at some point.

Chapter 31

It felt like I was operating on autopilot as I gave Kate and Luke the details of what I'd gleaned from the Wynbridge Autumn Festival. I didn't stay long and with Erik's gift zipped safely into my jacket pocket I headed to the Grow-Well. Graham set me the task of weeding and digging over a patch of land, which I threw myself into.

By the time I'd finished I was exhausted, dirty and although delighted to have accepted the dream job, Erik's sudden and silent disappearance didn't sit well with me. Cross, hurt and confused best summed up my emotions, despite my former determination to go with the flow, as I checked the bulbs in the bothy and then later lay in an Epsom salt enhanced bath. I tried not to keep looking at the gift which I still hadn't opened, but my gaze was constantly drawn back to it.

After a night spent tossing and turning and once Rafe had shouted up the stairs that he was off to see Grandad George, I padded down to the kitchen with the present in my hand. I sat at the table with a coffee, and the cats nearby, and gently pulled the red ribbon undone and lifted the lid on the box.

'Oh Erik,' I breathed as I lifted out a pendant I'd fallen in love with during our look around the Wynbridge market.

The top of it featured an exquisitely hand-sculpted fly agaric and this was set above a beautiful rose quartz crystal. I had never seen anything like it before and had regretted not buying it at the time. Erik had obviously seen how much I liked it, even though I hadn't specifically commented on it, and gone back for it. How intuitive he was.

As much as I adored it, I wasn't sure I would be able to wear it. That would depend very much on whether our friendship was going to survive the challenge it was facing. I knew I'd think of Erik every time I put it on, and for the moment, I couldn't bear that.

As incredible as the night I'd spent in his arms had been, potentially losing him for good felt like the highest price to pay for it. We'd gone to so much trouble to set out the ground rules to protect our relationship, but with him disappearing and making no attempt to contact me, it felt like we shouldn't have bothered.

But then there was the gift of the pendant . . . Though that, I then remembered, must have been bought before we'd tumbled into bed together. That said, whatever Erik's reason for buying it, I still wanted to thank him for it.

'Thank you for the pendant,' I read croakily as I typed. 'It's every bit as beautiful as I remembered. Kate and Luke have told me you've gone away. I hope everything is okay . . .'

My finger hovered over the keys as I dithered over how to sign off. I couldn't decide whether to add 'love' or not. In the end I opted for my name with a lower case 'x' after it, then set the phone aside and repacked the gift into its box.

⋆

'That Erik is in the paper again!' declared Freddie Fanshawe when he found Rafe and I talking to Grandad George in his room the next morning.

We'd gone in early so I could chat ahead of my usual Thursday volunteering hours, and my grandfather was sitting in a chair with a blanket over his legs and looking, just as he'd predicted, very much better.

'Not with you this time though, Skylar,' Freddie laughed as he handed the paper to Rafe. 'This is a different lass. That fella certainly gets about. I remember those days! A different girl on my arm every weekend.'

Grandad George rolled his eyes, and I willed my face not to flush.

'I can imagine you were quite the gadabout,' he tutted at Freddie.

'Did you know Erik was in London?' Rafe asked me.

'Yes,' I said. 'Kate and Luke mentioned it earlier in the week.'

'This says the woman he's with is a sports presenter,' Rafe frowned. 'I wonder what that's about?' With Freddie still listening in, I decided not to mention Erik's job offer. 'Do you want to see?' he asked me.

'Not especially,' I said, but took the paper anyway. I glanced briefly at it before handing it back to Freddie. 'They look good together, don't they?'

I remembered Mabel saying the same thing about Erik and me.

'Very,' Freddie agreed. 'Right, I'll leave you three to chat.'

Whistling, he sauntered off towards the dayroom. It felt rather like he'd lit the touchpaper and left. I didn't want to feel so impacted by the photo, but I did and I wished I wasn't in company while I processed it. It couldn't mean anything other than Erik had gone to London to accept the TV job and then gone out with the stunning presenter, who was likely his co-host, to celebrate. If I'd really friend-zoned him again I wouldn't have felt any response to seeing them together, but I did and it was a decidedly queasy sensation.

'I can't imagine that photo meant anything,' Rafe said.

'I was just thinking the same thing,' Grandad George joined in. 'After all, those ones of you and Erik didn't mean anything did they, Skylar?'

'The press love nothing more than to twist a story into something that will sell their papers,' Rafe continued. 'I was a victim of it myself when I was supporting a married actor chum and the media made out—'

'I don't know why you're thinking I'm troubled by it,' I cut in. 'I'm annoyed rather than upset. Erik must be sick of being constantly snapped. It got on my nerves when it happened and it's far worse for him.' I remembered how fed up he'd been, but then if he was going to work in TV maybe he'd resigned himself to it. Perhaps his presenter pal was helping him come to terms with the intrusion. 'Anyway, forget about Erik. I have something exciting to tell you.'

I hoped that didn't sound selfish, but I really wanted to share my news while they were both together.

'You do?' asked Grandad George.

'Yes, I do. I'll go and find an extra chair and then all will be revealed.'

I took my time finding a chair and by the time I returned, I was feeling much better and my well-meaning relations had thankfully finished talking about Erik.

'So, what have you got to tell us?' Grandad George asked, once Rafe and I were settled. 'Good news, I hope.'

Rafe looked a little uncertain.

'The best.' I smiled at the pair of them. 'I've got a job!'

My declaration was met with a stunned silence.

'A job?' Rafe swallowed. 'Already?'

'Yes,' I said. 'I was offered it about a week ago. I haven't mentioned it before because . . . well, never mind why, but I've accepted it and I'll be starting in the new year.'

'Oh, my dear,' Grandad George said. 'I want to be thrilled for you, but I can't deny I'm a little sad, too.'

'Why?' I said, playing innocent.

I knew it was a bit mean to not immediately put them out of their misery with regards to the location, but I was enjoying building up to the best bit.

'Because we love you being with us, Skylar,' Rafe said sadly.

He sounded forlorn and I couldn't keep the pretence up, even though just a second before I had been planning to string it out for maximum impact.

'Well,' I said, 'I'm relieved to hear you say that, because I'm not going anywhere!'

'You're not moving out?'

'Not when I've only got to walk across the road to go to work,' I laughed.

'What do you mean?' Grandad George demanded, sounding confused.

'The job's at Prosperous Place,' I was delighted to declare. 'I'm going to be an events planner across the road from the square and working collaboratively with Kate and Luke rather than flying completely solo.'

'Well, I never!' my grandfather clapped.

'Do you mean it?' said Rafe.

'Every word,' I confirmed.

'Oh, my darling girl!' he sobbed. 'I can hardly take it in.'

'You're pleased?'

'Over the moon!' he said and jumped up, pulled me to my feet and enveloped me in the longest hug.

'As am I,' joined in Grandad George and Rafe and I hugged him too.

'I feel like Christmas has come early,' Rafe proclaimed as we sat down again.

'Me too!' I laughed. 'It's the most amazing prospect, isn't it?'

'It certainly is,' he agreed. 'So, will you be working with Erik over there?' he asked and I wished he hadn't.

'If there's any meaning behind that news story Freddie's waving about,' I said lightly, 'then no, I don't think so.'

'Oh?' my father frowned.

'Just between us, Erik told me he'd been offered a job as a television sports commentator and it's my guess that he's gone to London to accept it.'

'That would explain the woman in the photo, wouldn't it?' Grandad George speculated.

'Yes,' I said. 'It would.'

'I can't help thinking that would be a bad decision,' Rafe said after a moment's thought. 'Both for him and for you, Skylar.'

I suddenly didn't feel like I wanted to continue refuting his insistence that Erik and I were, or had been given the current silent situation, attracted to each other.

'Well,' I said, 'that looks like what's going to happen. And I admit it, you were right to think we did have some feelings of attraction for one another, but we're over them now and each moving on with our lives.'

'Are you really?' Rafe asked, rather than grumble about all the time I'd denied there was anything between Erik and me. 'Is that how you truly feel?'

'Almost,' I confessed. 'We both needed a friend when I arrived in Norwich and that's what we've now agreed to return to being.'

Rafe's gaze became more intent.

'So, that means there was a time when you weren't friends,' Grandad George stated. 'When you were more than just friends, I mean?'

'Briefly,' I said succinctly. 'But it's all done with now.'

'For both of you?' Rafe said.

'I think so . . .'

'It sounds to me like there's a conversation that still needs to be had,' my father said. 'An honest one and the sooner the better.'

'I can't see the point now,' I sighed. 'Not if what Freddie showed us tallies up with the job Erik talked about. I want what's best for both of us, so I'm happy to move on. I really am,' I added because neither of them looked convinced.

'Must be hard though,' Rafe said. 'You're not someone who gives her heart easily, are you, my love?'

'Who said anything about my heart,' I said casually, again thinking about Mabel's advice that I should follow it. 'Now, I'd better go and find Beth before she comes looking for me. I'm supposed to be volunteering this morning in case you've forgotten!'

I ducked out of the room knowing that I was going to be the hot topic of conversation. Hopefully it would be exhausted by the time I was finished for the morning.

I didn't look at my phone until Rafe and I were back at home that day and I had mixed feelings when I saw there was a message from Erik waiting for me. Part of me wanted to read it straightaway but another wanted to delay. I had a feeling that whatever he'd sent was going to lead us further to the end of something I still didn't really want to finish.

My private feelings completely contradicted the public ones. I'd never put on a braver face. Loath as I was to acknowledge it, my father had been entirely accurate when he'd said that I wasn't someone who easily gave her heart away. There could be no denying that mine now belonged to Erik, and I hoped that in time and with some distance between us, I'd find a way to reclaim it and lock it up tight again. With hindsight I knew I'd felt more than attraction for him from practically the moment we'd met, but some love stories simply weren't meant to be.

In my sitting room that evening, with Plato on my lap as my loving support pet, I finally opened the message.

I'm so pleased you liked the pendant, Skylar, and I'm sorry I came away without telling you. I regret that now. I should be back late on Saturday night. Can I come and talk to you on Sunday? There's something I need to tell you. Erik x

I didn't know if I could bear to see him, even though I had previously craved to, but Sunday was still a few days away. Perhaps I'd be able to properly get a handle on my feelings by then, once and for all. I'd keep myself busy. Throw myself into housework, gardening, ideas for more events at Prosperous Place . . . oh, who was I kidding? It was going to be hell, but I'd bear it. I'd have to.

Great! I typed back. *I'll see you Sunday. In the morning would be ideal. No worries about not telling me and I love the pendant. Thanks again!*

It was a breezy response but there was no signing off with a kiss that time. From that moment on, and purely for self-preservation, I had to harden my heart rather than follow it.

Chapter 32

By Sunday morning, the house had never been cleaner, the garden had never been tidier and even the Grow-Well was looking winter ready, thanks to my forty-eight-hour spree. I, on the other hand was looking rather frayed around the edges because it didn't matter how much I exhausted my body, my brain was still wide awake and keen to torture me with thoughts and memories I could neither stop nor control.

'Hugh and I thought we'd drive up to the coast to see the geese today,' Rafe said as he served up a cooked breakfast I wasn't sure I would be able to eat. 'Give you a bit of peace.'

I had told him that Erik was going to be calling round at some point, and he'd obviously engineered a trip to give us some privacy. I appreciated that more than I felt able to say, so I simply nodded and buttered some toast.

'Oh, my darling—' he began but I cut him off.

'Don't,' I begged. 'Please, don't. If you're nice to me, I'll cry.'

We hadn't talked further about how I was feeling but Rafe was a sensitive and intuitive man and had homed in on my true emotions, despite my efforts to hide them.

'We'll probably be home quite late,' he said softly. 'But if you want us at any point, just message and we'll head straight back.'

'Okay,' I swallowed. 'Thank you.'

Someone knocking on the front door called time on the conversation and I practically jumped out of my skin.

'I'm certain that will be Hugh,' Rafe said to calm me down. 'I'm sure Erik won't be calling this early.'

He was right and when Hugh walked into the kitchen he was carrying a beautiful bouquet of dahlias and chrysanthemums in stunning autumnal colours.

'Your father assumed these were for him,' he smiled at me. 'But they're for you, Skylar. I thought they'd complement your sitting room seasonal décor.'

'Oh, thank you, Hugh,' I smiled back and jumped up to take them. 'They're stunning and yes, they'll look perfect with the new decorations I picked up in Wynbridge.'

Every thought and conversation seemed to lead back to that weekend away.

'That's what I hoped,' he said. 'Now come on you,' he chivvied Rafe, 'we should be off. Have you got your thermals on? There's a sharp frost this morning.'

With the pair away, I ate a little of my breakfast, then tidied up and arranged the flowers. There were enough to fill two jugs, so I set them at either end of the mantelpiece. I would have liked to place one on the hearth or windowsill, but I didn't want to risk the cats taking a bite out of them. None the more for that, they would have looked beautiful regardless of where they were displayed and I was thankful not only for the gift of them, but also the time it took to display them because it had kept me occupied.

With everything done, and me washed and dressed there was nothing to do but wait for Erik's arrival. It came sooner than I expected and I felt relieved when he knocked on the door but dismayed when I opened it to find him wearing the ruby coloured henley shirt and looking every bit as attractive as the last time I'd seen him. It might have been my imagination, but his eyes looked even bluer than I remembered.

'Hello,' I said, the word catching. 'Come in.'

'Hey, Skylar,' he said as he crossed the threshold.

With the door closed he moved to give me a hug, but I managed to sidestep that, though not before his familiar aftershave had filled the air around me.

'Coffee?' I offered.

'Yes, please,' he pulled off his boots and left them on the mat. 'Thanks.'

'Come through to the kitchen.'

'Thanks.'

I wondered how long the stilted conversation was going to last. Would it be just today or for ever? That was assuming we remained friends for ever.

'You're not wearing your pendant,' he commented while I was making his drink.

'No, I've been cleaning and didn't want to catch it. I do love it though. Thank you again for buying it for me.'

'You're very welcome,' he smiled. 'I knew you'd fallen in love with it.'

I wasn't going to allow talk of love of any kind.

'You said in your message you have something to tell me,' I reminded him.

Given the way my head and heart had reacted to the sight

and now the sound of him of him – swoon and thump, thump – I wanted to get this over with as quickly as possible. My attempt to turn him back into my PPO had clearly failed and I was already thinking that it was a good thing he was moving away because working with him would have been torture. Him becoming a distant friend would hopefully make the situation more bearable.

'I do,' he nodded. 'And to show you, too. Do you have a MacBook by any chance?'

'Yes,' I frowned. 'But why do you need that?'

'There's something I recorded while I was in London that I need you to see. I'd really appreciate your opinion on it.'

Oh god! He was going to show me something to do with his commentary interview. It was most likely a studio set-up where the commentators chatted about an imaginary rugby match or something to see how they came across on camera. Despite my thinking that his leaving Prosperous Place was ultimately going to be a good thing, him chatting with his potential co-host was the last thing I wanted to see.

'Can't you just show me on your phone?' I asked.

'I'd rather not,' he said and wrinkled his nose. 'It's better on a bigger screen.'

I took a deep breath and braced myself to be a better friend. After all, this was what friends did for one another, wasn't it? Each supported the other. I'd already accepted that Erik had stuck to our ground rules better than I had so it was time to up my game to match him before he guessed something was amiss. My breezy response to his phone message might have fooled him, but in person I was in danger of giving the game away.

'In that case, I'll go and get it,' I swallowed.

It took no time for him to set everything up. I had eschewed the space next to him on the sofa and plonked myself in my armchair thinking that a bit of distance might help me.

'Can you see from there?' he asked as he tried to adjust the angle so we could both watch. 'You'd be better off sitting here really.'

I moved to perch next to him but as close to the end of the sofa as I could get.

'Better?'

'Much,' he smiled. He looked a little nervous now, but that was probably because he was hoping I wouldn't laugh or something.

'Show me then.'

'Before I do,' he said. 'I should just warn you that it might come as something of a shock, and if it does, then I'm sorry.'

'Look Erik,' I said. I was becoming impatient. 'I saw you in the paper with that presenter so I know you went to London to accept the commentary job and even if this is your first time in front of a camera in a studio, I can't imagine you made that much of a hash of it. Just play it, will you?'

Apparently, I was a snappy friend who preferred tough love to the softly, softly approach. Erik looked slightly taken aback but didn't say anything and started the video. He sank back against the cushions, and I leaned forward so I couldn't see him watching me, which I had a feeling he was.

'You know,' he said and moved to turn it off, 'I'm not sure about this now.'

'Leave it,' I said and batted his hand away.

My guess had been right. There was a desk set up with a

screen behind it and into the frame walked Erik looking nothing like he usually did. His hair was tidy and I couldn't imagine the clothes were his own but then I'd only seen him in a casual setting.

'You look very smart,' I commented.

'I felt like an idiot,' he groaned. 'My father was with me and insisted a suit would make the best impression. He's standing right next to the camera.'

I watched on as Erik made himself comfortable behind the desk and someone wearing a headset fussed around him setting up an earpiece.

'How did you get this?' I asked. 'Are you supposed to have a copy?'

There was no sign of his co-presenter.

'Just wait,' he said. 'I'm about to do a test piece ahead of the actual interview.'

I leant even further forward as Erik looked directly at the camera. Someone gave him the signal to start talking and he took a deep breath.

'Okay Dad,' he said, his gaze shifting to where I imagined his dad was standing. *'This is for you. I've not actually come here today to try out for this job.'*

'What?' I gasped and Erik shushed me.

'Someone close to me and so very special too suggested that to get through to you, I should give a shock tactic a go and that's what this is. I don't want this job, I never asked you to find me this job. The work I'm going to do is back in Norwich at Prosperous Place and when we're through here that's where I'll be going. I know you're going to be furious, but you'll get over it in time. Sorry guys,' he then apologised as he looked around, and I imagined everyone

looking amazed. *'I didn't mean to waste your time, but it was the only way to say this and hopefully make an impact.'*

With my heart racing, I then continued to watch as he pulled the earpiece out, stood up and walked towards the camera. Erik paused the screen, but I continued to stare at it with my mouth open.

'You do realise you're the person who I described as being close to me and very special, don't you, Skylar?'

'Uh huh.'

I had realised that because it was me who suggested that he should try a shock tactic to get through to his dad.

'But what I didn't say in that video is that along with wanting the job here, I also want you. Last Sunday, when I asked if you thought we'd made a mistake, you shut me down, and knowing then that you were going to play by the rules, it didn't feel appropriate to explain that I meant I thought that the *rules* themselves had been the mistake. *Not* our night together.'

I slowly turned to face him. 'What?' I asked breathlessly.

My head and heart were filled with burgeoning hope, but I needed him to spell out in more detail exactly what he was saying before I would embrace it.

'I'm saying,' he said, 'that I've been going out of my mind all week because last weekend I realised that I haven't only been *thinking* about you Skylar, I've been falling for you, and I have been from the moment we met.'

'You've been falling for me?' I whispered as the hope of a genuine Big Love blossoming began to edge its way further in.

'Hook, line and sinker,' he said. 'And I know you don't feel the same about me because you've been playing by our rules, but I had to tell you—'

'I do feel the same,' I blurted. 'I absolutely do.'

'Really?'

'Cross my heart,' I promised. 'I only didn't say anything because I thought *you* were going along with what we'd agreed, and when you went away this week, I just assumed you were happy to move on.'

'I was trying to distance myself,' he explained as the crossed wires were untangled. 'But I couldn't do it. I knew as soon as I'd gone that I wanted to be here, and more than that, I wanted to tell you that I want to be with you.'

'I know this isn't what either of us expected to happen . . .'

'But I'm so happy it has.'

Without another word we embraced and the distance between us we'd both attempted to keep was banished for good. We didn't kiss straightaway but held each other close as the misunderstanding ebbed further away and the joyous prospect of what was to come sank in. It was in those seconds that I let the hope rush all the way in, and it immediately turned into a feeling of unbridled excitement and unadulterated joy. At last, I was following my heart.

'We're both staying in Norwich,' Erik whispered.

'And we're staying here together.'

We kissed for a long time and then I led Erik up the stairs to my room where we stayed for the whole of the day making up for the week we'd lost.

It was late in the afternoon when hunger of a different kind drove us downstairs to the kitchen. Erik fed the cats while I made a huge plate of sandwiches. Knowing that Rafe and Hugh wouldn't be back until later, neither of us were properly dressed.

Erik was barefoot and wearing his trunks and I had pulled on his henley shirt. It swamped me, but it felt thrilling to be wearing something I'd long admired him in.

'You still haven't told me who recorded that video so you could see it on your phone,' I reminded him. 'Or how your dad reacted to it.'

Given what Erik had previously told me about him, I couldn't imagine his shock tactic had been well received.

'Catlyn, who would have been my co-presenter, recorded it,' Erik grinned. 'We'd gone out one evening, hence the photo in the paper, and I'd filled her in on what I intended to do. I thought it was only fair.'

'Oh, my goodness!' I gasped. 'Whatever did she say?'

'When she heard there was a love story at the centre of the plan, she became a willing accomplice. She said she's a romantic at heart and that it was only fair that you got to see what I did with the good advice you'd given me.'

'I rather like the sound of Catlyn.'

'She was great and my agent was understanding, too.' I hadn't even thought about them! 'With regards to Dad,' Erik carried on. 'Let's just say he took a while to calm down, but when he did and I'd talked to him some more, he *finally* began to see the situation from my point of view. He didn't even baulk when I suggested he might consider grief counselling. Mum's passing might have happened a long time ago, but I know Dad still hasn't mourned her properly.'

'I'm so pleased you were finally able to have an honest conversation about that,' I said, feeling relieved that the impact of what Erik had done had hit its mark and been accepted.

'It's still going to take a lot to change the parameters of our relationship,' he went on, 'but thanks to you we're on the same page.'

'I can't take the credit,' I told him. 'You were the one who acted on what I suggested and that was so brave. I'm not sure I would have had the courage to do what you did.'

'Oh, now you tell me!' Erik grinned and rushed over to tickle me.

I squealed and shoved the plate of sandwiches between us.

'Offering advice is one thing,' I laughed, 'but acting on it is another. Now, come on, we need to eat.'

We were cosily snuggled under a blanket in my sitting room when Rafe and Hugh arrived back.

'I don't think I should come right in,' I heard Hugh say. 'I'll wait here while you get the lie of the land.'

Erik looked at me and frowned.

'They knew you were coming to see me today,' I whispered, 'and thought I might well end up heartbroken.'

'Oh Skylar,' Erik swallowed and kissed me. 'We've been such fools, haven't we?'

'We have.'

'Skylar!' Rafe called.

'In here!' I called back. 'You can come in.'

His head appeared around the door.

'Oh,' he gasped. He looked amazed, then grinned. 'If that photographer could see you now!' he laughed. 'Come and look at this, Hugh.'

My father walked right in and Hugh followed.

'Well, I never,' he applauded. 'This is a happy homecoming.'

'They've finally got their act together,' Rafe grinned.

'Hey!' I objected.

'I don't think you can refute that, Skylar,' Erik laughed. 'It has taken us a while.'

'Um, it has. Did you have a nice day?' I asked my father and Hugh.

'Fabulous,' Hugh smiled.

'Though perhaps not as good as yours,' Rafe said. 'Now, who fancies a takeaway?'

Chapter 33

The following week felt magical and with perfect timing the weather took an even chillier turn. Autumn was ushered out as the preparations for the Nightingale Square festive switch on got underway. I was especially thankful for the change in the weather because it kept me cool when being with Erik left me feeling searing hot. It was a total joy to be able to gaze into his blue eyes and then act on the feelings my staring aroused, and I was hard-pushed to believe we'd held back for so long.

However, the change to the parameters of our relationship had led to more than physical intimacy. We spent hours talking, immersed in lengthy soul baring conversations which led to genuinely revelatory moments.

We had both arrived in Norwich because of unwanted change which had been thrust upon us. Neither of us had chosen the abrupt endings we had endured but the love and kindness we'd found in the city, from family, found family and friends, had meant we'd worked through them, and in the end, found our way to each other, too.

When I had moved to the square at the end of the summer

I'd had no idea what I was going to find. Falling for someone and finding a Big Love hadn't been on my radar but now both were very much front and centre. As were mine and Erik's new jobs. Next year was going to be so exciting and living with Rafe would enable me to keep my work–life balance in check. And if I started to fail at that, I knew my father would be there to gently remind me to pull back a little.

I had sent Alisha an email telling her about Erik and my new job, as well as describing the Grow-Well, and I knew it was the most thrilling I'd ever written. I told her that if she ever visited the UK, then she must come and see us and she extended the invitation to us if we fancied booking a holiday to Canada. Now I was going to have proper breaks from work, that might one day become a possibility.

I'd also let Mum know what had happened, but in true Flighty Faye style, I hadn't yet had a reply. Madeline and Tobias however had been thrilled.

'Are you ready, Skylar?' Rafe called from the hall. 'I don't want to be the last to get ours up!'

'Coming!' I shouted back. 'Do you think I'll need a hat?'

We were both wrapped up for the task ahead. In theory, it shouldn't take us long, but we'd be standing about a bit, and the wind was in the north and making its presence felt.

'It was kind of Heather and Glen to leave us these, wasn't it?' I said as I followed my father into the front garden.

He was carrying a lidded plastic crate of outdoor Christmas lights which had been left behind by the family who had owned the house before us.

'It was,' he agreed. 'Classic Nightingale Square community spirit. I hope they've found it wherever they've moved to.'

'Or taken it with them and spread it about,' I suggested. 'Now come on, let's get this done.'

As this was our first attempt at outdoor illuminations, working out how best to arrange the lights for maximum effect draped over and about the hedge took us a little while. We had turned them on and off a couple of times to try and see how they looked and I was becoming increasingly excited for the party on the green Saturday evening when every house would be lit up in the same way.

'How are you getting on?' Lisa asked, carrying over two mugs of hot chocolate. 'It's not easy to see how they look in the daylight, is it?'

She handed the mugs to Rafe and me, and we gratefully wrapped our cold hands round them.

'Thank you, Lisa,' I smiled. 'You couldn't have timed this better and you're right about the lights, but I think we're almost there now.'

'I noticed you'd been out here a while, and I thought you might need warming up.'

It was embarrassing to think that the day I'd moved in I had been worried that she might be an overbearing nosy nuisance when now I saw her for what she genuinely was, a kind-hearted and generous friend.

'Aren't you supposed to be writing?' Rafe quizzed her.

'All right bossy boots,' she pretended to huff. 'Just because you've typed "the end" weeks ahead of your submission date.'

'You haven't!' I gasped. 'Why didn't you tell me?'

'Oops,' Lisa grimaced. 'Was it supposed to be a secret?'

'No,' Rafe smiled. 'Not really. I was going to mention it, but not until I've also finished writing the book I'm supposed to be working on.'

'But I thought this one was . . .' Lisa began and stopped.

'Don't tell me, Rafe,' I said and rolled my eyes because I had an idea as to what was going on even if she didn't, 'you've been writing the shiny new idea you mentioned back in September, haven't you?'

'I have,' he confirmed.

'And the book you're supposed to be writing is still languishing in a desktop folder half-written.'

'That's pretty much it,' he nodded, sounding unconcerned. 'But,' he quickly carried on before I could take him to task, 'now I've got the other one out of my system, I know exactly how the pending one is going to continue and I'm all set to get on with it.'

'Well, I wish you luck with that,' Lisa said, sounding awestruck. 'I've no idea how you've managed to get another book under your belt with one waiting, but I'll be happy to hear all about it. Doubling my output would be very helpful.'

'This is strictly a one-off,' Rafe laughed. 'And given that you have a full house to manage as well as books to write, I have nothing but respect for you. And don't worry Skylar,' he smiled at me, 'I'll be finished sometime between now and the new year and my agent and publisher will be none the wiser.'

'But what about Christmas?' I demanded, sounding closer to three than thirty. 'It's our first one together. You can't be writing the whole time.'

'Says the woman who has already bagged the best present to play with!' Lisa guffawed. 'I'm sure Erik will keep you amused while your dad's hard at work.'

I blushed at that, but she was right.

'Fair point,' I grinned and drained my mug. 'Now,' I said and handed it back to her, 'let's get these lights finished and go and see if Luke needs a hand with the tree.'

When I opened the bedroom curtains on Saturday morning, I felt as excited as if it was Christmas day. Lisa had been right about me bagging the best present, and once I'd finished admiring the almost naked oak in the neighbour's garden, I turned around to appreciate Erik, the gift at the top of my wish list, who was almost naked too and fast asleep in my bed. It was a shame to wake him, but with the switch on party happening that afternoon and lasting, so Rafe and I had been told, well into the evening, it was time we had breakfast and got ready to help with the finishing touches.

As well as the massive Christmas tree on the green and lights around the square being turned on, there was also going to be music and all sorts of vendors. The variety of food that was going to be available had made my mouth water when Luke took us through the list and the memory of it made my tummy rumble now.

'Hey, sleepyhead,' I whispered to Erik as I climbed back into bed. 'It's time to get up.'

Erik stretched out and as I planted soft kisses along the length of his body starting at his throat and stopping around his navel, he groaned in pleasure. I felt his muscles react as I made my slow way back up again, shifting to sit astride him.

'If it's time to get up,' he said as he rested his warm hands on my thighs, 'why are you torturing me with kisses that can come to nothing?'

I smiled at that.

'I just thought it might be nice to give you something to look forward to once the party has finished tonight.'

'Do I really have to wait?'

'Breakfast!' my father's voice shouted up the stairs.

'You do if you want breakfast,' I grinned and nimbly climbed off. 'Hugh promised he'd make kedgeree this morning.'

It was the first time both Hugh and Erik had stayed over, and I liked the thought of the four of us starting the day together.

'In that case,' Erik said as he slowly sat up and reached for his pyjama bottoms, 'we'll put this on hold.'

As I watched him pull a T-shirt over his head I wished I'd woken him sooner.

'Hugh,' Erik, who was now wide awake, applauded, when we arrived in the kitchen, 'this smells amazing.'

'It does,' I agreed. 'You need to stay over much more often.'

'That can be arranged,' Rafe said, setting the table.

Both cats were winding their way around Hugh's legs, so they obviously knew there was something new on the menu, too.

'I hope you enjoy it,' Hugh said as he began to fill the plates. 'I won't give you too much in case you don't like it.'

'I already know I'm going to love it,' Erik insisted. 'Load me up, please.'

With bellies full of the delicious dish, Erik and I walked over to Prosperous Place and found Luke checking over the list of vendors. When he'd mentioned at the beginning of the week that it was always stressful with vehicles parked everywhere during the set up, I had suggested he could contact everyone and allocate them arrival slots. That way their cars and vans could be moved to Prosperous Place ahead of the next wave turning up.

'Which is exactly why we're so happy to have you on board!' Kate had gratifyingly said when I proposed the idea.

'How's it all looking?' I asked Luke.

'Far less demanding than usual thanks to you.'

'I'm delighted to hear it. And the weather is hopefully going to be kind, which would be a blessing.'

I couldn't imagine a switch on in the rain would be quite so much fun.

'Cloudy but dry according to the forecast,' Erik said and showed us his phone.

'Perfect,' I smiled.

'The earlier the light goes the better it will be for today,' Luke said. 'The actual switch on is scheduled for six so visitors bringing little ones won't have to be out too late.'

'How many people are you expecting?' I asked.

Given the number of food stalls coming, I guessed more than lived around the square.

'It's always a bit of an unknown,' Luke shrugged. 'But dry weather helps and going on previous years, there have been a growing number of people coming along.'

'Fantastic,' I smiled. 'Now, what can we do to help?'

Luke, Erik and Finn spent the day helping the vendors and sorting out any niggles while Neil, Freya, Lisa and I checked the lights and decorations. Graham asked for some help with his and Carole's outdoor set and Carole made us all tea and filled us up on homemade ginger cake, which was delicious.

By mid-afternoon everything was ready and we all headed back to our respective homes to get changed.

'People will start arriving from around four I should think,' Kate said. She'd walked over with the girls who were now tearing around the green. 'And we'll be back here then, but you guys don't need to be. Just come out when you're ready.'

'My lot are ready now!' Lisa laughed and pointed at the three eager faces pressed against an upstairs bedroom window. 'Even Tamsin the bad-tempered teen has been looking forward to this!'

It seemed we were all excited and when I went home and looked out of an upstairs window I too could appreciate why. The square already looked wonderful, so my excitement was going to be at fever pitch by the time the lights were turned on. Even though I didn't have little ones to keep an eye on, I loved that the green had railings all the way around so there was no danger of them getting carried away and running out onto the road.

'Don't forget we have to switch our lights on before we go out again,' I reminded my father who had, as promised, been writing for much of the day, and this time on the book he was supposed to be working on. 'We don't want to be the house that breaks the chain!'

'We most certainly do not,' he said with a shudder. 'I love that every house has the same lights adorning their hedges. It feels like the most wonderful symbol of what a fabulous community exists here. Rather like our homes are all holding hands.'

'I couldn't agree more,' I beamed. 'And we're a part of that community now. How lucky are we?'

'Truly blessed,' he said and kissed my cheek.

'I hope you know that I'll always be grateful to you for inviting me here,' I said, feeling a little choked.

'And I'll always be grateful that you accepted,' he said and pulled me to him for a proper hug. 'I think we're both going to be very happy here for many years to come.'

'I don't doubt it,' I swallowed.

There was a knock on the front door, and I went to answer it.

'Delivery!' said Beth who I found on the doorstep with Grandad George, Freddie, Mabel and Harold.

I knew that Harold would be coming because he had been born, raised and lived his entire life in the square and was now a Cavell Care resident, but Mabel was a surprise. A very happy one!

'Hello all,' Rafe greeted them.

'I thought it would be easier to get everyone here in one go in the minibus,' Beth told us. 'Can you handle all four of them?'

This remark earned a mixed reaction.

'I don't need handling,' Harold protested. 'But Freya has very kindly said she and Finn will accompany me this evening.'

'And Rafe and I can manage the other three,' Hugh said, who with perfect timing also arrived. 'Don't worry, we'll keep them in check.'

Mabel was still looking adoringly at Rafe so there would be no fear of losing her among the crowd.

'Good luck with that,' Beth said. 'Though I'm delighted to report that Mabel is proving a calming influence on the Dynamic Duo.' Mabel laughed. 'I'll meet you all here at seven to take you back. Latecomers will be left behind.'

She went off to find Eli, and Rafe quickly turned our lights on. They looked perfect and as we looked around we could see some others were already lit up, too.

'Doesn't it look lovely?' Mabel said to me. 'I think this is going to be the happiest Christmas I've had in a while.'

'Me too.'

'Following your heart is working out for you then?' she nudged.

'It certainly is. Thank you for the advice. Erik's the only gift I wanted under the tree this year and he's already been delivered and he's filled my heart, too!'

'I'm delighted to hear it,' she said and then looked down at her legs. 'I've also had an early present.'

I glanced down.

'Mabel! Are you wearing leg warmers?'

'I am,' she confirmed with a chuckle. 'They were a gift from your father.'

'And very good they look on you, too Mabel,' Rafe said and she blushed. 'Now, would you all like to come inside? I just need to see to the cats and get myself wrapped up and then we can go.'

'I'm so pleased that you're well again,' I said to Grandad George who hadn't followed the others to the kitchen but waited in the hall.

'As am I,' he nodded. 'I wouldn't have wanted to miss this. It's a long time since I've made much of a fuss about the festive season.'

'You'll be here on Christmas Day, won't you?'

As well as him, Hugh and Erik would be with us too, so it was going to be a wonderfully packed house. I couldn't wait!

'I certainly will. I'm looking forward to it. I'm looking forward to a lot of things now you and Rafe are living nearby.'

'That makes me so happy,' I sighed contentedly. 'And you

know, being with you both has made me feel that I'm finally part of a real family.'

'Oh, Skylar.'

'As you know, Mum has never been motherly, and as much as I loved being with Madeline and Tobias and visiting Rafe in LA, this is completely different. The bond with my father is so much stronger now.'

'Everything's worked out well for you, my dear,' Grandad George nodded.

'Everything's worked out well for all of us,' I amended.

'Aren't you supposed to be meeting, Erik?' Rafe came out of the kitchen to remind me. 'There you are Dad. I thought I'd lost one of you already.'

'I am,' I said, 'but I don't mind sticking with you.'

'No, no,' Grandad George insisted. 'You go and find that fella of yours. We'll no doubt see you in a while.'

I looked at my father.

'You heard the man. Go on.'

I didn't have to look for Erik because he was already walking towards the house. Wearing a dark jacket and with a scarf wrapped around his neck he looked taller and broader than ever, and I was pleased that he was happy to be out among people and not worrying about any press photos that might materialise as a result.

'Are you warm enough?' he asked me. 'It's going to be chilly tonight.'

'Plenty,' I said and pulled him towards me for a kiss.

I could feel the comforting weight of the pendant against my skin as he held me close. The rose quartz had invited so much love into my life already.

'That's a shame,' Erik tutted. 'Because I was looking forward to warming you up again later.'

'I'll lose a layer before we go home. That way there'll be some work for you to do.'

'Hey, you two,' Freya said as she and Finn bounded up. 'Have you seen Harold? Beth said she dropped him here.'

'He's inside,' I said with a nod back to the house. 'They'll be out in a minute.'

'Good,' Finn said, 'because I'm starving and I want to treat Harold to one of those waffles he loved last year.'

Along with the chocolate and cream covered waffles, there were chestnuts and candied almonds, raclette and huge sausages from a local butcher served in Blossom's baguettes, with Poppy's pickles and chutney on the side.

'Oh my god,' I groaned as I later bit into a pickle covered sausage. 'This is divine.'

'So's mine,' Erik said after he'd swallowed a huge mouthful. 'Poppy has got a stand here tonight. A last-minute addition. I'm going to stock up on her stuff. Kate was saying earlier that once it's gone it's gone and we don't want to miss out.'

'In that case, I'll get some, too,' I said and we went to look for Poppy's stand.

'Going forward, I'm going to have to think about what I serve up with these pickles,' Erik said, once we'd each filled a bag. 'I need to keep trim.'

'You look perfect to me,' I said as I looked him up and down.

'Thanks,' he grinned, 'I need look the part.'

'Who do you need to look the part for?'

'Anyone who takes my exercise classes.'

I stopped walking and he halted, too.

'What exercise classes?'

'I'm going to do some training next year to teach seated aerobics and Pilates in care homes,' he told me. 'I didn't want to drop the fitness training completely and with the knee situation, I thought this would be ideal.'

'That's brilliant!' I said and put my bag down to give him a hug. 'But why am I only hearing about it now?'

'Because Beth has only just confirmed that I can work at Cavell Care,' he explained. 'I didn't want to mention it in case it didn't pan out, and I had to look for somewhere else. The guy offering the training I want to take likes to see the classes in action, so I needed somewhere where he can assess me while I'm getting the hang of it. Do you really think it's a brilliant idea?'

'I think it's amazing!' I hugged him again. 'Mabel has already got some leg warmers, so I bet she'll be the first to sign up.'

Erik was delighted with my response. 'Come on,' he said, 'let's take these bags to your place.'

Once we'd dropped them off, we realised the music had been turned down and that the crowd were looking towards the tree in the middle of the green. I'd heard more than one person say how much they wished they lived in Nightingale Square and how it was a shame that the houses rarely came up for sale. I felt even luckier to be there when I heard that.

'Okay everyone,' Luke said, standing on a small platform, 'it's time to turn the lights on! Are you ready?'

'Yes!' the crowd enthusiastically responded, Erik and I included.

'Apparently not,' Luke joked and scratched his head. 'I said . . . are you ready?'

'Yes!' everyone bawled even louder.

'That's more like it!' he laughed. 'Right, here we go then! Ten, nine, eight . . .'

We all joined in and the moment we shouted 'one' the Christmas tree, the railings, in fact the whole of the square was lit up and everyone cheered as the music was turned up again and the speakers belted out the classic festive favourite Wizzard was famous for.

'Do you wish it could be Christmas every day?' Erik asked me.

I took a moment to look around. I could see Hugh and Rafe dancing together with Grandad George and the others and Beth and Eli laughing and watching on. I could also see Freya and Finn, Mark and Neil and Lisa, John and their brood, too. Kate was on the dais hugging Luke, and Carole and Graham were watching from chairs outside their front gate.

'I don't have to wish,' I said, snuggling closer to Erik and relaxing into his embrace as I looked up at him, 'because since I've fallen for you, that's exactly what it's felt like.'

We sealed the moment with the longest kiss, both of us excited to step into the future that our move to Nightingale Square had bestowed upon us and knowing that, best of all, we were doing it together.

Acknowledgements

So here we are again! Back in Nightingale Square for the sixth time and what an absolute joy it has been to catch up with old friends and make some new ones.

I've mentioned before that writing every book is a different experience and *Falling for You*, once I'd decided who would move out and who would move in, felt like one of those stories that told itself. I'm not saying it was a doddle, because no novel is, but I started it on Boxing Day and wrote every day until I reached the end. And practically the whole time I was at the keyboard, I had a smile on my face!

As always, there are many people to thank for their wonderful support. My editor Phoebe Morgan, Emma Capron (fantastic to be working with you again) and the entire S&S Team. My incredible agent and cheerleader, Amanda Preston, who tirelessly goes above and beyond. Thank you all.

Mum, Dad, Lia, Sue, Jenni, Clare, Kate, Ian and Claire: I might not see much of you when I'm head down, but I know you're all there counting the words along with me. Thank you.

And, as always, a huge thank you to the bloggers, librarians, content creators, booksellers and magazine journalists, who champion the books and encourage more readers to become lifelong members of the Swainette Squad!

Wishing you all a wonderful autumn and a very merry end to the year. I can't bring myself to type the festive word just yet . . . but until the next time we meet, may your bookshelves, be they virtual or real, be filled with fabulous fiction!

With love

Heidi x

About the Author

Heidi Swain is a *Sunday Times* Top Ten best-selling author who writes feel good fiction for Simon & Schuster. She releases two books a year (early summer and winter) and the stories all have a strong sense of community, family and friendship. She is currently writing books set in three locations – the Fenland town of Wynbridge, Nightingale Square in Norwich and Wynmouth on the Norfolk coast, as well as summer standalone titles.

Heidi lives in beautiful west Norfolk. She is passionate about gardening, the countryside, collecting vintage paraphernalia and reading. Her TBR pile is always out of control!

Heidi loves to chat with her readers, and you can get in touch via her website or on social media.

All Wrapped Up

Heidi Swain

In Wynbridge, the scent of autumn is on the breeze and love is in the air . . .

After a very public heartbreak back in her hometown, Clemmie has been cosied up in the Fens renovating the beautiful Rowan Cottage, near the quaint town of Wynbridge. After a period of isolation, she's ready for a fresh start.

A chance encounter with co-owner of The Cherry Tree Café, the bubbly Lizzie Dixon, pulls her into organizing Wynbridge's first-ever Autumn Festival, and her once quiet life is soon a distant memory. With the whole town rallying behind the event, she discovers a new sense of purpose.

And when local vet Ash falls hard for Clemmie, she begins to wonder if she's ready to move even further on from her past and fall in love again . . .

Available now in Paperback, Ebook & Audio

SIMON &
SCHUSTER